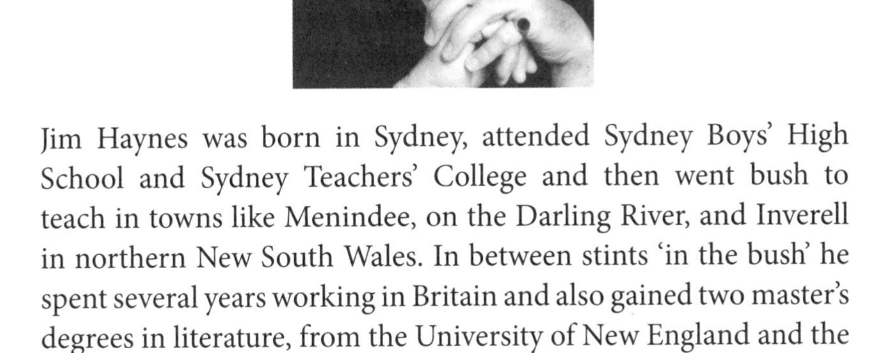

Jim Haynes was born in Sydney, attended Sydney Boys' High School and Sydney Teachers' College and then went bush to teach in towns like Menindee, on the Darling River, and Inverell in northern New South Wales. In between stints 'in the bush' he spent several years working in Britain and also gained two master's degrees in literature, from the University of New England and the University of Wales.

Throughout his teaching career, Jim was usually in a band or group as a singer. He started the Bandy Bill & Co Bush Band in 1977 and also worked in radio on 2NZ Inverell and the ABC's popular *Australia All Over* program.

A major career change in 1988 saw him signed as a solo recording artist to Festival Records. Other record deals followed, along with hits like 'Mow Ya Lawn', 'Since Cheryl Went Feral' and 'Don't Call Wagga Wagga Wagga'. He created the first morning variety shows at the Tamworth Country Music Festival and toured his own shows, as well as touring with artists like Slim Dusty, Melinda Schneider and Adam Brand. He has hosted the Pat Glover Memorial Story Telling Awards at the Port Fairy Folk Festival for almost twenty years.

Jim has written and compiled over twenty books and released many albums of his own songs, verse and humour. He still works as an entertainer and has a weekend Australiana segment on Radio 2UE's long-running *George and Paul* show.

Jim lives at Moore Park in Sydney with his wife, Robyn. He collects colonial art, plays tennis twice a week, supports the Sydney Swans and can walk to Randwick Racecourse in ten minutes.

AUSTRALIA'S BEST UNKNOWN STORIES

AND TALES YOU THOUGHT YOU KNEW . . .

JIM HAYNES

First published in 2014

Allen & Unwin
83 Alexander Street
Crows Nest NSW 2065
Australia
Phone:(61 2) 8425 0100
Email: info@allenandunwin.com
Web: www.allenandunwin.com

Cataloguing-in-Publication details are available
from the National Library of Australia
www.trove.nla.gov.au

ISBN 978 1 76011 178 6

Set in 12/15 pt Minion Pro by Midland Typesetters, Australia
Printed and bound in China by Hang Tai Printing Company Limited.

10 9 8 7

Dedicated to the memory of James Dellit
1947–2014

CONTENTS

Part 2 Characters Aussies Should Know About 123

Part 3 Unlikely Tales From Small Towns 255

INTRODUCTION

The *raison d'etre* for this collection is to give a few insights into bits of our history that may have escaped the school textbooks and which might, at the same time, serve to amuse and enlighten readers.

The aim of these stories and anecdotes is to make readers raise their eyebrows and exclaim, 'My goodness, I never knew that!'

Of course, it is a moot point if any of these stories contain what many people would consider to be 'essential information'. Some of us are, however, of the general opinion that you can never know *too* much.

After all, you never know when a certain fact or insight might be useful in some way, even if just to flaunt useless knowledge in the face of a tedious bunch of friends at a dinner party.

On the other hand, some of the information contained in these stories might actually help you to better understand the Australian psyche or just get a firmer grip on our history—or widen the horizon of your knowledge of Australia generally and meet a few characters from our past who deserve to be remembered but somehow weren't.

In this modern world where all knowledge seems to be available at the touch of a google, it is, perhaps, more fun to go seeking information we may not need right away. Information which might add to the rich tapestry of our life in less immediate ways.

Take the wombat, for example.

How many of you knew that wombat poo is cubic in shape?

Evidently the wombat needs to mark his territory, perhaps her territory also, and cubic poop stays on hillsides far more easily than the usual shaped stuff.

The wombat is, indeed, a mysterious creature.

Did you know that no one had ever seen wombats mating until 1987 when the process was finally filmed using infrared cameras? You might catch the movie on the adult pay TV channel one day.

That enigmatic explorer George Bass, who discovered the truth about Tasmania at the age of 27 and then sailed off and disappeared in the vast Pacific at the age of 31, and was never heard from again, managed, in his short life, to achieve the honour of being made a member of the Royal Society for his treatise on the anatomy of the wombat, which he dissected himself.

I bet you didn't know that.

You see, you're already more knowledgeable and the book has hardly begun.

We live in the only nation on earth that is also a continent. It is the driest and flattest continent on the planet and only one quarter of its surface can support agriculture.

The first European settlers in Australia drank more alcohol per head of population than any other community in the history of mankind.

Crimes for which you could be transported to this alcoholic haven included receiving stolen goods, setting fire to undergrowth, starting a union, stealing fish from a pond, being suspected of supporting Irish terrorism and 'recommending that politicians get paid'.

Once you were here you could do pretty well as you pleased. In fact, in 1832, in what was described as a 'rare moment of collusion', 300 female convicts from the Cascade Female Factory mooned the governor of Tasmania during a church service. The result of this mass mooning, believed to be the first of its kind in the world, was that 'the ladies in the governor's party could not control their laughter'.

Australia had a prime minister who was famous for his ability to drink 2.5 pints of beer in eleven seconds and New South Wales had a premier who famously drank a pint of rum every morning for 35 years of his life. (Bob Hawke and Sir John Robertson respectively.)

We needed two referenda before we decided we wanted to become a nation. Then one state, Western Australia, voted by a huge majority of almost 70 per cent to secede from Australia in 1933, only to be told by the Commons Joint Committee of the British parliament, from whom they sought permission to become a separate nation called 'Westralia', that, while it had the power to do what was required, it could not change the Australian constitution in order to do it!

Furthermore, the joint committee said, the state of Western Australia had no right to alter the Australian constitution and, consequently, Western Australian remained part of the Commonwealth.

We are an odd lot, us Aussies. Supposedly we have a distinctive character and, as Australians, exhibit many unique and lovable traits, which set us apart from other nationalities.

Yet we were reluctant to even become Australians at all. The constitution of our nation does not contain the word 'citizen' but speaks of us only as 'subjects'.

There was no such thing as an 'Australian citizen' until a law was passed enabling us to become such, in 1948. Before that date we were all British subjects. The first Australian passports were issued in 1949. Married Australian women, however, had to wait until 1983 before they were finally able to apply for passports without their husband's permission.

After 1949 you could be an Australian citizen in one of three ways: If your father was born here you were in, but mothers didn't count. If you were British and lived here and were 'of good character', or had lived here a year, were 'of good character' and swore allegiance to the Queen of Britain, you were okay too. Oh . . . and being white helped a lot.

Of course, these days you simply know if you're an Aussie or not—it's easy.

You know you're Australian if you understand the true meaning of the phrase 'a group of women wearing thongs' and you also understand that, unlike Britain and the USA, Australia does have a plural form of 'you'—it's 'youse'.

And, if you're really Australian, you need to know our own history, the quirky, the unknown and the forgotten . . . it helps.

PART 1
STUFF AUSSIES SHOULD KNOW ABOUT

The Australian history we were told about at school was only ever a small part of what happened to make our nation the place it is for us to live in.

Fads and trends come and go in education and at times, during some eras of education in different states, the curriculum didn't really include a lot of Australian history at all.

Of course, being young is never the best time to learn certain things. Kids are not that interested in the past, they want to be engaged in what is happening now and think about the future.

A desire to know about our past and what makes us who we are is more often than not a thing that comes with age.

Most of these stories fall into the category of things that most of us were not taught at school but they are stories which, hopefully, help us to understand how Australia developed into the kind of place it is today.

I am often annoyed by the simplistic attitude taken by teachers to history. The desire to pigeon-hole personalities and events into 'good' and 'bad' gives kids a very wrong impression of how things were in the past.

During my own education, I often had teachers who taught history as if it was mathematics: this person was bad, this event was good, etc. There was little attempt made to make history a continuum of consequences or a human story.

When I did strike a teacher who gave a class some idea of the complexity of the past and made history come to life by explaining the consequences of events, and describing the characters involved as real people, history became a 'story' and suddenly I was interested!

History is really only useful if it can help us to unravel and explain why things are the way they are today. We need to understand the present by looking at the past but, in order to make people look into the past, the past has to be made interesting.

So, some of these stories are attempts to help us understand who we are and why things happened to make our society the way it is.

There is also, however, another reason for the inclusion of some of these yarns. I have quite an obsession with researching things that are presented to us as 'facts' in order to find out if there is another side to the story. In doing so, I often discover that the 'facts' have, in fact, just been made up to suit someone's agenda and the truth lies elsewhere. Those stories, where a commonly held belief is proved to be wrong, are often the most interesting. People love to know stuff others don't.

Then, of course, there are the facts and stories that are fascinating and amusing for no other reason than they are unusual or odd or just funny!

I hope you enjoy this section, and maybe find out something about Australia you didn't know.

IT AIN'T NECESSARILY SO

There are always going to be more things you *don't* know than things you *do* know. It goes without saying.

As Hamlet (or was it Bill Shakespeare?) reminded us a few centuries ago, there are more things in heaven and earth than we can dream of.

What is sometimes very strange, however, is what we do know and what we don't. Even more fascinating, to me at least, is what we *think* we know, but what may not be true at all.

Let's start with an obvious one.

THE GHAN

Ask any Aussie why the train that runs from Adelaide to Darwin is called the *Ghan* and anyone who has an answer at all will tell you it is named as a tribute to the Afghan cameleers who carried goods through the outback before there were trains or roads.

That is what the railway publicity tells you and it's in all the encyclopediae and is a widely accepted 'fact'.

It is not true.

The Southern Section of the Great Northern Railway was begun in 1877 by the South Australian government and finally came to a halt in 1929 when the Commonwealth government completed the section from Rumbalara to Stuart, which later became Alice Springs.

The train was a 'limited mixed' which meant it had passenger carriages and goods vans, and it was given the official title of the *Oodnadatta Night Train*, until the route was extended. Then it reverted to being known as the limited mixed once more.

So, the legendary *Ghan* only came into existence on 4 August 1929 when the first passengers arrived in the town of Stuart, which would later be renamed Alice Springs. The train was two and a half hours late and the name was adopted as a private staff joke at the expense of George Gahan, Commissioner of the Commonwealth Railways, who was on that first train.

Commissioner Gahan had an obsession with building the line through to Stuart and arrived in a special commissioner's carriage he'd had built. The carriage cost £7584 of the Commonwealth government's money and featured an observation saloon with curved glass, four sleeping compartments, a bathroom, a dining saloon, a kitchen and a compartment to accommodate two male servants. The interior of the car was made from the best Tasmanian oak.

The train was regarded as unnecessary by many, including most of the railway staff at the time. The commissioner's carriage was seen as an extravagant toy and the rail line itself as a waste of federal money. Staff on the train often outnumbered passengers and the train was never going to cover its costs. The line was beset by problems of washaways and derailments and notoriously sloppy work practices prevailed.

Commonwealth Railways, which operated the service, was often referred to as the 'Comical Railways'.

As the train was considered slow and useless by railway staff, they took great delight in christening the train the *Gahan*, as a derogatory jibe at their commissioner.

So, the popularly believed story about the name *Ghan*, which most people believe, because they are told it over and over, is a 'furphy', which is an Aussie term for a false rumour or fib.

Here's another one.

AUSTRALIA'S CAR

It has long been a national legend that the Holden was 'the first car specifically designed for Australian conditions'.

Well, that's not a *legend*, it's a *myth*.

During World War II the government, along with both Ford and General Motors-Holden, explored the possibility of a locally produced affordable motorcar.

The Holden company began life in 1856 as saddle and harness makers. In 1908 the company moved into the automotive field before becoming a subsidiary of US company General Motors (GM) in 1931.

After the war General Motors-Holden continued to pursue the idea. Managing director Laurence Hartnett wanted a local design, while the company preferred to see an American one.

The final design for 'Australia's Own Car' was based on a US designed, but previously rejected, post-war Chevrolet.

The name 'Holden' was chosen, incidentally, in honour of Sir Edward Holden, the company's first chairman. Other names considered were 'GeM', 'Austral', 'Melba', 'Woomerah', 'Boomerang', 'Emu' and 'Canbra'.

THE ASHES

Contrary to what Aussies believe, and what we have been told for more than a century, that tiny vase, which is actually a ladies' scent bottle, does not contain the ashes of stumps, bails, balls or anything vaguely connected with the game of cricket.

It contains the ashes of a lady's hat veil.

When England lost at home for the first time to Australia, in 1882, a mock obituary was inserted in the *Sporting Times*, which read:

> In Affectionate Remembrance of ENGLISH CRICKET, which died at the Oval on 29th AUGUST, 1882, Deeply lamented by a large circle of sorrowing friends and acquaintances R.I.P. N.B.—The body will be cremated and the ashes taken to Australia.

This was the beginning of the Ashes legend.

When the Eighth Earl of Darnley, Ivo Bligh, led the English

team to Australia in the following English winter, the English press joked that he was going to 'bring back the ashes'.

When his team won two of the three official tests, a group of Melbourne ladies, including Bligh's future wife, Florence Morphy of Beechworth in Victoria, and Lady Clarke, who had, along with her husband, entertained the English team in Melbourne, made a joke presentation to him of a terracotta scent bottle, which contained some ashes.

The Countess of Darnley presented the urn to the Marylebone Cricket Club (MCC) after her husband's death. She died in August 1944. Replicas of the urn are used as trophies for the Ashes Series but the original remains with the MCC in London.

In 1998 Darnley's 82-year-old daughter-in-law said the ashes were the remains of her mother-in-law's hat veil. MCC officials, however, still persist with the nonsense that they are '95 per cent certain' that the urn contains the ashes of a cricket bail, most likely one used in a social game between the English team and a team chosen by Sir W.J. Clarke.

While 'bail' and 'veil' are very close in sound, and a misunderstanding is plausible, anyone understanding the nature of the joke presentation (and how hard it is to actually cremate a cricket bail and recover the ashes) will realise that 'the ashes' are, in all likelihood, derived from something much easier to incinerate than a wooden bail or a leather ball. At least, that's my opinion.

AUSSIE, AUSSIE, AUSSIE–OY! OY! OY!

While this is a perfectly fine patriotic chant, and I am not suggesting for a second that we stop using it to inspire our athletes, it's about as Australian as a Welsh pastie—literally.

Like the Cornishmen, who are famous for their pasties, the Welsh have a long history of working underground in the mining industry and also have their own local version of the miners' daily lunchtime pastry—the 'oggie'.

The original idea of the pastie was that it contained an entire meal, meat and vegetables, or often meat and vegetables at one end and jam or fruit and custard at the other, all wrapped in a baked pastry cover. The miners' wives would make the pasties with a ridge of crust along one side so that the miners could hold them in their filthy hands while eating their lunch underground. The crust was then discarded for the rats, which lived in the mines. This kept the creatures from attacking the men while they were eating.

Oggie sellers would push carts along the docks and working areas of Cardiff and other Welsh cities and call 'Oggie, oggie oggie!' to advertise their wares. The reply 'Oy, oy, oy!' was a response from anyone wishing to purchase. It was a signal for the oggie salesman to stop and wait until the customer could catch up and make a purchase.

Famous entertainer Max Boyce based his entire act on 'being Welsh' with Welsh songs, jokes and anecdotes about rugby and mining. Boyce was hugely popular in the 1960s and 1970s and adopted the call of the oggie salesmen as a gimmick to use with his audiences.

Australian entertainer Frank Ifield was touring the theatre circuit in Britain with Max Boyce in the 1970s and saw how Boyce had made the call a rallying cry for audiences. It was also used at rugby matches and in other contexts as a light-hearted method of asserting anyone's 'Welshness'. When I lived in a Welsh-speaking college at Aberystwyth University, it was often used between songs when spontaneous singing occurred in the dining hall (often rather 'anti-English' satirical songs or Celtic rebel songs).

While following Max Boyce around the theatre circuit, Frank decided to tease audiences with a version of the chant which asserted his Australian nationality.

'I did it as a joke, just for fun,' says Frank. 'Knowing that Max had used his "Oggie, oggie, oggie!" chant to warm up the audience, I'd parody the chant by yelling "Aussie, Aussie, Aussie!" to get the same response. It was just light-hearted fun.'

So, there you have it. Our fine patriotic chant is, genuinely, about as Australian as a Welsh miner's lunch.

Not only are there many things we don't know, we should never be too sure about the things we are sure we *do* know!

SPORTING STUFF YOU PROBABLY DON'T KNOW

Aussies are obsessed with sport. So here's a selection of trivial and astounding facts that you probably didn't know—some of the greatest victories, successes and failures ever in our sporting history.

THE FASTEST

Athletes run, swim and cycle faster and faster every year, possibly due to better equipment, training, diet and scientific methods of preparing. But how about the fastest ever *results* in Aussie sport?

Well, the shortest Australian boxing title fight was between Herb Narvo and Billy Britt. On 3 April 1943 in Newcastle, Narvo knocked out Britt 25 seconds after the opening bell—and that included the ten seconds taken to count Britt out! There is no record of whether or not patrons asked for a refund.

That is, however, not the shortest fight in Australia, not by a long shot. On 26 June 1991 in Brisbane, Paul Rees scored a TKO victory over Arne 'Charlie' Hansen in a bout that lasted exactly five seconds. The stitching on Rees's glove lacerated his opponent's eye with the first punch.

Jimmy Carruthers was reputed to have the fastest *hands* in boxing history and was the first world champion boxer in any division to retire without a loss or draw. As a professional Carruthers won fourteen straight fights before defeating Vic Toweel to claim the world title in Johannesburg in 1952.

Carruthers knocked out Toweel in 2 minutes and 19 seconds. The match was a sell-out and many fans were still finding their way to their seats when it ended. Judges scored Carruthers as throwing 110 punches in 1 minute and 40 seconds—Toweel threw one, which missed.

Carruthers then defended his title three times and retired undefeated. Sadly, he made a comeback eight years later and lost four of his seven fights.

As an aside—Australia also holds the record for the only boxing match in history where a draw was declared when both fighters were knocked out. In the second round of their bout at St George Leagues Club on 21 September 1965, middleweights Stan Simpson and Tony Lythgoe clashed heads, cinched, tumbled from the ring and were both knocked out cold.

In rugby league history the fastest sending off occurred at the Sydney Cricket Ground on Anzac Day 1986 when Peter Kelly, playing for Canterbury, was sent off after six seconds had elapsed. Canterbury kicked off and Kelly immediately charged at Souths' winger Ross Harrington and flattened him with a high tackle.

A bugler had just played the 'Last Post' in the centre of the ground, after a minute's silence had been observed as a mark of respect to the fallen. The bugler was still walking off and stopped and held open the boundary fence gate in front of the Members Stand for Kelly to leave the field.

Harrington was carried off on a stretcher some minutes later, unconscious.

On the subject of send-offs . . .

After an all-in brawl, Queensland country referee Kevin Hauff sent all 26 players to the sin bin for ten minutes in a game between Barcaldine and Blackall in 1990. When the game resumed, tempers had cooled but one Barcaldine player was sent off later for punching.

In rugby history Jim Baker is believed to be the only linesman ever sent off. Baker received his marching orders when he hit a player with his flag in a game at Chatswood Oval in Sydney in 1968.

THE BIGGEST

These days with World Cup matches between tiny countries and great sporting nations, huge scores in soccer are not uncommon, but the biggest defeat in international soccer at the time was England's 1951 trouncing of Australia 17–0 in Sydney after defeating the same side 13–0 in Adelaide three days earlier.

You won't believe this, but it's true—the Australian goalkeeper's name was . . . wait for it . . . Norman Conquest!

One of my favourite trivia questions concerns the biggest crowd ever to see a baseball game live—it was at the Melbourne Cricket Ground and 110,000 spectators turned up to see a demonstration game between Australia and the USA for the Olympics in 1956.

Our biggest haul of swimming and diving medals came at the Jamaica Commonwealth Games in 1966, when every member of the Australian swimming and diving teams won a medal. The tally in the pool was seventeen gold, thirteen silver and twelve bronze.

Conversely, Australia's poorest ever result at an Olympics—one silver and four bronze—came at the 1976 Montreal games. We finished 32nd in the medal count and the result led directly to the setting up of the Australian Institute of Sport.

THE LONGEST

Essendon's Albert Thurgood is famous as having the longest recorded kick ever—107 yards 2 feet 1 inch or 98.48 metres! Thurgood played for Essendon in two spells in the 1890s and won the grand final almost single-handedly against Collingwood in 1901. In between he played in Perth for Fremantle for three seasons and helped them win two premierships.

Of course Australian rules football is the oldest football code in the world. While the first recorded mention of the game being played in Australia dates from 1829, there is no record of what rules were used. In 1858, however, Tom Will and Henry Harrison wrote the first ten rules of the Australian Football League (AFL), thus becoming the first people in the world to codify a kicking-ball game. These rules predate those of rugby, soccer, Gaelic football and American football.

The odd thing about this world first is that the rules were written, and the game was first played, a long way from Tom's old school, Rugby in the UK, where he had had the idea.

C.J. Dennis had a different version of how the game began. He wrote this poem in the Melbourne *Herald*, explaining the origins of AFL, at the start of the footy season in 1930.

THE GAME

C.J. DENNIS

'Tis many and many a long year now
Since first a fellow killed a cow
And robbed the creature of its hide.
Then, when he'd scraped the hairy side,
He tanned it in a noisesome pit
And made a little bag from it.
But, finding it would not hold air,
He wandered to a forest where
There grew strange trees, and found that some
Contained a queer resilient gum.

So, being quite a clever chap,
He lined his leather bag with sap
Then took a long, long breath and blew.
Red in the face he puffed anew
Until the bag was blown up tight:
A thing elusive, hard yet light,
That to the slightest blow would yield.
And then he flung it in a field.
A score of tribesmen gathered there
Beheld the object, light as air
That bounced along, and, as it came,
'A game!' they shouted. 'Here's a game!'

One seized the thing and rushed away.
(Man had discovered how to play.)
He ran, he stumbled, almost fell,
And after him they rushed, pell-mell,
Each seeking madly to secure
And hold this strange elusive lure,
The whole excited, yelling tribe.
'Tis hardly fitting to describe
The scene that followed after that –
The scene where men cursed, struggled, spat,
Bit, gouged, kicked, and madly tore
From other men the skins they wore.
The scene of many wounded men
Lying on the ground, and then,
The sight of spent men out of breath,
Of battle riot, sudden death.

But all agreed, when it was o'er,
They'd never had such fun before,
And all agreed it closed too soon
A very pleasant afternoon.
And yet if you go down today,
And hear the yells and watch the play,
You'll find the prehistoric game
And modern football's much the same.
You'll notice your subconscious rise,
Responding to the savage cries,
Until the primal man once more,
Uprising, as he did of yore,
Impels you to stand up and hoot,
'Yah! Knock 'em down! Put in the boot!'
And, though you blush for what you've done,
You can't deny it's lots of fun.

WHY AUSSIE KIDS SHOULD LOVE NUGGET COOMBES

Australians under 60 years of age would have no idea what 'school milk' means.

For Aussies over 60, however, the taste of the free school milk remains vividly in the memory. The milk was rarely refrigerated and if you forgot to shake the bottle before opening you got a mouthful of warm, lumpy cream.

At the school I attended we could not leave the quadrangle until we had finished our milk. There was not a plant left alive in the gardens around the quadrangle and the whole place smelled of sour milk.

How did this happen? It was a conspiracy between some medical do-gooders and the nation's dairy farmers.

At the State Education Convention in 1941, Dr Noel Gutteridge of the British Medical Association proposed a scheme to provide a daily ration of one half-pint of milk to all Australian school children. He claimed it would 'double the normal growth rate of children and have positive effects on behaviour at school, athletic prowess, absenteeism and dental health'.

Only the Queensland Teachers' Union opposed the idea.

Milk producers, of course, loved the idea and lobbied hard. Milk production in the early 1940s had reached an historic high without a corresponding increase in consumption. Exports of butter were down. School milk schemes were industry subsidies on a huge scale.

In July 1950, Prime Minister Menzies proposed a free milk scheme. Commonwealth and state health ministers met in

Canberra and it was decided the Commonwealth Department of Health would operate the scheme with state authorities acting as agents. The act was passed in December 1950 and by October 1951 all states except Queensland were participating.

In Queensland, the Hanlon government said the scheme was inappropriate in a state with a tropical climate and huge distances between centres, but Queensland ultimately joined in 1953.

Implementing the scheme was a nightmare. The Department of Public Instruction (later Education) was responsible for the day-to-day tasks of administration and organisation including processing tenders for the supply of milk and straws, comparing school statements of actual supply with vendors' claims and record-keeping.

The scheme was limited to children under the age of thirteen and was supposedly a voluntary activity. Parents' permission was required to participate. Many schools reversed this to make administration easier, so you had to opt *out*!

The Whitlam government *Review of the Continuing Expenditure Policies of the Previous Governments* (June 1973), headed by Dr Nugget Coombes, recommended the scheme be stopped based on significant evidence that benefits to diet were minimal beyond age seven. The scheme ended in 1973.

Thanks, Nugget!

ACCIDENTAL DISCOVERIES

It is a fact that many of the great discoveries in our pioneering history were accidental. While the early exploration of Australia was often carried out systematically by surveyors like Major Mitchell, Charles Sturt and others, some areas were opened up and explored, and then settled, due to quite random events.

The need for farmland and expansion led to the exploration west of the Blue Mountains and south of Sydney after about 30 years of European settlement, but both Newcastle and Port Macquarie were established as a result of piracy and pursuit!

One thing they never told us at school was the number of attempts made by convicts to steal boats and escape from Sydney Cove.

While the obvious option was for convicts to escape overland, they usually met their death in the bush from starvation or fatal encounters with the various Aboriginal tribes. The other alternative was escape—and most probably death—by sea. Escape of any kind was highly unlikely to succeed, but life was grim for the convicts whether they stayed or ran. After all, the whole point of sending criminals to 'Botany Bay' was that the lord commissioners of the treasury knew it was a place 'from whence it is hardly possible for persons to return without permission'.

'Hardly possible' perhaps, but not entirely impossible.

In September 1790 a former seaman and highwayman, John Tarwood, stole a leaky boat from the South Head lookout station and set off for Tahiti with four other convicts. Five years later the four survivors of this daring escapade were found alive but somewhat emaciated at Port Stephens, where they had survived due to the generosity of the Aborigines.

Also in 1790 and against all odds, the convict Mary Bryant escaped but she successfully returned to her home in Cornwall—what's more, she received a pardon.

Unlike the spontaneous or opportunistic break-outs that occurred from time to time, the escape of William and Mary Bryant, their two children and seven other convict companions was carefully planned and well prepared.

William Bryant was a Cornishman and knew boats and the sea. He maintained the colony's small boats and helped with the fishing, as he was the most skilled and capable man for the job.

But he had a grievance; he knew he was technically a free man, he had served his time but Governor Phillip was waiting for the convict indents to arrive and had no record of which had served their time and which had not. So Bryant took extra care to maintain the government cutter, stole stores and stockpiled them, waited until there were no ships in the colony capable of pursuit, then escaped.

The escape was so well planned that after the boat was overturned in a squall, Bryant restored it to first-class order with new sails and masts and a complete refit, all supplied by the government. He and Mary had also stashed away 100 pounds of rice, the same of flour, as well as salt pork, water, tents and tools.

They survived storms in which they were lost in 'mountainous seas' and encounters with hostile Aborigines who chased them out to sea in large canoes. They navigated the Great Barrier Reef, regularly coming ashore for water and supplies, and crossed the Arafura Sea and finally made it safely to Koepang, on Timor, after 70 days at sea. There, they were arrested after their story of shipwreck failed to convince Captain Edwards, who had arrived there in the longboat from the wrecked HMS *Pandora*, and they were sent back to Britain. Due to disease and accidents at sea, only Mary and four of the others survived the journey home and were eventually pardoned.

While the Bryants and their crew were well prepared and knew exactly where they were headed, there was a general feeling among the more geographically challenged convicts that China was not far away and could be somehow reached by land or sea from Sydney Cove.

Twelve convicts undertook one of the most misguided escapes in the first decade of the colony. They took off by stolen boat and six of them were eventually found in 1798 living on an island near Western Port in what was later named Bass Strait. The man who found them, a very surprised George Bass, was supposedly the first European to explore the area.

Naturally Bass asked them what were they doing on an island off the south coast of the continent. They replied that they had been trying to sail to China!

The six had been abandoned on the island by the other six. We can only assume that the six who sailed off all perished attempting to find China somewhere in the Great Southern Ocean.

After rescuing the castaways, Bass set four ashore with directions to Sydney, a compass and rations, and took the two weakest on board for the return trip to Sydney. The four set ashore were never seen again.

Some 40 years later, in an act of daring piracy, a bunch of desperate convicts did steal a ship, the brig *Cyprus*, and sail to China, and there were other daring escape attempts in the meantime. One of which led to the discovery of Newcastle and its coal deposits.

In September 1797 John Shortland, in pursuit of convicts who had stolen the *Cumberland*, the colony's best boat, discovered Newcastle, with its rich coal deposits, accidentally. On 10 January 1798, Governor Hunter wrote to the Duke of Portland:

> I have now to inform your Grace that on the fifth day of September last, as our largest and best boat belonging to Government, was on her way to the Hawkesbury River, carrying stores, and to bring from thence some articles wanted here, a service on which she was constantly employed, she was taken possession of by a part of

> the crew, assisted by a few men in another boat, who threatened the life of the coxswain and all who dared to oppose them.
>
> They put him and three others on shore at Broken Bay, and went off with the boat we know not whither.
>
> I am of opinion it had been a long concerted plan. Not having any fit vessel to pursue upon such occasion, I dispatched two row boats, well armed; the one went about sixty miles northward along the coast and the other forty miles southwards, but without success, a gale blowing soon after the escape.

Another account from the same time, written by the colony's Judge Advocate, David Collins, tells us what happened next:

> One of these boats returned in a few days, without having seen any thing of them; but Lieutenant Shortland proceeded with the other, a whale boat, as far as Port Stephens, where he thought it probable they might have taken shelter; but on the 19th, having been absent thirteen days, he returned without discovering the smallest trace of them or the boat.
>
> His pursuit, however, had not been without its advantage; for on his return he entered a river which he named Hunter River, about ten leagues to the southward of Port Stephens, into which he carried three fathoms water, in the shoalest part of its entrance. Finding deep water and good anchorage within. The entrance of this river was but narrow, and covered by a high rocky Island, lying right off it, so as to leave a good passage round the north end of the island, between that and the shore. A reef connects the south part of the island with the south shore of the entrance of the river.
>
> In this harbour was found a very considerable quantity of coal of a very good sort, and lying so near the water side as to be conveniently shipped; which gave it, in this particular, a manifest advantage over that discovered to the southward. Some specimens of this coal were brought up in the boat.

So the colony lost a boat but gained a supply of coal, and a new settlement was formed, which soon became a 'hell-hole' with some nice dirty work for convicts who misbehaved in Sydney!

Because of Shortland's accidental discovery we now have the city of Newcastle, named, of course, after the most famous coal-producing city in Britain. It is the second largest city in the state of New South Wales—and a fine city it is, too.

The Port Macquarie area was also opened up after a pursuit of runaways, 'pirates' if you will.

While we have no idea what happened to the convicts who stole the *Cumberland*, we do have an account of what happened to the cast of characters involved in the second accidental discovery—and it's a fairly sad and gruesome story.

In September 1816 the brig *Trial* was anchored up near the Sow and Pigs Reef, at Middle Head in Sydney Harbour, waiting for a favourable wind to make a trading trip to Launceston, then known as Port Dalrymple.

The *Trial* was owned by ex-convict and successful merchant Simeon Lord, who would spend many years attempting to get around the restrictions placed on his trading by the fact that he was an ex-convict and also by the monopoly of the British East India Company in Asia.

A party of thirteen convicts who had escaped from the Hyde Park Barracks seized the *Trial* on 12 September 1816. They not only seized the ship, they kidnapped the captain and crew and the passengers who were on board, including a stowaway—the escaped convict Anne Shortis, who had been smuggled aboard by a crew member. It is not even known with accuracy who was on the ship—the passengers and crew numbered between eight and ten and there were probably three women and one child.

It was an unlucky Friday 13 for Governor Macquarie, who immediately declared the event an act of piracy, labelled the desperados with the strange old-fashioned word 'banditti' (meaning a gang of cut-throats) and noted in his journal:

> **Friday 13. Sept**—About 12,O'Clock this Day, Capt. Piper the Naval Officer sent me a written Report, stating that in the middle

of last Night or early this morning before Daylight, a Banditti of Runaway Convicts went on board of the Brig Trial (belonging to Simeon Lord Esqr.), seized and Piratically carried off from Watson's Bay near the Heads—where she lay at anchor waiting for a fair Wind, and by Day-break She was out of Sight.

Immediately on receiving this intelligence I directed the Colonial Brig Rosetta to be hired and armed to be sent after the Fugitive Pirates, and She accordingly sailed [sic] at 5,O'Clock this Evening, having a Party of Soldiers on board.

Exactly two weeks later the governor noted:

Friday 27. Sept Evening about 7,O'Clock, the Colonial Brig Rosetta—which had been fitted out and sent in Pursuit of the Brig Carried off in the Night of the 12th. Inst. by a Banditti of Convict Pirates—anchored in Sydney Cove, after cruising for a Fortnight in hopes of seeing and retaking the Trial but without Success. The Rosetta extended her Cruise to the Northward as far as Howe's Island—and then returned—not having seen or heard any thing of the Trial.

What actually did happen to the *Trial* was mostly pieced together from conversations with Aborigines who gave accounts to Captain Thomas Whyte of the government ship *Lady Nelson*. She had sailed from Newcastle in January 1817 to search for the *Trial* after reports of a wreck were received from outposts near Port Stephens.

Whyte found remains of the brig and a canvas tent on a beach about 60 miles north of Port Stephens, but there was no trace of any survivors.

Using sign language and drawing in the sand, a story was put together that the *Trial* came in to shore, probably to find water, and was wrecked by the surf after being run aground on a sand bar. After some time ashore the escaped convicts constructed a makeshift boat from the timbers of the wreck and a group of them headed back out to sea. The boat was swamped within sight of the shore and all aboard drowned in the surf.

It seems, though, that some of the *Trial*'s passengers and crew, along with several convicts, including Anne Shortis, did not attempt to leave in the makeshift boat. Instead, they remained on the beach near the wreck.

It is fairly certain that the men who remained on the beach were killed by the Aborigines and it appears that Anne Shortis and Emily Bardon, wife of the captain of the *Trial*, survived for some years, separately, living with the Indigenous people.

There were many reports over the ensuing years of a 'white lubra' and the resulting searches for the missing pirates and their hostages led to the exploration of the area, which had been the far northern limit of the colony when the wreck occurred.

As a consequence, Port Macquarie was established as a penal colony in 1821, and the bay where the wreck was found was called Trial Bay. A reward offered for knowledge of survivors of the wreck led to a woman, said to be Emily Bardon, being restored to her family in 1831. She was in a wretched and distracted state and died shortly afterwards.

The Kempsey area was opened up by cedar cutters in 1836 and the following year two 'renegade' Aborigines were tracked down by police after attacking settlers. One was shot and the other, named Billy Blueshirt, told the troopers that his mother was the white woman from the wreck, Anne Shortis.

It's a rather sad start for what would become the lovely city of Port Macquarie we know today.

THE LOVE BOAT

The convict transport *Janus* arrived at Port Jackson on 2 May 1820. She carried 104 female convicts from the port of Cork in Ireland. Her captain was Thomas Mowat and her first mate was John Hedges.

Governor Macquarie's secretary, John Campbell, had the unenviable task of inspecting each newly arrived ship and the convicts each vessel brought to the penal settlement of Sydney. Campbell didn't much like this part of his job as often the convicts were diseased and starving due to the ship owners cheating on rations, and other essentials to a healthy life, during the long five-month voyage from Britain. It was his duty to sign off on each new shipment so that the contractors could be paid for delivering their sad cargo.

To his delight the *Janus* seemed an exemplary vessel. The female convicts were healthy and happy, as were the captain and crew. So Campbell signed off on the shipment, the women were assigned to various families as servants, and the ship remained in port being reprovisioned and repaired.

All seemed in order.

Soon, however, things started to become a little more complicated.

Two female convicts assigned to Nicholas Bayley, Mary Long and Lydia Esden, entered a complaint to the governor via their new master. Mary claimed she was expecting Captain Mowat's child, Lydia was pregnant to first mate Hedges.

But this was only the tip of the iceberg, so to speak.

Soon complaints were flooding in from others who had been assigned the female convicts from the *Janus*. Dozens of the girls were expecting!

The governor ordered a full enquiry, a full bench of magistrates was assembled, and the girls and the crew, along with two clergymen who had been aboard, were all summoned to appear.

Commissioner Thomas Bigge was in New South Wales at the time to investigate concerns that transportation was no longer an effective deterrent of crime or a good method of reforming convicts. In effect, he was there to inspect the colony and report back to the British government. Bigge spent seventeen months in the colonies travelling around New South Wales and Van Diemen's Land and returned to England in 1821.

He was present at the enquiry into the voyage of the *Janus* and wrote a report on the proceedings:

> The circumstances that took place on board the female convict ship Janus are detailed in the minutes of evidence that were taken by myself upon the investigation, ordered by Governor Macquarie, of the complaint of two female convicts that had been assigned to Mr. Bayley.
>
> It is to be remarked, that the advanced state of pregnancy in which these women were found to be previous to the departure of the captain and mate of the ship from Port Jackson, occasioned their complaints to be preferred through Mr Bayley, their master, to the governor, although, at the muster that took place on board the ship, no complaint of any kind is recorded by Mr. Secretary Campbell to have been made to him, nor was any complaint addressed to any other quarter.
>
> From the evidence, however, it appears, that all the evils that unrestrained intercourse between the crew of the ship and a number of licentious women could produce, existed to their full extent in the voyage of the Janus from England . . . until its arrival at New South Wales.
>
> It appears that the attempts of the captain . . . to check the profligacy . . . were neither sincere nor effectual. With the

> knowledge, indeed, that the sailors could not fail to obtain of his participation, as well as the mate's, in the same intercourse in which they had so freely indulged, it was not to be expected that their admonitions, if sincere, could have been effectual.
>
> The captain has denied that his intercourse with Mary Long was of an improper or immoral kind; but the testimony of the Rev. Mr. Conolly and Mr. Therry both agree in the frequency and long duration of the visits of this woman to the captain's cabin; and it is also to be observed, that he has not denied the allegation made by her upon oath, of his being the father of the child with which she was pregnant when the inquiry took place.

The Full Bench of Magistrates ruled that the allegations were 'most fully and clearly proved'.

'Amorous activities,' they said, 'did prevail to a great degree on board the ship *Janus* throughout the voyage to Australia.'

Poor Governor Macquarie, with Commissioner Bigge looking over his shoulder to judge his reaction, was keen to punish the captain and crew as severely as possible. When Macquarie and his secretary investigated what powers they had over the crews of visiting vessels, however, they realised there was not really much they could do except refuse to sign the certificate that said the ship had delivered its cargo 'in good condition'.

As a result of Macquarie's refusal to sign the certificate of release, the *Janus* would never again be hired to transport convicts for the British government. Captain Mowat and his crew decided to try their luck at the newly profitable activity of whaling in the Southern Ocean and went off chasing whales, instead of women.

AUSTRALIA'S BEST-KNOWN SONG

What is Australia's best-known song?

All Aussie kids are taught the national anthem and most of us know at least the first verse. (It's something about 'Australians all eat ostriches' and some 'dirt by sea', I think.)

In spite of our great athletic and Olympic successes, however, few people outside of Australia have any idea about our anthem. In one of the first Olympics the Austrian national anthem was played when an Aussie won gold!

Is our best-known song 'Waltzing Matilda'? Well, maybe it is here in Australia, but there is another song much better known around the world.

Jack O'Hagan's classic 'Along the Road to Gundagai' was recorded and played thousands of times by the great violinist Stephane Grappelli; 'Pub with No Beer' was a big hit, too. But it isn't either of them.

The best-known Aussie song, worldwide, is, in fact, 'The Wild Colonial Boy'.

But just who was the *real* Wild Colonial Boy?

Jack Donohue was born in 1806 in Dublin and transported for 'intent to commit a felony' (which was probably related to the crime of having 'rebel sympathies or connections') on a ship named the *Ann and Amelia* in 1825.

Donohue was assigned for a short period to a road gang and then as a labourer to Major West, a surgeon who owned land at Quakers Hill, west of Sydney.

In 1827 he and two others absconded and committed 'highway robbery', which meant exactly that—they robbed some travellers on the Windsor to Sydney road. While that may sound romantic, the 'travellers' were actually a number of bullock drays.

The three men were sentenced to death twice. That is, they received two death sentences each for their crimes.

The other two were duly hanged, (just once each seemed to do the trick), but Donohue escaped while being taken from court to the jail in George Street and, over the following two years, he became the most celebrated bushranger in Australia.

The official 'Wanted' posters, which offered £20 reward, described Donohue as '22 years of age, 5 feet 4 inches in height, with a brown freckled complexion, flaxen hair, blue eyes, and a scar under the left nostril'.

His gang included various characters but the main members were Webber, Walmsley and Underwood. The gang covered a lot of territory and robbed settlers as far afield as Bathurst to the west, Yass to the south and the Hunter Valley to the north.

Finally, on 1 September 1830, a patrol of mounted soldiers and police caught up with the gang in the Bringelly scrub near modern-day Campbelltown.

Donohue boldly challenged the police and troopers to come and get him, using what the newspaper later described as 'the most insulting and indecent epithets'.

Unfortunately for him they did just that and he was killed by a pistol ball fired by Trooper Michael Muggleston. The ball entered Donohue's left temple and he died almost instantly.

After being caught during the encounter, Webber was hanged and Walmsley was reprieved. Underwood escaped but was shot dead in a chase in 1832.

Donohue's courage won him many admirers and his death was big news in Sydney. An enterprising tradesman fashioned a new style of clay pipes, which had bowls fashioned in the shape of the bushranger's head, complete with a bullet hole. These were very popular for many years, as were the ballads about his adventures and death.

The surveyor and famous explorer Major Mitchell obviously admired Donohue. He visited the morgue and made a quite beautiful pencil drawing of Donohue which is now in the Mitchell Library. Under the drawing Mitchell added a quotation from Byron:

> No matter; I have bared my brow.
> Fair in Death's face – before – and now

Donohue was seen as a 'Robin Hood' character, especially among the colony's ex-convict and Irish population. He is reputed to have robbed surveyor William Cox without realising who he was. Upon discovering his identity, Donohue returned Cox's valuables because he was 'a good master'.

Legend also has it that, on meeting Captain Sturt farming his land at Varroville near Camden, Donohue told his gang, 'Stand back, boys, it's Captain Sturt, and we don't rob him.'

Unfortunately this story breaks down somewhat in credibility when we learn that Sturt did not own the Varroville farm until 1837, seven years after Donohue died. Still, Sturt could have met the bushranger . . . somewhere else and some other time.

Many people ask, why are there so many versions of 'The Wild Colonial Boy'?

Well, there was already an Irish folksong about a scallywag named 'Bold O'Donohue'. Secondly, there were both Irish and Australian versions of the convict's bushranging adventures, and both versions changed as time passed.

Another reason for the bushranger having so many different names in the different versions of the song is that Governor Darling made singing the song a crime in the colony of New South Wales and a pub could lose its licence if the song was heard being sung on the premises. As a result of this ban, singers simply altered the lyrics slightly so names and facts were changed to disguise the hero. The bold bushranger was sometimes John Duggan, Jim Doolan, etc., but the initials were always J.D.

Another confusing element is that it seems there may have been another Victorian bushranger named Doolan many years later.

In some 1860s versions of the song the hero is born in Castlemaine and robs a coach near Beechworth—both in Victoria. In earlier versions of the ballad the hero is born in Dublin or Castlemaine in County Kerry, Ireland.

Outside Australia, 'The Wild Colonial Boy' was made famous by Burl Ives, Doctor Hook and The Clancy Brothers, who all recorded it—and Mick Jagger sang it in the film *Ned Kelly* in 1970. It was also used in the pro-Irish film *The Quiet Man* directed by John Ford and starring John Wayne.

So, there you have it, our most famous song—ever—is 'The Wild Colonial Boy'.

That is, of course, if you accept that it is Australian. The Irish think of it as Irish and it is considered an Irish rebel song as much as an Aussie ballad.

Here's my favourite version of 'The Wild Colonial Boy'. It is anonymous. There is no mention of Trooper Muggleston. Perhaps the name didn't rhyme with anything, which is a shame, because Harry Potter fans would have loved it.

I reckon it's an Australian song.

THE WILD COLONIAL BOY

There was a wild Colonial Boy; Jack Doolan was his name,
Of poor but honest parents he was born in Castlemaine.
He was his father's only hope, his mother's pride and joy,
And dearly did his parents love the wild Colonial Boy.

Chorus:
Come, all my hearties, we'll roam the mountains high,
Together we will plunder, together we will die.
We'll wander over valleys, and gallop over plains,
And we'll scorn to live in slavery, bound down with iron chains.

He was scarcely sixteen years of age when he left his father's home,
And through Australia's sunny clime a bushranger did roam.
He robbed those wealthy squatters, their stock he did destroy,
And a terror to Australia was the wild Colonial Boy.

In sixty-one this daring youth commenced his wild career,
With a heart that knew no danger, no foeman did he fear.
He stuck up the Beechworth mail-coach, and robbed Judge
MacEvoy,
Who trembled, and gave up his gold to the wild Colonial Boy.

He bade the judge 'Good morning', and told him to beware,
That he'd never rob a hearty chap that acted on the square,
And never to rob a mother of her son and only joy,
Or else you might turn outlaw, like the wild Colonial Boy.

One day as he was riding the mountainside along,
A-listening to the little birds, their pleasant laughing song,
Three mounted troopers rode along – Kelly, Davis and FitzRoy –
They thought that they would capture him, the wild Colonial Boy.

'Surrender now, Jack Doolan, you see there's three to one.
Surrender now, Jack Doolan, you daring highwayman.'
Jack drew a pistol from his belt, and waved it like a toy,
'I'll fight, but not surrender,' said the wild Colonial Boy.

He fired at Trooper Kelly and brought him to the ground,
And turning then to Davis, he received a fatal wound.
A bullet pierced his proud young heart, from the pistol of FitzRoy,
And that was how they captured him – the wild Colonial Boy.

THE COLONY THAT COULDN'T BE PREVENTED

The colonial administration in Sydney, in the early days, was always reluctant to allow other settlements to develop for fear that they would be outside its control. While there was some apprehension about European powers, especially France, settling parts of the continent, it was feared that other settlements springing up could stretch the administrative and military capability to breaking point and threaten the very existence of the colony, or be outside that control altogether.

Necessity drove Governor Hunter to send ships and men south in 1797. The ship *Sydney Cove*, carrying rice and supplies from Calcutta, was run aground on Preservation Island in Bass Strait after rounding Van Diemen's Land (Tasmania). The ship had been slowly sinking for weeks and her captain thought that grounding her in a sheltered cove was his only chance of preserving the cargo and the lives of the crew.

Seventeen men set out for Sydney in the longboat but it was driven ashore and wrecked by massive surf in a storm on the south coast. The group set out to walk to Sydney but hunger, exposure and attacks by hostile Aborigines had reduced the number to three when they were found just south of Sydney by a fishing boat on 15 May 1797.

Governor Hunter immediately sent the government schooner *Francis* and her tender *Eliza* to rescue the rest of the crew and the precious cargo.

Sadly, the *Eliza*, along with her crew and eight survivors of the *Sydney Cove*, was lost on the return journey, but the *Francis* made two more trips to the wreck, in December 1797 and February 1798. On the last occasion one of the officers on board was Matthew Flinders.

News of the wreck and the rescue voyages awakened interest in the area. Hunter himself, as captain of the *Sirius*, which circumnavigated the world just above the Antarctic Circle in order to bring supplies from Capetown to the starving colony in 1789, had detected strong currents in the area, and speculation grew about a passage between the mainland and Van Diemen's Land.

George Bass had arrived as ship's surgeon on the *Reliance* in 1795, along with Flinders and John Hunter, who was returning to the colony as governor. In December 1797 he took a whaleboat and a crew of six volunteers and explored the south coast. Past Wilsons Promontory he kept sailing until he reached 40 degrees south, where howling gales and mountainous waves forced him to turn back. He then followed the coast westward for more than 100 kilometres.

Bass made two remarkable 'discoveries' on that voyage. One was his realisation that the waves and wind he had encountered coming from the west indicated that there was no land to the west and Van Diemen's Land was indeed an island.

The second discovery was more mundane but just as surprising—he found six escaped convicts living on a small island just off the coast near Western Port. They had been part of a group of twelve who had stolen a boat and attempted to make their way to China, but had been abandoned by their companions on the island.

Bass could not take all the men back to Sydney; his boat was only 28 feet long and supplies were short. He took two who were weak from illness and put the others ashore with some fishing lines, a compass and directions to Sydney. They were never seen again.

Settlements were established in Van Diemen's Land in 1803 and 1804, and soon whalers and sealers who worked the coast from the island to South Australia were regularly visiting Western Port and Port Phillip Bay.

Port Fairy and Portland, to the west, were inhabited permanently by the 1820s and substantial settlements were established in both of those places in the 1830s, in defiance of the governor's edict prohibiting settlements that might destabilise the convict colony and lead to expansion beyond the control of both his powers and the British.

Hamilton Hume and William Hovell reached Port Phillip in 1824. They actually thought they were at Western Port, to the east of Port Phillip and, two years later, a small convict settlement was established at Western Port in order to give Britain some presence on the south coast. It lasted just thirteen months before being abandoned.

In November 1834, Edward Henty, whose requests for permission to settle across Bass Strait had been left unanswered by Lieutenant Governor Arthur in Hobart, ignored the edict about new settlements and started a township at Portland Bay. In early 1835, spurred on by Henty's example, John Batman crossed Bass Strait and in June he infamously secured land on the western shore of Port Phillip Bay 'by treaty' from the local Aboriginal tribe.

Batman had explored the shores of Port Phillip Bay and chose a site for what he called 'a village'. Within a year the township of Melbourne began to grow on the banks of the Yarra River.

Attempts to stop other settlements had proven futile and, in 1837, the township of Melbourne was surveyed and named and a magistrate, Captain William Lonsdale, was sent from Sydney to maintain law and order. A new colony was born.

Victoria became a separate colony in 1853. There was great resentment over the reluctance of the Sydney government to allow the area to be settled—spawning a rivalry that has lasted to the present day.

First, there was the problem of the river. The border between New South Wales and Victoria is the high-water mark on the southern bank of the Murray River.

When the Mildura Irrigation Company was being set up by the Canadian Chaffey brothers, with the support of the Victorian government, Sir Henry Parkes complained that it was illegal as New South Wales owned the Murray River and thus the water. Years later when the Victorian town of Echuca flooded, the mayor telegraphed New South Wales parliament to 'come and get your water out of our town'.

Then, there was sport. When the first cricket test was played in 1877 between the touring Englishmen and a Combined Australian XI, attempts were made to compromise between the two colonies but there was controversy right from the beginning. Due to the bitter inter-colonial rivalry that existed at the time, the two best bowlers in the country were absent although both were selected. Victorian Frank Allen decided to go to the Warrnambool show instead, and New South Wales bowler Fred Spoffoth would not bowl to the Victorian wicketkeeper Jack Blackham and refused to play.

In 1878 New South Wales announced it was changing its name to 'Australia', because not only was it the first colony but more native Australians had been born there than in all the other colonies put together. When a Victorian member of parliament asked the Victorian premier, Graham Berry, to rename Victoria 'Australasia', he replied: 'No, because then New South Wales might call itself the Southern Hemisphere.'

THE RACE THAT DIVIDED THE NATION

Some of the most obvious examples of rivalry between New South Wales and Victoria can be seen in horseracing. One of the main reasons for the Melbourne Cup being established was to assert Melbourne's superiority over Sydney both as a city and financial and sporting capital.

So the Victoria Turf Club announced the running of a great new race. It was to be an egalitarian affair, with the best horses carrying extra weight to make the race more equal. The trophy was a gold watch and the prizemoney of £710 was the most ever put up for a race in the colonies.

A horse from parent colony New South Wales winning the great new race was exactly what was not supposed to happen! When the unthinkable did happen, it was the start of the wonderful tradition of rivalry, myths, legends and larger-than-life stories that has become the Melbourne Cup.

In 1861, the New South Wales horse Archer, trained by Etienne de Mestre, won the first Melbourne Cup convincingly by 6 lengths from Mormon. Seventeen horses started and a dreadful fall resulted in two being killed. A crowd of some 5000 saw the race and de Mestre, who had prepared his horse for the race away from prying eyes at St Kilda, backed Archer from 10 to 1 into 6 to 1 and made a killing, taking untold amounts of Victorian 'gold' back to New South Wales.

The story of Archer's two victories in the first two Cups is the stuff of legend. On both occasions he is supposed to have walked from his home near Nowra, on the New South Wales south coast, to Melbourne—but the truth is that Archer went by steamship. He made the sea voyage three times to compete in Victorian spring races, in 1861, 1862 and 1863.

The irony of a New South Wales horse winning a race organised to display Victorian superiority was reinforced when Archer started favourite and won again the following year, this time defeating Mormon by 8 lengths in spite of carrying 10 stone 2 pounds.

A further insult, which modern racegoers may not realise, is that there was no prize at all for running second.

The story of how Archer missed running in a third Melbourne Cup is also part of the race legend and inter-colonial rivalry. Although Archer was given the massive weight of 11 stone 4 pounds by the handicapper in 1863, de Mestre accepted, sending a telegram on the due date. However, while that particular day was a normal working day in New South Wales, it was a holiday in the colony of Victoria and the telegram was not delivered until the following day; the entry was not accepted. All the interstate entrants pulled out in protest and only seven local horses ran.

It is another delightful irony that the public holiday which enabled this act of unbridled inter-colonial perfidy to be perpetrated was Separation Day, the day that Victoria celebrated its official division from New South Wales in 1851.

The debacle of the third Melbourne Cup had positive results. The two Melbourne racing clubs, realising that parochialism was not the best policy, merged to form the Victorian Racing Club and the Cup recovered its prestige and went on to become our number-one sporting event.

But just to prove that old rivalries run deep and last long, in 2013 the Sydney Turf Club announced a new Autumn Carnival, with more prizemoney than what is offered during Victoria's Spring Carnival.

SAFE PASSAGE TO MELBOURNE

The rivalry between Sydney and Melbourne is deep-seated and has a long and complex history. Reluctance to allow settlement at all, followed by Sydney's perceived neglect of the fledgling colony in its early days, were the factors that caused the rivalry to develop and grow. It was, however, the loss of life in Bass Strait, especially of migrants bound for the new settlement, that was the catalyst for demands for separation from New South Wales.

In 1839 Charles La Trobe was appointed superintendent of the Port Phillip District and the colony established its own police force, customs office and lands office. The new colonial government in Sydney negotiated with the Land and Emigration Board for Melbourne to receive much-needed migrants, free settlers with trades, farming skills and families.

In 1844 Joseph Robinson was elected to represent Melbourne in the Legislative Council of the colony of New South Wales under the new colonial constitution, which expanded the council. One of his most pressing concerns, and the frequent subject of his speeches in Macquarie Street, was the building of lighthouses in Bass Strait. The council had approved a study to locate the best positions for lighthouses in 1842, but nothing had been done due to lack of funds.

The need for lighthouses was obvious. Among many other shipping disasters in Bass Strait's brief maritime history, the tragedy of the *Neva* was foremost in the minds of any captains who used the passageway to Sydney, and more lately to the new settlement of Melbourne.

The *Neva* was a barque of 327 tons. She sailed from Cork for Sydney, commanded by Captain Benjamin Peck, in January 1835, with 150 female convicts, nine wives of convicts, 55 children and 26 crew. The voyage was uneventful, there were three deaths and one birth and slow easy sailing until the weather worsened approaching Bass Strait.

When the sextant reading was taken at noon on 12 May, the ship was running before a strong wind and huge seas at a position Peck calculated as 90 miles west of King Island. He set course to pass well to the north of the reefs at the island's northern tip. On the afternoon of 13 May, land was seen on the horizon ahead and Peck changed course to sail north. At about 5 p.m. breakers were seen ahead and the *Neva* suddenly struck a submerged rock and lost her rudder.

The ship was carried onto the main part of the Harbinger Reef, rudderless and broadside, with such force that the hull buckled and the prison section below was sprung open.

With the giant surf breaking over her decks, the *Neva* filled with water and stuck fast on the reef. Cutting away the masts made no difference. As the ship broke up on the reef, some of the women broke open the rum store and quickly became drunk. Such was the panic that the ship's boats and longboat were overcrowded and sank as they were launched.

When the ship finally fell apart and sank, two sections of the deck floated to the surface and were used as rafts by those left alive. The chief officer and eighteen others were carried right onto the beach on one raft while the other, with Captain Peck aboard, had part of the mast still attached and became grounded almost a mile from shore. Only Peck and two others from the second raft made it to safety.

During the first night ashore four women and a boy died of exposure and the next day two more survivors died from the effects of drinking rum from a full cask that washed ashore. Those who survived the first night stayed alive using food washed ashore until they were found by sealers and finally rescued in June.

An inquiry exonerated Peck of any blame and stressed the dangers of navigating Bass Strait. The loss of a ship carrying convict women was tragic, but it took a tragedy of even greater proportions, involving the loss of free settlers and more than 180 children to finally prompt the building of lighthouses in Bass Strait.

The *Cataraqui* was carrying assisted migrants to the relatively new settlement of Melbourne in the colony of New South Wales under a scheme originally set up in 1832 by the Land and Emigration Board. It was just eight years since Melbourne had been surveyed and named and the arrival of some 369 new citizens would have added substantially to the population of the town. There were 13,500 settlers already living in Melbourne in 1845, and the 62 families, 33 unmarried women and 23 single men aboard the *Cataraqui* would have added 3 per cent to Melbourne's population just by reaching the dock, but it was not to be.

On 12 March 1845 the secretary of the Land and Emigration Board, Mr Walcott, wrote to the relevant naval officer, Lieutenant Henry, in Liverpool as follows:

> Sir,
> The Messrs. W. Smith & Sons having apprized the Board that they propose to take up for the conveyance of emigrants on bounty to Port Phillip, the barque 'Cataraque,' [sic] 712 tons, O.M., and that she will be placed in the graving-dock next week, I am to instruct you to make a strict and thorough examination of the vessel while in dock, and to request that you will report the result to the Commissioners, and whether you consider her in every respect eligible for the intended service. You will also report the number she can legally carry.

The number was set at 260 adults and the migrant vessel *Cataraqui* sailed from Liverpool for Melbourne on 20 April 1845 with 369 assisted emigrants. The number of adults was well within the legal limit set, as more than 180 of her passengers were children under sixteen.

The *Cataraqui* had a crew of 46, under the command of Captain Christopher Finlay. She was a good strong ship, just five years old, built in Quebec and named after a Canadian River.

She had a relatively safe passage until she reached the Southern Ocean. Only five infants had died en route of natural causes, one crewman was lost overboard and several babies had been born, all fairly normal for that number of people on a voyage of 100 days in 1845.

The *Cataraqui* approached Bass Strait in a raging 'Roaring Forties' storm, which pushed her relentlessly towards her destination for ten days. It was probably what we would class today as a 'one in ten year' event. With modern equipment, waves have been measured at more than 20 metres high in storms like the one the *Cataraqui* was caught in. One captain who sailed through the same storm called the weather that week 'fearful'.

In the early nineteenth century navigation had been much improved by the use of chronometers to calculate longitude. At first, chronometers were often almost as expensive as the ship itself but, by 1825, all British naval ships had them. Migrant ships were expected to be well equipped with navigational aids as well and vessels were inspected before being accepted as part of the assisted migrant programme.

Accurate navigation for latitude still relied on sun and stars. The angle of the sun and stars measured by sextant gave latitude when used in conjunction with accurate charts. But even with a good chronometer a 'fix' was needed on the sun at noon to calculate longitude. In poor weather, with cloud cover obscuring sun and stars, navigation was a matter of 'dead reckoning'. This was more or less guesswork based on distance travelled, which was calculated by the compass and by measuring the ship's speed by timing how long she took to pass a floating object.

Captain Finlay's problem was that he had not seen the sun or stars for more than a week. He had to take the *Cataraqui* into Bass Strait between Cape Otway and King Island to make his way into Port Phillip Bay. He knew that using dead reckoning in the conditions he was sailing in was madness, but he had nothing else to go by, apart from an 'indifferent observation' on 31 July by which he made a calculation, noted in the ship's log, which he obviously didn't trust as accurate.

There is a gap of about 90 kilometres between King Island and Cape Otway at the entrance to Bass Strait. There were no lighthouses in Bass Strait in 1845 and Finlay was fearful of the 'shipwreck coast' and did not want to risk being too close to Cape Otway, so he took the *Cataraqui* southward.

Still unsure of his position and unwilling to risk the lives of his crew and the assisted migrants, he stood off for eight hours, holding his ship against the wind through the night, hoping that dawn might bring him some sight of land. He expected to sight Cape Otway sometime on 5 August, hopefully after the storm abated and visibility returned.

The situation, however, was dire. The ship was in a cauldron of wind and massive waves and Finlay feared she would go down. At 3 a.m. on 4 August, the storm abated slightly and Finlay decided he had to sail east.

As he had suspected, his calculated position was completely wrong and the *Cataraqui* crashed without warning onto jagged rocks 150 metres offshore near Fitzmaurice Bay, on the desolate south-west coast of King Island.

Finlay attempted to drive the vessel over the rocks, thinking it was a hidden reef, and the ship stuck fast on the rocks and was slowly smashed to pieces by the massive waves. The crew managed to get all the emigrants on deck but about half were swept overboard and drowned or battered to death on the rocks. The masts were cut away in the hope that the wreck would clear the reef and be driven ashore, but the *Cataraqui* was full of water and remained on the rocks.

The crew struggled to launch the longboat in the teeth of the howling wind and raging sea. As they were about to do so, an enormous wave hit the ship and swept away the boat and the crewmen and all in front of it.

Daylight found about half the ship's passengers and crew still alive. Several hours later, with the storm still raging, the ship's last remaining longboat was launched in an attempt to get a line ashore, but it immediately capsized, drowning the six men who were in it. Captain Finlay was still alive and he ordered some of the crew to descend into the hold and find ropes. Then an attempt was made to float a line to the shore attached to an empty barrel, but it was caught up in the kelp about 20 metres from shore.

By this time the *Cataraqui* was breaking up and splitting slowly into two halves across the deck. Those left alive were trapped at either end of the vessel. The remaining crew strung ropes as best they could so that the survivors had something to cling to or tie themselves to the wreck with, but huge seas continually swept the decks and washed scores of passengers overboard; those that did not drown immediately were dashed to their death on the rocks by the massive surf.

Sometime in the afternoon the ship's hull parted across the middle of the deck and half of those left alive were swept away.

During the second night, quite close to dawn, the stern section of the vessel collapsed into the sea and completely disintegrated, leaving alive only those on the front section of the wreck.

By dawn on 5 August just 30 survivors remained. Captain Finlay then attempted to swim ashore and secure a line, but the waves and fierce current forced him to turn back as the line was again fouled by kelp.

The ship was slowly disintegrating and, when the front section broke in two and the bowsprit was washed away, Captain Finlay made his final decision. The only hope of staying alive was to attempt to swim or float to shore on the wreckage. He ordered the lines securing survivors to the wreck to be cut and it was 'everyone for themselves'.

Some attempted to make it, while others remained on what was left of the front section of the *Cataraqui* and awaited their fate.

The ship's chief officer, Thomas Guthrie, crawled to the front of the ship and swam to the bowsprit section, which had broken away and was nearer to shore. He then reached the shore by clinging to some planking. He found two men already there, a crewman named John Robertson and Samuel Brown, an emigrant; both had been washed ashore clinging to wreckage during the night.

Some crewmen who were still alive on the wreck saw that Guthrie had made it and leapt into the sea to follow. Six more made it ashore, exhausted and bruised from the rocks.

Then, as they watched, the remaining section of the wreck collapsed and the *Cataraqui* disappeared forever beneath the waves.

The nine castaways, who assumed they were on the mainland somewhere west of Cape Otway, were lucky to be found two days later by one of the island's only four inhabitants, seal hunter David Howie, an ex-convict who had secured a lease of 10 acres on the island. He and another sealer named Oakley and two Aboriginal women, known as Maria and Georgia, were living at Yellow Rock sealing station 40 kilometres away from the wreck site.

Howie had leases on several other islands but was himself marooned on King Island at that time. Having lost his own small boat in a storm, Howie was waiting for the arrival of the 10-ton cutter, *Midge*, which regularly visited the island.

Attracted to the scene of the tragedy by the large amount of wreckage drifting past their camp at Yellow Rock sealing station, Howie set out and found the survivors in such a poor state that they could not walk to the hut. Howie, Oakley, Maria and Georgia made several round trips with food, and Howie left a note on the hut door explaining the situation.

It was five weeks before the *Midge* arrived at Yellow Rock on 7 September and her master, John Fletcher, read Howie's note. He set off immediately to find the wreck and the survivors. In his account of the tragedy, published in the *Melbourne Courier* after the group arrived at Port Melbourne on 13 September, Fletcher described the scene of the tragedy quite vividly.

He stated that the entire west coast of King Island was the 'wildest and most dangerous that can be imagined' and described the area where the *Cataraqui* struck as one where 'you find reefs extending 9 miles seaward, and at this distance off one or two of the points, a wall of enormous rollers breaking towards the shore'.

Fletcher was able to approach the wreck site only with extreme caution and it took him three days to get the survivors safely aboard. At one point he managed to get onto the 40-foot high rocks that formed a part of the reef, over which part of the wreck had been lifted and thrown.

'Perhaps in the annals of shipwreck,' Fletcher stated, 'a more calamitous event is not to be found.'

He described the coast for 5 miles as being strewn with wreckage and bodies. The *Midge* recovered what bodies it could from the reefs and the beaches.

Many of the dead had been buried by the survivors and the four inhabitants of the island while they waited for the *Midge*. David Howie was contracted to return to the island and find, identify and bury all that could be found. Eventually 342 victims of the tragedy were buried in four mass graves.

With a death toll of 400, the wreck of the *Cataraqui* is still Australia's worst civil maritime disaster.

Ironically, the New South Wales Legislative Council was listening to the member for Melbourne, Joseph Robinson, attempting to put forward a motion to have lighthouses built in Bass Strait on 9 September, while the nine survivors of the wreck were being rescued by the *Midge*.

By 1850 lighthouses had been built in Bass Strait at Cape Otway, Deal Island, Goose Island, Swan Island and Cape Wickham on King Island. The King Island lighthouse was replaced in 1861 and another was built further south on the island in 1879.

The Cape Wickham lighthouse, which warns ships that they are approaching the southernmost point of Bass Strait and the treacherous coast of King Island, is the tallest lighthouse in the Southern Hemisphere.

Although the lighthouses were finally being built, the damage had been done, the resentment and rivalry between the two colonies was cemented into the Australian psyche. The loss of the *Cataraqui* and her cargo of potential Melburnians was the final straw for the embittered settlers of the unwanted outpost.

On 1 July 1853, Victoria achieved separation from New South Wales.

THE WRECK THAT MODERNISED SYDNEY

> Sydney was, yesterday, thrown into a state of great anxiety and alarm, by the report that, during the previous night, a large ship, with a considerable number of passengers, had been wrecked outside the South Reef at the Heads.

That was the report with which the *Sydney Morning Herald* announced to its shocked and disbelieving readers, on Saturday, 22 August 1857, that the worst tragedy in the city's 80-year history had occurred. It was a tragedy that would eventually bring down the newly created government of the colony of New South Wales and cause a massive modernising of Sydney Harbour's shipping operations.

The ship was the 1321-ton *Dunbar*, the largest vessel built in the Sunderland shipyards in the north of England. At the end of May 1857, she was ready for her ill-fated second voyage to the colony. Many well-to-do Sydneysiders had visited the Old Country with the *Dunbar* and were on the homeward voyage.

Confidence in the ship's seaworthiness was so great that the cargo was not even insured. The cargo holds were 22 feet deep and she carried beer, wine, spirits, dates, figs, raisins, candles, hardware, haberdashery, and confectionary valued at £73,000. Her first-class cabins were large and airy with 7-foot ceilings. She was the very best ship of the day, the epitome of maritime luxury and quality. A sleek vessel more than 200 feet long, she had extra copper sheeting and copper fittings throughout and her main mast weighed more than 9 tons.

The only knowledge we have of her second voyage to Sydney was provided by the only man who lived to tell the tale, 23-year-old Irishman James Johnson, a sailor since the age of twelve, who had joined the ship just before she departed.

On the final day of May 1857, the *Dunbar* sailed for Sydney then made her way uneventfully through the Atlantic, down the coast of Africa, and across the Southern Indian Ocean, with no more drama than some early seasickness among her 45 first-class and 22 'intermediate' (steerage) class passengers.

Johnson testified that the ship reached Bass Strait in mid-August. Running before a strong westerly wind, they sighted King Island and the Cape Howe Light and started the run up the east coast in misty weather with Captain Green steering well out to sea and keeping a constant watch as the wind was known to veer from the north-east at that time of year, which would put the ship on a lee shore.

Sailing ships were often wrecked when trapped on a lee shore, with the wind blowing towards the shore and the ship unable to tack away out to sea. It seems that Captain Green was mindful of this and acted accordingly as he approached Sydney. He stood the *Dunbar* well out to sea as she headed north into worsening weather but a strong wind, coming now from the north-east and developing into a gale with torrential rain and huge swells, put his vessel on a lee shore. A lee shore in which he had to find the small opening that would take his ship into the safe haven of Port Jackson.

After 81 days at sea, the *Dunbar* approached Sydney Heads in treacherous weather conditions, with heavy rain squalls severely reducing visibility and obscuring the cliffs at the entrance.

Captain Green was a veteran of eight previous visits to Sydney and knew the approach to Sydney Heads, he knew the Macquarie lighthouse beam rotated every 90 seconds from a position high on the cliffs south of the heads, and he knew the only other light was the one in Middle Harbour, at Sow and Pigs Reef.

Green planned to wait till first light to enter the harbour but the storm worsened in intensity and at 11.30 p.m. he posted three lookouts, called all hands on deck and turned the *Dunbar* so she ran before the wind towards the heads.

It seems that the Macquarie light was visible only at intervals due to the torrential rain and pitch black, but it did appear to port as they approached the coast. When next it appeared it was directly above the masts and the *Dunbar* was about to hit the reef at South Head. The lookout had just shouted, 'Breakers ahead!' when the light was seen again. Then the ship turned to starboard, hit the reef side on and was smashed to pieces within minutes.

Perhaps Captain Green, overshooting the harbour entrance to the north and thinking that the breakers indicated North Head, tried to make a quick turn into what he believed was the harbour? Perhaps the officers on watch mistook The Gap for the entrance to the harbour?

An indentation in the massive cliffs just south of Sydney Heads, The Gap has become infamous as a 'jumping off' place for suicides. The Macquarie lighthouse is much closer to it than Sydney Heads.

When the ship hit the cliff the masts came down, the lifeboats were all lost and all the crew and passengers were either drowned or smashed to death on the rocks by the massive seas.

All, that is, except one—James Johnson who was miraculously thrown onto a small ledge of rock while clinging to some planking. When the huge wave that deposited him there receded, he used the interval between waves to haul himself up onto a relatively safer and larger ledge some 10 metres above the waves, where he remained unseen as the wreckage and cargo of the *Dunbar* washed around him, along with the shattered bodies of those who had been on board. He was eventually spotted and rescued more than 30 hours later.

The official death toll from the *Dunbar* has always been 121. However, there is good reason to believe there were a few more lost than that. When the official passenger and crew list was found and released three months later in London, it did not contain the name of James Johnson, and Johnson said he knew of two others on board whose names did not appear, either.

South Head was a long way from the city in 1857 and Sydney was unaware of the tragedy until reports of wreckage in and around the harbour began appearing on Friday.

The first knowledge of the disaster apparently appeared as a supernatural premonition. There was a signal station at South Head, manned by a signal master and an assistant. The signal master, Mr Graham, was woken by his wife around the time the *Dunbar* struck. With the storm raging outside, she cried out that a great ship was sinking near the heads and a man was on the rocks below South Head.

Mr Graham calmed his wife and assured her that it was a nightmare and no ship could possibly be near the harbour in the conditions. She went back to sleep only to wake again within minutes and beg her husband to go and look over the cliffs. She even ran down the hall and woke the assistant, Henry Packer, pleading with him to go and look and then attempted to leave the station herself in the raging storm. Finally Graham and his assistant gave the hysterical Mrs Graham a sedative and got her to sleep.

Next morning Graham and Packer forced their way against the howling easterly to the cliff top, saw the wreckage of the *Dunbar* far below and realised that Mrs Graham's nightmare had come true.

Mrs Graham was present when James Johnson was winched to safety. When he was untied and turned to face the crowd, Mrs Graham reportedly said, 'That's the man I saw in my dream, but no one will believe me.'

Meanwhile, Captain Wiseman, of the paddle-steamer *Grafton*, reported huge amounts of wreckage and cargo as he entered the harbour from the north coast. He'd had to stop and clear debris from his ship's paddles several times. The massive swell ahead of a wind, which had turned more southerly, was washing everything from the wreck through the heads and into the harbour.

With the wreckage came the bodies, or what was left of them.

Sydney was about to be plunged into a frenzy of disbelief, rumour, horror and mourning as its famous safe harbour was filled with death.

Phillip Cohen, proprietor of the Pier Hotel at Manly, salvaged several bodies from the water and had one body taken from his grasp by a large shark as he stood waist-deep attempting to get the body ashore.

Considering how long it took for the truth of the tragedy to become known and for action to be taken, it is remarkable how quickly the inquest, parliamentary debate and funeral followed the event.

By Sunday afternoon a jury was sworn in for the inquest and inspected the bodies and parts of bodies at the George Street Deadhouse, as the morgue near the Circular Quay was then called. One juror fainted and several others had to be taken outside. Only seven of the 24 bodies were identified. The inquest was then adjourned to the following day, which was also the day of the funeral for the victims.

It is hard to imagine how the *Dunbar* tragedy hysteria gripped the city of Sydney over those few days. The newspapers talked of nothing else, parliament debated little else and all business came to a halt on the Monday afternoon to watch the funeral procession travel from the deadhouse at the bottom of George Street to the cemetery at Camperdown.

Seven hearses carried seventeen coffins and almost a hundred carriages followed with official dignitaries and mourners. Hearses contained multiple coffins whose contents were officially listed in such pathetic terms as: 'portions of human bodies', 'a female unknown', 'a boy supposed to be Master Healy', 'trunk of a female unknown', 'parts of human bodies picked up at The Heads', and so on.

There are many reasons why the wreck of the *Dunbar* had a devastating effect on the people of Sydney: of course, many citizens of the city were lost on the ship, and Sydney was still small enough for everyone to know anyone of consequence. But it also threatened the stability of the colony itself.

The colony had recently achieved self-government; transportation was a distant memory, having ended almost twenty years before. There was a feeling that Sydney was a real city and the colony was ready to take its place in the world. The city, however, depended entirely on the sea for contact with the outside world and the 'mother country'. The sea was also its only link to the other major towns and cities of the colony. The last ship into port before the *Dunbar* was wrecked was the Shoalhaven steamer SS *Nora Creiner*, and the first ship in after the wreck was the paddle-steamer *Grafton*. The sea was Sydney's lifeline; its safe harbour was its greatest pride and joy.

The *Dunbar* had been the toast of the town the previous year; she was the best ship of the best shipping company in the world and Captain Green was a respected and experienced seaman.

'Here was a vessel built as strongly as teak timber and honest English shipwrighting could make her,' the *Sydney Morning Herald* declared, 'commanded by a cautious, vigilant and experienced sailor who, both as mate and master, had frequently entered the port before and knew it well. If we had dared to predict a safe voyage for any vessel it would have been the Dunbar under Captain Green.'

If it was not safe for the *Dunbar* to enter the port, then perhaps Sydney was not the city of the future that its citizens had imagined it to be.

It is also a fact that Melbourne, mainly due to gold, was seriously challenging Sydney as the main city of Australia. Victoria had become a separate colony in 1851 and the rivalry between the two cities was already intense. Melbourne was a prosperous and wealthy city, which would overtake Sydney in population size within a decade. Sydney's self-esteem and confidence were shaken by the shadow of doubt suddenly hanging over its famous harbour, the one thing it had that Melbourne could never match.

What was the problem? Was Sydney not the safe, modern, cosmopolitan destination its complacent leaders and citizens assumed it was? The city was about to be dragged into the 'modern world' of the post–Industrial Revolution nineteenth century.

Just one year earlier the great engineer John Whitton arrived in Sydney to take charge of the colony's railway construction. Here was a man highly regarded in Britain, who had helped construct some of England's finest railways and worked with the greatest engineer of the new age, Isambard Brunel. Whitton would go on to pioneer mountain railway construction by building the world's first zigzag railway and give New South Wales the finest railway system in the world. Yet his first task on arrival was to convince the government of the colony, led by Governor Denison, that its proposal that he build a horse-drawn narrow-gauge railway system was not exactly a great idea.

Seen through other eyes, Sydney in 1857 was still an isolated backwater of antiquated colonial thinking at the very end of the world, caught in a time warp of eighteenth century technology and practices.

The conjecture as to whether Captain Green thought he was too far north or south of the harbour entrance when he lost his ship was soon forgotten and replaced by a tidal wave of self-analysis, finger-pointing, guilt and recrimination as the city of Sydney turned on itself and debated the efficiency, practicality and modernity of the way it ran its harbour. Critics came out of the woodwork to attack Sydney's inadequate and outdated harbour facilities.

At the inquest, Captain Wiseman of the *Grafton* stated that Captain Green was correct in attempting to enter the harbour rather than stay at sea in the storm. He also stated, 'The Gap . . . is very apt to lead captains of vessels astray . . . the North Head is the more fitting place for a beacon to point out the entrance to the harbour.'

Captain Fletcher, skipper of the SS *Nora Creiner*, was the last man to see the *Dunbar* afloat as his steamship passed her to enter the harbour earlier on the night she went down. He testified that the pilot arrangements for the port were 'not adequate to provide assistance for vessels in distress'.

It made no sense that large vessels should have to wait all night for pilot assistance in poor weather. Fletcher made his point by declaring, 'On that night no vessel could have held on by her anchors outside Sydney Heads.'

A letter appeared in the *Sydney Morning Herald* on the Wednesday after the event from a retired seaman, 'D.P.', challenging the supposed safety of the harbour entrance: 'with a strong wind blowing on the land, the ship scudding and thick showers of rain—the characteristic of our east winds—making the darkness impenetrable, there is perhaps not another port in the world more terribly confusing to enter than the loudly lauded one of Sydney.'

This was the first of many letters criticising the way the harbour was run and suggesting improvements. Many of them defended Captain Green and blamed the inadequate harbour facilities for the tragedy; others simply criticised the outdated harbour management and lack of proper lights, and said the *Dunbar* was merely a tragedy waiting to happen.

The mass of evidence was growing against Sydney being a safe port.

The Macquarie light was in bad position, too far south of the entrance, and could not be seen at all if a ship was under the high cliffs on which it stood. The conditions in which the *Dunbar* was wrecked were not uncommon in winter, yet the pilot station was inside the harbour and the signal station was useless in the dark and in stormy weather. The pilot boats were small man-powered vessels that could not operate in bad conditions. The Gap was deceptive, the heads were unlit, and a floating light inside the harbour was the only other reference point apart from the poorly situated lighthouse.

The newspapers picked up the criticisms and began a tirade of questioning: surely the citizens of Sydney deserved a better service than this, not to mention those who chose to travel as migrants and visitors to 'the finest harbour in the world'!

The Sydney Chamber of Commerce met on the Thursday after the tragedy and passed a resolution that the governor be petitioned to ensure that the proposed telegraph line to South Head be built immediately. Many members of the chamber, including chairman Captain Robert Towns, had maritime business interests. Virtually all members of the chamber relied on the harbour to conduct their businesses; the entire colony needed a safe harbour to continue to prosper.

In the parliament of New South Wales the questioning and finger-pointing began even before it was known that the wrecked vessel was the *Dunbar*. The probing and criticism was led by the leader of the opposition, Mr Charles Cowper. The main target of the criticism was the premier and colonial secretary, Henry Parker.

When asked, on the Friday afternoon, if it was true that a large migrant ship had gone down the previous night, Parker replied that he could not give out information that may be incorrect and that the government was doing 'all in its power, not only for the relief of the sufferers but to ascertain information as to what had happened'.

It is hard to know what Mr Parker thought his government was doing to relieve the suffering of the as-yet-unknown drowned victims from the as-yet-unknown ship that had been wrecked. The man doing 'all in his power' was actually the portmaster, Robert Pockley, who had ridden out to the signal station on receipt of the letter from Mr Graham, organised a search using the manpower and boats from the pilot station, and announced a £3 reward to anyone who could identify the ship.

Mr Cowper was soon back on the attack on the Monday, asking questions that implied that the government's response to the tragedy was reactive and inadequate. The tirade continued in parliament through the week.

Hadn't the government agreed a year before to install a telegraph line from South Head to the city? Why had it not been done? Wasn't the Macquarie light poorly situated for ships wishing to enter the harbour? Shouldn't there be a light on North Head, or South Head, or both? Did the government consider that a small light on a floating barge at Sow and Pigs Reef inside the harbour was sufficient to guide large ships into Sydney? Were there enough pilots and did they do their job well enough? Were the pilot boats modern enough to cope with the demands of a busy harbour in safety? Why couldn't there be a pilot station at Botany Bay so ships could be brought in safely from there?

The government was now under siege as the whole colony looked for answers and suddenly questioned the efficiency and safety of their port. Within days the government presented a 'Light, Navigation and Pilot Board Bill', proposing a board be set up to advise and consult with the government.

This was grist to opposition leader Cowper's mill. 'No action . . . jobs for the boys . . . the telegraph was supposed to be built last year and the same thing happened . . . etc. . . . etc.'

The bill was never passed; it was obviously about to fail and bring down the government so it was amended to be set aside for six months. Henry Parker's government, however, was doomed. Parker lost a lot of public and political support when he suggested that the harbour was safe to enter and perhaps Captain Green had acted 'rashly'. Two weeks after the *Dunbar* was wrecked, the government was defeated on an electoral bill and lost office. Elections were called and six weeks later Cowper was victorious at the poll.

Just nine weeks after the wreck of the *Dunbar*, on 24 October, the clipper ship *Catherine Adamson* ran onto the reef inside North Head in a south-westerly gale and was smashed to pieces. Twenty-one lives were lost and the ship completely destroyed; once again the harbour was full of wreckage.

This was the last straw—Sydney was now spoken of as a 'port of shame'.

Again the competence of Sydney's pilots and harbour management was called into question. The pilot, Mr Hawkes, had argued heatedly with the captain of the ship, Captain Stuart, about what should be done as the ship drifted towards the rocks. Although it was later revealed that the *Catherine Adamson* had trouble steering due to worn blocks, Pilot Hawkes was blamed by many for the wreck, in spite of the fact that he remained on the ship and drowned while Captain Stuart left the ship and survived.

Cowper was now premier and questions were asked of the new government as Sydney again wallowed in a pit of shame and recrimination. Just four days later the detailed plans were announced for the building of the lighthouse at South Head and it began operating the following year. In true colonial fashion Governor Denison named it after his father-in-law, Admiral Hornby.

The telegraph between South Head and the city was operational by February 1858 and a complete overhaul of the pilot system followed, with the practice of pilots boarding ships outside the harbour becoming standard and better vessels being bought for the purpose.

Sydney has never forgotten the *Dunbar* and church services are held annually at St Stephen's Church in Camperdown to this day. The mass grave was badly vandalised in the 1970s but has been restored since then. There have been other tragedies in and around the harbour since, but none of them has produced an effect like the shock and horror of the event that changed Sydney forever, when the *Dunbar* was lost at South Head and 'the finest harbour in the world' was filled with bodies.

THE GREAT ZIGZAG

Few Australians realise today that one of the world's greatest engineering marvels was constructed here in the 1860s.

The Blue Mountains, that section of the Great Dividing Range just west of Sydney, had provided a barrier to the colony's development since the first settlement in 1788. It was 25 years before the mountains were even officially crossed in 1813.

That enlightened governor, Lachlan Macquarie, wasted no time in having a road built in 1815 and establishing Bathurst as the first inland town that same year. By 1860, however, William Cox's famous convict-built road of 1815—the Great Western Highway—was the only link between the port of Sydney and the prosperous inland farming areas and the coal and iron ore deposits found in the Lithgow valley. The colony's development was slowed to the pace of bullock teams.

John Whitton changed all that when he took the railway across the Great Dividing Range.

Whitton, a Yorkshireman, was engineer on the Manchester, Sheffield and Lincoln railway when he was just 28 and, at 33, he was chosen to replace the greatest engineer of them all, Isambard Brunel, as resident engineer on the Oxford, Worcester and Wolverhampton railway.

In 1856, John Whitton was offered, and accepted, the commission to become engineer-in-chief of the New South Wales Government Railways at an annual salary of £1500. He arrived with his family in 1857, and not only designed and built the NSW rail system, he also became the first to design a true 'mountain railway' which paved the way for others around the world and was the engineering wonder of the age.

Penrith, 35 miles from Sydney, is just 88 feet above sea level. From there the railway had to climb 3658 feet in just over 50 miles to enter the proposed Clarence Tunnel. The construction of this line, including the first zigzag at Lapstone Hill, and its continuation west into the Lithgow valley, was one of the greatest engineering and construction feats of the time.

The idea itself was simple: build a track in the form of a giant Z. The train went along the top or bottom of the Z to a set of points, switched in the middle to another set of points and then forward again on its way. It took a lot of shunting and engines had to 'run around' their trains, which made it a slow process. But it made previously impossible grades possible. The problem was finding a way to carve the two giant Zs into the incredibly wild, rugged terrain of the Blue Mountains.

Whitton began by designing the first zigzag, which raised the line 520 feet to the summit of Lapstone Hill. He had to design and build a bridge over the Nepean River and a massive stone viaduct across Knapsack Gully. The bridge, named the Victoria Bridge, had three spans of 200 feet and the viaduct required seven arches and rose 126 feet at its centre. The steepest gradient here was 1 in 30.

The construction of this zigzag was, however, mere child's play when compared to the building of the one that was necessary on the western side of the Great Dividing Range.

The Lithgow valley zigzag, which became known as the Great Zig-Zag, carried the line from the Clarence Tunnel down a descent of 687 feet to the valley floor in three great sweeps across the mountain sides. The gradient was 1 in 42 and Commissioner John Rae wrote that it 'passed through a deep and rugged ravine where formerly there was scarcely footing for the mountain goat and where the surveyors' assistants had occasionally to be suspended by ropes in the performance of their perilous duties'.

John Whitton himself spent many hours sitting in a basket

suspended over these enormous spectacular cliffs while he surveyed and checked the progress of the construction.

An old colleague of Whitton's, George Cowdery, was the resident engineer for this section of the line. Cowdery had worked under Whitton building the Oxford, Worcester and Wolverhampton railway in Britain. He migrated to Victoria in 1856, during the goldrushes, and had worked as an engineer on the Melbourne to Bendigo line.

Many British workers, including more than two thousand Scots, both skilled and unskilled, arrived in the colony to help build the line across the mountains. Construction lasted three years, from 1866 to 1869, and the project was a source of fascination in the colony.

In January 1867, part of the mountain blocking the line near the first reversing station needed to be removed by blasting. This was to be the most massive explosion ever seen in Australia. Using the new process of electrical detonation, 40,000 tons of rock was to be cleared in one huge explosion. Twenty-five holes were drilled 30 feet into the mountain face and more than 3 tons of blasting powder was inserted.

It became a great social occasion and the theatrical nature of the event was enhanced by two failed attempts at detonation. The first attempt failed at one o'clock and a second some 30 minutes later. Finally, at five minutes to two, after more wire had been replaced, the third attempt was successful. The governor's wife, Lady Belmore, pushed the detonator and Commissioner Rae reported that the resulting explosion 'tore the mountain asunder, heaving huge masses of rock into the valley . . . leaving the face of the parent mountain almost as plain as if it had been cut with chisels'.

After the entertaining event, the *Sydney Morning Herald* reported:

> A large number of ladies from different parts of the district being in the immediate vicinity by invitation . . . the party, numbering upwards of fifty persons, sat down to an excellent luncheon served in No 1 Tunnel. A better or cooler place for a luncheon, considering the intense heat of the weather, could not be conceived.

The Great Zig-Zag line was completed with much fanfare in September 1869. A reporter from *The Empire* newspaper described his first trip on the completed line thus:

> The descent is commenced along the back of the tortuous ridge dividing the impassable gullies descending on the right to the Grose River and on the left to Cox's River . . . approaching the verge of the precipices where the Zig-Zag commences . . . the various traverses of the line are seen crossing each other at intervals below and to look down from the windows of the railway carriages almost makes the traveller dizzy. The track runs along the side of the cliffs cut through the solid rock in most places, in others carried on lofty arches of masonry.

Many thousands of passengers had similar feelings of awe and excitement while making the journey across the mountains by rail. Finally, as Henry Lawson said:

> The flaunting flag of progress is in the West unfurled,
> The mighty bush with iron rails is tethered to the world.

Now goods, passengers and mail could flow reliably and quickly across the mountains in either direction. The port of Sydney and overseas markets were open to primary products; inland isolation was overcome; the city and the bush could unite in new developments. News and letters were only a day or two away for people of the Western Plains. Mail was sorted on the trains as they sped through the night to the west.

While Henry Lawson bemoaned the passing of the 'golden days' of bush life, Banjo Paterson celebrated the new era of communication to the remotest parts of the bush:

> By rock and ridge and riverside the Western Mail has gone,
> Across the great Blue Mountain Range to take the letter on.
> A moment on the topmost grade while open fire doors glare,
> She pauses like a living thing to breathe the mountain air.

Then launches down the other side across the plains away
To bear that note to 'Conroy's sheep, along the Castlereagh'.

In the building of this railway the colony truly came of age. No longer a quaint colonial backwater, New South Wales now had an engineering marvel to impress the world, along with all its strange plants, animals and natural wonders.

And many people were mightily impressed, not only the locals but also visiting foreigners, like French diplomat Edmond La Meslee, who wrote a wonderful account of crossing the mountains by train in 1880:

> Beyond Mount Victoria the line continues to follow the crest of the Blue Mountains till it begins to descend the western slopes. Here we came to the second zigzag, the masterpiece of Australian engineering.
>
> It seems miraculous that human brains and brawn should have been able to conceive and construct the zigzag along the fearful face of this escarpment. The mountainside falls away dizzyingly here, and when the engineers made their first preliminary surveys, they had to be lowered down the precipice by ropes to measure their angles. Later, to build the three viaducts that carry the line, the workmen in their turn had to work on the foundations, while dangling suspended by ropes from above.
>
> One shuddered to think what terrible accidents could occur on such gradients without those safety precautions.
>
> Soon we were bowling along on the valley floor. To see the crest of the mountainside, more than a thousand feet above, one had to lean right out of the window. In fact, until the train entered the Lithgow valley, it was not easy to catch a glimpse of a patch of blue sky.

From 1869 until 1910 every train across the mountains in either direction used John Whitton's zigzags. By 1910, however, traffic was so heavy that bottlenecks delayed trains constantly and there were some spectacular, though relatively harmless, accidents. A new line was designed, using what became known as the 'ten-tunnel deviation'. The old track was torn up and the bush slowly reclaimed the land. Where the great scar of the railway had existed since the massive destruction of bushland caused by the line's creation in the 1860s, peaceful walking tracks through new-growth forest are all that remain of Whitton's marvel.

The Great Zig-Zag was regarded as one of the engineering wonders of the Victorian Age. A by-product of its construction was the development of locomotive boilers, which could cope with steep grades. This, along with Whitton's other engineering innovations and construction techniques, made it possible for mountain railways to be built all over the world. Mountain railways everywhere are, to some extent, the legacy of this Yorkshireman and his vision, tenacity, honesty and pursuit of perfection. The Great Zig-Zag became the model for mountain railroads worldwide. But, more than that, Whitton gave the extremely lucky colony of New South Wales a railway system built on sensible ideas, good engineering practice, and a minimum of political and economic interference and corruption.

The fact that he gave up a promising career in his native land, where railways had been in existence for several decades, to take up a position at the end of the earth and attempt to build railways through what was still uncharted wilderness, tells us a lot about this dour Yorkshireman. The fact that he remained engineer-in-chief of New South Wales Railways for 34 years, and chose to live out his life here in Australia, tells us even more about this remarkable man.

He died in February 1898, aged 80, at his house in St Leonards and was buried in St Thomas's Cemetery, North Sydney. Twenty years earlier *The Town and Country Journal* published what could have been a fitting epitaph:

> Among the public men of the colony who occupy professional positions . . . none is more distinguished for ability than Mr John Whitton, the Engineer-in-Chief of Railways, none, it may be said, is equal to the grandeur of his achievements.

THE GREAT ESCAPE

The Irish Republican Brotherhood was formed in 1858 by James Stephens, who had led an ill-fated uprising against British rule in 1848 and then fled to Paris, returning to Ireland in 1853 to start the *Irish People* newspaper.

His partner in planning the 1848 uprising was John O'Mahony, who fled to the USA and started the Fenian Brotherhood there.

The Irish Republican Brotherhood grew in Ireland during the 1860s, money was sent from the USA and the movement had a cache of weapons and 50,000 willing recruits.

A planned uprising in 1865 was poorly organised and ended in a series of skirmishes. In September that year, the *Irish People* was shut down by the government and Stephens and others were arrested and sent to prison. Stephens subsequently escaped and fled to the USA.

Anyone suspected of being involved with the Brotherhood was arrested and some units of the British army based in Ireland, believed to be sympathetic to the cause, were moved out of the country.

In 1866 the British government suspended *habeus corpus* in Ireland, which meant people could be held without trial indefinitely, and hundreds of men were arrested. Civilians were treated as political prisoners; men from the army were treated as traitors and the letter 'D', for deserter, was branded on their chests.

The British government transported most of the 'Fenians' to Australia. The Perth settlement was the last in Australia to receive convicts, having asked for them to be sent when the colony was struggling for manpower in the late 1840s.

There were 62 Irish political prisoners among the 280 convicts on board the *Hougoumont*, the last convict ship to ever sail to Australia. Also on board, acting as an assistant warder of convicts, was Scotland Yard detective and British spy Thomas Rowe.

Many of the Irish political prisoners were well educated; some were schoolteachers and journalists. Among them was John Boyle O'Reilly, born in 1844 during the Great Potato Famine. He was the son of a schoolteacher and began work on the local paper at age fourteen. He moved to Lancashire and worked on the local newspaper in Preston and joined the Lancashire militia, the 11th Volunteer Rifles, and then returned to Dublin and joined the 10th Hussars in 1863. About a year or so later, he joined the Irish Republican Brotherhood.

O'Reilly was arrested in 1866 for recruiting fellow soldiers to join the Fenians. He was court-martialled and sentenced to hang but the death sentence was commuted to twenty years transportation to Fremantle. O'Reilly, however, was undeterred. While sailing on the *Hougoumont*, he and another convict even produced a weekly shipboard newspaper called *The Wild Goose: A Collection of Ocean Waifs*.

The *Hougoumont* arrived in Western Australia in January 1868 and O'Reilly was sent with a convict work party to Bunbury. He spent the year at Bunbury planning his escape, with the help of local Irishmen and a priest, Father McCabe.

In February 1869 O'Reilly escaped in a rowboat and rowed 12 miles up the coast to wait for an American whaling ship, the *Vigilant*, which Father McCabe had arranged to pick him up. All went well until the ship failed to meet him. He spent days hiding in sand dunes being hunted by police and Aboriginal trackers until a second whaling ship, the *Gazelle*, was organised to collect him.

The plot thickened when a convict named James Bowman got wind of the plan and blackmailed the conspirators into allowing him to join O'Reilly on the *Gazelle*.

Father McCabe had arranged for the *Gazelle* to take O'Reilly to Java but bad weather forced the ship to Mauritius, which was a British colony in 1869. There, police boarded the *Gazelle* and a magistrate demanded that the escaped convict be handed over. The captain hid O'Reilly and gave them Bowman.

Realising that this would happen again at the next port of call, St Helena, the *Gazelle*'s captain arranged to transfer O'Reilly onto the American cargo ship *Sapphire*. The transfer was carried out at sea and O'Reilly sailed to Liverpool in the *Sapphire* where he was secretly transferred to another American ship, the *Bombay*. On 23 November 1869, O'Reilly landed at Philadelphia and was warmly greeted by members of the Irish community there.

O'Reilly settled in Boston where he worked on *The Pilot*, a newspaper aimed at the Irish-born population. He made lecture tours, wrote poetry and a novel, married a journalist named Mary Murphy, and set about planning the escape of his fellow Fenians, still in Fremantle Prison.

British policy on Ireland had softened and, by 1869, most of the Irish civilian political prisoners at Fremantle had been freed. This reprieve did not apply, however, to military prisoners.

In 1875, John Devoy came to O'Reilly with a plan to storm Fremantle Prison and rescue the remaining Fenians by force. Devoy had orchestrated the recruitment of Irish soldiers in British army units for James Stephens back in the 1860s and been imprisoned then exiled to the USA.

One of the Fremantle exiles, James Wilson, had written to John Devoy in June 1874:

> This is a voice from the tomb . . . we have been nearly nine years in this living tomb since our first arrest . . . it is impossible for mind or body to withstand the continual strain that is upon them. One or the other must give way.

O'Reilly suggested a less drastic plan, one similar to that which worked for him. Instead of relying on the goodwill and honesty of ships' captains, however, his idea was to raise funds and buy a ship for the sole purpose of rescuing the prisoners. That way they could choose a captain who could be trusted and the ship could easily pose as a legitimate vessel. A whaling ship was the obvious choice.

Devoy and O'Reilly formed a committee to plan the whole venture and set about raising funds with the help of the American Irish Republican Brotherhood, Clan na Gael. There was no shortage of donations, which was just as well as the plan required a large amount of money and manpower in order to work.

Devoy knew a shipping agent, John Richardson, who helped them purchase a three-masted barque, the whaling ship *Catalpa*, at a cost of US$5200. The ship was bought in the name of one of the committee, James Reynolds. Richardson also put the committee in touch with his son-in-law, a whaling captain sympathetic to the Irish cause named John Smith Anthony.

The *Catalpa* was set up as an operational whaler and merchant ship, and departed from New Bedford, near Boston, at the end of April 1875. Only Captain Anthony and one of the committee, Dennis Duggan, who was on board as the ship's carpenter, knew the real purpose of the voyage.

The ship headed for the Atlantic whaling grounds then sailed on to the Azores to unload 200 barrels of whale oil. Most of the crew deserted the ship there and Anthony recruited a new crew and headed for Australia. A savage storm delayed the ship and severely damaged her foremast, but she arrived off Bunbury, south of Perth, on 27 March 1876.

The bad luck Anthony experienced in losing the crew and having the ship damaged in the storm was offset by a stroke of amazing good luck.

Catalpa met the trader *Ocean Beauty* in the Indian Ocean and her captain happened to be the former master of the *Hougoumont*, which carried the Fenians into captivity at Fremantle. Captain Anthony told him they were headed for the whaling grounds off Western Australia and he happily provided them with navigation charts of the Western Australian coastline.

Meanwhile, in late 1875, two Fenian spies, John Breslin and Thomas Desmond, had travelled to Perth from the US to organise the local side of the rescue operation. Desmond set himself up as a carriage builder in Perth, and Breslin posed as a wealthy American businessman, James Collins, in Fremantle.

The plot worked so well that Breslin, now known as Collins, was able to befriend the assistant superintendent of Fremantle Prison and be taken on a tour of the establishment. He managed to make contact with six of the twelve remaining Fenian convicts, either personally or through local Irish residents, and explain the plot to them.

Of the other six Fenians, one was in a high-security section of the prison, two were assigned to work out of the district and could not be contacted, another two had tickets-of-leave and could not be found either, and the final member was considered unreliable and a security risk.

When the *Catalpa* berthed at Bunbury on 29 March, Breslin met the ship and he and Anthony took passage to Perth on the steamer *Georgette*, which would reappear in the drama later. There they met Desmond and other sympathisers to make their final plans.

The escape was originally planned for 6 April, but the arrival of several British warships in Fremantle Harbour meant a postponement. It was rescheduled for the 17th, Easter Monday, when the British ships had departed and the Perth Yacht Club Regatta would be a good distraction. Thomas Desmond was to provide transport and arrange for sympathisers to cut the telegraph lines connecting the colony to the rest of Australia, and the *Catalpa* would be waiting offshore from Rockingham Bay, south of Perth, in international waters between Rottnest and Garden islands, having sent a whaleboat ashore to collect the escaped prisoners.

The plan almost came unstuck yet again when Captain Anthony went to send the crucial coded telegram at Bunbury and discovered the telegraph office was closed for Good Friday. Somehow he was able to locate the telegraph operator and get the message sent to Fremantle telegraph office, which was open for business.

Before sunrise on Easter Monday, James Wilson, Robert Cranston and Michael Harrington, who were working outside the prison, slipped away and made their rendezvous with a carriage provided by Desmond. Around the same time James Donagh, Thomas Hassett and Martin Hogan escaped from the prison's minimum-security section and were picked up by another carriage.

The two carriages raced to Rockingham where the whaleboat was waiting, but no sooner had they shoved off than a local resident—a timber cutter named Bell who had spoken to the men and thought their abandoning carriages and horses on the beach very suspicious—mounted up and headed for Perth. He arrived at 1 p.m. and informed the police that he had seen an American whaleboat, manned by sailors armed with rifles, take nine men, some in prison clothes, from the beach at Rockingham.

The police only had a small vessel, a single-masted cutter, which put to sea as soon as possible. But within several hours they had also commandeered, by authority of the colonial governor, Sir William Robinson, the schooner-rigged coastal steamer *Georgette*, which headed out to sea with a hastily assembled group of volunteers from the quaintly named 'Enrolled Pensioner Force'.

Meanwhile, out at sea, the whaleboat came within sight of the *Catalpa* just on sunset, but a sudden fierce squall hit and they lost sight of her and spent the night battling the storm.

Next morning the group in the whaleboat relocated the *Catalpa* but saw the *Georgette* heading to the whaling ship and stayed away, lying down in the whaleboat to avoid being seen.

Superintendent Stone of the Water Police, aboard the *Georgette*, hailed the *Catalpa* and requested to be allowed on board to search for escaped convicts. The request was denied, although the fugitives were not yet on board, and the *Georgette* followed the *Catalpa* for several hours until the former was forced to return to Fremantle to refuel.

As the *Georgette* disappeared towards Fremantle, the police cutter appeared on the horizon. The men in the whaleboat rowed hard for the *Catalpa* and made it on board as the police approached. The cutter also lingered within sight of the *Catalpa* for some time before heading back to shore.

The governor was now determined to recapture the convicts and had the *Georgette* fitted with a 12-pound howitzer field gun overnight. Both the police cutter and the *Georgette* set out to find the *Catalpa* the following day, Tuesday, 18 April. The Pensioner Guards were all armed and eager on board the *Georgette*, along with the howitzer.

The *Catalpa* was spotted on the horizon that afternoon but it wasn't until 8 a.m. the following day that the *Georgette* overhauled the whaling ship and fired shots across its stern and bow. Captain Anthony hove to and parlayed with Superintendant Stone.

Stone demanded to be allowed to board the *Catalpa* but Anthony refused the request.

Stone had British law on his side, and the *Georgette* had might on her side; a cannon and 30 or more eager armed militiamen.

Captain Anthony bluffed it out with style. He reminded Stone that they were in international waters, then he pointed to the stars and stripes, at the masthead and challenged Stone to create a diplomatic incident.

The taunt was deliberately intended to remind Stone that several years earlier the USA had sued Britain over a maritime breach of neutrality in the American Civil War and the case had been settled in Geneva in September 1872, with Britain paying compensation of £3 million.

Firing on or attempting to board the *Catalpa* without permission, Anthony declared, would be nothing short of an act of war against the USA.

The *Catalpa* then made sail and proceeded westward.

With no other option, the *Georgette* followed until she was low on fuel then turned back to Fremantle as the *Catalpa* disappeared into the vastness of the Indian Ocean. The complex rescue plan, over two years in the making, had worked.

Due to the successful cutting of the telegraph wires by Thomas Desmond's two recruits, John Durham and Denis McCarthy, it was June before news of the escape reached London.

Meanwhile, the *Catalpa* managed to avoid British ships and make its way back to the USA. Captain Anthony even chased a few whales on the way home but the *Catalpa* proved to be better at catching escaped convicts than whales—no kills were made.

John Boyle O'Reilly finally learned of the escape in early June and publicised the event to the world, provoking anger in Britain, jubilation in Ireland and the USA, and mixed sentiments in the various colonies of Australia.

The *Catalpa* arrived in New York Harbour on 19 August 1876 and was given to Captain Anthony, with shares going to his two chief officers, as a reward for their part in the adventure.

In the colony of Western Australia there was embarrassment and paranoia about a Fenian invasion. The assistant warden who had shown Breslin through Fremantle Prison attempted suicide unsuccessfully and then resigned. The prison controller and several other officials were sacked, and all tickets-of-leave for Fenians were revoked.

In spite of this, all Fenians were freed by 1878. The traditional song which follows, written at the time, was banned in the colony of Western Australia.

THE CATALPA

A noble whale ship and commander,
Called the *Catalpa*, they say,
Sailed out to Western Australia
And took six bold Fenians away.

Many long years they had served there
And many more years had to stay,
For defending their country, Old Ireland,
For that they were banished away.

You kept them in Western Australia
Till their hair it began to turn grey,
Then a Yank from the States of Americay
Came out here and stole them away.

The *Georgette*, all armed with bold warriors,
Went out the brave Yank to arrest,
But she hoisted the star-spangled banner
Saying, 'Now you'll not board me, I guess.'

They landed them safe in Americay
And there they were able to cry,
'Hoist up the green flag and the shamrock,
Hurrah, for Old Ireland we'll die!'

So remember those Fenians colonial
And sing out these verses with me,
And remember the Yankee that took them
To the home of the brave and the free.

Come all you screw-warders and gaolers
Remember Perth regatta day.
Take care of the rest of your Fenians,
Or Yankees will steal them away.

POETIC PARODIES

Here is a story about three great poets and a connection between them of which few Australians have ever been aware.

With his knowledge of literary forms and old ballads, Adam Lindsay Gordon was a master of rhythm and rhyme. One of his most famous galloping ballads is the starting point for this wonderful tale of parodies.

Both Banjo Paterson and C.J. Dennis wrote parodies of Gordon's steeplechasing poem 'How We Beat the Favourite' using the same metre and rhyme scheme but slightly changing the title to give a new twist to a racing story of their own time and gently poking fun at the man they said was their most admired predecessor.

Their poems are quite well known and Banjo's is often recited and anthologised. Although 'How the Favourite Beat Us' is famous and much loved, I have never met one reciter or bush verse aficionado who knew that both it and C.J. Dennis's poem, 'How We Backed the Favourite', about Peter Pan's first Melbourne Cup win, were tributes and parodies of the poem written in the middle of the nineteenth century by Adam Lindsay Gordon.

Here is Gordon's original, a stirring tale of the underdog beating the favourite in a steeplechase, told by the jockey wearing the scarlet colours and riding the mare Iseult, who finishes in a near dead heat with the favourite, The Clown, ridden by Dick Neville wearing green.

It takes some working out to realise which horses are which and how the race unfolds, but it's very stirring stuff!

HOW WE BEAT THE FAVOURITE

ADAM LINDSAY GORDON

'Aye, squire,' said Stevens, 'they back him at evens;
  The race is all over, bar shouting, they say;
The Clown ought to beat her; Dick Neville is sweeter
  Than ever – he swears he can win all the way.

'But none can outlast her, and few travel faster,
  She strides in her work clean away from *The Drag*;
You hold her and sit her, she couldn't be fitter,
  Whenever you hit her she'll spring like a stag.

'And p'rhaps the green jacket, at odds though they back it,
  May fall, or there's no telling what may turn up.
The mare is quite ready, sit still and ride steady,
  Keep cool; and I think you may just win the cup.'

Dark brown and tan muzzle, just stripped for the tussle,
  Stood *Iseult*, arching her neck to the curb,
A lean head and fiery, strong quarters and wiry,
  A loin rather light, but a shoulder superb.

'Keep back on the yellow! Come upon *Othello*!
Hold hard on the chestnut! Turn round on *The Drag*!
Keep back there on *Spartan*! Back you, sir, in tartan!
  So, steady there, easy!' And down went the flag.

We started, and Kerr made a strong run on *Mermaid*,
  Through furrows that led to the first stake-and-bound,
The Crack, half extended, looked bloodlike and splendid,
  Held wide on the right where the headland was sound.

I pulled hard to baffle her rush with the snaffle,
  Before her two-thirds of the field got away;
All through the wet pasture where floods of the last year
  Still loitered, they clotted my crimson with clay.

The fourth fence, a wattle, floored *Monk* and *Bluebottle*;
  The Drag came to grief at the blackthorn and ditch,
The rails toppled over *Redoubt* and *Red Rover*,
  The lane stopped *Lycurgus* and *Leicestershire Witch*.

She passed like an arrow *Kildare* and *Cock Sparrow*
  And *Mantrap* and *Mermaid* refused the stone wall;
And Giles on *The Greyling* came down at the paling,
  And I was left sailing in front of them all.

I took them a burster, nor eased her nor nursed her,
  Her dark chest all dappled with flakes of white foam,
Her flanks mud bespattered, a weak rail she shattered,
  We landed on turf with our heads turned for home.

We crashed a low binder, and then, close behind her,
  The ground to the hooves of the favourite shook,
His rush roused her mettle, yet ever so little,
  She shortened her stride as we raced at the brook.

She rose when I hit her, I saw the stream glitter,
  A wide scarlet nostril flashed close to my knee,
Between sky and water *The Clown* came and caught her,
  The space that he cleared was a caution to see.

And forcing the running, discarding all cunning,
  A length to the front went the rider in green;
A long strip of stubble, and then the quick double,
  Two stiff flights of rails with a quickset between.

She came to his quarter, and on still I brought her,
  And up to his girth, to his breastplate she drew,
A short prayer from Neville just reached me, 'The Devil!'
  He muttered . . . locked level the hurdles we flew.

A hum of hoarse cheering, a dense crowd careering,
  All sights seen obscurely, all shouts vaguely heard;

'The green wins!' 'The crimson!' The multitude swims on,
And figures are blended and features are blurred.

'*The Clown* is her master!' 'The green forges past her!'
'*The Clown* will outlast her!' '*The Clown* wins!' '*The Clown*!'
The white railing races with all the white faces,
The chestnut outpaces, outstretches the brown.

On still past the gateway she strains in the straightway,
Still struggles, '*The Clown* by a short neck at most!'
He swerves, the green scourges, the stand rocks and surges,
And flashes, and verges, and flits the white post.

Aye! So ends the tussle, I knew the tan muzzle
Was first, though the ring men were yelling, 'Dead heat!'
A nose I could swear by, but Clarke said, 'The mare by
A short head.' And that's how the favourite was beat.

You will notice how the rhyme scheme of two close rhymes, followed by long lines, which also rhyme with each other, gives the exact feeling of a galloping horse. The metre is a variation of a form called 'amphibrachic', where three syllables are used and the middle syllable is accented. It really doesn't matter how Gordon did it, what matters is that the rhythm and rhyme sweep the story along at a galloping pace and the reader can't help but get excited and swept along at the same time.

ENTER THE BANJO

Andrew Barton Paterson was born on 17 February 1864, at Narambla, New South Wales, not far from Orange. He was the son of a Scottish immigrant, Andrew Bogle Paterson, from Lanarkshire, who had arrived in Australia in the early 1850s, and Rose Barton, daughter of a pioneering family. Rose's parents had both emigrated from England and owned a property in the Riverina.

Paterson's early life was spent on family properties in the Riverina and near Yass. Here, he became acquainted with the colourful bush characters that he wrote about so vividly in his later life.

His early education took place at home under a governess then at the bush school in Binalong, the nearest township. From about the age of ten he attended the Sydney Grammar School. He lived with his widowed grandmother, a cultivated woman who had been educated on the continent and wrote verse, which was published privately.

'Barty', as the family called him, spent much of his early life around horses, and his lifelong love of horseracing and polo is reflected in many of his poems. He was a member of the first New South Wales polo team to play against the Victorians.

He had a very light touch on the reins which he always attributed to the fact that he was dropped by his nurse as a small child and suffered a badly fractured right arm. The nurse was afraid to tell anyone about the accident; she was an Aboriginal girl and doubtless feared the consequences. The damage was not detected for some time and then young Paterson had to undergo a series of operations, which left his right arm considerably shorter than his left. He attributed his success at polo and racing to this fact. He won the Polo Challenge Cup in 1892 on his horse The Shifter, and also competed in races at Rosehill and Randwick as an amateur, or 'gentleman' rider.

After completing school the sixteen-year-old Paterson was articled to a Sydney firm of solicitors, Spain and Salway. He was admitted as a solicitor in 1886 and formed the legal partnership, Street and Paterson. His first poem was written in 1885 and he wrote his first 'racing' poem, 'A Dream of the Melbourne Cup', on 30 October 1886. In the poem Paterson dreams that the Cup is won by the New South Wales horse Trident:

But one draws out from the beaten ruck
And up on the rails by a piece of luck
He comes in a style that's clever;

'It's *Trident*! *Trident*! Hurrah for Hales!'
'Go at 'em now while their courage fails;'
'*Trident*! *Trident*! for New South Wales!'
'The blue and white for ever!'

In the dream Paterson has backed the winner at 'a million to five' but, true to colonial rivalry perhaps, the bookie had not paid him when he finally 'woke with indigestion'. (Several days later Trident ran fourth behind Arsenal in the actual race.)

Paterson's verse began appearing in the *Bulletin* from 1885 under his nom de plume, 'The Banjo', which was the name of a racehorse his father had once owned. It was not until 1895, on the publication of *The Man from Snowy River and Other Verses*, that the public finally discovered his identity.

Paterson worked as a journalist, was a war correspondent in the Boer War and became editor of the *Sydney Evening News*. He was almost 50 when war broke out in 1914, but he enlisted in the Australian Imperial Force and worked in France as an ambulance driver before joining the First Australian Remount Unit as a lieutenant and then rose to the rank of major.

In 1922 he became editor of the *Sydney Sportsman*, a weekly sporting newspaper. Paterson retired in 1930, was awarded the CBE for his services to Australian literature in 1939 and died in 1941. He remains Australia's best known and most loved poet.

Banjo Paterson always said he admired and was inspired by Adam Lindsay Gordon. In 1894, Paterson wrote a parody of Gordon's famous galloping rhyme 'How We Beat the Favourite', which used the same rhyme scheme and scansion as the original but reversed the roles and added the double twist of a betting coup gone terribly wrong.

The poem was called 'How the Favourite Beat Us' and appeared in the race book for the Rosehill meeting on 9 November, the Saturday following the Melbourne Cup. It tells how an owner tries to back his horse, fails to get a price, attempts to get the jockey to pull up the horse and is ironically defeated in his trickery by a mosquito . . . and his own horse. The poem appears to be set in Newcastle, as the mosquito in question is one of the infamous 'Hexham greys' from the mangrove swamps near the Hunter River.

HOW THE FAVOURITE BEAT US

A.B. PATERSON ('THE BANJO')

'Aye,' said the boozer, 'I tell you it's true, sir,
I once was a punter with plenty of pelf,
But gone is my glory, I'll tell you the story
How I stiffened my horse and got stiffened myself.

''Twas a mare called the Cracker, I came down to back her,
But found she was favourite all of a rush,
The folk just did pour on to lay six to four on,
And several bookies were killed in the crush.

'It seems old Tomato was stiff, though a starter;
They reckoned him fit for the Caulfield to keep.
The Bloke and the Donah were scratched by their owner, –
He only was offered three-fourths of the sweep.

'We knew Salamander was slow as a gander,
The mare could have beat him the length of the straight,
And old Manumission was out of condition,
And most of the others were running off weight.

'No doubt someone "blew it", for everyone knew it,
The bets were all gone, and I muttered in spite
"If I can't get a copper, by Jingo, I'll stop her,
Let the public fall in, it will serve the brutes right."

'I said to the jockey, "Now, listen, my cocky,
You watch as you're cantering down by the stand,
I'll wait where that toff is and give you the office,
You're only to win if I lift up my hand."

'I then tried to back her – "What price is the Cracker?"
"Our books are all full, sir," each bookie did swear;
My mind, then, I made up, my fortune I played up
I bet every shilling against my own mare.

'I strolled to the gateway, the mare in the straightway
Was shifting and dancing, and pawing the ground,
The boy saw me enter and wheeled for his canter,
When a darned great mosquito came buzzing around.

'They breed 'em at Hexham, it's risky to vex 'em,
They suck a man dry at a sitting, no doubt,
But just as the mare passed, he fluttered my hair past,
I lifted my hand, and I flattened him out.

'I was stunned when they started, the mare simply darted
Away to the front when the flag was let fall,
For none there could match her, and none tried to catch her –
She finished a furlong in front of them all.

'You bet that I went for the boy, whom I sent for
The moment he weighed and came out of the stand –
"Who paid you to win it? Come, own up this minute."
"Lord love yer," said he, "why you lifted your hand."

''Twas true, by St. Peter, that cursed "muskeeter"
Had broke me so broke that I hadn't a brown,
And you'll find the best course is when dealing with horses
To win when you're able, and *keep your hands down*.'

THEN ALONG CAME DENNIS

In 1931, when Peter Pan was a hot favourite for the Melbourne Cup, C.J. Dennis dipped his poetic lid to his two predecessors, Gordon and Paterson, and wrote his parody of 'How We Beat the Favourite'. It is a typical C.J. Dennis piece, which captures the mood of the day and shows how well Dennis knew the average bloke and how his mind worked. Its title and the word 'backed' shows how Dennis's emphasis was always on the common punter rather than the actual race itself.

HOW WE BACKED THE FAVOURITE

C.J. DENNIS

'Sure thing,' said the grocer, 'as far as I know, sir,
This horse, Peter Pan, is the safest of certs.'
'I see by the paper,' commended the draper,
'He's tipped and he carries my whole weight of shirts.'

The butcher said, 'Well, now, it's easy to tell now
There's nothing else in it except Peter Pan.'
And so too the baker, the barman, bookmaker,
The old lady char and the saveloy man.

'You stick to my tip, man,' admonished the grip-man,
'Play up Peter Pan; he's a stayer with speed.'
And the newspaper vendor, the ancient road mender,
And even the cop at the corner agreed.

The barber said, 'Win it? There's nothing else in it.
I backed Peter Pan with the last that I had.'
'Too right,' said the liftman. 'The horse is a gift, man.'
The old jobbing gardener said, 'Peter Pan, lad!'

I know nought of racing. The task I was facing,
It filled me with pain and unreasoning dread.
They all seemed so certain, and yet a dark curtain
Of doubt dulled my mind . . . But I must keep my head!

I went to the races, and I watched all their faces.
I saw Peter Pan's; there was little he lacked.
And as he seemed willing, I plonked on my shilling
And triumphed! And that's how the favourite was backed.

So there it is—a wonderful trifecta of poems, all using the same rhyme and metre, by three of the best poets that ever lived in Australia. Yet many verse reciters who have entertained audiences across Australia with Banjo's 'How the Favourite Beat Us', and have made it, and to a lesser extent C.J. Dennis's, famous, have no idea that both poems are tongue-in-cheek tributes to the writers' hero, Adam Lindsay Gordon.

Although the original is hardly remembered today, I think they are three of the most recitable of all Aussie verses and are certainly among my all-time favourites. I enjoy the way each verse illustrates so accurately a different aspect of the Australian obsession with horseracing. I enjoy the excitement and honesty of Gordon's poem, and I enjoy the two different styles of humour displayed by Paterson and Dennis, and the respect that you sense in their efforts to closely parody the style of the man they both admired.

Parody is, perhaps, the ultimate compliment.

WATTLE THEY THINK OF NEXT

You may be surprised to know the real reasons why our coat of arms features the kangaroo and emu and why the floral emblem in the background is the golden wattle.

Most Aussies assume that we simply chose the largest native animal and bird, and threw in 'golden' wattle to match the national colours, or because of the goldrushes, or the importance and status of gold—or because gold is . . .well, gold!

All of the above assumptions are, however, wrong.

For a start, our national colours of green and gold are a very recent development, but that's another story.

According to legend, the reason for choosing the kangaroo and emu was that supposedly neither of those creatures could step backwards. This was meant to represent the fact that our new nation was a forward-looking society, interested in a future rather than a past history.

In fact, both those creatures can move backwards but rarely do, which is good enough as far as that theory goes, I guess.

The reason for our national floral emblem being the golden wattle is rather more strange and complicated.

The approach of Federation brought the desire for national symbols. In 1891 a Melbourne *Herald* reader, David Scott, advanced fourteen reasons why wattle should be the national emblem.

Why did we need to be convinced that wattle was the best choice?

Well, many colonists wanted the waratah, *Telopea speciosissima*, to be chosen, but there was strong opposition to that idea outside of New South Wales. As usual, there was rivalry and disagreement between New South Wales and Victoria.

Henry Lawson was a proud 'Sydney-sider', as New South Wales residents were known (being 'Sydney side' of the Murray River). All for the waratah, he wrote:

> Waratah, my Mountain Queen,
> Grandest flower ever seen,
> Glorious in shade or sun,
> Where our rocky gullies run.
> There is nothing, near or far,
> Like our Mountain Waratah.

The logical argument put forward for the waratah was that it is *only* found in Australia whereas acacia, or wattle, is found in many parts of the world. Botanist R. Baker, advocating the waratah as the national floral emblem, wrote: 'The expression "the land of the Waratah", applies to Australia and no other; it is Australia's very own.'

The problem with the waratah as a 'national' emblem was that it is found naturally only in three of the six states—New South Wales, Victoria and Tasmania—and was already associated as an emblem with New South Wales.

The conflict which existed about the choice of the Australian national flower is seen in the inclusion of both waratah and wattle flowers as decoration on the three golden trowels used by the governor-general, Lord Denman, the prime minister, Andrew Fisher and the minister for home affairs, the Hon. King O'Malley, for the laying of foundation stones in Canberra, the national capital, on 12 March 1913.

David Scott's fourteen reasons why wattle should be the national emblem mostly related to the universal nature of wattle around Australia and the historic connections with the early settlers using wattle to build huts and shelters. In fact, the common name 'wattle' is derived from the verb 'to wattle', which means to use pliable branches mixed with mud and woven to make huts which were then coated with more mud. The process was called 'wattle and daub' and was used for building huts in Celtic and Saxon times in Britain.

Early European settlers in Australia, including the first-fleeters, found acacia the best plant for this purpose and the word was then associated with the plant and became used as a noun.

Scott suggested that there were three species of wattle that might be suitable for a national emblem due to their generic distribution around the continent and the beauty of their blooms: silver wattle, black wattle and golden wattle.

You may think that he suggested golden wattle merely because of the name, but this is not the case. Nor did he choose it for the depth of colour, as the flower of black wattle is much brighter than golden wattle. In fact, he decided that *Acacia pycnantha* had 'the highest value' because of its importance in the Australian tanning industry.

Few Aussies these days can imagine the importance of the leather industry back in the 1890s. As a kid I remember when the suburbs around Botany Bay were home to dozens of tanneries and the industry employed thousands of men in the suburbs of Botany and Mascot, and it was the same all over Australia. Before the advent of synthetic substitutes, leather was a mainstream product in everyday life and very valuable to Australia as an export as well as essential for local needs.

Golden wattle is far and away the best species for tanning as its bark has a higher content of the tannin used for leather making than other species of acacia. Even today golden wattle is grown abroad in temperate regions for its bark, and it is also used in perfume making.

There is an irony in Scott's choice of the golden wattle. One of his arguments against the waratah as a national emblem was that it was only found naturally in three states. Golden wattle also only occurs naturally in three states—South Australia, New South Wales and predominantly in Victoria—though it is true it will grow prolifically anywhere in a temperate climate. It has even become a pest in parts of Western Australia!

It is true, however, that wattle species are universal to our continent and are far more obvious and noticeable than the reclusive waratah. There are more than 900 species of *Acacia* in Australia. There is only one species of waratah.

Perhaps, though, Scott was being parochial in his choice, as the state of Victoria is really the home of the golden wattle as a common and highly visible species of acacia.

After Scott's letter was published in 1891, the golden wattle seems to have been accepted as the first choice for a floral emblem.

Archibald Campbell founded The Wattle Club in Victoria in 1899 to promote Wattle Day, 1 September, stating that 'Wattle is almost exclusively Australian, and should undoubtedly be our national flower'. Wattle Day was celebrated in Sydney in 1909. Victoria and South Australia participated in 1910, and Queensland in 1912—the year that the adoption of wattle as the national flower was confirmed by its introduction into the design of the Australian arms.

The big problem facing Wattle Day is the fact that wattle blooms far earlier in the northern states than it does in the south. There is still some good old-fashioned bickering about which day it should be. New South Wales still feels cheated that 1 August wasn't chosen. Most wattle has bloomed well and truly before September in New South Wales, and in Queensland the flowers are finished and fading!

Still, we all acknowledge that wattle heralds the spring. Veronica Mason wrote:

> The bush was grey a week today,
> Olive green and brown and grey,
> But now it's sunny all the way,
> For Oh! the Spring has come to stay
> With blossom for the Wattle.

Acacia pycnantha was not actually proclaimed as the national floral emblem until 1988, at a ceremony at the Australian National Botanic Gardens when Hazel Hawke planted a golden wattle. In 1992, 1 September was formally declared 'National Wattle Day' by the minister for the environment, Ros Kelly.

Golden wattle grows 4 to 8 metres tall. It tends to be short-lived in cultivation and regenerates freely after fires, which usually kill the parent plants but stimulate the germination of seeds stored in the soil if rain follows soon after. Another reason it was thought to be suitable as symbolic of a nation that survives disasters and goes on growing.

For better or worse, golden wattle is our national floral emblem, all because of the leather industry, and good old colonial rivalry!

WARATAH AND WATTLE

HENRY LAWSON

Though poor and in trouble I wander alone,
With rebel cockade in my hat,
Though friends may desert me, and kindred disown,
My country will never do that!
You may sing of the Shamrock, the Thistle, the Rose,
Or the three in a bunch, if you will;
But I know of a country that gathered all those,
And I love the great land where the Waratah grows.
And the Wattle-bough blooms on the hill.

Australia! Australia! so fair to behold –
While the blue sky is arching above;
The stranger should never have need to be told,
That the Wattle-bloom means that her heart is of gold.
And the Waratah's red with her love.

Australia! Australia! most beautiful name,
Most kindly and bountiful land;
I would die every death that might save her from shame,
If a black cloud should rise on the strand;
But whatever the quarrel, whoever her foes,
Let them come! Let them come when they will!
Though the struggle be grim, 'tis Australia that knows
That her children shall fight while the Waratah grows,
And the Wattle blooms out on the hill.

WHAT SMITHY DID BEFORE HE WAS FAMOUS

We all know that Charles Kingsford-Smith flew across the Pacific with three companions and went on to be our most famous aviator. What most of us may not know is what he did before that memorable flight.

'Smithy' was one of seven children of William Smith and his wife, Catherine Kingsford, whose family were important people in Brisbane. William went into real estate in Canada in 1903 and worked as a clerk with the Canadian Pacific Railways before the family returned to live in Sydney at the end of 1906.

Not long after the family returned, Smithy, aged ten, became the first person to be rescued using the new life-saving reel, at Bondi Beach. He was partly educated in Vancouver and at St Andrew's Cathedral Choir School, Sydney, then at Sydney Technical High School. At sixteen he was apprenticed to the Colonial Sugar Refining Co. Ltd.

When he was eighteen, World War I broke out.

Here he tells the story of his wartime and post-war adventures, before his history-making flight across the Pacific in 1928.

WAR AND CIRCUSES

CHARLES KINGSFORD-SMITH

There comes a time in the lives of most young men when they have to make decisions—I mean decisions which will affect the future course of their lives.

Some of us are born to the humdrum, placid existence of city life; some are born wanderers; others are impatient of the yoke and are a law unto themselves, and some are content to drift along in the path that leads nowhere.

I do not know in which category to place myself. I think perhaps that my future was determined on that day in 1915, my eighteenth birthday, when I presented myself at the Recruiting Office in Sydney Town Hall and enlisted in the Signal Engineers A.I.F.

Not that there was anything special about that. Everyone was joining up in those hectic days, but from that hall in Australia to France and England in war time was a short cut. That, in itself, meant a violent change in one's life.

Until then, I had been an Australian schoolboy, 'messing about' with electric gadgets and interested in engines of all kinds, and consequently apprenticed by my parents to the electrical engineering trade.

Most men look back to their war days with disgust and horror. So do I, but I must confess that I didn't dislike it at the time. The war meant to me a change of scene, a plunge into a big adventure, a new life, new countries. But first there were early days of training as a soldier in the Australian army, in my first unit, the 19th Battery A.I.F. Somehow or other, guns did not appeal to me, so I got a transfer to the Signal Corps, and it was with the Signallers that I found myself in Egypt and thereafter in Gallipoli, where we remained until the evacuation.

That was certainly an exciting enough adventure for most of us who were still in our teens, but it was hardly the sort of adventure we had visualised in our hot young dreams.

From Gallipoli to France via Egypt was but a step, a step that led to another change for me, from the Signal Corps to the motorcycle despatch riders, a more interesting occupation for one whose thoughts were largely centred on speed, and on gadgets devised to produce it.

I might have been a despatch rider for the 'duration'; returning when demobbed to Australia, like many thousands of my cobbers, to the humdrum life of peace. But there came a day in 1916 when an opportunity offered itself to become, if not an airman, at least to have the chance of training for a commission in the then Royal Flying Corps.

It was the chance of a lifetime; it proved to be the chance of my flying life, and it was a decision I made without a moment's hesitation. I was not peculiar in this respect. There were hundreds, thousands situated like me, each of whom would have given their soul cases to have been selected for the R.F.C. But although many were called, few were chosen, and those of us who were selected left for our new life, envied by our fellow Diggers whom we left behind.

The story of the 'War Birds' over France in those hectic days of 1917 and 1918 has been told by many. I will not linger over them myself, except to remark, in passing, that they were great days. There were giants in the sky then—Albert Ball, Jimmy McCudden, Mannock, Bishop and the Frenchmen Nungesser, Guynemer, Garros and others.

And on 'the other side' there were foemen worthy of our steel, and of our Lewis-Vickers guns; such as Immelmann of 'The Turn,' the slickest and quickest method of doubling in one's track, Richtofen and his circus and others.

The names of these great fighting pilots stand out, but there are hundreds of others of equal calibre whose names are unknown except to their own comrades and to those in their immediate circle who knew of their deeds, and their exploits with the flying gun.

And the machines we flew!

The old names recur to me like wraiths from the past. Maurice Farman, the B.E.'s, the Martinsydes, the D.H.2, Camels and Pups, the wonderful S.E.5, noted for its speed, and last but not least, the machines with which my own squadron, the 23rd, was equipped—the famous French 'Spads.' And on 'the other side,' the Rumplers, Albatross and Fokkers, whose machine-guns were timed to fire ahead through the propellers.

Queer old antediluvian craft they seem now, looking back across the years, but what tricks we performed in them, what feats of daring were accomplished.

I came into the world of flying at its dawn, and what a glorious dawn! There was barely a glimpse of dawn in those dark drear days of 1914 when the sole idea in air warfare was that the machines were designed, and the men were trained, for reconnaissance only.

They were to be scouts, the eyes of the army. But long before Armistice Day arrived, the flying forces of all the combatants had reached a pitch of development in design, speed, fighting power which, two years earlier, had hardly been dreamt of.

Everything was in a state of flux, so rapid were the developments taking place almost from day to day. And among the pilots was a keen and friendly rivalry to outdo each other, which nothing could dampen.

When we were not dodging the German 'Archies' we were on patrol, or loosing off drums of Lewis or Vickers bullets, or engaged in performing terrific stunts in fighting aviation known as the 'zoom' or the 'roll,' or the 'dive.'

Our planes flew and fought at 15,000 feet, a tremendous ceiling in those days; the Spads had a top speed even then (and that was nearly twenty years ago) of 130 m.p.h. and a ceiling of 20,000 feet.

Sometimes our squadrons would sweep the sky in bands twenty strong, looking for trouble in the shape of the Hun machines, and generally finding it. We flew low over enemy aerodromes and trenches, ground strafing and attacking anything in sight with our drums of Lewis fire.

At other times we flew high, waiting at 15,000 feet to pounce on our enemies, and there were exciting and adventurous occasions when we deliberately cultivated a spinning nose dive in an effort to avoid attack, or with nonchalant abandon rolled carefree.

But, underneath this youthful impetuosity and superficial gaiety, there was a deadly concentration of purpose and superb nervous stability. You hardly ever heard of an airman having a nervous breakdown in those days, though how we managed to avoid them with all that immense output of energy, I do not know.

I expect it was just youth living on its nerves. Another memory of those days comes to me—of the long summer evenings of 1918 over the famous old Salient; there is, too, still in my nostrils the unmistakable odour of the German tracer bullets as they streamed past like a jet from a hose, and I recall the joy of battle when one first 'bagged one's own bird' and had the inexpressible relief of seeing the enemy going down to disaster.

But why linger over those hectic days on the Western Front? In our funny old machines, prodigious feats were performed by 'intrepid airmen' in things tied up with bits of string, and when it was not unknown for the *London Gazette* to announce that a packet of Military Crosses had been handed out to as many young subalterns and airmen for 'distinguished service'.

I managed to shoot down a few 'Huns', as we called them in those good old days, and I managed to get wounded and shot down myself. It was service all right, though I doubt whether it was very distinguished, but all the time we were youngsters learning a lot. We were imbibing an immense store of flying experience and technical knowledge, and we were learning something which to my mind is far more valuable—the capacity to look after yourself, the instinct to do or to die, the desire for action, without thought of the risks and dangers.

For one thing, you had to be wounded, and I duly received my 'Blighty', a fact which enabled me to take further and more advanced courses in flying, with the result that by the summer of 1918, when I was barely twenty-one, I became an Instructor.

It might seem a little presumptuous to many people that a youth not yet twenty-one should take upon himself the style, title and dignity of 'Instructor R.A.F.'.

The truth was that I, and many more like me, felt in those days that we could instruct anybody in anything. We thought we knew everything, from how to win the war down to the stripping and re-assembly of any aero engine you liked to place in front of us.

We were a care-free, cigarette-smoking, leave-seeking lot of young devils who feared nothing; except being brought down behind the enemy lines.

Looking back on that slap-dash, careless, nonchalant time, we seem to have been coldly efficient. We did our job to the best of our ability in what seem to be the craziest old antiquarian contraptions imaginable—the machines of the Royal Flying Corps. And we were up against an enemy that was ahead of us in aircraft design, and certainly not our inferiors in courage, elan and dash. And then suddenly it was all over.

The tumult and the shouting died, and there was I, with the remains of a war wound, a war gratuity and a war decoration, and with the wide world before me.

I also had two friends, ex-officers like myself, named Maddocks and Rendle—stout fellows both. We clubbed together and purchased two ex-war-time machines. D.H.6's, I think they were, and with these we carried on sundry commercial jobs, joy-riding, taxi-flights and so on.

We bought these machines very cheaply from Air Ministry war stocks, which were surplus to requirements, and as we crashed them we would dash back and buy others to replace the crashed machines. We were young and full of beans, and ready for anything. In fact, the new days of Peace seemed strangely dull and flat after the old days of war.

One day I remember passing over some coverts, and with the 'war bird' fever still strongly working in us, we shot a brace of pheasants and landed to capture our bag.

The irate farmer suddenly appeared and accused us, not of shooting pheasants, but a hare, thereby breaking some ancient feudal law. The penalty for this, according to the farmer, was deportation or transportation for the term of our natural lives to Australia, from which we had recently come to fight for King and country.

There was considerable excitement over the incident; the farmer declined to be mollified and we were 'taken to Court', as they say. Fortunately, another law intervened on our behalf. The prosecution could not prove that we had actually shot the hare, and the case was dismissed.

About this time we three became associated with the Blackburn Aviation Company.

The year 1919 had come in with a rush and, almost before we realised it, new marvels were being accomplished. Alcock and Brown had flown across the Atlantic; Harry Hawker had become a national hero, and to us, a tempting prize was held out by the Commonwealth Government which offered £10,000 to the first Australian who should fly from England to Australia.

Ten Thousand Pounds seemed a lot of money to us. It *was* a lot of money. Furthermore, it was just such a venture as this that appealed to people like us and to others like us, too. There were dozens of Australian airmen in England at that time, and they all began feverishly to lay their plans for the flight.

Our idea was to fly in a Blackburn Kangaroo twin-engined machine, and it seemed a very good idea, too. But there was a nigger in the wood-pile in the form of Mr. W. M. Hughes, our war-time Prime Minister, who was all powerful in those days. When he heard of our plan, he put his foot down. We were too young; we were too inexperienced; particularly, we had no navigation knowledge or experience for such a tremendous journey. He absolutely forbade it and that was the end of our plan.

We sold the machine after an official veto had been placed on our venture by the Air Ministry. There was nothing else to be done, but a short time later two other Smiths, Ross and Keith, flew their Vickers Vimy out to Australia in 28 days, winning the prize of £10,000 and knighthoods for this magnificent feat.

My mind was filled with aviation to the exclusion of everything else. The fact was, though I did not realise it then, that the time had come when decisions were being made for me.

The course of my future left solid ground and soared up into the sky. But to where it would lead me, I had not the slightest notion. Having spent what little money I had, the pressing necessity arose of finding a job—obviously a job connected with aviation.

Looking for something that an airman could do, I heard of the great rich opportunities offering to bold young fellows who were ready to perform at Hollywood.

Stunt flying for film purposes was then in its infancy when I joined up with the film people, under contract as a 'stunt pilot' and 'wing walker,' hanging by my legs from undercarriages. I very soon realised that my flying life would be short indeed if I continued at that game very long.

The people who attended these exhibitions were too bloodthirsty for my taste. They wanted too much for their money. They were not satisfied with flying and wing walking and other pleasant manoeuvres. I could see what they wanted. They wished to see a body or two carried off the field, and I did not want to be the body.

I felt, like Lord Clive, that I was reserved for something better.

Besides, the owners of the circus were unable to pay my wages, so I left.

There was, however, one further experience for me, before I left California to return to my native land. I undertook the role of 'Flying Scarecrow' on the Rice Patrol, a monotonous task of which I soon tired, of shooting duck from an aeroplane over the rice crops and spraying trees from the air. It was a sort of anti-climax to shooting down the Boche over the Western Front.

Leaving duck shooting to others, I took ship and returned to Australia—still seeking the elusive job.

By now I was an airman, a pilot whose destiny had already been decided. But aviation in Australia in 1921 offered little professional scope.

It would be untrue to say that there was no aviation in Australia in 1921; but there was very little of it.

A little group of Diggers, with more optimism than cash, had pooled their resources and started 'Diggers Aviation Ltd.,' a company formed to supply air services to the public, such as joy-riding and taxi work. I worked with them for a time, and then I received an offer to join the newly-formed West Australian Airways as pilot.

West Australian Airways was a pioneering service, struggling along with inadequate capital. Nevertheless, it was an interesting time, including a forced landing on a very remote beach on the north-west coast. We were there for three days before being picked up, and we were so sunburnt that we were confined to bed in great pain for a week afterwards.

For two years I flew backwards and forwards on this service, covering thousands of miles, acquiring experience and gradually becoming bored with the monotony of it all.

Then I heard of a motor truck transport service operating from Geraldton and joined that as a working partner, but the West was no place in which to get on in those days.

'Go West, young man!' became for me 'Go East!' I had scraped enough money together to enable me, with my chum, Keith Anderson, to pick up a couple of old Bristol machines. We decided to fly these machines across Australia to Sydney, and off we went, taking each a passenger, one of whom, Mrs. Marshall of Cottesloe, was thus the first woman to fly across Australia.

Well, there we were in the big Smoke of Sydney, stony-broke, but with a fund of flying experience and a couple of old planes.

Smithy, Anderson and Charles Ulm formed Interstate Flying Services in 1927 and just one year later Smithy and Ulm, with Americans Harry Lyon and Jim Warner, made the first flight across the Pacific in the *Southern Cross*.

THE RED BARON'S AUSSIE SEND-OFF

It is fairly certain that Australian gunners were responsible for ending the career and life of Baron Manfred von Richthofen, the World War I German flying ace known as the Red Baron. He was certainly buried with full military honours by the Australian forces.

Private Alfred Fowler, a soldier with the 40th Australian Battalion, witnessed the Red Baron's death. He recalls delivering a message to a gunner at the 11th Battalion, who opened fire on von Richthofen's plane and claims to have seen the bullets pierce the cockpit. Running to the wreckage, Fowler himself saw the bullet wounds in von Richthofen's chest and was convinced he had been killed by the Aussie gunners, although surgeons who conducted von Richthofen's autopsy formed the opinion that the angle and nature of the bullet wounds ruled out being shot from the ground, and concluded that his injuries were were probably caused by bullets from the guns of Canadian pilot Roy Brown.

In hindsight, it appears more than likely that Australian Lewis guns on the ground killed the Red Baron.

The last surviving member of the Australian Flying Corps, Howard Edwards, who passed away in 1998, remained certain it was Australian 3rd Squadron field guns that killed von Richthofen. Here is his story:

> We used to see the Red Baron's three-decker plane, and there was deal of 'scare' attached to him because he had the name of being a

successful aeronaut. He certainly was a force to be reckoned with. But he had an umbrella, as I call it, of other aeroplanes all around him. He'd have eight to ten other planes making a great circus—we used to call it the Red Baron's Circus. Not infrequently he would be up very early in the morning. At daybreak you'd find this circus up in the air waiting for some of our people to come out, and then they'd just sink down onto them and surround this one plane and let the Baron have the pleasure of shooting him down.

We felt it wasn't fair sportsmanship. What it was, was war, and as they say, 'all is fair in love and war'. We were more than delighted when we heard Richthofen had been brought down.

As I understand it, he was following one of our aeroplanes down. Our fellow dived to get away and he was following. When they got down near the ground he levelled off. He had flown some half a mile, or a mile, on the level, a few hundred feet above the ground, when he was brought down. He couldn't have done that if he'd been shot from above, but he was shot by ground forces while he was on the parallel, chasing our aeroplane.

Our squadron was commissioned to go out and collect his crashed machine. When they got out to the scene of the crash (it was in no-man's land and under pretty close observance by the enemy) it was felt that it was not wise to attempt to bring in the plane under the circumstances, so they decided to wait until night. But in the meantime they wanted to get the body of Richthofen out, so one of our corporals, Corporal Collins if I remember rightly, went out with a rope and put it around the Baron's body so that by pulling the rope they could pull him out. Then they pulled the Baron's body to their cover and brought him back and Scotty Melville and I were deputed to take it in two-hour turns to guard the body in one of our hangars until the authorities had verified the authenticity of it being the Red Baron.

Richthofen was very poorly dressed. He didn't have any sort of coat on, just what I considered to be a rather shabby kind of shirt and an undershirt, a singlet. I was rather amazed that one in his position could be so poorly dressed.

> He had a stern, set face it seemed to me and there were several marks, indentations and wounds. I could touch four or five on his face, but I didn't think any of them were bullet wounds. I felt they were wounds from the crash. What brought him down, undoubtedly, was a bullet that went through his right side, right underarm, and came out just in front of the left arm, just below the heart.

Howard was an instrument fitter and he was ordered to engrave the nameplate for von Richthofen's coffin. He commented:

> You do what you are told when you are in the Army or the Air Force. So I made up little engravers from bits of wire from the aeroplane's steel wires, polished them up and cut them suitably, then did the engraving.

When the results of an exhaustive investigation into the death of von Richthofen were published in 1997 in *The Red Baron's Last Flight* by Norman Franks and Allan Bennett, they seem to prove that the bullet that killed the flying ace could not have come from Brown's plane but had to have been fired by Australians on the ground.

Baron von Richthofen was buried on 22 April 1918 in the small village of Bertangles. British and Australian troops gave him full military honors. A British pilot dropped a note into German territory containing the news. Germany went into deep mourning.

In 1925, von Richthofen's younger brother Bolko recovered the body and the Red Baron was given the largest funeral ever seen in Berlin.

However, there is a strange twist to the tale. Some years later, author and historian P.J. Carisella reopened the grave in search of the coffin plaque made by Howard Edwards. He found the well-preserved bones of Baron von Richthofen, all intact except for the skull. He didn't find the plaque.

HOW TWO HEROES SWAPPED PLANES

Two of our nation's greatest heroes, polar explorer Hubert Wilkins and pioneer aviator Charles Kingsford-Smith, have an odd connection—they bought planes from each other to attempt flights into history.

Both men were decorated heroes of World War I, Kingsford-Smith as a pilot and Wilkins as a photographer.

When Wilkins returned to England from photographing the battlefields of Gallipoli in 1919, he learned that our government had offered £10,000 for the first all-Australian crew to fly an aeroplane from England to Australia.

Charles Kingsford-Smith had intended to enter the race in a Blackburn Kangaroo, but was banned by the rules set up by the prime minister, Billy Hughes, as he had no navigational qualifications and was not allowed to fly solo. Hughes was fearful that tragedies during the race would reflect badly on his idea to open up the air route from Britain to Australia by offering the huge prizemoney and encouraging reckless behaviour.

Kingsford-Smith was annoyed and decided to head off to California instead and work in the 'movies' doing stunts and flying for the cameras.

Wilkins then purchased the Blackburn Kangaroo from Kingsford-Smith and entered the race with a crew of three. They left England on 21 November 1919 but problems were experienced with the engines and the plane was forced down over France. Repairs were made and the flight continued, but eventually, with engine problems over the Mediterranean Sea, they were forced to turn back and look for land and the plane crash-landed in Crete. Oddly enough, the plane crashed in the grounds of a hospital for the mentally ill; there is a graphic photo of the plane resting across the wall of the hospital in the Byrd Polar Research Center Archive at the Ohio State University, where all Wilkins's papers are held.

After completing a successful expedition to tropical Northern Australia in 1926, Wilkins planned to fly over the unexplored areas north of Alaska. He first purchased two Fokker aircraft but found them too large for landing on ice and he crash-landed in one of the planes and broke his arm.

He sold one of the planes, which was called *The Detroiter* after a newspaper that had sponsored the attempt, to Charles Kingsford-Smith, who was in the USA looking for financial backing to attempt the first flight across the Pacific Ocean.

The plane had to be salvaged from where it was stranded in Alaska and flown to California, where it was fitted with new propellers supplied by the US government and renamed the *Southern Cross.*

With Kingsford-Smith and his crew on board, it became the first plane to fly across the Pacific Ocean.

GREAT TRAIN ROBBERIES

There have been some uniquely 'Aussie' train robberies in the outback.

About a year before the railway line was completed between Oodnadatta and Stuart (later Alice Springs) in 1929, a robbery occurred from the brakevan of a train which had stopped at the navvy camp called, rather obviously, the 'sixty-one mile', to the north of Oodnadatta.

The railway line construction was a huge task, being undertaken with Commonwealth government funding, and there were camps all along the line. Wages had to be paid and trains often carried large amounts of money.

There were more than 600 men at the 'sixty-one mile' camp at the time and the chances of recovering the money seemed slight at best.

Railway managers and police decided to use the services of an Aboriginal tracker and, sure enough, they were soon able to make two arrests, and as a result the money was recovered and the two men convicted.

The two desperadoes had attempted to conceal their ill-gotten gains by quite a few ingenious methods, which included hiding some of the loot in a rabbit burrow, and hanging some in calico bags from trees, to make it appear to be food kept in the shade away from vermin. The Aboriginal tracker was not fooled for a moment! Justice prevailed and the robbers were duly apprehended.

The only train in the Northern Territory for many years was the one that ran from Darwin down to Pine Creek. As you would expect, this train also had a unique Territory character. In *We of the Never Never*, Jeannie Gunn described it as 'a delightful train—just a simple-hearted, chivalrous, weather-beaten old bush-whacker, at the service of the entire Territory'.

At the end of World War I, work began on extending the line to Emungalen, on the banks of the Katherine River. This was so that the Vestey company could get their cattle to the Darwin meatworks. As labour was short, Greeks, Russians and even Patagonian migrants were brought in. Many settled in the Territory to add to its melting pot.

The wildness of railway gangs in Katherine was legendary. One gang of thieves, rumoured to be railway workers, built a spur track running off the main line into the bush, removed the goods in two vans, set the vans alight and covered their tracks by removing the rails.

But the most daring outback train robbery of all was the Great Ghan Gold Robbery of 1935—which was never solved!

Somewhere between Alice Springs and Quorn, a mailbag containing fifteen and a half kilos of gold ingots mysteriously disappeared from the safe in the brakevan of the *Ghan*.

The *Ghan* was officially known by the erroneous title of the *Northern Express* and it was, in railway parlance, a 'limited mixed service', which meant it had both freight and passenger cars. But it was hardly any kind of 'express'. The official memorandum stated that the robbery took place somewhere between the 28th and 30th of May, as that was how long it took the train to make the journey.

The gold was from three mines in the Tennant Creek district and it had been delivered to Alice Springs under armed guard and taken on board and locked in the safe. The guard and stationmaster had locked the safe together with the unmarked registered parcel, now officially the responsibility of the postmaster-general's office, safely inside. The guard then placed the key in his coat pocket, where he claimed it stayed until the train reached Quorn.

Sending gold by unmarked registered mail had, up until this time, been standard practice despite railway commissioner George Gahan expressing some concern about the prospect of theft. The post office was not greatly concerned, replying that as its liability was limited to £50 ($100) in the event of any registered parcel going missing, it was the consigner's problem. Naturally nothing was done to improve the situation.

Although the guard had gone off duty and then back on duty throughout the journey, he had remained on the train when off duty and the key stayed in his pocket the entire time and was not passed back and forth between the guards on duty.

When the safe was opened in the presence of the guard by the booking clerk at Quorn, the door was found to be a little stiff and the gold was gone.

I will let the *Adelaide Advertiser*, that revered Murdoch newspaper, take up the story:

> **Gold Stolen—Safe in Train Rifled**
> The type of safe used on the train is very old. It is not large, and has an ordinary old style lock. There is no combination, and it is thought it would be an easy matter for anyone to make a duplicate key. It was stated tonight that in competent hands the safe could easily be opened with a piece of wire. Articles of considerable value are carried on the train both ways.
>
> The view is held here that the work is that of someone with an inside knowledge of the railways. The safe was in perfect order when the train reached Quorn except that the door was a little stiff.
>
> The safe is thought to have been robbed while the train was at a siding and when the guard was assisting in shunting. The other guard would then be off duty resting.
>
> The theory was advanced tonight that a thief might even have taken the key (a bulky one with a brass tag) from the tunic of the guard on duty, as often before shunting, the guard removes his tunic and hangs it in the van.

Commissioner Gahan issued a statement declaring that the maker's certificate claimed the lock on the safe could not be picked and a duplicate key had been used.

Adelaide detectives were sent to investigate and came up with the amazing theory that the crime had 'probably' occurred in the dark of night at either Oodnadatta, Abminga or Edwards Creek, when the guard was otherwise occupied.

A reward was offered but the crime was never solved.

In the public service bureaucratic railway traditions of the day, someone had to be officially blamed. This was in spite of the fact that the gold was sent as normal certified mail and not labelled 'gold' or even 'valuable'.

The postmaster-general's office, with its £50 liability for registered mail, wasn't too bothered.

So the Commonwealth Railways fined the guard who had the key ten shillings for 'carelessness in respect of one value package of mail [when] . . . you failed to hand over the key of the brakevan safe to the Guard who relieved you, and to obtain his receipt for it . . .'

The other guard on the train was fined fifteen shillings. The extra amount was not related to the gold robbery, it was a fine for a previous offence. On an earlier trip he had left behind two railway carriages, which were supposed to go to Port Augusta and Port Adelaide, at Oodnadatta by mistake.

IN VAIN SACRIFICE

What we all tend to forget is that war takes many lives, not just the lives of those who make it to the war zone. Many young Australians have sacrificed their lives for their country without ever getting a chance to join the conflict.

Pilot Officer Michael Dicken was on a morning training flight when he died. The accident that took his life occurred 15 miles out from Mildura airport, which was a pilot training centre during World War II. The crash took place near the village of Iraak in far north-western Victoria.

The Wirraway aircraft in which he was flying was seen to pull out of a steep dive and one wing broke off, causing the plane to crash into the ground immediately. Dicken and his instructor, Flight Officer Power, were both killed instantly.

Pilot Officer Michael Dicken was just twenty years old when he died but he had a fascinating short life. His father was in the British foreign service and Michael was born in Egypt and raised in Morocco. When war came in 1939, North Africa was certainly not a safe place for a teenager, nor was Britain during the Blitz, so young Michael was sent to far-off Australia to finish his education at Melbourne Grammar School.

His father was posted to India soon after Michael left, so, when he finished school during the darkest period of the war, there was no option for Michael to rejoin his parents. Instead he enlisted in the Australian air force and was sent to Deniliquin where he completed the first stage of his flying training.

It was at Deniliquin that Michael met a local girl named Joan. They became sweethearts and he told her many stories of his childhood in the exotic lands of North Africa, where arum lilies grew. One evening he said that, if he died during the war, he would like her to plant an arum lily in his memory.

While Michael Dicken's background was uncommon, his fate was, sadly, not.

At the Number Two Officer Training Flight Unit at Mildura alone, a total of 52 men were killed in accidents while engaged in pilot training during the chaotic years of World War II. They were all either training officers, repatriated from the war zones, or youngsters whose lives ended abruptly before they had a chance to fight or serve.

That sort of thing happened all over Australia, of course. The difference is that, in Mildura, a genuine attempt to remember the sacrifice of so many young lives is being made.

As well as the well-kept graveyard where the crash victims were laid to rest, and the memorial in the Royal Australia Air Force Museum at Mildura, there are now plaques at the various crash sites. Each plaque is dedicated separately with a memorial service attended by the mayor of Mildura, a chaplain, local historian Ken Wright, and any friends or relatives that can be traced.

The landowners on whose properties the crashes occurred are also often present to pay their respects. Indeed, in some cases the landowners erected markers and memorials themselves and have kept the crash sites maintained as memorials to the victims.

During the war, the owner of Keera Station, 30 miles west of Mildura, was Tom Grace. When two Boomerang training aircraft collided over his property and crashed, he erected crosses and planted two tamarisk trees in memory of the airmen who died.

Tom Grace and the owner of nearby Lybra Station, where the second plane crashed after the collision, allowed the families of the airmen, flight officers Syd Knapman and Roger Byrne, to place plaques at the sites. Subsequent owners of the properties continued to look after the sites. When the official plaques were unveiled more than 60 years later, friends and descendants of the property owners, along with friends and family of the two airmen, including Flight Officer Knapman's widow, attended the memorial service.

The official memorial plaques were the brainchild of Ken Wright OAM, a former mayor of Mildura and the driving force behind having the RAAF Museum set up in the reconstructed headquarters of Number Two Officer Training Unit.

The granite memorials have bronze plates attached and it is no surprise to discover that 60 per cent of them will be located within the grounds of Mildura airport or close by.

Interestingly, the first memorial erected is actually right in the city boundaries and marks the spot where Pilot Officer McGowan crashed and died in a Kittyhawk. Three other fatalities occurred in the populated part of the city in January 1943, when two Wirraways collided over the streets of suburban Mildura and the two planes involved crashed into San Mateo Avenue and Etiwanda Avenue. Plaques now mark all these sites.

It is, perhaps, typical of the people of a rural area like Mildura to want to remember the past in this fashion. Civic pride has always been strong in the city, which is proud of its unusual history as an independent, planned and regulated town. The Canadian Chaffey brothers founded the Mildura Irrigation Company in 1887 and Mildura became an oasis in the desert, Australia's first irrigated colony.

Civic-minded individuals like Ken Wright were determined that the 52 young men who died in training at Mildura were not forgotten. The sadness that their deaths engendered among their friends and families, and also among the people whose lives they touched while training in Mildura and on whose properties they crashed, will be remembered when passers-by stop to read the plaques.

On occasions such as Anzac Day and Remembrance Day the plaques will serve as shrines and memorials to those men and many others like them who may not have died in battle but who nonetheless gave their lives as a result of the call to duty and as a sacrifice to their country.

On 17 August 2004, on the roadside at Iraak, at a spot nearest to the crash site that it is possible for the public to access, Archdeacon Colin Tett dedicated a memorial plaque to Flight Officer Power and Pilot Officer Michael Dicken. Among those in attendance were the mayor of Mildura, Peter Byrne, instigator of the memorial scheme, Ken Wright, and Mrs Joan Ward.

Sixty-one years previously, Mrs Ward had been the sweetheart of Michael Dicken, and the ceremony concluded with the planting of an arum lily beside the memorial.

THE ENEMY WE WERE NEVER TOLD WAS THERE

The enemy below

These days Australians are more worried about shark attacks on out coastal beaches than submarines. But in World War II the dangers of subs lurking just off our beaches was very real—except no one told us about them!

By 1942 the Japanese controlled the seas to our north and could use aircraft carriers operating in Australian waters to bomb Darwin with impunity from February. Indeed Australia was bombed on 97 separate occasions, Darwin more than 60.

When Japan entered the war, Australia was exposed to a calculated onslaught on coastal shipping by Japanese submarines which, had all the facts been known at the time, would have added considerably to the justifiable paranoia felt by the nation.

At the start of the Pacific War, the Imperial Japanese Navy had 63 submarines. Most of them were the massive 'I Class' vessels: 400 feet (120 metres) long, 2900 tons, with crews of 100 or more.

The Japanese built 126 more submarines after entering the war in late 1941, bringing their total to 189, of which 131 were lost in action by the end of the war.

At least 28 Japanese submarines, many of them of the huge 'I Class', patrolled in Australian waters. A total of 40 patrols were undertaken around our coastline from the Japanese naval base on the island of Truk, north of the Solomon Islands. Each patrol lasted several months.

'I Class' submarines were all-purpose vessels that could stay at sea for months at a time. They laid mines, reconnoitred enemy ports, collected weather and shipping data, attacked merchant ships and bombarded shore installations. Some carried float planes or midget submarines secured to the outer deck, which were used for reconnaissance of enemy ports and shipping.

The two-man submarines we refer to as 'midget' were actually 80 feet (25 metres) long and weighed almost 50 tons. Each carried two torpedoes and they could be used to attack enemy ships and installations, as happened in Sydney Harbour in May 1942.

When you realise that these 'midgets' were carried strapped to the deck of the 'I Class' submarines, you get some idea of just how big the 'I Class' subs were.

The 28 Japanese submarines known to have operated around Australia in 1942, 1943 and 1944 attacked at least 50 merchant vessels. The Japanese hoped to cut off supply lines to the war zones in New Guinea and the north, and separate Australia from the rest of the Pacific.

Losses were often not reported due to military censorship and there was also uncertainty as to the definite cause of sinking in many cases. More than twenty sinkings were officially confirmed by the Allies to be the result of Japanese submarine attacks and another dozen or more were claimed by the Japanese submarine commanders but unconfirmed by the Allies. More than 150,000 tons of merchant shipping was sunk and it is believed that 467 people died in the attacks, including those killed when HMAS *Kuttabal* was sunk in the midget attack in Sydney Harbour.

The three midget submarines that caused terror and chaos in Sydney Harbour were from a fleet of five 'I Class' submarines operating off the coast of Sydney in May 1942.

Two of these carried float planes which made reconnaissance flights around Sydney Harbour on 23 and 30 May. The first flight was undetected and the second was seen by many and assumed to be a plane from the visiting warship USS *Chicago*.

The *Chicago* and battle cruiser HMAS *Canberra* were the targets for the three midget subs which all entered the harbour undetected on the night of 31 May 1942. One of the midgets reversed into a submarine net after hitting a harbour light support and was spotted by harbour patrol boats and destroyed by depth charges. Another self-destructed after her torpedoes became jammed in the tubes, and the third fired her two torpedoes at the USS *Chicago* then escaped back out to sea.

Neither torpedo reached its target. One ran up into Garden Island and failed to detonate. The other hit the sea wall beneath the converted ferry HMAS *Kuttabal* and exploded, sinking the ship and killing the 21 sailors who were using the vessel as accommodation.

The whole affair was a comedy of errors on the Australian side.

The submarines were spotted and fired at by a variety of small patrol boats manned by enthusiastic 'Dad's Army' types who reported the subs' presence as early as 8.15 p.m. No official response was made until almost 10 p.m. and the harbour's submarine action plan wasn't activated until 10.27 p.m.

At least one of the submarines registered on the defensive magnetic detection loop as it entered the harbour. Although the device was manned, it was so often faulty that no one ever took any notice of it. When it registered a vessel crossing just before 2 a.m. it was thought another submarine had entered the harbour and more panic ensued. What registered on the loop at 2 a.m. was almost certainly the submarine that sank the *Kuttabal* leaving the harbour!

The man in charge of the harbour's defences, Admiral Muirhead-Gould, was at a dinner with the captain of the USS *Chicago* and both were reported to be noticeably drunk later in the evening when attempting to deal with the situation.

Several ships opened fire on what they thought was one of the submarines near the Harbour Bridge and shells from the *Chicago* managed to hit parts of the harbour's north shore.

Scared by the idea of submarines inside the harbour, four warships, including the prime targets USS *Chicago* and HMAS *Canberra*, fled out to sea, where five Japanese 'I Class' submarines waited. Japanese fleet Commander Sasaki thus missed a perfect opportunity to sink the very vessels he had sent three small and rather ineffective submarines to find.

The midget submarines had poor handling capability and their torpedoes and diving apparatus often malfunctioned. M–24, the submarine which sank the *Kuttabal*, left the harbour and headed north to a pick-up point near Broken Bay. It was found resting on the seabed off the northern beaches of Sydney in 2006. It is assumed the crew of two died from fumes or lack of oxygen when it malfunctioned and sank.

Two of the 'I Class' submarines returned a few nights later and shelled parts of Sydney from a few miles offshore, causing panic in the city and a fall in real estate prices in the eastern suburbs.

Newcastle was also shelled and a number of merchant ships were torpedoed and sunk off the coast of New South Wales in the following weeks.

Few Australians during World War II were aware how many vessels were lost in Australian waters. A probable list, as accurate as can be compiled from Japanese accounts by individual submarine commanders, reads like this:

20/1/42 *Eidsvold* 4184 tons—near Christmas Island
1/3/42 *Modjokerto* 8806 tons—South of Christmas Island
1/3/42 *Parigi* 1172 tons—off Fremantle
1/3/42 *Siantar* 8867 tons—200 nm NW of Shark Bay
4/3/42 *Le Maire* 3271 tons—NW of Cocos Islands
5/5/42 *John Adams* 7180 tons—120 nm SW of Nouméa
7/5/42 *Chloe* 4641 tons—35 nm from Nouméa
31/5/42 HMAS *Kuttabal* 448 tons—Sydney Harbour
3/6/42 *Iron Chieftain* 4812 tons—27 nm east of Sydney
4/6/42 *Iron Crown* 3353 tons—40 nm SW of Gabo Island
12/6/42 *Guatemala* 5527 tons—40 nm NE of Sydney
20/7/42 *George S. Livanos* 4883 tons—15 nm E of Jervis Bay
21/7/42 *Coast Farmer* 3290 tons—25 nm E of Jervis Bay
22/7/42 *William Dawes* 7176 tons—off Tathra Head
25/7/42 *Cagou* 2795 tons—NE of Sydney
25/7/42 *Tjinegara* 9227 tons—92 nm SE of Nouméa
30/8/42 *Trawler Dureenbee* 233 tons—off Moruya
18/1/43 *Kalingo* 2047 tons—110 nm E of Sydney
18/1/43 Tanker *Mobilube* 10,222 tons—60 nm E of Sydney
22/1/43 *Peter H. Burnett* 7176 tons—420 nm E of Sydney

29/1/43 *Samuel Gompers* 7176 tons—500 nm NE of Brisbane
30/1/43 *Giang Ann* (unknown tonnage)—30 nm E of Newcastle
8/2/43 *Iron Knight* 4812 tons—21 nm off Montagu Island (one of the few ships sunk while in an escorted convoy)
10/2/43 *Starr King* 7176 tons—150 nm E of Sydney
11/4/43 *Recina* 4732 tons—20 nm off Cape Howe (sunk while sailing in an escorted convoy)
24/4/43 *Kowarra* 2125 tons—160 nm N of Brisbane
26/4/43 *Limerick* 8724 tons—20 nm SE of Cape Byron
27/4/43 *Lydia M. Childs* 7176 tons—90 nm E of Newcastle
29/4/43 *Wollongbar* 2239 tons—off Crescent Head
5/5/43 *Fingal* 2137 tons—off Nambucca Heads
14/5/43 AHS *Centaur* 3222 tons—30 nm E of Moreton Island
16/6/43 *Portmar* 5551 tons—250 nm NE of Sydney (sunk while sailing in an escorted convoy)
22/6/43 *Stanvac Manila* 10,245 tons—off Nouméa
22/6/43 two PT boats (each approx. 50 tonnes)—off Nouméa

*nm = nautical miles

Coastal shipping convoys were introduced early in the war and only six ships were lost while in a convoy or having fallen behind due to engine problems. All other ships lost to submarine activity were travelling independently, including the one ship Australians remember as being sunk by a Japanese submarine, the AHS *Centaur*.

The best known and most infamous submarine attack in Australia's WWII history occurred at 4 a.m. on 14 May 1943, when the hospital ship AHS *Centaur*, a converted merchant vessel travelling just north of Brisbane with her markings fully lit as per the Geneva and Hague conventions, was torpedoed by the Japanese KD7-class submarine *K177* captained by Lieutenant Commander Hajima Nakagawa.

Although the *Centaur* should have been in normal merchant shipping lanes further out to sea, her captain decided to travel closer to land, which made the hospital ship a perfect target. She was fully lit; there was land on the portside, deep open sea (perfect for submarine operations) to starboard and a convenient island for a submarine to hide behind.

A torpedo from *K177* hit a fuel tank below the waterline of the *Centaur*, causing an explosion, which instantly killed many on board. The explosion started a fire, which then killed many others. The *Centaur* sank too quickly for lifeboats to be put to use.

Most on board were asleep and, although probably half of the 332 lived through the explosion and fire, there were only 64 survivors. They stayed afloat on wreckage and barrels and gathered on two lifeboats that had broken free as the ship went down. They were picked up two days later.

Of the eighteen female nurses on board the *Centaur*, only one, Sister Ellen Savage, survived. She was awarded the George Medal for providing medical care, supervising the distribution of rations, boosting morale and leading the survivors in prayer and song, despite her jaw being badly broken when she jumped from the burning ship and was sucked under as the vessel sank.

Survivors heard and saw a submarine surface and then submerge amid the wreckage. But the Imperial Japanese Navy denied any involvement for decades, until an official history finally admitted, in 1979, that *K177*, commanded by Hajima Nakagawa, sank the *Centaur*. Nakagawa was never convicted of the crime but served time as a war criminal for other atrocities, including machine-gunning survivors of the ships he sank and murdering prisoners of war.

The sinking of the AHS *Centaur* outraged Australians and fuelled hatred of the Japanese. Prime Minister Curtin called it 'an entirely inexcusable act' and General MacArthur said it demonstrated the 'limitless savagery' of the Japanese.

The incident was used to boost the war effort and silence pacifists. Posters showing the sinking were used to encourage enlistment in the armed services; the slogan was 'Avenge the Nurses'.

That sort of propaganda was useful in supporting the war effort, getting men to enlist to fight, women to join up in the ancillary services and generally keeping Aussies focused on supporting the government's policies during the war.

The actual reality of the threat, the number of ships being lost and the proximity of the enemy to our beaches was, however, best kept a deadly secret!

Some early Japanese tourists

Many Australians are unaware that Japanese troops actually landed on the mainland on at least one occasion in World War II and also used Murray Island in Torres Strait as a source of fresh water and vegetables several times in 1942.

Murray Islanders gave accounts of landing parties from a Japanese submarine coming ashore. The submarine apparently surfaced beside Dauar, one of the three volcanic islets that make up Murray Island. Crewmen came ashore to take on fresh water from the wells at the sardine factory located there, collect fruit and vegetables from the islanders' gardens and obtain information about the area. The submarine also cruised slowly on the surface along the length of Murray Island.

Evidently a crew member of the submarine was a bêche-de-mer (sea slugs, a delicacy in Japan) boat skipper in the Torres Strait before the war and knew the islanders well. There are accounts of the submarine making quite a few visits to Murray Island.

In April 1942 the Japanese submarines *RO–33* and *RO–34* were sent to search for convoy routes and anchorages in advance of the planned Japanese invasion of Port Moresby. They were later ordered to blockade Port Moresby and, on 7 August 1942, *RO–33* sank the Burns-Philp motor launch *Mamutu*, which was taking women and children further along the coast to Daru to escape the Japanese bombing of Port Moresby.

The *RO–33* attacked on the surface and sank the *Mamutu* with her guns and then machine-gunned many of the passengers in the water just north of Murray Island. Only 28 of the 120 on board survived.

RO–33 was a small but well-armed submarine of 940 tons with a crew of 42 officers and men. It was almost certainly the *RO–33* that regularly visited Murray Island and put landing parties ashore during July and August.

On 29 August 1942, the destroyer HMAS *Arunta* used depth charges to sink *RO–33* 10 miles out of Port Moresby. There were no survivors.

Eighteen months later, in January 1944, a Japanese army

reconnaissance party of ten soldiers and fifteen Timorese, led by Lieutenant Susuhiko Mizuno, left Timor in a fishing vessel, the *Hiyoshi Maru*. Their mission was to investigate reports received by Japanese navy sources that the United States navy was building a base at Admiralty Gulf in Western Australia.

They were given air cover for part of the voyage by a light bomber from the 7th Air Division. This plane had a crew of two and they spotted, fired at and attempted to bomb an Allied submarine they encountered en route.

The *Hiyoshi Maru* reached Browse Island at about 10 a.m. on 18 January and stayed there for about three hours. The ship left the island at 1 p.m. that day and next morning entered an inlet on the West Australian coast.

The Japanese anchored near shore at about 10 a.m. and camouflaged the ship with tree branches. Three landing parties led by Lieutenant Mizuno and two sergeants explored different areas of the coast for about two hours.

They all returned to the ship and discussed what they had seen (mostly red rocks, small trees and old campfires). They went ashore again next day and explored until 2 p.m. and then returned to Timor with 8-mm movie footage of what they saw.

The area they explored was actually only 15 miles from the site of the proposed RAAF Truscott Airfield, construction of which started several weeks later.

German raiders

Throughout World War II a fleet of German raiders was also operating in the Indian Ocean and at times along the Australian east coast as well. The navy knew this and had photos and descriptions of the ships.

One of them, the ship known as the *Schiff41/Kormoran*, sank the battle cruiser HMAS *Sydney*, which was lost with all 645 hands, in November 1941.

The shock that the nation felt over the loss of the *Sydney* is hard to imagine 70 years after the event. Add to that the devastating bombing of Darwin three months later, and a major sea battle in the Coral Sea off the east coast three months later again, and you begin to realise just how like an island under siege Australia felt to its citizens in 1942.

More than 50 enemy warships operated in the oceans around Australia between 1940 and 1945. Some were 'normal' Japanese naval vessels, carriers, cruisers and destroyers, some were 'German raiders' (Hilfskreuzers or auxiliary cruisers disguised as merchant ships) and 28 were submarines.

During their stay in Australian waters the German raiders laid extensive mine fields off the coasts of Tasmania, Victoria, New South Wales, South Australia and Western Australia, as well as in Bass Strait.

In 1940 the German raider *Schiff36/Orion* placed mines in the entrance to the port of Albany in Western Australia. In 1941 *Schiff33/ Pinguin,* accompanied by a captured Norwegian tanker *Storstad,* which had been converted to an auxiliary minelayer and renamed *Passat*, sailed through Bass Strait and the two ships laid mines along the coast of Victoria, New South Wales and South Australia.

The *Schiff33/Pinguin* was the most successful of the Hilfskreuzers. She was responsible for capturing sixteen ships and sinking sixteen more between June 1940 and 8 May 1941, when she was blown apart by the cruiser HMS *Cornwall* near the Seychelles in the Indian Ocean.

The Hilfskreuzers were converted freighters armed mostly with WWI guns and torpedo tubes. They were given the official name *Schiff* and a number. The captain of each vessel chose a name for his ship. Captain Kruder, in command of the *Schiff33*, decided to call his vessel *Pinguin* when he was ordered to patrol the Southern Ocean after taking command in June 1940.

Most Hilfskreauzers could disguise themselves as several different merchant ships, depending on the area of the ocean in which they were operating. Their task was to capture or destroy merchant ships by guile, pretence, and force when necessary. They were, however, under orders to run up their true colours before taking any aggressive action.

On 7 October 1940 the *Schiff33/Pinguin* captured the

9000-ton Norwegian motor tanker *Storstad*, off Christmas Island. Loaded with 12,000 tons of diesel oil and 500 tons of heavy fuel oil, *Storstad* was on her way from British North Borneo to Melbourne. She was taken to a remote spot between Java and the north-west tip of Australia and converted into an auxiliary minelayer. One hundred and ten mines were transferred to her from the *Schiff33/Pinguin*.

The *Passat/Storstad* laid her mines in Bass Strait and along the west and east approaches to Melbourne, while the *Schiff33/Pinguin* headed for the ports of Sydney, Newcastle and Hobart, and later laid mines off Adelaide.

Between 28 October and 7 November, the two ships laid their mines without being detected and then rendezvoused in the Indian Ocean.

On 7 November 1940 the mines off Wilsons Promontory claimed the 11,000-ton British refrigerated cargo liner *Cambridge*, which was making its twenty-first trip to Australia. Next day the MS *City of Rayville* struck a mine off Cape Otway and became the first US merchant ship sunk in World War II.

The USA had not entered the war when the *City of Rayville*, which had the stars and stripes painted on both sides of her hull, hit a German mine laid by *Passat/Storstad* between Cape Otway and Apollo Bay.

In a letter to Prime Minister Menzies, the 37 crewmen who survived the sinking of the *City of Rayville* wrote:

> Since the time of our rescue by the fishermen of Apollo Bay, through our stay at the Ballarat Hotel at Apollo Bay, and since our arrival in Melbourne, we have received every consideration and courtesy from our Australian friends. We cannot adequately express our deep appreciation of this kindness.

It was a portent of things to come—a friendship which would help save Australia in the years ahead.

A month later, on 5 December 1940, the Australian freighter MV *Nimbin* hit a mine laid by the *Schiff33/Pinguin* and sank off

Norah Head, north of Sydney, with the loss of seven lives. Two days later the British freighter *Hertford* hit a mine at the entrance to Spencers Gulf but managed to limp into Port Lincoln for repairs which enabled her to be towed to Adelaide.

The trawler *Millimumal* hit one of *Schiff33/Pinguin*'s mines off Barrenjoey Head, just out of Sydney, in March 1941, and seven of her crew of twelve died.

Some of the mines washed up on the coast of South Australia and the first men killed on Australian soil as a result of enemy action were two members of a REMS (Rendering Mines Safe) patrol who responded to reports of a mine which a fisherman found floating in Rivoli Bay near Beachport, South Australia, and towed to shore on 12 July 1941.

Naval headquarters in Adelaide were advised and a patrol of one officer and two ratings arrived at Beachport the next day. Able seaman Thomas Todd and William Danswan were killed when a wave picked up the mine and dropped it on the shore, causing it to detonate as they attempted to disarm it.

The rogue U-boat

It is also true that not all the Axis submarines operating in Australian waters were Japanese. The 1800-ton German U-boat *U862* gained the rare distinction of being the only German submarine to sink a vessel in the Pacific Ocean during the war when it torpedoed the 7180-ton SS *Robert J. Walker* off Moruya on Christmas Eve 1944.

Indeed the *U862* was the only German submarine known to operate in the Pacific at all in World War II!

The *U862* was part of a U-boat fleet based in Penang, in Japanese-controlled Malaya. She had made a successful sortie to the African coast in July and August 1944, sinking five Allied merchant ships and shooting down a Catalina aircraft before returning to base in Penang.

She has been described in some war histories as a 'rogue German U-boat' whose captain, Heinrich Timm, apparently decided on a whim that he would cruise around Australia on the way back to Europe because he had sailed in Australian waters before the war as an officer on a merchant ship.

It is far more likely that he was assigned to the task by the fleet command in Penang, although he may well have suggested the idea. The *U862* moved its base to Batavia (now Jakarta) in preparation for the voyage. She left in November 1944 and headed down the West Australian coast. Timm then turned east across the Great Australian Bight and fired on the Greek tanker SS *Illios* 130 miles south-east of Adelaide. *Illios* returned fire with her 4-inch gun and *U862* submerged and headed south.

A search was mounted by three corvettes, HMAS *Lismore*, *Burnie* and *Maryborough,* and Beaufort aircraft flying from a base near Sale in Victoria, but the *U862* escaped, went around the bottom of Tasmania and turned north. Proceeding up the New South Wales coast, she encountered the *Robert J. Walker* off Montague Island and used six torpedoes to sink her.

The *U862* then headed east, sailed around New Zealand and entered the harbour at Napier, undetected at night, before recrossing the Tasman and retracing her course back to Jakarta.

On 6 February 1945, 700 miles south-west of Fremantle, *U862* sank the liberty ship SS *Peter Sylvester*, which was heading from Melbourne to Colombo, with US army supplies, 107 troops and 317 mules. The *U862* once again used six torpedoes to complete the sinking. Thirty-three lives were lost and some survivors of the *Peter Sylvester* drifted on rafts for 38 days before being picked up by Allied ships.

U862 was at sea testing radar equipment when Germany surrendered in May 1945. On arriving at Singapore the crew were arrested by the Japanese as 'enemy personnel' and the submarine was seized and became the IJN *I–502*. It was surrendered to the Allies at the end of the war and scuttled by the British in the Strait of Malacca in February 1946.

The crew of the *U862* survived the war and were repatriated home in 1947. They were lucky. Being a submariner did not do a lot for your life expectancy. Not one of the five 'I Class' submarines off the coast of New South Wales in May and June 1942 survived the war. Indeed only a small percentage of Axis submarines did survive. Japan lost 131 of her 189 submarines, while Germany had 1152 subs in operation during the war and lost 785. In each case that is almost 70 per cent.

(On the other hand, the USA had 390 submarines and lost 52; Britain had 220 and lost 75; and Russia lost 109 of its fleet of 282. So Allied losses amounted to around 26 per cent of available submarines.)

There is an interesting sidelight to the Australasian cruise of the *U862*.

For decades after World War II there were stories of enemy troops on Australian soil, although most of these stories were fanciful paranoid conspiracy theories at best, all part of the fear generated by the 'ring of menace'.

However, there *were* enemy troops on Australian soil; it did happen, and it happened several times.

After the war an ex-crew member of *U862* visited his brother who lived, like so many German-Australians, in South Australia. While fishing with his brother's mates on the Coorong, south-east of Adelaide, he commented that the area had not changed since he and other crew members of *U862* had gone ashore there looking for fresh water in 1944.

It has also been reported, and is quite probable, that German sailors went ashore from the *Passat/Storstad* near Wilsons Promontory to look for fresh water supplies in November 1941.

Australians, so used to living safely on their island nation at the bottom of the world, felt vulnerable after the loss of the HMAS *Sydney* so close to home. Perhaps it's just as well the censor kept hidden many of the facts about how close the war really was.

Much damage was done around our coast by Japanese submarines and German raiders and many lives were lost—the threat *was* there and the enemy *was* here.

Australia was totally unprepared to protect its enormous coastline in World War II. Axis submarines and German raiders operated with relative impunity all around our coasts—laying mines, sinking merchant ships, and even coming ashore to find fresh water and explore the countryside.

Australia came out of the war with a standing army, a firm alliance established with the USA, a policy of 'populate or perish', and a much less complacent attitude to protecting her borders.

The Australia which we know today is a result of the shock realisation, brought home to us by the events of World War II, that we are indeed 'girt by sea'.

PART 2
CHARACTERS AUSSIES SHOULD KNOW ABOUT

Certain characters from our past fascinate me, often for no obvious reason, but history is an odd business. Some characters get great press and become iconic, famous, notorious, household names, included in school history lessons . . . remembered!

Others, just as important, just as worthy of our respect, just as talented, and often more renowned and important *in their own lifetime,* are forgotten with the passing of years. Sometimes they are forgotten within a generation!

In our brief Australian-European history there are umpteen examples of this phenomenon.

Historic figures, I can understand. Human history, whether it be social, political or military, is so complex that we like it to be packaged up in simple black and white terms. We also like to pigeon-hole historic figures into 'goodies and baddies', when we all know that human nature is never that simple! The story of Samuel Marsden is a good example of that.

Engineers and journalists tend to make their mark then fade from memory rather quickly; I guess that's due to the nature of their work. How anyone in Western Australia could be allowed to forget Charles O'Connor is beyond me, however.

The thing that really puzzles me is how often the great literary and artistic figures of a certain age are randomly remembered or forgotten. I cannot for the life of me understand why certain poets are revered and anthologised over and over again, usually being represented by the same poems over and over again, when so many other poets, considered their equals *in their day*, are completely forgotten. Nor can I understand why only certain poems by great poets are read over and over, while hundreds just as good by the same writers remain unpublished for decades.

It's the same with artists. Why can you buy a stunning landscape by that great painter Will Ashton for a few thousand dollars, while similar works by the artists who have had better press, like Arthur Streeton and Tom Roberts, fetch millions? I have no idea, to be honest. There is no real logic to it.

My interest in verse is rather obvious in this section. Quite a few of the 'forgotten Aussies we should not have forgotten' are poets, but there are several other types of forgotten characters as well. For me, it's not about whether they are great poets, engineers or explorers—it's about the fact that they are worth remembering!

Truth is always stranger than fiction and many of these characters are proof that some lives are so full of coincidences and complicated beyond our comprehension that they can't but astound readers and make the exaggerated fictions of Hollywood appear mundane.

Why film-makers don't pick up on some of these characters rather than retelling the stories of Robin Hood, Superman and others over and over is beyond me. The Ned Kelly story has been filmed at least five times but, to my mind, characters like Jim Kelly and Adam Lindsay Gordon provide equally interesting material for rip-roaring movie epics!

In this section I hope you meet a few interesting characters you never knew about, or had forgotten.

THE POCKET PICKING POLICEMAN

George Barrington was one of the most famous criminals ever sent to 'Botany Bay', as the British public called the penal settlement at Sydney in the early days of our European history.

While it is true that our nation's first European citizens were law-breakers, it is probably not fair or accurate to call them all cut-throats, cold-blooded murderers and hardened criminals. Those sent here were mostly petty thieves and miscreants convicted of minor crimes—any 'real' criminals who were caught were hanged!

In the late eighteenth century, when New South Wales was established as a convict settlement, it was up to the jury to decide not only guilt, but also the value of any goods allegedly stolen in cases of theft and robbery. If a person was found guilty of stealing goods valued at more than a shilling, they hanged.

This explains why many convicts seem to have been transported for stealing items of little value. If the jury took pity on the thief, or felt he or she deserved another chance in life and was perhaps the victim of poverty and circumstance, they could value the goods stolen at less than a shilling and thus save the convicted person's life. The penalty was then transportation.

Which brings us to the strange case of the most famous convict ever sent here, George Barrington.

Barrington was the best-known criminal of his day. He was once caught in the act, and convicted, of attempting to steal a golden snuff-box from the Russian Count Gregory Orloff at the Drury Lane Theatre. It was valued at £30,000. He was also convicted of stealing a gold watch and chain at Enfield racetrack, obviously worth rather more than a bob! He stole expensive jewels and goods valued at well over a shilling many times.

Why didn't Barrington hang? Well, he had a silver tongue and was so famous in his day that society women reputedly boasted about being robbed by the dashing, handsome and elusive 'prince of rogues'. He mixed in the best circles and was the talk of the town in London, and the darling of the press, who often attributed all sorts of crimes and adventures to the notorious and charming gentleman thief.

Barrington was, according to the newspapers of the day, the Scarlett Pimpernel, Robin Hood and Beau Brummel all rolled into one. He mixed freely in the best of social circles and picked pockets at the Royal Court during the Queen's birthday celebrations in 1775. He was also a master of disguise and often dressed as a minister of religion and picked pockets and stole jewellery while wealthy women were actually wearing it.

London society was all agog at the exploits of this famous thief and expert pickpocket. He was so well-liked that, although he was arrested more than a dozen times and convicted at least eight times, he was actually pardoned more than once and 'let off' lightly by judges on quite a few more occasions. Often he was able to talk his way out of being convicted at all. His silver tongue, eloquent speeches, fashionable dress and genteel manners often convinced a jury that it was 'all a terrible mistake' or a misunderstanding, or even that he had merely found misplaced items and was returning them!

Barrington was not, however, 'to the manor born', he was simply a very good actor and an excellent pickpocket.

He was born in 1755, somewhere near Dublin, possibly at the village of Maynooth where his mother worked as a midwife. He claimed to be the illegitimate son of Captain Barrington, the commander of a nearby English garrison, but we should not take the claim too seriously. At different times in his life, both Barrington and the newspapers of the day claimed that he was the illegitimate son of various noblemen, even royalty.

He was more than likely the son of a silversmith named Waldron. Although his early life in Ireland is confused by various romantic versions, it appears his parents gave him some early education and he served briefly as an apprentice to an 'apothecary' or village doctor and pharmacist until a minister of the Church of Ireland saw some promise in him and arranged a scholarship to the famous 'Blue Coats', a charity grammar school attached to Trinity College in Dublin.

At the age of sixteen it seems he was involved in a fight with another schoolboy and resorted to stabbing his opponent with his penknife.

(All literate men carried a penknife in those days—the term originally applied to a small clasp knife used to make a quill pen from a feather by shaping and forming a nib. The nib lasted a short while before another was required to be made with the 'penknife'.)

Barrington was given a severe flogging by the headmaster for his crime and took it rather badly. He actually retaliated by committing the first of many robberies, including stealing twelve guineas and the headmaster's gold watch, and absconding. Some accounts say he was expelled, which he no doubt was, but he did, in fact, expel himself by running off to Dublin and embarking on a life of crime.

He soon joined a 'theatre company', which was in fact a group of petty criminals and strolling players whose leader was John Price, a conman and thief who was already wanted by the police in England. Price taught young Barrington to pick pockets and he was so good at it that he and Price set up in partnership on their own, picking pockets and thieving, first in Dublin then in London.

When Price was finally tracked down, arrested and transported to the American colonies in 1773, Barrington continued his career solo and used his acting skills and good manners to enter society, posing as a gentleman or even a nobleman. It is said that he 'stole the hearts of influential friends as readily as their purses'.

He was arrested but escaped conviction several times, often because those he robbed refused to press charges but, finally, in

1776, he was arrested for stealing a pair of silver studs, a silk purse, half a guinea and three shillings and sixpence from a widow, Ann Dudman, in the pit of Drury Lane Playhouse.

Poor Barrington was sentenced to three years working on the coal hulks on the Thames. This must have come as quite a shock to the 21-year-old, who had appeared in court tastefully and expensively dressed with a gold-tipped cane and gold buckles on his shoes. He was described in one newspaper as 'the genteelest thief ever to have been seen at the Old Bailey', although a witness in the case stated that Barrington lived in lodgings in the down-market inner London neighbourhood of Charing Cross.

As it was his first offence, officially, Barrington was free within twelve months due to his excellent behaviour and influential friends. He went straight back to mixing in the best circles and stealing and was, consequently, back in court within six months. Giving his profession as 'surgeon' (perhaps based on his brief apprenticeship to an apothecary as a boy), he was convicted of stealing a watch, three pounds, a silk watch string and a glass seal on 15 March 1778 from one Elizabeth Ironmonger in the crowded St Sepulchre's church while 'a special sermon was being delivered'.

This time he received a five-year sentence on the hulks. While serving the sentence Barrington hit a low point in his life and showed the first signs of a mental instability, which would return in later years. He attempted to escape and when he failed to do so, he attempted suicide, again using his penknife.

While recovering from his wounds he contracted tuberculosis and almost died.

The authorities took pity on the gentleman thief and he was freed and pardoned, due to the efforts again of influential friends, on the condition that he leave England and never return.

He went back to Ireland but found that he was wanted there for earlier crimes and eventually, after more robberies in Ireland and Scotland, he fled back to London.

In 1783 he was arrested for breaking the terms of his pardon and served a year in prison. On his release he returned to his former life, mixing with and stealing from 'the brightest luminaries in the globe of London'. Although he was arrested many times, his friends and his gentlemanly bearing, manners and eloquence almost always led to his acquittal.

But his luck ran out in 1790 when he appeared at the Old Bailey charged with stealing a gold watch and chain at Enfield racecourse. Although the most famous defence council in London, William Garrow, acted on his behalf, Barrington was convicted. The newspapers recorded that Barrington's speech in his own defence, and pleas not be executed, brought tears to the eyes of the jury. Although found guilty he was sentenced only to transportation, not hanging, and for only seven years, not the fourteen years or life sentence that he could have received.

Although the newspapers carried stories of Barrington organising break-outs and escaping from Newgate Prison disguised as a woman, he was sent to Sydney on the convict transport ship *Active* in September 1791, along with 2000 other convicts of what was called the Third Fleet.

His arrival in the settlement caused quite a stir and Governor Phillip had no idea what to do with a gentleman convict like Barrington, whose conduct he described as 'irreproachable', so he made him a policeman and put him in charge of the government stores at Parramatta.

In 1792 Governor Phillip actually granted him a conditional pardon. This was not the usual 'ticket-of-leave' that convicts received for good behaviour—it was actually a pardon.

In 1796 this pardon was made an absolute pardon by Governor Hunter who, at the same time, appointed Barrington chief constable of the settlement at Parramatta and granted him 32 acres of land. Barrington had a fine house built and bought another 50 acres on the Hawkesbury River where he farmed, with the help of convicts assigned to him as workers and servants.

By all known accounts Barrington never committed one crime in his new-found home; it seems the fresh air in sunny New South Wales cured his criminality for good.

He did, however, like a drink, and in 1800 he resigned his post as head constable due to a serious 'infirmity', which may have been alcoholism or perhaps mental illness of some kind. He was allowed to keep half his salary as a pension.

Soon his mental health was so poor that a commission was appointed to look after his affairs and care for him. He died on 27 December 1804. He wasn't quite 50 years old.

Barrington's fame lasted long after his death. He is credited with so many adventures and crimes and daring deeds that he would have needed to live three lifetimes to have done them all.

While on the voyage to Sydney he was credited by the press as having prevented a mutiny. Then a long sentimental letter, begging forgiveness and swearing repentance to his long-suffering wife, appeared in the London newspapers, although he almost certainly never wrote it.

Although absent from England, his notoriety continued. In a popular broadside ballad, 'The Jolly Lad's Trip to Botany Bay', a group of convicts laugh about being transported and swear that the first thing they will do in New South Wales is take over the colony and appoint a king, 'for who knows but it may be the noted Barrington'.

Despite the stories crediting him with many publications, letters, journals and theatre pieces, he probably never wrote most of them. He certainly never wrote the three books that appeared in his name. Two books, *A Voyage to New South Wales* and *A History of New South Wales*, were selling in London shops in the last years of his life and another, entitled *A History of New Holland*, was published four years after his death.

All these books sold very well but no one to this day knows who wrote any of them, though one seems to have been based on the published journals of Judge Advocate David Collins. No doubt some enterprising journalists and publishers of the day colluded and cashed in on Barrington's name—it sounds familiar, doesn't it?

We know for sure that Barrington wrote none of them and was also certainly not the author of the much-quoted speech supposedly given by him as a prologue at the opening of the first Australian theatre in Sydney in 1796.

He is credited with having said, in his own defence and to avoid hanging, that he 'never pilfered *any* man of his fair name'.

There are many stories about George Barrington's real and imaginary adventures and one of them, by colonial author John Lang, based on a 'real event' that occurred after his arrival in New South Wales, appears in Part 3 of this collection.

THE EVANGELISING BLACKSMITH

Was he a cruel, arrogant prig . . . or a caring, generous and pious Christian role model?

Reverend Samuel Marsden is often caricatured, in simplified versions of Australian colonial history, as the 'the flogging parson', a cruel religious zealot and upper-class snob who abused convicts and had all the characteristics that Aussies love to hate.

In New Zealand, however, the very same man is revered as a pioneer missionary who brought peace and Christianity to the Maori people, helped protect them from exploitation and conducted the first Christmas church service in New Zealand's history. He is the man who brought Christianity and sheep to New Zealand and helped establish the wine industry. Several landmarks are named after him and a huge cross, erected in his memory at a point called Marsden Cross, is a famous tourist attraction.

How can this be the same bloke?

Marsden was a strange man . . . but he has had very bad press in the more simplified versions of Aussie colonial history, where everyone has to be either a 'goodie' or a 'baddie'. He is invariably painted as a 'baddie' in spite of the fact that he grew crops to help the starving colony, developed a flock of sturdy sheep suitable to local conditions and took wool back to Britain before John Macarthur. (His efforts were rewarded when he was given sheep by King George III himself to take back to New South Wales.)

When his life is researched a little more sympathetically, in light of the attitudes of his time, we can understand a lot more about this complicated character from our earliest colonial days.

Samuel Marsden really only had one 'failing'—he truly believed that it was his Christian duty to spread the gospel and obey the laws of the Christian God he believed in.

Unfortunately that brought him into direct conflict with those who were trying to develop a colony on rather more 'realistic' lines, or should I say 'pragmatic', given the material and circumstances they had to work with!

As far as being 'cruel' goes, it appears Marsden was as cruel a convict master as some others but less cruel than many. He did, however, believe that men should be punished for their sins. It is odd that he reported Governor Macquarie for being cruel and excessive in handing out punishment, especially to non-convict prisoners and miscreants. Marsden's sentence of flogging in order to get information about hidden weapons, for which he is most often labelled 'cruel', was more than likely the decision of another magistrate with which he concurred.

You see, Reverend Marsden believed in punishing the wicked, and he reported corruption whenever he saw it occurring because he believed it was wrong. Others in the colony believed certain behaviour was 'expedient' and 'sensible', and they were, in retrospect, probably right. That doesn't necessarily make Marsden 'wrong'—he certainly believed in what he did and took the high moral ground always.

The problem was that taking the high moral ground was often not likely to help the colony function too well.

As far as being upper class, that's pure nonsense.

Marsden was the son of a small-scale Yorkshire farmer and blacksmith; his mother was a weaver. Young Samuel himself worked in the blacksmith's shop and on the farm. He attended the village school in Hull and was a Wesleyan lay preacher as a young man before switching to the Anglican Church and training as a missionary.

That is the secret to understanding Samuel Marsden—he was an evangelist with a missionary zeal. He was a noted preacher and was spotted and chosen to be trained by an evangelical branch of the Anglican Church, the Elland Society.

The Elland Society sent Samuel to grammar school at the age of 24 and then paid for him to attend Cambridge University for two years. His only claim to being a 'gentleman' was his unfinished education and his ordination. He was, in fact, of much humbler origins than many of the convicts.

Marsden was also not a typical Anglican clergyman. Not only was he 'low born' but very few Anglican priests were evangelical at the time. Marsden was a zealot, converted to evangelical Christianity as a young man and determined to take the word of God to all men, to the ends of the earth.

He was about as a typical an Anglican minister of the period as you could find. He could shear a sheep, sow grain, plant crops and harvest them, and teach Maoris how to work a forge. He could also trade, haggle and barter; he dressed like a farmer and talked like one. He could walk for miles through the bush and work as hard on the farm as any convict or free labourer.

These qualities meant he was often looked upon with some disdain by the officers and gentlemen of New South Wales. He managed to get along more or less with governors Hunter, King and Bligh, but he clashed violently with the liberal-minded, pragmatic Lachlan Macquarie.

Macquarie found him a nuisance and an impediment to his efforts to get the colony operating as a normal settlement by bringing ex-convicts into society and encouraging them to engage in trade and commerce. Marsden's high-mindedness infuriated Macquarie so much that he banned Marsden from attending functions that he himself attended!

When Marsden spoke out against supposed wickedness and the evils of letting miscreants become decent citizens, once they had served their time, Macquarie accused him of spending too much time working his farm and not enough ministering to his flock.

Even worse for Marsden's reputation in the rough and ready colony was the fact that he drank very little and disapproved of horseracing and gambling . . . and he spoke his mind openly when he saw his moral and religious beliefs being ignored, by convicts and authorities alike.

He was disliked by convicts and emancipists because of his strict adherence to church law and authority, and he was disliked by the officers and gentlemen because of his humble origins and interference in the pragmatic running of the colony.

The big problem for Marsden was that what the colony needed was someone to minister to the practical needs of the population in the more normal, acceptable way expected of the Anglican Church.

He was expected to support the authority of those governing, turn a benign blind eye to the way things were made to run smoothly, and minister to the everyday, practical needs of those being governed. This was not what Samuel Marsden saw as his duty, however—he was a missionary!

Marsden was trained specifically. After two years at Cambridge he was offered the post of second chaplain to the colony of New South Wales and accepted, but he still saw himself as an evangelist, rather than the chaplain of a young British settlement.

Reverend Johnson was the colony's chaplain so Marsden took up his post at St John's Parramatta and remained there long after Johnson left the colony in 1800, finally becoming the colony's senior chaplain in 1810 after a visit back to England, which meant he avoided the Rum Rebellion.

It is indicative of various governors' dislike for Marsden that he was the colony's only Anglican minister for ten years before receiving the official position and stipend of 'Senior Chaplain'.

Marsden was given land, and bought more; he farmed and bred sheep to help support his growing family. A son and five daughters survived to adulthood. He ended up with more than 3000 acres and requested more, but was refused.

There is, however, a whole other side to Marsden's life and reputation, one that most Aussies don't even realise exists.

Across the Tasman, New Zealanders regard him as an iconic figure in their colonial history. Marsden is revered as a great friend to the Maori, a civilising force and the man who introduced sheep, grapevines and viticulture to the country.

Marsden made an amazing seven voyages to New Zealand, at a time when they were difficult, expensive and dangerous undertakings!

It is true that Marsden saw himself as more of an evangelist than a chaplain—it was what he was trained to be and, as well as being principal chaplain for New South Wales and minister of St John's, he was also an agent for two missionary societies. One was the inter-denominational protestant London Missionary Society that operated mainly in the Society Islands; the other was the Church of England Missionary Society,

Marsden was instrumental in establishing missions in the Bay of Islands. He visited England in 1807 and recruited personnel to start the missionary settlements and purchased a ship from his own funds to set up the missions. He visited, guided and controlled the settlements until his death in 1838.

Marsden's Christmas Day service at Oihi Bay in the Bay of Islands in 1814 is considered to be the first in New Zealand. The service marked the beginnings of the Christian mission to New Zealand.

(Mind you, on Christmas Day 1769, the French explorer Jean François Marie de Surville and his crew were in Doubtless Bay in far northern New Zealand. On board the *Saint Jean Baptiste* was a Dominican priest, Paul-Antoine de Villefeix. It therefore seems highly likely that such an important occasion would have been marked with a mass. In the absence of hard evidence, New Zealand's English colonial traditions have always favoured Marsden's claim to fame.)

So, why did the man sent to minister to the spiritual needs of the young colony, full of sinners, make such an effort to civilise the natives of another country and save their souls instead?

It has been said of Marsden that he complained of the depravity of the convicts but did little about it, other than request more ministers be sent to the colony. He seems to have decided that the depravity of the convicts and officers was so bad that redemption was not a possibility . . . and he gave up on them.

He attempted to preach to the Aborigines, but found them unprepared for conversion. He wrote: 'The natives have no Reflection—they have no attachments, and they have no wants.'

In short, they seemed ill-prepared to be 'saved' and took no interest in European ways, and Marsden had lost interest in trying to save the souls of the Aborigines by the time Macquarie established the Native Institution, in which Marsden took no part.

To Samuel Marsden, civilisation and Christianity went hand in hand. His practical Yorkshire mind seemed to believe that some people could be saved, and others were doomed to perdition for their sins or primitive, uncivilisable nature.

He was much more excited about the possibility of missions aimed at the people of the Pacific Islands. He met Tahitians and Maoris in Sydney and had a Maori chieftain's son brought to live with him.

On his long visit back home in 1808–09 he met Ruatara, a Maori chief who had sailed to London as crew on a whaler and was returning home, very ill. Marsden nursed him back to health and took him in when they arrived in Sydney, teaching Ruatara good English and farming and crafts while he, in turn, learned Maori language and culture. He taught Ruatara how to grow wheat and grind flour and Ruatara gifted Marsden with tribal land for the establishment of missions.

In his determination to take God to the Maoris, Marsden displayed tenacity, sacrifice and resourcefulness, qualities that have made his reputation in New Zealand so different from how he is thought of in Australian history.

At his own expense Marsden hired craftsmen to go with him and Ruatara to teach the Maoris carpentry, shoemaking and ropemaking. Having formed the 'New South Wales Society for Affording Protection to the Natives of the South Sea Islands and Promoting their Civilisation', they set out, in November 1814, in the brig *Active*, which he had bought for £1400, to maintain the Maoris' contact with civilisation.

Marsden made seven voyages to New Zealand between 1814 and 1837 and persevered, largely at his own expense, to make the missions work, despite massive problems caused by the behaviour of the crews of passing ships, the violence of the Maori lifestyle, and the ever-increasing cost of supplying blankets, clothes, tools, and rice and potatoes for the mission villages and schools. In order to pay the salaries of the New Zealand settlers, the *Active* was sent whaling.

There were also many difficulties with the missionaries as petty politics took hold and temptations caused men to stray from the straight and narrow: one left his wife and took a chief's daughter as his partner, and some missionaries traded guns for Maori products. Marsden dealt with all these problems in the face of continuing criticism from Macquarie and later governors to the effect that he was neglecting his duties.

Australia's 'flogging parson' is considered to be the man responsible for making New Zealand's history of early contact with the Maori a story that contains goodwill and Christian charity.

Marsden shows us that history can be merely a matter of 'spin'—or perhaps it simply demonstrates the fact that most men are a complex mix of good qualities and human failings.

OUR FIRST HOMEGROWN HERO

The first generation of native-born children of migrant settlers and convicts were called 'currency lads' and 'currency lasses', to distinguish them from the non-convict British settlers, who were known as 'sterling'.

The currency lads and lasses were quite different from the migrants.

The terms used referred to the fact that New South Wales did not use British currency (sterling) until 1822. There were insufficient coins to establish a sterling currency and any coins usually left the colony on each ship that departed. Rum was used as currency until Governor Macquarie ordered 40,000 Spanish dollars, which arrived in November 1812 from the East India Company in Madras on board the HMS *Samarang*.

The convict forger William Henshall then cut the centres out of the coins and counter-stamped both pieces. The 'holey dollar' was worth five shillings and the 'dump' was worth fifteen pence. The makeshift currency stayed in New South Wales, as it was obviously useless outside of the colony.

So the terms 'currency lads' and 'currency lasses' were originally derogatory, but soon became terms of pride for those to whom they referred. The currency lads were also referred to as 'cornstalks' because they were mostly taller than their British counterparts and had a distinct way of talking.

Commissioner John Thomas Bigge reported in 1820 that the children of convicts were generally industrious and surprisingly free of any criminality. He described them as taller, fairer, stronger and healthier than the 'free' migrant settlers. They were also better educated and more literate; in Sydney and Parramatta more than 80 per cent of the men and 75 per cent of the women signed their own name on the marriage register. The boys excelled at sport and usually won when running, field sports and boxing contests were organised between 'currency' and 'sterling' athletes.

James 'Jim' Kelly was a currency lad and the first Australian-born child to ever become a ship's captain. Sadly, today his name is long forgotten, except perhaps in Tasmania, where several places are named after him.

Ask mainland Aussies if they know who James Kelly was and they would probably say, 'Wasn't he Ned's dad?' Well, no, he wasn't; Ned's dad was John Kelly, known as 'Red'. Red Kelly was born in County Tipperary three decades after Jim Kelly's birth at Parramatta and, at the age of 21, Red was transported to Tasmania for the very 'Irish' crime of stealing pigs.

But, back to Aussie-born 'currency lad' Jim Kelly. His mother, Catherine Devereaux, was Irish and was probably from Dublin. She was certainly in Dublin Prison in 1791, having been sentenced to death for theft. We don't know what she stole, but it probably wasn't a pig. Instead of being hanged she was transported.

Eighty-five prisoners from Dublin Prison left from Cork on the convict transport *Queen*, along with more than a hundred other Irish prisoners. The *Queen* was the first convict ship to ever sail directly from Ireland to New South Wales. Among the 85 prisoners from Dublin Gaol were two women condemned to death. One woman, who we know only by her surname of Rositer, had stolen linen. The other was Catherine Devereaux, aged 30.

There is a story that Jim Kelly's father was James Kelly, a cook on the *Queen* who might have taken that job to enable him to travel to Australia with his pregnant, but condemned, girlfriend, Catherine Devereaux. It's a good story and might be partly true. Jim Kelly's father was either James Kelly or an English soldier.

What cannot be true is that James Kelly knew Catherine was pregnant. The *Queen* sailed in early April 1791 and arrived in

Sydney in September. Catherine's child was born on Christmas Eve 1791. So, assuming positions aboard the *Queen* were being filled in late March 1791, it is hardly likely that James Kelly applied for a position knowing Catherine was pregnant. Indeed, she might have conceived while on board or just before.

What we do know is that the child was christened James Devereaux and later changed his name to Kelly. He may have grown up on a farm at Parramatta where Catherine and James Kelly Snr lived quite happily, but he was already working on sailing ships at the age of twelve.

A month after turning thirteen, having already made several voyages out of Sydney, he was apprenticed to boat builders and traders Kable and Underwood and sailed on sealing expeditions along Bass Strait until 1807. He then sailed to Fiji for sandalwood and as far as India on trading voyages.

Kelly became chief officer of Kable and Underwood's *Campbell Macquarie* and was on watch one night in June 1812 when the vessel became caught on a lee shore in storm and fog off the coast of Macquarie Island, off western Tasmania. The ship was driven onto rocks and wrecked, but Kelly and the ship's captain managed to get all men into boats and make it ashore. Four months later they were picked up by the sealer *Perseverance,* which sailed back to Sydney but could not enter the harbour due to a savage storm. They took refuge in Broken Bay north of Sydney and Kelly walked overland to be reunited with his fiancé, Elizabeth Griffiths.

He married Elizabeth, a 'currency lass' and the daughter of a former marine, later that same year and was given the command of the sealing vessel *Brothers*, which left Sydney on 24 December 1812, Kelly's 21st birthday, for an expedition to Bass Strait. Kelly returned five months later with more than 7000 sealskins. Soon Kelly was in demand by merchants and ship owners.

A few months later, in command of William Collins' ship the *Mary and Sally*, he set out on another very successful sealing voyage and, on his return in March 1814, he was employed as captain of the schooner *Henrietta* which sailed between the ports of the colonies.

The *Henrietta* was owned by Thomas Birch and was also used to explore the coast of Tasmania searching for new seal colonies; those along Bass Strait were almost wiped out by sealers within twenty years of the first settlement at Sydney Cove. While engaged in the search Kelly was reputed to have circumnavigated the island, then known as Van Diemen's Land, and discovered Macquarie Harbour and Port Davey.

Kelly decided to move his family to Hobart and, in 1817, settled his family into a stone house he built on the banks of the Hobart Town Rivulet that runs from Mount Wellington into the Derwent River.

Thomas Birch was given a monopoly on huon pine as a reward for the discoveries made by Kelly and he next sent Kelly across the Tasman Sea, in the ship *Sophia*, to explore trading possibilities in New Zealand. Accompanying Kelly were his brother-in-law and several friends interested in trade possibilities, including William Tucker, who had lived with the Maori in the Otago area previously.

It seems they sailed into a dispute between tribes and, after an original friendly greeting, the party separated into two groups, one of which was suddenly attacked a few days later and Tucker, Kelly's brother-in-law, and another man were killed and eaten. It seems that previous contact with Europeans had made the Maori distrustful and cautious, but to Kelly it was simply an unprovoked act of treachery, murder and cannibalism.

Kelly's retaliation certainly did little to help relations between Europeans and Maoris. He shot and killed quite a few Maori warriors then set about destroying their canoes and burning the Maori town of Otago, reputed to have had 600 houses, to the ground.

Kelly was evidently a fearless fighter and a crack shot with a pistol. On his return to Sydney in 1818 he led an armed detachment, which scoured the islands of Bass Strait searching for escaped convicts. Kelly had earlier reported that sealing and whaling was being made a dangerous business by bands of escaped convicts who attacked parties of sealers or crewmen coming ashore to get water and fresh food.

According to the Jim Kelly 'legend', the young captain had previously killed a few of these desperate escapees, on earlier voyages around the area, with a pair of long-barrelled duelling pistols he always carried.

The hunting party arrived back in Sydney to much celebration and congratulations and Kelly prepared to visit his family at Parramatta, but he heard a whisper along the docks that an attempt was to be made by a certain group of convicts to seize a ship and escape. Kelly quite rightly suspected that they had designs on the *Sophia* and knew that he was planning to ride to Parramatta.

He rode away towards Parramatta before doubling back to Sydney. He then went aboard and prepared his crew to defend the ship.

Here is the account of what happened next, as reported in the *Sydney Gazette* on 20 June 1820:

> On Thursday night, or rather at an early hour yesterday morning, a daring attempt was made by a set of ruffians in a boat, to board and carry off the brig Sophia, (Mr James Kelly master) from her moorings in Sydney Cove. Happily, owing to a judicious measure of Police some time since adopted in consequence of the frequent piratical attempts made on the shipping in Port Jackson, the design was completely frustrated and the party well peppered by a brisk discharge o' musketry under the direction of Captain Kelly, who was fully prepared for the occasion, and exerted him self so successfully in repelling the attack, as to leave no doubt that some of the party were severely wounded.
>
> Immediately on the firing being heard on shore, a boat, well-manned, set out under the direction of Mr Williams, His Excellency the Governor's coxswain, in pursuit of the desperadoes, but they were not for fortunate enough to fall in with them, though little doubt remains that the vigilance of the Police, combined with the circumstance of one or more of the party being wounded, will quickly lead to the complete discovery of the miscreants, and drag to public punishment a set of monsters who were bent on embruing their hands in the blood of their fellow creatures, the master and crew of the vessel.
>
> The time chosen for effecting their diabolical purpose was when it was supposed Mr Kelly was at Parramatta, whither it was known

he had gone in the morning; and this circumstance, which lulled the assailants into a perfect security as to their success, eventually proved the means of their discomfiture, for the whole of their plan was well known to those whose duty it was to repel it.

Viewing the above attempt, and all the circumstances attending it, with its final defeat, and the exposure and punishment awaiting this band of pirates, we have no hesitation in saying that were that constant vigilance observed on the part of the masters and crews of vessels, which the faithful discharge of their duty to their owners and employers demands, and equal intrepidity as that of Captain Kelly, when attempts such as we have now described were made, we would not have to lament the different losses sustained in this way by the merchants and ship owners of New South Wales.

We hold out to public view and admiration the bold spirited faithful conduct of Captain Kelly, which cannot be too highly commended or appreciated; and the masters and crews of the colonial shipping in particular are called on, by every principle of duty, to show an equal zeal and promptitude in defence of the persons and property entrusted to their charge, whereby they will not only secure the good will and favour of their employers, but also render their own persons and property safe against the attempts of such midnight assassins, and merit, at least, public good opinion, if not public remuneration.

It is with no little satisfaction, we understand, that it is a contemplation, with the merchants and ship owners of Sydney, to present Captain Kelly with a handsome piece of plate, inscribed with the record of his manly and successful exertions, in repelling a strong and desperate party of sanguinary pirates, in their attempt to seize the brig Sophia under his command, on the morning of the 19th instant; and we hope a liberal consideration, proportioned to their respective situations and exertions, will be also extended to the meritorious crew.

Captain Kelly was duly rewarded for his actions and presented with a commemorative plate.

His heroics also brought him to the attention of Governor Macquarie and he was offered the position as pilot and harbourmaster at Hobart. In 1821 he took up the position and, in the *Sophia*, also helped transport convicts to the newly established penal station at Macquarie Harbour, which he had discovered in 1815. In 1825 he also helped to set up the convict settlement on Maria Island.

Kelly turned his attention to establishing the whaling industry in Hobart in 1826, sealing having become harder with the virtual extermination of most seal colonies. He became actively engaged in whaling and part-owned several ships. He was so busy with his business interests, which included farming on Bruny Island as well as whaling, insurance and property development, that he had resigned his positions as harbourmaster and pilot by 1831.

The swashbuckling Captain Kelly settled down to being a respectable citizen. He was a director of the Derwent and Tamar Fire, Marine and Life Assurance Co., helped build the Theatre Royal and was on the Regatta Committee. He sent two of his sons to be educated at Bath Grammar School in England.

But fortune did not always smile upon him. In 1831 his wife died and three years later his ship *Australian* was lost and another of his ships, the *Mary and Elizabeth*,was attacked and burnt by Maoris in New Zealand. Then in 1841 his eldest son was killed while chasing whales, and another son drowned in the Derwent River. In fact, seven of his ten children died before their father.

Kelly was financially ruined when Depression hit the colonies in the 1840s and returned to working in a government position as assistant harbourmaster.

Fame and fortune can be fickle things. In his day Captain Jim Kelly was about as famous as you could be in the colonies of 'New Holland'. He was so famous that ballads were written about him. His name was given to the steps at Battery Point in Hobart, which he built, as well as Kelly Island and Kelly Basin at Macquarie Harbour. Kelly Point on Bruny Island was named after him, but the name was later changed to Dennes Point as the memory of Jim Kelly faded.

UNKNOWINGLY QUOTED BY MILLIONS

Back in the first two-thirds of the twentieth century almost every young Aussie had an 'autograph book'. They were sometimes used to obtain celebrity signatures but far more commonly they were a record of friendships and acquaintances. Anyone who passed through your life, intimately or casually, was asked to write some remembrance, witticism or message in your autograph book. Millions of Australians in those decades wrote four short lines in countless autograph books:

> Life is mostly froth and bubble,
> Two things stand like stone,
> Kindness in another's trouble,
> Courage in your own.

But few, if any, of those millions of autograph writers would have known whom they were quoting, let alone the sad and strange story that accompanied his verse. The lines are merely a fragment from a much longer and long-forgotten poem by Adam Lindsay Gordon titled 'Ye Weary Wayfarer'.

Why no one has made a movie of the remarkable life of this heroic, talented, doomed and tragic character is completely beyond me. Gordon is remembered today, if he is remembered at all, for two things. He is revered by literary historians as the father of Australian rhymed verse, the creator of that great tradition that gave us Banjo Paterson, Henry Lawson, Will Ogilvie and

C.J. Dennis, and he is remembered by racing aficionados as an outstanding and daring horseman and steeplechase jockey.

The Australian love affair with rhymed verse goes hand-in-hand with our love of horseracing, and it all began with this ex-patriot Brit, a man of Scottish descent, born on a Portuguese island and raised in England, who wanted to be taken seriously as a poet, but ended up being remembered for his galloping rhymes and his riding ability.

Gordon's disappointment at not having his 'serious' poetry taken seriously, along with financial and personal troubles and injuries sustained while steeplechasing, eventually led to his suicide. Yet the very same factors made him the inspiration for our most famous ballad writers and are the reason he is so revered.

Adam Lindsay Gordon was born in the Azores in 1833 while his parents were staying on his grandfather's plantation, probably for the sake of his mother's health. His father was a retired Bengal cavalry captain who had married his first cousin.

The family was an old and famous one, which had produced many distinguished men, and also the bloodthirsty Adam O' Gordon, the leading figure in the famous Scottish ballad in which a band of 50 Gordons commit grisly atrocities against the Campbell women and children and are slain in retaliation.

On the family's return to England, young Gordon was sent to Cheltenham College. He had constant trouble at school and was there for only a year before he was sent to a church school in Gloucestershire.

At the age of fifteen he was sent to the Royal Military Academy, Woolwich, where he was good at sports but undisciplined and not inclined to study. In 1851 his father was asked to withdraw him and, after another spell at Cheltenham College, where, rumour has it, he was finally expelled, he finished his education as a private pupil of the headmaster of the Worcester Royal Grammar School.

Gordon lived with an uncle in Worcester but began to lead a wild and aimless life, contracted debts, and was a great anxiety to his father. He also fell in love with, and proposed to, a young woman at this time, but she refused him. Finally it was decided that he should go to Australia and make a fresh start.

This was a common procedure at the time with 'respectable' families. Sons who got into trouble with debt or women were often shipped off to the colonies and sent money at regular intervals to keep them there. Breaker Morant was another of these 'remittance men'.

Gordon was just over twenty when he arrived at Adelaide in 1853. He immediately obtained a position in the South Australian mounted police and was stationed at Mount Gambier. He was a tall man and handsome in the saddle but, out of the saddle, his posture was bad and his eyesight very poor. He was shy, sensitive and inclined to be moody.

In 1855 he resigned his position and took up horse breaking in the south-eastern districts of South Australia. An interest in horseracing, which he had developed as a youth in England, continued in Australia and he had a reputation for being 'a good steady lad and a splendid horseman'.

His father died in 1857 and his mother about two years later. He received the then massive amount of £7000 from his mother's estate towards the end of 1861. In 1862 he married seventeen-year-old Margaret Park and bought a cottage where they lived for two years at Port MacDonnell, near Mount Gambier. This cottage, which Gordon gave the rather twee name of 'Dingley Dell', is preserved to this day.

In 1864 Gordon had his first poetry published and also came third in the Border Watch Handicap Steeplechase, the most famous Mount Gambier horse race. The day after, he made his famous leap on his horse, Red Lancer, over a high fence between Leg of Mutton Lake and the Blue Lake. He landed on a small 1.8 metre ledge above a 60-metre drop into the Blue Lake below. An obelisk, erected in 1887, now marks the spot.

In 1865 he was asked to stand for parliament and was elected by three votes to the South Australian House of Assembly. He spoke several times but had no talent for speaking in public and made a poor politician. He resigned his seat in November 1866.

Gordon was earning himself a reputation as a rider over jumps and often won or was placed in local hurdle races and steeple-chases. He was also contributing verse to various magazines. Around this time he also bought several properties, including one in Western Australia, which he visited in 1867, but he lost money, and all his land purchases proved to be disappointing.

Next he moved to Ballarat in Victoria where he rented livery stables and set up a general horse business as a dealer and breaker. Gordon, however, had no head for business and the venture was a failure. In March 1868 he had a serious accident when a horse smashed his head against a gatepost.

Finally he was bankrupted by a fire in his livery stable later that same year and, to add to his misery, his infant daughter died just short of her first birthday and his wife also left him for some time.

In spite of being short-sighted he was becoming very well known as a gentleman rider, and on 10 October 1868 actually won three steeplechase races in one day at the Melbourne Hunt Club meeting at Flemington racetrack. He began riding for money but was not fortunate and had more than one serious fall. He sold his business in 1868 and moved to Brighton, in Melbourne.

In Melbourne, Gordon succeeded in straightening out his financial affairs, made a little money from race riding, and became friendly with literary figures of the day such as Marcus Clarke and Henry Kendall.

In March 1870 Gordon again injured his head in a bad fall while riding in a steeplechase at Flemington and he never completely recovered from the accident. To make matters worse, in June he learned that his claim to his family's ancestral land in Scotland had been rejected on a legal technicality.

His last book, *Bush Ballads and Galloping Rhymes*, was published on 23 June 1870. Gordon had just asked his publishers what he owed them for printing the book, and realised that he had no money to pay them and no prospects. His marriage had also failed irrevocably.

That day he bought a package of cartridges for his rifle and went home to his cottage at Brighton. Next morning he rose early, walked into the scrub at Brighton Beach and shot himself.

Gordon wrote volumes and volumes of 'serious' poetry. All through his short adult life he wrote poetry in the very ornate, literary style of the old ballads and the romantic poets. Most of his verse seems tedious and old-fashioned today, but then so does most of Tennyson's poetry.

He was finally recognised as a literary figure of some standing and, in 1934, his bust was placed in Westminster Abbey. He is the only Australian writer to receive that honour, although he was, of course, actually British.

When he is remembered by Australians these days, it is generally not for his serious poetry or his place in the literary world. He is remembered as the poet who wrote galloping rhymes, like 'How We Beat the Favourite', and sentimental verses like 'The Sick Stockrider', and inspired Paterson, Lawson, Harry Morant, Ogilvie and a host of other verse writers. All four poets mentioned said Adam Lindsay Gordon was their favourite poet and their inspiration, so it is fair to call him the father of Australian 'bush' verse.

He is also remembered by racing historians for his daring deeds as a horseman and steeplechase jockey, and for his rather romantic and tragic life.

And his memory still lives on, albeit anonymously, when he is quoted verbatim by many older Australians who remember four short lines of his poetry.

In fact, the poem from which the couplet is taken deals with death as well as what is important in life. To quote a few more lines seems an appropriate way to end this story of the tragic life of Adam Lindsay Gordon:

Question not, but live and labour
Till yon goal be won,
Helping every feeble neighbour,
Seeking help from none;
Life is mostly froth and bubble,

Two things stand like stone,
Kindness in another's trouble,
Courage in your own,
Courage, comrades, this is certain,
All is for the best –
There are lights behind the curtain –
Gentles let us rest.

THE FRENCHMAN WHO PUT ON A SHOW

The first Easter Agricultural Show was held in 1823 at Parramatta. It was organised by the newly formed Agricultural Society of New South Wales, established under the patronage of Governor Brisbane who also set up an agricultural training college and encouraged the importing of livestock.

The aim of the show was to help the colony's rural industries to improve and develop by providing displays and competitions for farm produce, horses, cattle, sheep, pigs and poultry, and it continued to be held at Parramatta until 1869, when it moved to Prince Alfred Park, in Redfern, near the edge of the city. At this time sideshows and other entertainments were added to the event.

This move was the brainchild of a remarkable Frenchman, Jules Francois De Sales Joubert, who was born in 1824 in Angouleme, France, and educated in Bordeaux and at the College Bourbon, Paris.

Jules's brother, Didier, was an agent for the wine company Barton Fils of Bordeaux and had migrated to Sydney and become a successful merchant, living in Hunters Hill.

In May 1839 Jules sailed as a passenger in the French frigate *Heroine*. After visiting New Zealand, he went to Sydney and took a post as interpreter on the French corvette *Aube,* which was on a goodwill visit to the Pacific. He returned in 1841 and became chancellor at the French consulate in Sydney and encouraged trade and good relations between France and the Australian colonies.

In 1848 momentous political changes in France saw

Napoleon III take over government from the Orleanists and Jules, a confirmed Orleanist, resigned his post. He also married Florence, daughter of wealthy Sydney landowner, politician and solicitor Robert Owen.

Jules was never a faint-hearted fellow and, needing to provide for his family, he moved to South Australia during the copper boom, invested in property and set himself up in business as a storekeeper and building contractor.

Tragedy struck, however, when both his children and then Florence died of typhoid, but the indefatigable Frenchman moved on to the Mount Alexander goldfield in Victoria, where he contracted to construct government buildings and ran a store at a place with the delightful frontier name of Sawpit Gully. He returned to Sydney in 1853 with the contract to supply the French forces that were busy annexing New Caledonia and, by 1854, he was on the high seas, trading with the French colony at Madagascar.

By 1855 he was back in Adelaide where he married Adelaide Levi and the couple immediately left for Sydney where Jules had been busily buying land at Hunters Hill.

Jules and his brother practically built the suburb of Hunters Hill by bringing 70 tradesmen from France to build stone houses. They also were given the common known as the 'Field of Mars' to develop and subdivide, in return for building bridges over the Lane Cove and Parramatta rivers. When Hunters Hill was given municipal status in 1861, Jules was the first chairman of the council and Didier became the first mayor in 1867. Jules had also established a ferry service and by 1865 he was chairman of the Parramatta River Navigation Co.

Jules's life, however, was often a roller-coaster ride between entrepreneurial success and disaster, and in 1866 he went bankrupt.

Undeterred, the plucky Frenchman threw his talents and energy into running the Agricultural Society of New South Wales, of which he'd been a member for some years. As honorary secretary in 1867, and later paid secretary, he revitalised the society, edited the society's journal, moved the annual show from Parramatta to Sydney, and enlarged it to include non-agricultural exhibits.

From 1870 the show was held in the society's new buildings in Prince Alfred Park.

Jules threw himself into the world of exhibitions and trade shows with his customary energy. In 1874 he sought united colonial representation at the 1876 Philadelphia Exhibition. In 1878, as secretary to the New South Wales commission, he organised the Australian exhibits for the Paris Exhibition and, while there, he arranged for French participation at the 1879 Sydney Exhibition, which was the brainchild of Jules himself.

In his homeland he was made a chevalier of the Legion of Honour for having sent £12,000 to French flood victims in 1875, but in Sydney local politics took hold of the planning for the exhibition and, on his return, Jules found he was excluded from the commission, which he had conceived and organised. Questions asked in New South Wales parliament by business rival and volatile roughneck public crusader John McElhone implied that Jules had private items shipped back from the Paris Exhibition at government expense.

Annoyed, disgusted and disillusioned, but never beaten, Jules and his friend Richard Twopenny went on to organise and present exhibitions in Perth in 1881, Christchurch in 1882 and Calcutta in 1883.

Finally tired of running exhibitions all around the world, Jules settled in Melbourne and tried his hand at theatrical promotion, building the Alexandra Theatre. Sadly the tide turned once more and he was again bankrupt in 1887, so he switched back to exhibitions and represented New South Wales at the 1888 Melbourne Exhibition. He then organised and managed an exhibition in Dunedin in 1889–90. It was at Dunedin that he launched his latest venture, a book of his experiences and reminiscences entitled *Shavings and Scrapes in Many Parts*.

Still restless and energetic in his 60s, he went to Tasmania where he organised exhibitions at Launceston in 1891–92 and Hobart in 1894–95.

Jules finally settled down in Carlton, Melbourne, where he died in 1907, survived by his second wife, eight sons and two daughters, whom he had somehow managed to raise, educate and provide for through all his adventures and ups and downs.

A truly amazing and energetic man, he helped create and build the suburb of Hunters Hill, was a visionary in the field of exhibitions and trade shows, and opened many doors for understanding and trade between Europe and Australasia. He was a citizen of the world.

But, of all his achievements, the greatest for me is the event he created which has been loved by millions of Sydney children, generation after generation. Sadly, though, those millions of kids almost certainly never heard the name of the man who gave them the Royal Easter Show.

In 1881, with the show having outgrown Prince Alfred Park, the New South Wales government gave land at Moore Park where it was held for the next 116 years. In 1998, the Sydney Royal Easter Show moved to a new showground at Homebush. The event has been around for more than 190 years. It has been held every year since 1869 except in 1919, when Spanish flu hit Sydney, and between the World War II years of 1942 and 1946.

The show as we know it today is the legacy of that remarkable, energetic, irascible and visionary Frenchman, Jules Francois De Sales Joubert. It was advertised as the 'Greatest Show On Earth' and the 'Biggest Event in the Southern Hemisphere' when I was a kid and it was a highlight on every child's calendar. Farm animals, woodchopping, showbags, sideshows, ferris wheels, ghost trains, fairy floss, dagwood dogs and night-time spectaculars including rocket men, daredevil car demonstrations and demolition derbies made the Easter Show a magic annual event in every Sydney kid's life.

I, for one, would like to say, '*Merci beaucoup, Monsieur Joubert!*'

TWO CLAIMS TO FAME

Christina Macpherson is not a name that would immediately mean much to many Aussies.

If you were aware of the history of our national song, 'Waltzing Matilda', it might ring a bell somewhere deep in your subconscious, but that's about all.

(You will note there that I said 'national song'. I am fully aware that it is not our national *anthem*. It is, however, very much our 'national song' whether officially or not—the song Aussies use to identify their nationality all around the world.)

It was Christina Macpherson who provided the original tune to the words written by Banjo Paterson.

In order to understand the connection between the two it is necessary to unravel a saga that involves such diverse locations as Wangaratta and Warrnambool, in different parts of Victoria, Winton in far north outback Queensland, and Sydney.

In 1854 the Macphersons and Rutherfords migrated together from Scotland and took up 150,000 acres of good grazing property near Wangaratta, which the families owned jointly. Ewan Macpherson married Margaret Rutherford and they had eleven children.

The ninth child was Christina Rutherford Macpherson, born in 1864.

The Macphersons were wealthy people and Christina was educated at Oberwyl Ladies School in the Melbourne suburb of St Kilda. There, she befriended Sarah Riley, whose father ran a

Sydney legal firm. His partner in that firm was none other than Andrew Barton Paterson, also of Scottish descent, a man who would become our best-known and best-loved poet—and the man who wrote the words of 'Waltzing Matilda'. He became engaged to Sarah Riley in 1887.

In 1894 Christina visited her younger sister Margaret, who had married Stewart MacArthur (later a Supreme Court justice in Victoria), at their property at Meningoort, in the western districts, and while Christina was there they attended the famous Grand Annual, a three-day race meeting still held every year in May at Warrnambool.

The Warrnambool Garrison Artillery Band played between races over the three days and the band frequently played a catchy march version of a Scottish song, 'Bonnie Wood O' Craigielea', which Christina liked and soon learned to play on the piano.

Christina's mother died later that year in December and her father, in early 1895, took his unmarried daughters Christina and Jane to visit another family property, Dagworth Station, in far north Queensland.

There had been a major riot on the property in September 1894, during the shearers' strike, when a group of shearers burned Dagworth shearing shed, which contained about 150 lambs. This act of violence ignited much outrage and police were sent to the area and the media had a field day; anarchy was loose in the bush!

Ewan Macpherson wanted to see the situation first-hand and thought a break away from home after the death of their mother would be a good thing for his two unmarried daughters. So, the scene was set for a meeting which would impact drastically on three lives and give us a national song.

Sarah Riley and her fiancé of eight years, Paterson, were visiting from Sydney, staying on Sarah's brother's property, 'Vindex', which adjoined Dagworth, so a house party was arranged between the two old school friends, Sarah and Christina.

It was during this time together that Christina played the tune she had heard at Warrnambool races on an auto harp, and Paterson began composing some words to the melody. His lyrics told, in a figurative way, the story of the suspected arsonist Samuel Hoffmeister, and the squatter and the police. The young poet had to be circumspect as he was a guest in the house of the man who may well have been an accessory to the murder of Hoffmeister. This is apparently the reason for the lyrics of the song being symbolic rather than factual.

The collaboration between Christina and Paterson evidently developed into far more than a songwriting exercise.

The late Dennis O'Keeffe, who spent many years researching the origins of the song and wrote the definitive book on the subject, was convinced there was a strong romantic bond—probably an affair—between the two, which led to the breaking of Paterson's engagement to Sarah Riley.

Whatever did happen at Dagworth, it is true that neither Sarah Riley nor Christina Macpherson ever married and Paterson was always dismissive of 'Waltzing Matilda', sold off the rights cheaply to the Billy Tea Company, and appears to have tried to put the whole episode out of his memory. He married many years later and his family were always reluctant to deal with the Dagworth episode in biographies after his death.

Christina Macpherson lived quietly as a spinster in Melbourne for the rest of her days, dying aged 72 in 1936. Her grave remained unmarked until the 1970s when interest in the history of the song led to some recognition of her role in its creation, and her niece placed a small plaque to mark her grave in the family plot at St Kilda Cemetery.

The tune most sung today is the one which was used after Paterson sold the rights for the lyrics to Billy Tea, a march tune composed by Mary Cowan, although many folk singers still use and prefer the tune first applied to the song by Christina, which is often called 'the Queensland version'.

Christina Macpherson appears to have been intelligent, cultured, unassuming and charming. She never attempted to take any credit for 'Waltzing Matilda'; she wrote a very humble and informative letter explaining how the song came to existence to Thomas Woods, a folklorist and historian, but never bothered to post it. The letter was a found among her papers when she died in obscurity in 1936.

Oddly enough, Christina Macpherson has another 'claim to fame' in our history, totally unconnected to 'Waltzing Matilda'.

On 8 April 1865, the psychotic bushranger, arsonist and murderer Mad Dan Morgan arrived at the Macpherson homestead 'Peechelba' near Wangaratta and held the family and their employees hostage at gunpoint in their dining room.

Morgan was the most wanted man in the colonies, having terrorised the population of New South Wales and Victoria for years. He was known for his erratic behaviour and sadistic tendencies. On one occasion he held up a station and wounded a man, then apologised and allowed another to ride for the doctor, changed his mind again and rode after the man and killed him.

On this occasion, having rounded up all the adults on the property and made them prisoners in the dining room, he allowed Alice Keenan, a nursemaid, to go and attend to a crying infant in the next room. The brave young Alice escaped by climbing through a window and ran to the other homestead on the property, which was the home of the Macphersons' relatives, the Rutherfords.

The Rutherfords notified the local police who arrived and laid a trap for Morgan in the early hours of the following day. Next morning as Morgan was leaving the homestead, a stationhand named John Quinlan, who was the best shot in the district, shot the bushranger in the back as he crossed the open ground between the house and the stable.

Morgan died of his wounds and the event was celebrated by the press with gruesome photographs of his body propped against the stable. The body was also mutilated by souvenir collectors before the bushranger was buried in the Wangaratta cemetery.

This infant whose crying caused Mad Dan Morgan to allow Alice Keenan to leave the room, and ultimately bring his life and career to a bloody and gruesome end, was fifteen-month-old Christina Rutherford Macpherson.

THE POET TIME FORGOT

The Australian rhymed verse tradition is as old as European settlement in this country. We worship our poets like Banjo Paterson, Henry Lawson and Mary Gilmore. Indeed, Australia is the only nation in the world to feature three poets, those just mentioned, on its currency!

For no really logical reason, however, some poets, no less talented or entertaining, have been completely forgotten.

One of those poets who was just as much admired and praised and read as any in his time, including Paterson, Lawson, Gilmore and many others like C.J. Dennis and Will Ogilvie, was Charles Souter.

I'd like to tell you about this wonderful poet and acquaint you with his verse in a modest way, but first let's look at how rhymed verse became popular in Australia and why some poets are remembered and others forgotten.

Early colonial poets like Charles Thatcher were very popular writers of comic satirical doggerel, and others like Charles Harpur and Henry Kendall popularised more lyrical rhymed verse which described Australian scenes, characters and events. Then, of course, Adam Lindsay Gordon came along and inspired a whole raft of versifiers with his sentimental and rousing rhymes.

Most of this early verse has been forgotten because the subject material was current events which are outdated, or because the language and style of verse used is rather too ornate and archaic to modern tastes.

In 1880 the *Bulletin* magazine was established by J.F. Archibald and John Haynes, and subsequently the rhymed verse tradition became well and truly confirmed and established as part of our 'national' heritage. Conversational and common vocabulary was more often used in verse writing, and poetry became more accessible and easily understood by the general public.

The first 'bush ballad' the *Bulletin* published was 'Sam Holt', in March 1881. The poem, by G.H. Gibson (known as 'Ironbark'), is a series of complaints addressed to a bushman who has struck it lucky and become a city 'toff'. It contained the common themes of 'city versus country' and what we now call the 'tall poppy syndrome':

> Say don't you remember that fiver, Sam Holt,
> You borrowed so frank and so free?
> I guess I may whistle a good many times
> 'Fore you think of that fiver or me.

The magazine nicknamed the 'Bully' or 'Bushman's Bible' regularly published the work of more than 60 verse writers and introduced Paterson and Lawson to the Australian public, along with Victor Daley, Mary Gilmore, C.J. Dennis, Will Ogilvie, Harry Morant, W.T. Goodge, 'John O'Brien', E.J. Brady, 'Jim Grahame' and the rest.

The *Bulletin* became the chief source of income for our best writers of verse. It was the magazine that sent Lawson on his inspirational trip to Bourke and supported many writers, as well as artists like the Lindsays, for many years. The importance of the *Bulletin* to our rhymed verse heritage cannot be overestimated.

Hundreds of writers were discovered and published by *Bulletin* owner J.F. Archibald and editors like A.G. Stephens, James Edmond and S.H. Pryor from the 1880s through to the 1920s. But, sadly, it is also from this age of plenty, in terms of rhymed verse, that many poetic treasures became lost.

What happened was that certain poets became very famous indeed. Paterson, Lawson, Dennis, and to a lesser extent Ogilvie and Gilmore, became the great names of Australian verse. Their most popular verses were much anthologised and recited, studied, learned and, indeed, loved by ordinary Australians. They were successful during their lifetimes and much of their work has remained popular long after their deaths.

Another group of *Bulletin* poets have fared much worse. These are writers like Dorothea Mackellar, W.T. Goodge, Barcroft Boak, Harry Morant and Thomas E. Spencer, who are mostly remembered for one or two well-anthologised poems. These 'one-hit wonders' were all writers of many excellent entertaining and moving poems.

The real 'forgotten' poets of our Australian verse heritage, however, are *Bulletin* poets like Charles Souter.

Souter's touching visions of bush life and the sailing days are wonderful, evocative and vividly visual poems that demonstrate a talent for accurate observation and human feelings. I think they are timeless verses. Written in an era when people had more time to read and ponder the human condition, his verses are still vibrant today and have, for modern readers, a lovely patina of nostalgia. Yet who today has heard of Charles Souter?

In his heyday he was as popular as many of those poets whose names we still remember and revere and whose verse is constantly anthologised and recited and enjoyed. Indeed, he was far more popular than some of them. Yet, when I set out to compile a collection of Australian rhymed verse in 2005, Souter's verse had completely disappeared from anthologies and his published collections had been out of print for 80 years.

I had discovered poems of his in the *Bulletin* archives, and went looking for more in the Mitchell Library.

It can be difficult to place the authors of verse printed in the *Bulletin*, as poets used various noms de plume when writing for the magazine. Some poets used different names at times, depending on whether they considered the poems they submitted to be serious, frivolous, satirical or merely doggerel.

It can often take quite a lot of research and guesswork to decipher who the poets were. Ed Dyson used the pen name

'Billy T' when writing light verse, and Victor Daley used his real name for lyrical poetry and the Irish nom de plume 'Creeve Roe' (red cross, referring to the Irish flag at that time) for his satirical and political verse.

Charles Souter was a qualified and practising physician and his verse appeared in the *Bulletin* under the names Charles Souter, 'Dr Nil' and 'Nil'. I can only assume he was having a joke at his own expense when he wrote a piece as 'Doctor Nothing' or merely 'Nothing'.

I remember being moved to tears, sitting in the silence of the Mitchell Library, upon discovering a poem of Souter's entitled 'Buckalong', in which an old bushman recalls his days as a boy on a South Australia outback station and bemoans the coming of motorcars, wire fences and modern attitudes. To me, this poem encapsulates the feelings we all have about the past, especially as we grow older. It is still one of my favourite poems. I can hear the old man's voice and close my eyes and picture him perfectly. Here it is:

BUCKALONG

CHARLES SOUTER

They have cleared them 'ills down Jarvis way, where the great tall
gum-trees grew;
An' where there was forests of she-oak once, you'll find but a scanty
few.
Wire fences runs 'longside o' the roads where once there was posts
and rails;
An' the old slab cottage 'as tumbled down an' so 'as the old cow-
bails.
The blacksmith's forge on the Ad'laide road 'as been gone this many
a year;
An' they've closed the pub McGonnigal kep', where we useter stop
for a beer.

But when I was young at Buckalong,
When fust I come ter Buckalong,

There wasn't much in life we missed,
Nor many girls we hadn't kissed,
An' the best man there had the hardest fist,
When fust I come ter Buckalong!

I've galloped all over them 'ills meself, after emus and kangaroo,
On Sundays, after we'd been ter church – an' the Parson, 'e come too.
An' the Trooper come, an' the Doctor come, an' some o' the gals as well;
We reckoned as some of *us* coves could ride, but them *gals* could ride like Hell!
We used no dogs fer runnin' 'em down, just rode 'em to a stand.
An' the cove as got ahead o' them gals was the proudest cove in the land!

They was bushmen then at Buckalong,
When I was a lad at Buckalong,
We didn't squat in motor cars
An' swap blue yarns an' green cigars,
An' we never let down the slip-rail bars,
In them early days at Buckalong!

Now the roads is like some city street, all bitcherman and tar!
They don't make tracks fer the horseman now, only the motor car.
A team o' bullicks 'ld bust themselves a-tryin' ter keep their feet,
An' there ain't no shade by the long wayside where a cove can spell in the heat.
The creeks is dry an' the paddicks bare, an' there ain't a patch o' scrub;
An' all yer can find is a petrol pump, when what yer want is a pub!

But when fust I come ter Buckalong,
When we was boys at Buckalong,
The bush WAS bush, an' the birds could sing,
An' a man could RIDE, an' an axe could ring,
An' yer life-blood flowed like a golden spring!
When I was a lad . . . at Buckalong!

Charles Henry Souter was born in 1864 at Aberdeen, Scotland. His father was John Clement Souter, a doctor, artist and writer who collected rare books, china and coins. The family moved to Nottingham when Charles was a child and, when he was eight, to London.

Charles was educated at Highgate and University College schools, and attended the Royal College of Surgeons from fourteen as a registered medical student under his father's tuition.

John's next move was to migrate with his family to Australia. Travelling as a ship's surgeon, he took his family to Sydney in 1879 and they settled in the bush town of Coonabarabran.

As a result of this move, fifteen-year-old Charles developed a keen interest in ships and the sea, as well as a love for the bush. He worked on the family farm and became an excellent horseman.

When he was eighteen he returned to Scotland, completed his medical studies at the University of Aberdeen and, aged 23, married Jane Raeburn, the daughter of a baker.

They returned to Australia and lived at Hillston in western New South Wales until Jane died after giving birth to a daughter in 1889.

Souter then worked for some time as a ship's surgeon before setting up as a GP in the town of Balaklava, South Australia, where he practised for fifteen years. He married again and had a son.

Souter, along with his father and younger brother, also practised medicine as *locum tenens* in various parts of Adelaide and Whyalla.

Souter contributed verse to the *Bulletin* from 1896. His poetry was much admired in his lifetime by critics and writers like H.M. Green and Vance Palmer, and he was a favourite of *Bulletin* editors J.F. Archibald and A.G. Stephens.

His first three published collections of verse—*Irish Lords* (1912), *To Many Ladies* (1917) and *The Mallee Fire* (1923)—were very popular and sold exceptionally well. His fourth collection, *The Lonely Rose* (1935), was less well-received, and by the end of World War II his work had been all but forgotten and was out of print.

Souter was an old-fashioned fellow with a handlebar moustache whose hobbies were drawing, singing old bush songs, playing sea shanties on his harmonica and imitating birdcalls on his flute. He was also, like Banjo Paterson, a radio personality and featured as an expert on 5AD's popular *Information Please* programme.

He was greatly influenced by the old bush songs and the other *Bulletin* poets, but also by the great British poets of the era, Alfred Noyes and Rudyard Kipling. Charles Souter's verse falls into four categories: sea poems, romantic verse, patriotic verse written during World War I and verse about life in the bush. Perhaps his best verse gives accurate and vivid depictions of everyday life on farms and grazing properties in the rural districts of South Australia.

Souter's sensitive and well-observed verse was of the highest quality of its type and he was much admired as an important poet of his day. Although critics considered that he made a significant contribution to Australian writing, his verse was all but forgotten by the 1960s and had not been anthologised from the 1930s until 2005, when I included many of his poems in an anthology of a thousand Australian rhymed verses.

Here is Souter describing the mundane task of unloading wheat at the silo in a small town while the wheat inspector assesses and values the harvest:

SLIDE ALONG

CHARLES SOUTER

When the cranky German waggon,
With its ten or fifteen bag on
Comes a-jerkin' and a-joltin' down the dusty, limestone street,
And the 'Norther's' blowin' blindin',
And the rollers are a-grindin',
And the agent jabs his sampler thro' the sackin' to the wheat,
Let 'em slide along the plank! slide along! slide along!
Sixty bushels for the Bank; slide along!

When your back is fairly breakin'
And your very fingers shakin'
With the heavin', heavin', heavin', in the blarsted, blazin' sun;
And the agent finds the spots out
And takes all his sample lots out
Where its rusty, pinched, or smutty – knockin' off five pound a ton;
Sling 'em over with a jerk! slide along! slide along!

Sixty days of wasted work! slide along!
Sixty days a-ploughin' mallee
In the God-forgotten valley
Of the creepin', crawlin' Murray, with the dingoes for your mates!
Sow and harrow, roll and reap it,
But you get no show to keep it,
For it's 'Boom and bust yer biler' when the cocky speculates!
Let the bankers take the lot: slide along! slide along!
Farmin' mallee's bloomin' rot – slide along!

Souter's patriotic poems are dated now, but still capture the feeling of the times, like this poem in praise of the 10th Battalion at Gallipoli:

THE TENTH

CHARLES SOUTER

No drums were beat, no trumpets blared,
The day they marched away;
Their wives and sweethearts watched them go,
And none would bid them stay!
They heard their country calling them,
And asked no second call,
The sacred voice of duty spoke;
They answered, one and all.
Hats off to The Tenth!

Untried they faced the deadly hail
Of shrapnel, shot and shell!
Untried they stormed the fire-swept ridge
Where earth was changed to hell!
Was there a man whose courage failed,
A boy who thought to flinch;
Did any soldier of The Tenth
Give ground a single inch?
Hats off to The Tenth!

Some of The Tenth are buried deep
On ANZAC's lonely shore,
The womankind who watched them go
Will look on them no more.
But when you see the colours
Of the famous 'double-blue',
You know you're looking on a Man
Who served his country true!
Hats off to The Tenth!

My favourite Souter poems are the nostalgic and romantic verses like 'Irish Lords', where a bushman visits the now-deserted homestead where he had courted a girl in his youth:

IRISH LORDS

CHARLES SOUTER

The clover-burr was two foot high and the billabongs were full,
The brolgas danced a minuet and the world seemed made of wool!
The nights were never wearisome and the days were never slow,
When first we came to 'Irish Lords', on the road to Ivanhoe.

The rime was on the barley-grass as we passed the homestead rails,
A 'Darling Jackass' piped us in with trills and turns and scales,
And youth and health and carelessness sat on the saddle-bow,
And . . . Mary lived at 'Irish Lords', on the road to Ivanhoe.

On every hand was loveliness, the fates were fair and kind;
We drank the very wine of life and never looked behind;
And Mary! Mary everywhere went flitting to and fro,
When first we came to 'Irish Lords', on the road to Ivanhoe.

The window of her dainty bower, where the golden banksia grew,
Stared like a dead man's glaring eye, and the roof had fallen
through.
No violets in her garden bed, and her voice . . . hushed long ago . . .
When last we camped at 'Irish Lords', on the road to Ivanhoe.

So, there you have it—a great poet, forgotten as the world moved on and others were remembered and revered or even, like Paterson, Lawson and Gilmore, had their faces placed on our banknotes. Yet none of them captured the Aussie vernacular as spoken by true bushmen like Charles Souter, not even the great C.J. Dennis, and few captured the restrained yet poignant nostalgia for the past that sailors and bushmen share yet rarely articulate.

I will leave this story with a poem by Souter about the passing of the great age of sail, told by an old sailor of the clipper days who can't face the prospect of looking at the harbour, with its steamships and diesel-driven freighters.

SEA FEAR

CHARLES SOUTER

I can't go down to the sea again
For I am old and ailing;
My ears are deaf to the mermaid's call,
And my stiff limbs are failing.
The white sails and the tall masts
Are no longer to be seen
On the dainty clipper ships that sailed
For Hull, and Aberdeen!

I can't go down to the sea again:
My eyes are weak and bleared,
And they search again for the gallant poop
Where once I stood and steered.
There's nought but wire and boiler-plate
To meet my wand'ring gaze.
Never a sign of the graceful spars
Of the good old sailing days!

So I will sit in the little room
That all old sailors know,
And smoke, and sing, and yarn about
The ships of long ago,
'The Flying Cloud', 'The Cutty Sark',
'The Hotspur' and 'The Dart' . . .
But I won't go down to the sea again,
For fear it breaks my heart!

I commend to you the poet Charles Souter, long forgotten but remembered here. Let's not forget him again.

THE MAN IN CHARGE OF EVERYTHING

This is the story of how an Irishman living in New Zealand came to be almost single-handedly responsible for the development of Western Australia.

Charles Yelverton O'Connor was born near Waterford, Ireland, in 1843 into a farming and business family.

Educated at Bishop Foy's School in Waterford and at Dublin University, he showed a gift for engineering and was soon working on the Waterford-Kilkenny railway construction. He later helped design and build water storage systems in the north of Ireland.

In 1865, aged just 21, he was offered the opportunity to join a company called Rowland Campion Long, which had secured a contract to survey the Waipa River area on the North Island of New Zealand.

Young Charles made rapid advancement in his new homeland, through his excellent work on projects such as surveying a route for the first road constructed across the Southern Alps of New Zealand. He was appointed surveyor of the Greymouth-Hokitika-Christchurch railway line when he was just 23 years old. By the age of 27 he was county engineer and, before he turned 30, he became district engineer for Canterbury province.

O'Connor's most important work over the next decade included designing and building water supply systems for the New Zealand goldfields and improving and developing harbour facilities around the colony. In 1880 he became inspecting engineer for the South Island and was elected to the Institution of Civil Engineers in London. He had a worldwide reputation for innovation and was considered an expert on colonial railways and harbour construction.

From 1883 he held the position of under-secretary for public works in New Zealand but, when the position of departmental head became vacant, in 1890, he was overlooked and moved sideways to the position of marine engineer for the whole colony.

O'Connor had married Susan Ness in 1874 and they had eight children. So, aged 47 in 1890, he began examining employment prospects elsewhere.

Meanwhile, far away on the other side of the continent of Australia, the Swan River Colony had been developing, albeit slowly. It was now known as Western Australia and, in 1891, the premier, Sir John Forrest, desperate to find someone who could help solve the colony's massive infrastructure problems, invited O'Connor to become the colony's engineer-in-chief. He offered O'Connor a 25 per cent increase in salary.

In response O'Connor asked whether he would be responsible for constructing railways or harbours or roads. In reply to this enquiry, he received a telegram, which said simply, 'Everything.'

O'Connor then said he would take on the Herculean task of engineering 'everything' for a massive and underpopulated colony—for an extra 20 per cent on top of the 25 per cent raise in salary. Forrest agreed.

When O'Connor arrived in Perth (via Victoria, where he presented a report on the state of colonial railways), he found that his position included being general manager of the government railways, as well as colonial engineer! Not only was he in charge of engineering 'everything', he had to run the railways as well.

Up until this time the port for Perth had been Albany, 400 kilometres away, as seagoing vessels could not berth near the mouth of the Swan River. A ramshackle railway line between the two towns carried mail to Perth. The line was partly government-owned and partly private, and the gauges were different!

It was believed by most 'experts' that problems with sand movement and coastal currents prevented a harbour being built at Fremantle and the plans presented to remedy this situation included a massive outside harbour, which was beyond the resources of the colony.

O'Connor did extensive research and surveys and personally interviewed fishermen and locals then presented a plan for a safe anchorage harbour at Fremantle for a fraction of the cost.

In spite of vehement arguments that he was wrong, Premier Forrest trusted his judgement and his plan was put into place. The O'Connor family set up house in Fremantle in 1892 and, five years later, the largest seagoing ships of the day were safely berthed in Fremantle Harbour, which would become the gateway to Australia for millions of migrants.

O'Connor was, at the same time, building a viable railway system throughout the south-west of Western Australia. He bought out the private lines and consolidated and upgraded existing tracks and extended the railways north, south and inland. Soon, efficient, well-maintained rail lines extended from Northam to Southern Cross; the Southwest, Donnybrook and Albany, and the goldfields of Kalgoorlie and Coolgardie.

O'Connor purchased better rolling stock and designed a railway that was suitable for West Australian conditions. As general manager of railways he was a great supporter of his staff whom he said were overworked, underpaid and endured poor working conditions; he instituted better education, recruitment and training systems for railway workers at all levels, from engineers to navvies. His railway management methods were so successful that, despite the massive expense, the railways began, for the first time, to make a profit.

Having developed the harbour, roads and railways, Charles O'Connor was faced with the biggest problem of his career. It's all very well to have communities living in arid areas serviced to rail and road, but without water, steam trains cannot run and people cannot survive.

The rushes that followed the discovery of gold at Coolgardie in 1892 and Kalgoorlie a year later severely exacerbated the water problem. The goldfields needed a water supply—people were dying every day of cholera, typhoid, dysentery or just plain thirst. Water was selling at more than a pound a gallon and steam trains were stranded with dry boilers.

What was required was an engineering feat of unbelievable and never-before-imagined complexity.

O'Connor had been working on a plan from around 1894—at the same time he was building a harbour, surveying, planning and constructing roads and railways, and running a railway system!

He had also become responsible for water conservation and storage as early as 1892 and set up a survey for water along the proposed route of the Northam–Southern Cross rail line, as a result of which rock catchments and groundwater tanks were constructed to provide water for the steam engines and railway workers.

O'Connor's proposal was, as usual, audacious and original. It would provide enough water for the mines, the railway and the townships that were expected to grow along with the mines and railway.

Water was to be dammed and stored west of the Darling Range, then lifted 1000 feet (300 metres) over the top of the range and pumped 330 miles (530 kilometres) to a reservoir at Coolgardie.

O'Connor estimated that 5 million gallons (23 million litres) of water a day could be piped through 30-inch steel pipes and delivered for three shillings sixpence per 1000 gallons (4500 litres). He estimated the time required for construction to be three years and the cost to be £2.5 million.

Premier Forrest accepted it. He had absolute faith in O'Connor but had to convince parliament, and persuade it to support the raising of a London loan.

The pipeline was open to much uninformed and malicious political criticism. Eventually O'Connor was accused of corruption. This was too much for the scrupulously honest and dedicated Irishman and he was forced to waste more of his precious time writing a detailed rebuttal of a long list of criticisms for both houses of state parliament.

In the face of hostile criticism of the project, O'Connor offered to travel to London to convince the necessary people that the scheme would work. He did so in 1897 and expert British engineers sanctioned his plans as perfectly feasible. While he was in London, Queen Victoria awarded him the order of St George and St Michael, which was presented by the Prince of Wales.

Finally, in 1898 the West Australian government signed contracts for the manufacture of the steel pipes, excavation began on the dam at Mundaring and the pipeline route was surveyed.

In February 1901 O'Connor lost an ally when John Forrest withdrew from state politics to enter the new federal parliament.

The coming of Federation placed more pressure on O'Connor as imported material for the project now attracted federal tax. On top of that, his old friend Forrest was now the federal minister for defence and requested that O'Connor research and cost a plan for an Australian transcontinental railway connecting Kalgoorlie to Port Augusta in South Australia.

Charles O'Connor duly took on the extra responsibility and somehow managed to complete the task with his usual efficiency and present the plans and estimates.

But the political sniping and criticism continued. Complaints were made about wasting public money and not compensating landowners for resumed land for the pipeline.

Finally it was all too much for the dedicated visionary who was suffering from neuralgia and insomnia caused by years of overwork.

On 8 March 1902 there was a successful pumping along 6 miles (9.6 kilometres) of the pipeline that proved the project was working as planned.

On 10 March 1902, O'Connor prepared for his daily early morning ride along the beach, which he usually took with his youngest daughter. She was not feeling well, so he rode alone along Fremantle beach past the new harbour he had designed and built. He then rode his horse into the shallow water at South Beach and shot himself through the head with a pistol.

After a decade of building roads, railways and a great harbour, and turning Western Australia from a convict backwater into a well-serviced colony, Charles O'Connor wrote a note, which started with the words, 'It has become impossible . . .'

His suicide letter contained detailed plans for the completion of the pipeline and construction phases of Mundaring dam and concluded:

> The Coolgardie Scheme is alright and I could finish it if I got a chance and protection from misrepresentation but there is no hope of that now and it is better that it should be given to some entirely new man to do who will be untrammelled by prior responsibility.

Within a year the pipeline, one of the world's greatest feats of engineering, was working and the final cost was within the budget set by O'Connor, except for the added customs duty imposed by the new federal government, which had been applied after O'Connor costed the project.

There was a grand opening and anyone who was anyone was there. When O'Connor's friend and ally Sir John Forrest turned on the water at Coolgardie and Kalgoorlie, he asked those present to remember 'the great builder of this work' whose efforts had brought 'happiness and comfort to the people of the goldfields for all time'.

O'Connor is buried in the Palmyra cemetery, overlooking Fremantle Harbour. His grave is marked by a huge Celtic cross erected by his staff. There is also a statue of him at Fremantle.

His wife and seven of his children survived him. Two of the sons became engineers and two of the daughters married engineers.

Western Australia owes Charles O'Connor an unfathomable debt of gratitude.

Sometimes being responsible for 'everything' is just too much.

THE DAWN AND DUSK DREAMER

Most Australians have never heard of him, or read one line of his verse, but Victor Daley was described by *Bulletin* magazine owner and editor J.F. Archibald as 'the rising poet of this country'.

Archibald included more of Daley's verse in *Bulletin* anthologies than that of Henry Lawson or Banjo Paterson, or any other poet for that matter.

Victor James William Patrick Daley was born in 1858 at Navan, County Armagh, Ireland. His father had been a soldier in the Indian army. Young Victor's grandfather told him the old Celtic tales and legends, and Daley always claimed that many of his relations were Fenian rebels and, as a child, he helped to make lead bullets for the rebels.

He was educated by the Christian Brothers but spent much of his childhood visiting ancient sites from Celtic history and daydreaming about the old legends and heroes.

After his father's death, Victor's mother remarried and the family moved to Plymouth in England, where Victor completed his education at a Catholic school and then became a clerk for the Great Western Railway Company.

Three years later, in 1878, he decided to migrate to South Australia where he had friends. He worked briefly in Sydney before taking up a position as a clerk in Adelaide where he also contributed writing to a newspaper called the *Star*.

Always a wanderer and bohemian, Daley had a desire to see New Caledonia and set out to travel there via Melbourne.

Evidently he lost all his money at the races in Melbourne and decided to stay there. He wrote about horseracing for the *Carlton Advertiser* and eventually joined the paper as a staff writer.

In 1881 Daley had enough money to commence his wandering once more and set out for New South Wales, where he worked on the *Queanbeyan Times* before moving on to Sydney. In the city he wrote for *Sydney Punch* and then the *Bulletin* which had commenced publication only a year previously.

Archibald loved Daley's verse and wrote, in 1882, 'We have not had more melodious and imaginative verses from an Australian writer.'

Daley's verse was far more lyrical and sentimental than most of the verse appearing in the *Bulletin* and featured regularly in the magazine until the poet's death in 1905.

Daley married Elizabeth Thompson while living in Sydney and they had six children in eight years. Four of the Daley children, two girls and two boys, survived childhood. The family also lived in Melbourne for about ten years and Daley attempted to live on his writing.

Although his freelance writings (short stories and articles as well as verse) were accepted by several newspapers and magazines, times were tough for the family. Victor Daley was, however, the first writer in Australia to live entirely on his income from writing.

In 1898 he returned to Sydney, where A.G. Stephens, at the *Bulletin*, had edited and helped to publish Daley's first book of verse, *At Dawn and Dusk*. The book received very favourable reaction from critics and sold well. Articles written by his contemporaries in praise of the volume took up one entire edition of the *Bulletin* literary section, the 'Red Page'.

The publication of this collection led to the formation, in 1898, of the 'Dawn and Dusk Club'. Named after his book, the 'Duskers' membership consisted mostly of those who had praised Daley's book and writers and artists associated with the *Bulletin*. It was a convivial 'men's drinking club' whose participants, including Henry Lawson and Norman Lindsay, discussed events of the day, read their work and satirised their contemporaries. Lindsay wrote an account of the club activities and profiled some of its members in a book titled *Bohemians of the Bulletin*.

Crusading newspaperman John Norton called the club 'a band of boozy, bar-bumming bards'. Daley was the elected chief of the club with the official title of 'Symposiarch' and there were seven 'Heptarchs', including Lawson.

Daley's best lyric poetry was mostly written in the earlier part of his career, in the 1880s and early 1890s, before he formed the Dusk and Dawn Club. It is rarely anthologised today, which is a shame as it has stood the test of time and offers an alternative to the 'bush verse' with which we are mostly familiar from that period.

Here are two examples of Daley at his best, writing on the power and timelessness of love:

PLAYERS

VICTOR DALEY

And after all – and after all
Our passionate prayers, and sighs and tears
Is Life a reckless carnival?
And are they lost, our golden years?

Ah, no; ah, no; for, long ago,
Ere time could sere, or care could fret,
There was a youth called Romeo,
There was a maid called Juliet.

The players of the past are gone;
The races rise; the races pass;
And softly over all is drawn
The quiet curtain of the grass.

But when the world went wild with Spring,
What days we had! Do you forget?
When I of all the word was king,
And you were my Queen Juliet?

There lives (though time should cease to flow,
And stars their courses should forget)
There lives a grey-haired Romeo,
Who loves a golden Juliet.

SONG

VICTOR DALEY

What shall a man remember
In days when he is old,
And Life is a dying ember
And Fame a story told?

Power – that came to leave him?
Wealth to the wild winds blown?
Fame – that came to deceive him?
Ah, no! Sweet Love alone!

Honour, and Wealth, and Power
May all like dreams depart,
But Love is a fadeless flower,
Whose roots are in the heart.

Commenting on a different aspect of love, and ageing, Daley wrote, in a poem called 'Over the Wine':

Long ago I did discover it was fine to be a lover,
But the heartache and the worry spoil the game;
Now I think, like an old vandal,
That the game's not worth the candle,
And I know some other vandals think the same.

Daley also wrote humorous satirical verse, social commentary, which was sometimes gentle, but often bitingly vitriolic. This type of verse was always written under the nom de plume of 'Creeve

Roe', and was considered as lighthearted doggerel, rather than serious literature, by Daley and his contemporaries.

In the guise of 'Creeve Roe' Daley delighted in satirising killjoys and wowsers:

LULLABY

VICTOR DALEY

Oh, hush thee, my baby, the time it has come,
For the nuisance to pass here with trumpet and drum.
Oh, fear not the bugle, though loudly it blows –
'Tis the Salvation Army disturbs thy repose.

He chose the nom de plume, which means 'red branch', as a reference to the legendary Irish hero Cuchulainn, the mythical warrior chieftain. Cuchulainn trained to become a member of the Knights of the Red Branch in the region of Ulster where Daley was born.

Strangely it was this verse, rather than his more highly praised lyrical verse, that attracted some minor attention long after Daley's death in the 1940s and a collection entitled *Creeve Roe* was published in 1947.

Being of Irish birth and Australian inclination, Daley loved the underdog. He often wrote in praise of the liberated rebel spirit and was scathing in his attacks on the British establishment and homogenising nature of British culture.

In a poem called 'When London Calls', he exhorted Australian writers not to toe the line and write to please the English critics or the English public. He bemoans the fact that all gifted creative writers and artists are drawn to London:

They leave us – artists, singers, all –
When London calls aloud,
Commanding to her Festival
The gifted crowd.

In the poem the city of London is personified as a greedy evil sphinx:

She sits beside the ship-choked Thames,
Sad, weary, cruel, grand;
Her crown imperial gleams with gems
From many a land.

From overseas, and far away,
Come crowded ships and ships –
Grim-faced she gazes on them; yea,
With scornful lips.

The garden of the earth is wide;
Its rarest blooms she picks
To deck her board, this haggard-eyed
Imperatrix.

Sad, sad is she, and yearns for mirth;
With voice of golden guile
She lures men from the ends of earth
To make her smile.

The student of wild human ways
In wild new lands; the sage
With new great thoughts; the bard whose lays
Bring youth to age;

The painter young whose pictures shine
With colours magical;
The singer with the voice divine –
She lures them all.

In a chilling conclusion, the artist's creative juices are sucked dry and his talent destroyed:

The story-teller from the Isles
Upon the Empire's rim,
With smiles she welcomes – and her smiles
Are death to him.

For Her, whose pleasure is her law,
In vain the shy heart bleeds –
The Genius with the Iron jaw
Alone succeeds.

And when the Poet's lays grow bland,
And urbanised, and prim –
She stretches forth a jewelled hand
And strangles him.

She sits beside the ship-choked Thames
With Sphinx-like lips apart –
Mistress of many diadems –
Death in her heart!

Criticism of mother England, or anything British, was pretty daring stuff in Daley's day, but the *Bulletin* was often vehemently anti-Empire and editors like Archibald loved including the attacks on the British that appeared in verse under the name 'Creeve Roe'.

Daley saved his most savage satire for the Jubilee of Queen Victoria. While the nation was going dotty with celebrations and royal hysteria, he wrote a poem entitled 'A Treat for the London Poor', which took an alternative view of the ageing queen's triumphant procession through the poorer areas of London. I am amazed that it didn't land him in prison for sedition!

A TREAT FOR THE LONDON POOR

VICTOR DALEY

They are hungry; they are ragged; they are gaunt and hollow-eyed;
But their frowsy bosoms palpitate with fine old British pride;
And they'll belt their rags in tighter and they'll hoarsely cry,
'Hooray!'
When their good queen's circus passes on sexagenary day.
Oh the thunder of the drums,
And the cry of, 'Here she comes!'
Will be better than a breakfast to the natives of the slums.

Sixty years their gracious Queen has reigned a-holding up the sky,
And a-bringing round the seasons, hot and cold, and wet and dry;
And in all that time she's never done a deed deserving gaol –
So let joy-bells ring out madly and Delirium prevail!
Oh her Poor will blessings pour
On their Queen whom they adore;
When she blinks her puffy eyes at them they'll hunger never more.
She has reigned – aloft, sublime –
Sixty years – let joy-bells chime!
And these God-forgotten wretches were her subjects all that time!

Victor Daley was a dreamer and a drinker and a bohemian 'ne'er-do-well'. He neglected his wife and family and rarely had two bob in his pocket, or a permanent safe roof over his head. He was, however, totally aware of his own failings and honest about them.

He could write very funny pieces aimed at his own poverty and fecklessness, as illustrated by the story regarding bailiffs, those men employed to collect debts and evict people who had stopped paying their rent. Bailiffs were the lowest of the low, and figures of fun and ridicule to Daley, who had a great deal of experience with them. That story appears in Part 3 of this collection.

Here is Daley describing his 'working day':

OMARISM – A SELF PORTRAIT

VICTOR DALEY

With pen in hand and pipe in mouth,
And claret iced to quench my drouth,
I sit upon my balcony
That overlooks the sparkling sea,
Serenely gay, and cool, and bland –
With pipe in mouth and pen in hand.

This life I think is beautiful,
When at the jug I take a pull.
The harbor shines like azure silk;
The claret tastes like mother's milk;
Then to the pipe I turn again –
And then I trifle with the pen.

The red-faced neighbors townward go;
The air is in a furnace glow.
I watch them scorching as they pass,
Like flies beneath a burning glass –
Each clutching at the red-hot hour
For coin; their folly turns me sour.

The Business Man may fret and sweat
In his black coat, for etiquette,
And grow in shop and office old,
And gather wrinkles with his gold –
I sit in shirt-sleeves cool and bland,
With pipe in mouth and pen in hand.

The white clouds – idle they as I –
Like dreaming gods, at leisure lie
Upon the hill-crests. Smoke upcurls
From chimneys lazily, and girls

Below me, with bare, brown arms fine,
Are pegging linen on a line.

The great ships, from the world outside,
Steam slowly in with stately pride,
Their giant screws now gently spin;
'Tis good to watch them gliding in
From East, and West, and North, and South,
With jug in hand and pipe in mouth.

These visions fill me with content,
And I remember not the rent.
When with cool breezes comes the night
It will be time enough to write.
Then you shall see me start the band –
With pipe in mouth and pen in hand.

By far my favourite poem of Daley's is called 'Moderation', in which he claims not to want fame, respect, beautiful women or spiritual enlightenment, just the mundane day-to-day pleasures that we all know we should avoid. It is a poem I often recite to many friends who always seem to instantly make some connection to the verse.

MODERATION

VICTOR DALEY

I do not wish for wealth
Beyond a livelihood;
I do not ask for health
Uproariously good.

I do not care for men
To point with pride at me;
A model citizen
I do not wish to be.

I have no dream bizarre
Of strange erotic joy;
I want no avatar
Of Helena of Troy.

I do not crave the boon
Of Immortality;
I do not want the moon,
Not yet the rainbow's key.

I do not yearn for wings,
Or fins to swim the sea;
I merely want the things
That are not good for me.

By 1900 Daley was suffering noticeably from tuberculosis. He went to stay with friend and fellow poet E.J. Brady in Grafton for his health but his condition became worse. The Daley family was living in an impoverished state and some of his friends raised enough money to send him, finally, to New Caledonia, the island he had set out for from Adelaide all those years ago and never managed to reach.

It was thought the tropical climate might improve his condition but it was all in vain. He returned to Sydney and died at his home in December 1905.

He is buried in the Catholic section of Waverley Cemetery, not too far from his dear friends and great supporters Henry Lawson and J.F. Archibald.

Victor Daley was a dreamer and bohemian who drifted through life avoiding what many would have seen as his responsibilities. He was the epitome of the 'devil-may-care' poet, almost a caricature of how creative types are perceived by the more conservative members of society.

He wrote this poem about himself:

DREAMS

VICTOR DALEY

I have been dreaming all a summer day
Of rare and dainty poems I would write;
Love-lyrics delicate as lilac-scent,
Soft idylls woven of wind, and flower, and stream,
And songs and sonnets carven in fine gold.

The day is fading and the dusk is cold;
Out of the skies has gone the opal gleam,
Out of my heart has passed the high intent
Into the shadow of the falling night –
Must all my dreams in darkness pass away?

I have been dreaming all a summer day:
Shall I go dreaming so until Life's light
Fades in Death's dusk, and all my days are spent?
Ah, what am I the dreamer but a dream!
The day is fading and the dusk is cold.

My songs and sonnets carven in fine gold
Have faded from me with the last day-beam
That purple lustre to the sea-line lent,
And flushed the clouds with rose and chrysolite,
So days and dreams in darkness pass away.

I have been dreaming all a summer day
Of songs and sonnets carven in fine gold;
But all my dreams in darkness pass away
The day is fading, and the dusk is cold.

Victor Daley left his family destitute. His friends organised benefits, publications, dinners and theatrical shows to raise money to support his widow, but she died within a year of her husband

and the four surviving children went their own way, no one seems to know where.

It is a shame that Daley's verses are not better known today; he was regarded by poets whose names *have* survived as the best of the bunch, the 'sweetest singer' of them all. His mates loved him for his wit, friendship and good nature, and mourned his passing as the end of an era. Henry Lawson foresaw the fact that he would not be remembered as he should be:

VICTOR DALEY

HENRY LAWSON

And his death came in December,
When our summer was aglow,
Like a song that we remember,
Like a child's dream long ago,
And it brought Australia to him,
Her sweetest singer dead,
While in silence friends who knew him
Bowed their heads beside his bed.

While Australians in their blindness
Fail to realise their loss,
Place the wreath of loving kindness
And raise the simple cross.
For he taught us to be brothers
And he taught us to be brave,
And we'll banish pride and envy,
With a hand-clasp by his grave.

THE MOST IMPORTANT AUSTRALIAN EVER

If you asked a thousand Aussies in the street if they had ever heard of George Morrison, I bet you wouldn't get a 'yes'.

Ask if the name 'G.E. Morrison' rang a bell, or if the name 'Chinese Morrison' meant anything, and you might get one or two answering in the affirmative, although they would probably not remember what he did, exactly.

Yet, in terms of world history and events, George Morrison was, and possibly still is, the most important Australian who ever strode the planet. And, boy oh boy, did he stride the planet!

In 1879, at the age of eighteen, having finished his schooling at Geelong College, he walked from Geelong to Adelaide around the coast of southern Australia, about a thousand kilometres.

Having arrived in town he decided to go to the cricket to see the great South Australian wicketkeeper-batsman Affie Jarvis play, still wearing his walking clothes and haversack, and later recorded in his diary that he was made fun of by other spectators for his dress and that Jarvis was run out first ball.

Morrison would later walk back from the mouth of the Murray River to Geelong, having travelled the length of the Murray from Wodonga to the sea by canoe; walk from the Gulf of Carpentaria to Melbourne; and walk from Shanghai in China to Rangoon in Burma, a distance of almost 5000 kilometres (it took three months and he spent the grand sum of £18 on the journey). On that walk Morrison 'cheated' by using boats and horses at times.

But that was all in front of the young man who walked from Melbourne to Adelaide to see a cricket match.

Morrison's father owned, and was principal of, the Geelong College and his eldest son was already an avid collector and diary writer when he left the school. These were two interests that he would keep all his life. As a boy he obsessively collected stamps and shells. As a man he amassed the largest collection in the world of Chinese books, maps and manuscripts—which he sold to a Japanese businessman in 1917 for £35,000. It became the foundation collection of the famous Oriental Library in Tokyo.

Everywhere you look in Morrison's biography you find surprises. How one man could have managed so many diverse and outstanding achievements in one lifetime is beyond the comprehension of most of us mere mortals.

His father and brother were noted educationalists, both being headmasters of the family-owned Geelong College, which was eventually sold to the Presbyterian Church and is still going today.

George, however, was not interested in the sedentary life of an educator. His first choice of career was medicine and he completed his first year of study at Melbourne University before adventure and an urge to be a journalist took over.

Having sold the story of his walk to Adelaide to a newspaper, he started thinking up other treks and adventures that might make good copy for newspapers eager to thrill their readers with tales of Australia's more exotic and far-flung regions and wildernesses.

To this end he signed on as a crewman on a blackbirding ship, the *Lavinia*, sailing out of North Queensland, and wrote reports that helped turn the tide of public opinion against the thinly disguised slave trade that provided a workforce for the cane fields. He was able to balance his exciting seagoing adventures to the exotic islands of the Coral Sea with enough moral indignation to both thrill and influence the readers of his reports.

The ability to switch between diverse careers and interests was one amazing feature of Morrison's personality. It's not a surprise to learn that his adventure down the Murray and his other sporting and collecting interests resulted in a failed exam in his second year.

This minor setback led to the career change from medical student to crewman on a sailing ship, then journalist and moral crusader. His return to medicine would be similarly serendipitous.

As he was in tropical waters, Morrison decided to visit Port Moresby and Thursday Island and then Normanton, on the Gulf of Carpentaria.

Only twenty years before, the Burke and Wills expedition had set out with twenty men, camels, horses and tons of supplies and equipment to cross the continent south to north. It had proved a tragic failure; the desert had defeated the best efforts of British know-how, technology and planning.

In typical style, however, Morrison decided to walk back to Melbourne following the route taken by the intrepid explorers, in the middle of summer, alone and on foot. He managed it easily and later described the journey, 3200 kilometres through mostly barren wilderness, as 'a pleasant excursion' which he did not feel was deserving of praise, as it was really 'no feat of endurance'.

The *Times* of London certainly thought it was a feat worthy of mention and called it 'one of the most remarkable of pedestrian achievements'. They already had their eye on Morrison who would become, in a later phase of his incredible life, their best and bravest foreign correspondent.

Until that point Morrison's articles had been syndicated through the *Leader,* a regional Victorian newspaper. On his return to Melbourne, however, he wrote a letter to the *Age* criticising blackbirding as 'the Queensland slave trade', which led to questions being asked of the Queensland government, and initiated the first serious enquiry into the trade in 'kanaka' labour in that state.

Although the Queensland government found no need to act to change things, the governor, Sir Anthony Musgrave, was able to diplomatically concur with Morrison's opinions in letters to influential friends in Britain and the days of the 'kanaka trade' were numbered from that time.

Another result of that letter, and the preceding articles written aboard the *Lavinia*, was that Morrison was employed and financed by the much-respected *Age* and *Sydney Morning Herald* to explore and cross New Guinea, recently annexed by the Queensland government as a protectorate.

He set out from Port Moresby, in July 1883, for the unknown interior with a party of 25, including renowned bushman John Lyons, some other European adventurers, two Malays and quite a few natives. They trekked into the unexplored jungles and mountains for 40 days until his adventurous spirit and bravery, accompanied by a good dose of youthful recklessness and arrogant bravado, almost cost him his life.

Morrison was all of twenty years old at the time.

The local tribes became increasingly hostile as the expedition penetrated the jungle. Finally there was an all-out raid on their camp and many of the supplies were carried away. In the midst of the attack, Morrison shot and killed a native. Next day there was a great sound of wailing echoing through the jungle and the men accompanying Morrison, both European and native, were adamant that retreat was essential, at least to neutral tribal territory.

Although Morrison was sick with remorse and 'felt like a murderer', he disagreed with the overwhelming general opinion and went ahead—the others followed reluctantly.

When crossed spears and a shield were found blocking the jungle path, his companions again urged discretion and retreat.

Once again Morrison insisted on continuing, past the grim warning, and once again his companions followed, at a distance, only to come across their intrepid leader lying in a pool of his own blood with spears protruding from his head, near his right eye, and his stomach.

Led by Lyons, who broke off the spear shafts and tended the wounds (and to whom Morrison always said he owed his life), the party retreated hastily the way they had come. With Morrison either strapped to a horse or carried in a blanket they reached Port Moresby, remarkably, in eleven days. There the young adventurer received some emergency medical attention but he did not reach the hospital at Cooktown for more than a month.

One day, on the ship returning to Cooktown, Morrison, in

constant pain and seriously ill, sat up and blew his nose—and an inch-long piece of wood flew out of his nostril.

In spite of what he saw as a failed expedition, Morrison's party had penetrated further into New Guinea than any European.

After a week in hospital at Cooktown, Morrison sailed to Melbourne where, 170 days after the attack, a surgeon removed the remainder of one spear, which had made its way to the back of his throat. This was done by taking it up through his throat and out of his nose—without anaesthetic.

The other spear was still embedded in his abdomen and his father decided to send young George to the famous surgeon John Chiene, professor of surgery at Edinburgh University, to have it removed.

Once the removal of a tapering spearhead 'the size of your second finger' was successfully achieved, Morrison decided that this was an excellent opportunity to resume his medical studies. He duly graduated as a Bachelor of Medicine and Master of Chemistry from Edinburgh University in August 1887.

After his graduation Morrison, having spent several years in the one place, decided it was again time to travel, so he headed to Canada, the USA and West Indies and worked as a medical officer in several places before returning to Europe, where he became the medical officer at the Rio Tinto mine in Spain.

Tiring of that position he travelled to Morocco and became physician to the Sharif of Wazan in Tangier, which gave him free time to explore the desert and mountain areas of Africa, where few Europeans had ever travelled.

Morrison had an interest in neurology, perhaps associated with his horrific head injuries suffered in New Guinea, and decided to seek out and study under Dr Jean-Martin Charcot, the pioneer of neurological medicine and anatomical pathology in Paris.

Having done that, the 27-year-old returned to Australia in 1890 and took up a position as resident surgeon at the hospital at Ballarat. He was there for two years before the wanderlust struck again and he was off, after a disagreement with the hospital committee.

This time he travelled through the Philippines, Hong Kong then into Siam (Thailand). He moved on to China and later Japan.

He studied the work of the missionaries and was often assumed to be one in China, where Christian missionaries where by far the most common Europeans.

While in Japan he decided it was time for another walk. He was now a mature 31-year-old and, for reasons best known to himself, decided he'd like to walk from Shanghai in China to Rangoon in Burma.

He set out in February 1894, unarmed and mostly staying with Christian missionaries along the way, or in villages. He had very little Chinese language and said openly that he started out with the typical racist opinions that most Australians had towards the Chinese. He hired guides from time to time and his diary noted that the entire journey cost something in the vicinity of £20.

From Rangoon he travelled through India and proceeded to Calcutta where he contracted a severe fever and almost died.

I have no idea how, but Morrison had somehow managed to complete his doctoral thesis sometime in between all his travels and adventures. He decided to recuperate in Australia then head back to Edinburgh and submit his thesis and gain his Masters degree, which he subsequently did.

His journal of his long walk through China was published as a book, *An Australian in China, Being the Narrative of a Quiet Journey Across China to Burma*, and was very successful and popular as a contemporary account of Chinese and Burmese provincial life.

It may astound readers to realise that all I have written about this remarkable Australian so far has been a mere preliminary prologue to what he is mostly remembered for in world politics and history. His real achievements were yet to come.

Morrison was approached by the *Times* to take up an appointment as a special correspondent in Asia. This was to be a 'secret' commission for two reasons. Firstly, it was the first position of its kind and the newspaper was not certain it would be a permanent one. Secondly, it involved Morrison working, for the first time but certainly not the last, as a secret agent for the British.

Late in 1895 he travelled via Saigon into Indo-China as far

as Bangkok, reporting on French activities in Cambodia. His superiors at the *Times*, and the foreign office praised his public and secret reports, and his position was soon made permanent. In March 1897 he was stationed in Peking (Beijing) as the first official Chinese correspondent of the *Times*.

Peking would be Morrison's home base for the next twenty years. He would become, in that period, the world's leading expert on the politics of China and the region and survive the Boxer Rebellion, in which he helped save countless lives and after which he wrote the most reliable and definitive history of the crisis.

He would also read his own obituary, be credited with precipitating the Russo-Japanese War, be chief advisor to the ruler of China, bring about China's entry into World War I and be part of the Chinese advisory team for the Peace Conference at Versailles after the declaration of peace.

The Boxer Rebellion, in which Christian Chinese and missionaries were slaughtered by a group called 'The Righteous Fists', whose members practised martial arts and were therefore called 'Boxers' by the Europeans, culminated in all ex-patriot and diplomatic foreigners being blockaded in the diplomatic enclave in Peking for 55 days—besieged by the Boxers and the Imperial Army, after the Dowager Empress decided to support the Boxers and ousted her nephew, the Emperor.

Morrison acted with his customary bravery throughout the siege, plotting and scheming with elements of the Chinese army who supported negotiation. He also fought his way in and out of the blockade at times to rescue Christian Chinese and European families who were being attacked.

At one point Morrison led a party of twenty British troops and a few Americans to a Christian area near Nanting Church where Christian converts were being tortured and slaughtered by Boxers. He reported that they found 46 Chinese Christians dead with their hands tied and a gang of Boxers about to kill another hundred. Morrison's patrol saved more than a hundred and he reported casually, 'All the Boxers were killed, only one dared to face us, I myself killed at least six.'

Those rescued joined thousands more in a safe area, a palace called 'The Fu', and Morrison and others made many daring journeys between the besieged legation and The Fu to make sure the people there were safe and to tend to the wounded.

On one such occasion his friend Captain Strouts was shot dead beside him and Morrison wounded as they made their way to The Fu with some Japanese military who were also trapped in the siege. He wrote:

> Another bullet had splintered and some fragments struck me . . . When they were cut out I fainted again and then vomited, the pain being intense, though I have no reason to believe it was one half as great as other pain I have suffered.

The following day a false report, posted by another newspaper but carried by the *Times*, reported that the Boxers had butchered all Europeans in Peking. The *Times* then ran an obituary of Morrison, praising him for being the most accurate and reliable reporter in China whose reports were always days ahead of, and more accurate than, any other news or 'official' bulletins.

Had they waited they would have received a more accurate account of the situation from the man whose praises there were singing in print, supposedly posthumously. As it was, Morrison was one of the few people in history who ever read his own official obituary.

The frightened besieged diplomats and their families saw the tall handsome Australian, often dishevelled and untidy, as a saviour. One American woman wrote:

> Not a foreign man on the place to protect us . . . we waited . . . and our reward came when we saw down the valley a dusty figure ambling along on a dusty Chinese pony, crossing from the direction of Fengtai . . . it was Dr Morrison.

When the siege was lifted with the arrival of British, German, Russian and French troops, the situation was reversed with suspected Boxers beheaded and many innocent Chinese slaughtered by rampaging troops, mostly Russian.

Morrison's next plan involved getting rid of the Russian threat to China. Russia challenged Britain's influence in China and therefore her empire states of India and Burma. When it became apparent that Russia, through demands and intimidation (about which Morrison had inside information), had taken over the Chinese warm-weather port of Port Arthur, Morrison declared, 'There must be war, there *shall* be war!'

There was war. Britain could not oppose another foreign power like Russia directly, so the Machiavellian Morrison decided the Japanese should take on the role of China's protector. He helped engineer the surprise attack on the Russian navy by Japanese troops at Port Arthur and rode into the captured city with the Japanese general who led the attack. Morrison was described as 'the author of the Russo-Japanese War'. Tsar Nicholas's determination to continue this unwinnable war was one of the factors that led to the Russian Revolution.

The influence on world affairs exerted by this doctor from Geelong would, however, grow to even greater dimensions. When the Manchu Dynasty finally ended with the abdication of the last emperor in 1912, the military powerbroker Yuan Shikai become the President of All China. In 1915 he declared himself Emperor. Morrison was his chief advisor, virtually the foreign secretary of China.

Although he was a supporter of Japan in order to prevent Russian pressures on China from escalating, and actually precipitated the war between Japan and Russia in 1904, he later saw Japan as a similar threat and warned Australian prime ministers Deakin and Hughes about Japanese expansionism. He was involved in negotiating the Japanese relationship with China and convinced the Japanese to water down their infamous Twenty-One Demands made to China in 1915.

Morrison campaigned for conscription in Australia in World War I, turned down the post of foreign editor of the *Times*, was instrumental in changing British policy on the opium trade in India, and considered taking the position of British Minister in China.

I think that will suffice to give a brief outline of the life and times of George Ernest 'Chinese' Morrison. Whole books have been written about him but, oddly, he is hardly remembered today.

His private and personal life was also quite fascinating, and his romantic and erotic adventures were recorded in his diaries in similar detail to the political and social observations.

He married his New Zealand-born secretary Jennie Robin in 1912. He was 50 and she was 22. They had three sons who all graduated from Cambridge University. Their eldest son, Ian, was killed while reporting on the Korean War for the *Times*.

Morrison did not live to see his sons graduate. His health began to deteriorate in 1919 and he realised he had little time left, so he retired to England where he died on 30 May 1920.

Banjo Paterson, in his role as a war correspondent, visited China to report on the Boxer Rebellion. Commenting on world political figures, he once wrote that he had met and spoken with Winston Churchill, Cecil Rhodes and George Morrison and, in his opinion, Morrison was the 'most impressive' of the three.

So, if anyone ever asks you to name the most important Australian that ever lived, don't hesitate to answer. You will certainly surprise them.

Just say, 'George Morrison—ever heard of him?'

VOICE OF THE INVISIBLE PEOPLE

She was born and brought up in the Melbourne seaside suburb of Brighton. Her parents were Australian born, respectable Catholics of Irish descent. Her mother was related to the Earl of Drogheda and her father was a successful and well-known real estate and finance agent.

Now, Brighton is a respectable middle-class suburb and hardly the place where you would expect to find a young girl who would one day become not only a great poet, but also a radical, freethinking pioneer of workers' rights and women's liberation.

She was educated at the Sacred Heart convent in nearby Glen Iris, and the Mary's Mount convent at Ballarat. When she was eight her father suffered financial ruin and went to Western Australia, leaving his wife to raise the four kids, of which she was the oldest. Her mother took in boarders and lived hand-to-mouth on family handouts and charity.

She was a sickly child who suffered from a congenital heart defect and had a severe attack of rheumatic fever as a child. Later, as an adult, she contracted tuberculosis, which ended her life prematurely at the age of just 36.

Her name was Lesbia Venner Keogh and she was one of the most remarkable women who ever lived in Australia.

Lesbia is remembered today by only a tiny handful of feminists and poetry historians and aficionados. For many years after her death, she was remembered by almost no one. Her poetry was all but lost. In her lifetime only a dozen or so poems ever saw the light of day, and for decades after her death it was assumed her writings had been lost in a fire.

Until the 1980s when a small limited edition of her poems was printed and distributed, no one had ever heard of Lesbia Keogh/ Harford, much less read her poetry.

Let me tell you about the other side of this young, sickly, Catholic girl from a respectable family.

She was one of the first women in Australia to graduate with a law degree.

It was only ten years since Ada Evans had broken the male dominance in law by being the first female in Australia to complete a law degree, only to be denied entry to the Bar on the basis of her gender. Lesbia enrolled at the University of Melbourne in 1912 and paid her way through by teaching art classes in schools. She graduated Bachelor of Laws at the end of 1916, ironically in the same graduating class as the great right-wing Australian politician, and later prime minister, Robert Menzies.

Lesbia was an openly bisexual advocate of free love. Later in her brief life she married Pat Harford, a socialist and sometime artist with a drinking problem. But, from an early age, she had affairs, some long term, with men and women, including the academic Katie Lush, philosophy tutor at Ormond College, and the famous communist leader Guido Barrachi, co-founder of the Communist Party of Australia, who was jailed for sedition in 1918 and who credited her with showing him the right way into the 'revolutionary working class movement'.

She renounced her Catholicism and joined the revolutionary socialist Christian reformer Frederick Sinclaire in his church of fellowship and took part in services with him.

She went to work in clothing factories and was state vice-president of the Federated Clothing and Allied Trades Union, and she campaigned against conscription in World War I and was a member of the IWW (International Workers of the World), or 'Wobblies', the socialist movement that swept the planet at that time.

In 1918 she moved to Sydney in order to campaign for the

release of the 'Sydney Twelve', who were notoriously framed and convicted on charges of arson, treason, sedition and forgery during the vitriolic conscription campaign and later exonerated after an inquiry into the trial.

Lesbia worked in sweat shops with working-class girls in Sydney in order to help them fight for better conditions, and she wrote scathingly about the wealthy. She was a maid to the Fairfax family for a brief time.

All this makes her a truly remarkable Australian character, but I haven't mentioned the main reason we should never forget Lesbia Harford.

She wrote truly exquisite, funny, tender, angry and satirical poetry, unmatched in our literary history for its brevity and colour and cutting insight into the world of a liberated woman of the early twentieth century and also the world of working-class girls and women of her time.

Her love poems, written to both men and women, are raw in their honesty and true expressions of everyday emotions surrounding those we love. They are alive with detail and humour. Her descriptions of domestic life are sharp and often poignant, even harsh. She was never self-pitying and always brutally honest in her verse, yet her poetry is filled with colour, life, accurate observation and wit.

I always think of her poetry as being the literary equivalent to impressionist art. Here is her impression of the Melbourne Cup:

THE MELBOURNE CUP

LESBIA HARFORD

I like the riders
Clad in rose and blue;
Their colours glitter
And their horses too.
Swift go the riders
On incarnate speed.
My thought can scarcely

Follow where they lead.
Delicate, strong, long
Lines of colour flow,
And all the people
Tremble as they go.

Here is one of her observational short poems about relationships and gender differences:

I BOUGHT A RED HAT

LESBIA HARFORD

I bought a red hat
To please my lover.
He will hardly see it
When he looks me over,
Though it's a fine hat.
Yet he never misses
Noticing my red mouth
When it's shaped for kisses.

Her poems about domestic life always make me smile. This one, with its description of a young couple's typical poverty and its openly sexual reference, is one of my favourites:

INVENTORY

LESBIA HARFORD

We've a room
That we call home,
With a bed in it,
And a table
And some chairs,
A to Z in it.
There's a mirror,
And a safe,

And a lamp in it.
Were there more,
Our mighty love
Might get cramp in it.

Her poetry about the nature of love and the phases of a relationship is unequalled in Australian writing. Few women wrote publicly at all in her day, and none wrote so honestly about their feelings regarding love and sex.

Some of her poetry of early romantic awakening is so direct and mundane that its simplicity belies the fact that it really describes feelings with which we immediately connect:

EVERY NIGHT I HURRY HOME

LESBIA HARFORD

Every night I hurry home to see
If a letter's there from you to me.
Every night I bow my head and say,
'There's no word at all from him today.'

When she became a 'liberated' woman, Lesbia was able to write with an honesty far ahead of her time, about sexual love and feminine feelings:

I USED TO BE AFRAID

LESBIA HARFORD

I used to be afraid to meet
The lovers going down our street.
I'd try to shrink to half my size
And blink and turn away my eyes
But now I'm one of them I know
I never need have bothered so.
And they won't mind it if I stare
Because they'll never know I'm there

Or if they do, they're proud to be
Fond lovers for the world to see.

She always managed to say a lot in a few words; that is what I like about her love poems. They are not prolonged descriptive ballads, just extremely short poems celebrating the joy of love—full of wit and honesty:

WHAT WERE THE GOOD OF STARS

LESBIA HARFORD

What were the good of stars if none looked on them
But mariners, astronomers and such!
The sun and moon and stars were made for lovers.
I know that much.

She also realised the realities of relationships and understood the marital condition in a time when it was not fashionable to be quite so pragmatic about marriage and long-term love:

I'M LIKE ALL LOVERS

LESBIA HARFORD

I'm like all lovers, wanting love to be
A very mighty thing for you and me.
In certain moods your love should be a fire
That burnt your very life up in desire.
The only kind of love then to my mind
Would make you kiss my shadow on the blind
And walk seven miles each night to see it there,
Myself within, serene and unaware.

But you're as bad. You'd have me watch the clock
And count your coming while I mend your sock.
You'd have my mind devoted day and night

To you and care for you and your delight.
Poor fools, who each would have the other give
What spirit must withhold if it would live.
You're not my slave, I wish you not to be.
I love yourself and not your love for me.

The self that goes ten thousand miles away
And loses thought of me for many a day.
And you loved me for loving much beside
But now you want a woman for your bride.
Oh, make no woman of me, you who can,
Or I will make a husband of a man.
By my unwomanly love that sets you free
Love all myself, but least the woman in me.

Of course, she did marry Pat Harford and it was as she predicted, a bittersweet experience that led eventually to separation and estrangement. They lived together for a time at her mother's boarding house in the Melbourne suburb of Elsternwick, and after they separated he stayed in Melbourne and later achieved some success as a painter in the impressionist school. Lesbia was able to recognise the things she loved in him, despite the fact that his character was mostly that of a dissolute, often aggressive, alcoholic:

Pat wasn't Pat last night at all.
He was the rain,
The Spring,
Young Dionysus, white and warm,
Lilac and everything.

Her verses also show a deep and even-handed understanding of gender differences—based upon the most obvious observations:

ALL KNOWLEDGE

LESBIA HARFORD

I know more about flowers,
And Pat knows about ships.
'Schooner' and 'barquentine'
Are words of note on his lips.
Even 'schooner, barque-rigged'
Has meaning for him. And yet
I don't believe he knows
'Hearts' ease' from 'mignonette'.
And whenever the daffodils,
Like visiting golden dames,
Honour our humble flat . . .
He has to ask their names.

Lesbia wrote out her verses in notebooks in copperplate script and was not keen to publish them during her lifetime. She often read or even sang them to tunes she composed and frequently sent them in letters to friends. When friends suggested publication, she said she was 'in no hurry to be read'.

Her poems, while being universal in their understanding of the human condition, and certainly still resonating with meaning to this male reader almost a century later, were deeply personal observations about her own life. She even wrote insightful verses about why she was the way she was:

FATHERLESS

LESBIA HARFORD

I've had no man
To guard and shelter me,
Guide and instruct me
From mine infancy.
No lord of earth
To show me day by day

What things a girl should do
And what she should say.
I have gone free
Of manly excellence
And hold their wisdom
More than half pretence.
For since no male
Has ruled me or has fed,
I think my own thoughts
In my woman's head.

Several of her poems were published in the journal of the Melbourne Literary Club in 1921 and, after her death, several were included in *An Australasian Anthology* in 1927. Nettie Palmer published four of her poems as a tribute to Lesbia when she died; then, in 1941, a small selection was published with Commonwealth Literary Fund assistance and distributed among friends. After she died her father took her notebooks and they were believed to be lost in a fire that destroyed his shack.

The real power in Lesbia's writing is apparent mostly in her poems about the lives of working women and the unfairness she saw in Australian society; almost always this was seen as between females, the wealthy and the poor who served them. She wrote touchingly about the squalid lives and seemingly inescapable drudgery of working-class women:

WORK-GIRLS' HOLIDAY

LESBIA HARFORD

A lady has a thousand ways
Of doing nothing all her days,
And so she thinks that they're well spent,
She can be idle and content.
But when I have a holiday
I have forgotten how to play.
I could rest idly under trees

When there's some sun or little breeze
Or if the wind should prove too strong
Could lie in bed the whole day long.
But any leisured girl would say
That that was waste of holiday.
Perhaps if I had weeks to spend
In doing nothing without end,
I might learn better how to shirk
And never want to go to work.

She understood also the horror of unemployment, when working people had no fallback position and lived day to day:

THE WIFE

LESBIA HARFORD

He's out of work!
I tell myself a change should mean a chance,
And he must look for changes to advance,
And he, of all men, really needs a jerk.
But I hate change.
I like my kitchen with its pans and pots
That shine like new although we've used them lots.
I wouldn't like a kitchen that was strange.
And it's not true
All changes are for better. Some are worse.
A man had rather work, though work's a curse,
Than mope at home with not a thing to do.
No surer thing
Than that he'll get another job. But soon!
Or else I'll have to change. This afternoon
Would be the time, before I sell my ring.

Her best polemics in verse, to me, are her satirical poems. Often these take the form of a working girl speaking her mind:

SKIRT MACHINIST

LESBIA HARFORD

I am making great big skirts
For great big women –
Amazons who've fed and slept
Themselves inhuman.
Such long skirts, not less than two
And forty inches.
Thirty round the waist for fear
The webbing pinches.
There must be tremendous tucks
On those round bellies.
Underneath the limbs will shake
Like wine-soft jellies.
I am making such big skirts
And all so heavy,
I can see their wearers at
A lord-mayor's levy.
I, who am so small and weak
I have hardly grown,
Wish the skirts I'm making less
Unlike my own.

As she never meant most of her verse to be published, her honesty often verged on the libellous. She worked as a maid in the Fairfax mansion at one stage and wrote this poem, unambiguously satirising one of the family:

MISS MARY FAIRFAX

LESBIA HARFORD

Every day Miss Mary goes her rounds,
Through the splendid house and through the grounds,
Looking if the kitchen table's white,
Seeing if the great big fire's alight,

Finding specks on shining pans and pots,
Never praising much, but scolding lots.
If the table's white, she does not see
Roughened hands that once were ivory.
It is fires, not cheeks, that ought to glow;
And if eyes are dim, she doesn't know.
Poor Miss Mary! Poor for all she owns,
Since the things she loves are stocks and stones.

Her brief spell working as a maid inspired her most sarcastic poem. It is in the form of a conversation between a wealthy woman seeking help from an employment agency and the voice of reality and social conscious:

A PARLOURMAID

LESBIA HARFORD

I want a parlourmaid.

Well, let me see
If you were God, what kind of maid she'd be.

She would be tall,
She would be fair,
She would have slender limbs,
A delicate air;
And yet for all her beauty
She would walk
Among my guests unseen
And through their talk
Her voice would be the sweet voice of a bird,
Not listened to, though heard.

And now I know the girl you have in mind
Tell me her duties, if you'd be so kind.

Why, yes!
She must know names of wines
And never taste them –
Must handle fragile cups
And never break them –
Must fill my rooms with flowers
And never wear them –
Must serve my daughter's secrets
And not share them.

Madam, you are no God, that's plain to see.
I'll just repeat what you have said to me.
You say your maid must look in Helen fashion
Golden and white
And yet her loveliness inspire no passion,
Give no delight.
Your intimate goods of home must owe their beauty
To this girl's care
But she'll not overstep her path of duty
Nor seek to share
Through loving or enjoying or possessing
The least of them.
Why, she's not human, by your own confessing,
And you condemn
Your rational self in every word you're speaking!
Please understand
You'll find the hollow maiden you are seeking
In fairyland.

For many years Lesbia had suffered from tuberculosis. She managed to complete her articles with a Melbourne law firm in 1926, but she died at St Vincent's Hospital aged 36 on 5 July 1927 of lung and heart failure, without ever practising law.

Although she renounced her Catholicism at an early age and lived a bohemian life in many ways, she remained a great believer in the power of the human spirit, the sanctity of life and the need for dignity in human affairs. Oddly, she also never lost her belief in the power of prayer:

I AM NO MYSTIC

LESBIA HARFORD

I am no mystic. All the ways of God
Are dark to me.
I know not if he lived or if he died
In agony.
My every act has reference to man.
Some human need
Of this one, or of that, or of myself
Inspires the deed.
But when I hear the Angelus, I say
A Latin prayer
Hoping the dim incanted words may shine
Some way, somewhere.
Words and a will may work upon my mind
Till ethics turn
To that transcendent mystic love with which
The Seraphim burn.

After Lesbia's death, her mother made some attempts to have her work published and, as previously stated, Nettie Palmer had a small print edition published through the National Library in 1941.

As it turned out, her exercise books of poems were not burnt and are now in the Mitchell Library archives.

Some renewed awareness of her work occurred in the 1980s and a feminist publication of some poems appeared which attracted little general interest. In Melbourne, the Victorian Women Lawyers' Association give a biennial speech in her honour.

It would be nice to think that her work will one day receive the attention and honour it deserves. She was a woman ahead of her time and, to me, an heroic woman and great Australian who was the champion, and the voice, of the 'Invisible People'.

THE INVISIBLE PEOPLE

LESBIA HARFORD

When I go into town at half past seven
Great crowds of people stream across the ways,
Hurrying, although it's only half past seven.
They are the invisible people of the days.

When you go in to town about eleven
The hurrying, morning crowds are hid from view.
Shut in the silent buildings at eleven
They toil to make life meaningless for you.

THE PRINCESS AND THE PIE

We are a nation of 'pie eaters' and it's mostly the fault of the Sargent family!

George Sargent was born in Warwickshire, England, in 1858 and trained as a baker. He migrated to Sydney and worked in a George Street bakery where he met a single mum, Charlotte Foster from Woolloomooloo, who managed a cake shop. Charlotte was pretty and popular and a good saleswoman with a young son to care for.

It was a perfect match. George and Charlotte were married in 1883 and ran a bakery in Glebe. They worked hard and were successful but lacked the capital to start their own business.

They had a stroke of luck when a win in the Tattersall's sweep gave them enough money to buy a small bakery in Darlinghurst and by 1890 they were baking 700 loaves of bread a day.

Then George became ill and they were forced to sell, so Charlotte went back to cakes and pastries and they opened a shop in Oxford Street, Paddington. It was there they began making small meat pies, which they sold for a penny.

It was a stroke of genius and the cheap tasty pies were a big success. Charlotte had a flair for promotion and theatrics and called herself 'The Princess' and gave George, with his handlebar moustache, the nickname 'The Colonel'.

Sargent's Pies were so popular that they moved the business into the city and set up in Hunter Street in 1895.

After five years of being the most popular fast food outlet in Sydney, they were able to sell the booming business, set up

Charlotte's son, Hartley, who was now 22 and had been part of the business all his life, in a bakery at Manly and set off on a world tour.

Hartley married in 1900 and by 1901 had opened two more bakeries in Pitt Street and refreshment rooms in George Street.

When George and Charlotte returned from travelling the globe and tried to restart their business, they were promptly sued by the company they had sold to in Hunter Street.

The solution was to join Hartley in a partnership and in 1906 they formed Sargents Ltd.

In 1909 Sargents became a public company with George as chairman. George took care of the business side of things while Charlotte looked after the customers and staff, and business boomed.

Sargents' refreshment rooms established a reputation for quality food and good service from attractive waitresses. They opened in Melbourne and soon had control of 36 outlets, restaurants and shops, a factory, a catering business and function centres.

The Sargents never forgot their humble origins and were famously generous supporters of charity. They raised more than £4000 for the war effort when Hartley was wounded and taken prisoner in World War I. They also helped returned soldiers and soldiers' wives, widows and children, and the company gave free meals to servicemen and their families.

George and Charlotte lived with their adopted daughter at Vaucluse, where George died in 1921. Charlotte continued to run the company until her death in 1924.

Hartley, who suffered from poor health after the war, died in a fall from a cliff near his home at Medlow Bath in the Blue Mountains just three months after his mother's death.

Hartley's five children stayed involved in the business which continued as a public company; it is still going today after many mergers and takeovers.

That great Aussie icon, the meat pie as we know it, was the brainchild of Charlotte and George Sargent, 'The Princess' and 'The Colonel'. God bless 'em!

THE BARD OF CUP WEEK

One poet that most Aussies *do* know is C.J. Dennis.

He was the most popular poet in Australia for many years at the beginning of the twentieth century and is known for *The Sentimental Bloke* and his children's verse. Poems like 'Triantiwontigongolope' and 'The Ant Explorer' are favourites even today and are among the most anthologised children's poems in Australian history.

What most Australians, especially those born outside of Victoria, do *not* know is that Dennis wrote more than 3000 poems about a huge variety of subjects, including whole series on birds, roads of Victoria, all the characters in a generic country town, the streets of Melbourne, a group of philosophising pensioners, and timely events like feats of aviation, new discoveries and the deaths of great Australians. He also wrote a whole book of political satire in verse called *The Glugs of Gosh*.

His daily poems, written for the *Herald-Sun* newspaper, are a chronicle of Australian social history from 1922 until his death in 1938.

For me, a real measure of his talent is shown in the fact that he wrote several poems each year about one event, the Melbourne Cup. No writer has ever captured the flavour of the city's Spring Racing Carnival like C.J. Dennis.

Dennis found new angles and perspectives time and again as he celebrated the wonderful 'Aussieness' of 'Cup Week'. His ability to find such variety for his racing verses provides proof for the old adage that racing reflects life itself and is truly the 'sport of kings and deadbeats'.

'Den', as he was known both to his work colleagues and readers during his time at the *Herald-Sun*, was the poet who best captured the common Australian character and lifestyle. He was an unpretentious observer and chronicler of the average Aussie.

Clarence Michael James Stanislaus Dennis was born in Auburn, South Australia, in 1876, to James Dennis and his second wife Catherine. Due to the boy's and the mother's ill health and frailty, Dennis was looked after in his early years by his mother's maiden aunts who lived nearby. His father ran the Beetaloo Hotel in the township of Laura.

Dennis's mother died in 1890 leaving his father with three sons and a hotel to look after. This was never going to work successfully, so two of his mother's unmarried sisters moved to Laura to help with the children's upbringing. For some time in his teens Dennis attended the Christian Brothers' College in Adelaide but had returned to Laura by the age of seventeen and took a job as a clerk.

At nineteen he published his first poem in the local newspaper, the *Laura Standard*. Some time later, after stints as a barman in his father's hotel and some time spent in Broken Hill, he worked as a writer on the staff of the *Critic*, an Adelaide weekly newspaper, finally ending up as the journal's editor.

In 1905 he started a threepenny weekly newspaper called the *Gadfly*, which lasted about three years. After two years of editing the *Gadfly*, Dennis left Adelaide and went to try his luck in Melbourne.

He worked as a freelance journalist in Melbourne and joined a small community of artists that had been established in a sort of camp in the Dandenong Ranges at a place called Toolangi, about 40 miles east of Melbourne. Apart from a brief interlude in Sydney, Dennis lived in this area for pretty much the rest of his life.

Songs of a Sentimental Bloke was published in 1916 and by 1917 Dennis was the most prosperous writer in Australia. The book has never been out of print.

The people who inhabit Dennis's poems are real men and women. Unlike Banjo Paterson, who wrote about larger than life characters and unusual, memorable events, Dennis wrote about everyday people and everyday things.

Although he was, like Henry Lawson, involved in Labor politics early in his life, Dennis's verse exhibits none of Lawson's polemic and social reform agenda. Where Lawson's verse reveals a striving for 'something better' and a sense of loss, Dennis is always happy with life 'as it is'.

Although both Lawson and Dennis struggled at times with the demon drink, their lives could not have been more different in terms of outlook and philosophy. While Lawson was a tortured soul and a 'sad case' in his later years, Dennis appears to have found peace of mind at Toolangi with his wife and his garden, and it shows in his verse.

There *are* stories of Dennis's wife holding his head under the garden tap in order to get him to work on his *Herald-Sun* poem, but his daily contribution always made the train and the quality of verse he could produce on demand is astounding.

Dennis not only wrote sometimes hilarious, sometimes touching, celebratory verse about current events, he often did so within hours of the event and the poem would appear in the *Herald-Sun* the following day.

He celebrated such momentous events as Bert Hinkler's landing at Darwin, the death of Nellie Melba, and Phar Lap's Melbourne Cup victory with verse that appeared in the *Herald-Sun* the next day. What astonishes me is that it is damn fine verse, too!

When it came to Cup Week in Melbourne, Dennis was in his element. Each year he would produce at least one, often two, poems celebrating the social phenomenon of the Spring Racing Carnival.

His keen observation was always directed at the real people for whom Cup Week came as a blessed relief from the rat race and everyday grind, especially in the years of the Great Depression.

In the year of Phar Lap's victory, 1930, Dennis produced one of his funniest Melbourne Cup poems. Entitled 'The Barber's Story', it is written from the point of view of a barber who, the day after the Cup, attempts to make conversation with a surly customer who has, rather obviously, backed the second favourite, Tregilla.

Phar Lap won the Cup of 1930 at the shortest price ever, 11 to 8. It was a small field of only fifteen, with the Depression and Phar

Lap's dominance of racing keeping many owners from starting their horses. The rest of the field were all at 16 to 1 or better, except Tregilla.

Many punters backed Tregilla, with 7 stone 9 pounds, to beat Phar Lap, who carried the huge weight of 9 stone 12 pounds, 15 pounds over weight for age. Tregilla was a talented four-year-old who finished second to Phar Lap at weight-for-age in the W.S. Cox Plate and the Melbourne Stakes in the lead-up to the Cup. He had won the Australian Derby earlier that year.

Phar Lap won easily by three lengths slowing down. Tregilla started at 5 to 1 and ran seventh. This verse by C.J. Dennis appeared in the *Herald-Sun* the following day.

Blithely unaware of the reason for his customer's surly mood, the barber goes on and on about how wonderful Phar Lap's victory was:

'Mornin',' I sez to 'im. Gloomy, 'e seemed to be.
Glum an' unsociable, comes in the shop
'Mornin',' I sez to 'im, 'e don't say anythin'.
'You're next,' I sez; and 'e sits with a flop.

'Great Cup?' I sez to 'im. Shakin' the wrappin's out.
He don't say nothin'; but jist give a grunt.
'Great win?' I sez to 'im, Smilin' encouragin'.
'Wonderful way that 'e come to the front.'

He don't reply to me. Sits sorta glarin' like.
'Phar Lap,' I sez to 'im. 'Wonder 'orse, what?
Have a win yestidy?' Still 'e don't answer me.
'Phar Lap,' I sez, 'He made hacks of the lot.'

The barber then goes on to compound the error by commenting:

'Champeen,' I sez to 'im. 'Wonderful populer . . .
This 'ere Tregilla, 'e never showed up . . .
'Phar Lap,' I sez to 'im, 'Must be a wonder 'orse.
But that Tregilla run bad in the Cup.'

Even when his customer vents his frustration with an outburst in which Tregilla is declared a 'Cab-horse!' the barber remains totally insensitive to his customer's state of mind:

'What?' 'e come back at me, lookin' peculiar,
Red in the face, so I thought 'e would choke.
'Cab-horse!' 'e sez to me, nasty an' venomous,
Real disagreeable sort of a bloke.

'Tregilla!?' 'e sez to me, glarin' real murderous.
'Tregilla!!?' 'e barks at me. 'That 'airy goat!'
Surly, 'e seemed to me, man couldn't talk to 'im . . .
'Hair-cut?' I sez to 'im. 'No!' 'e sez . . . 'Throat!'

It was a favourite device of Dennis's to find some aspect of Aussie life outside racing and fasten on that as his focus for the Cup each year. In 1931 he delighted in the news that the Australian Naval Squadron just 'happened' to be stationed in Melbourne during Cup Week.

Typically, Dennis saw no harm in this amazing 'coincidence' and celebrated the Aussie predeliction for making the most of the situation and putting 'pleasure' before 'business' when it suited and if at all possible.

In 1931 he wrote a rollicking sea shanty in praise of our brave sailors, which was, in fact, another poetic celebration of what Mark Twain described as 'The Australasian National Day'. Dennis prefaced this 1931 verse with the tongue-in-cheek comment that, 'Through the usual coincidence many ships, including the Australian Naval Squadron, have reached Melbourne just prior to Cup Week.'

SAILING ORDERS

C.J. DENNIS

Up the hook, the bosun said;
(Ho, me hearties, ho!)
There's heavy weather on ahead

(Tumble up, below!)
There's dirty weather coming down,
Our course is set for Melbourne town
And a queer thing that should be!
So show a leg and tumble up,
And pick your fancy for the Cup
With the good ship running free.

Funny thing, the boatman said,
(Ho, me hearties, ho!)
But when November looms ahead
(Tumble up, below!)
To Melbourne Port the orders say,
And nothing's left but to obey,
For the likes of you and me.
And what's a sailor to do,
When duty calls, but see it through,
With the good ship running free?

If I should win, the boatman said;
(Ho, me hearties, ho!)
I'll buy myself a feather bed
(Tumble up, below!)
And never put to sea again.
Yet luck ain't kind to sailor men,
But I'll get my fun, said he.
And every man shall have his lass,
And make his bet and drink a glass,
To a good horse running free, said he,
And that's the life for me!

Two years later the poet turned his attention to the phenomenon of radio.

In a nation as large and sparsely populated as Australia, the coming of 'the wireless' meant quite dramatic changes to everyday life. Australia became a nation of 'listeners' able, for the first time, to communicate quickly and share in world events as they happened.

This phenomenon only enhanced the importance of the Cup as an essential part of Aussie culture. Dennis realised the impact that radio was having and, in one of his Cup Week poems of 1933, he celebrated this new way of being involved in the thrill and excitement of the race.

THE LISTENING WEEK

C.J. DENNIS

This is the listening week of the year –
 Listening-in.
A-cock and alert is the national ear –
 Listening-in.
All over the land in the country towns,
From the back of the Leeuwin to Darling Downs,
Layers of 'quids' or the odd half-crowns,
 They are listening-in.

On the far-flung farms they are round each set,
 Listening-in.
The work and the worry they all forget,
 Listening-in.
Wherever an aerial soars in space
To the Cup, or the Oaks or the Steeplechase,
To the roar of the ring and the lure of the race
They are listening-in.

In the far outback there are sun-tanned men,
 Listening-in.
Where the woolshed stands by the drafting pen –
 Listening-in.
Old Dad's come in from the Ninety Mile;
He scored on the Cup and he wears a smile,
And he 'reckons this game is well worth while',
 So he's listening-in.

To the edge of the desert the sound-waves go;
  And, listening-in,
Ned of the Overland, Saltbush Joe,
  Listening-in,
Recall the giants of years long past,
And the loneliness of these spaces vast;
But they reckon that life's worth living at last
  With this listening-in.

Although he often wrote about the 'mug punters', Dennis rarely concerned himself with the feats of the actual horses, or the jockeys, trainers or owners. He was able to convey the effects that Cup Week had on all and sundry. During Cup Week in 1932, he even wrote about the effect of the Spring Carnival obsession on himself, and other poets:

GALLOPING HORSES

C.J. DENNIS

Oh, this is the week when no rhymster may rhyme
On the joy of the bush or the ills of the time,
Nor pour out his soul in delectable rhythm
Of women and wine and the lure they have with 'em,
Nor pen philosophic (if foolish) discourses,
Because of the fury of galloping horses.

Galloping, galloping thro' the refrain –
The lure and the lilt of it beat on the brain.
Strive as you may for Arcadian Themes,
The silks and the saddles will weave thro' your dreams.
Surging, and urging the visions aside
For a lyrical lay of equestrian pride,
For the roar of the race and the call of the courses,
And galloping, galloping, galloping horses.

This is the week for the apotheosis
Of Horse in his glory, from tail to proboscis.

That curious quadruped, proud and aloof,
That holds all the land under thrall of his hoof.
All creeds and conditions, all factions and forces,
All, all must give way to the galloping horses.

Galloping, galloping – sinner and saint
March to the metre, releasing restraint.
If it isn't the Cup it's the Oaks or the Steeple
That wraps in its magic the minds of the people.
Whether they seek it for profit or pleasure,
They all, willy-nilly, must dance to the measure.
The mood of the moment in all men endorses
The glamorous game and the galloping horses –
Galloping horses – jockeys and courses –
They gallop, we gallop with galloping horses.

Dennis used the fervour and excitement of Cup Week to celebrate all aspects of the Aussie character and human nature. Even the less admirable machinations of married middle-class couples were grist to the mill of his perceptive and humorous verses.

One of Dennis's favourite writing styles was the 'one-sided conversation' in which the reader is presented with only one voice in a conversation and the humour comes, in part, from guessing the obvious 'other side' of the dialogue.

In several Cup Week poems Dennis used this device to great effect to illustrate, and comment on, the never-ending 'cold war' of Machiavellian plotting, game-playing and deceit that is a part of the age-old battle of the sexes in middle-class marriages.

In 'Listen, Elaine!' the husband is slowly stripped of his Cup Day punting money by a wife keen on using the race as the excuse to obtain an entire new wardrobe. The only voice we hear is that of the husband, firstly making unsuccessful attempts to keep his wife in her old dress. Of course, the punter's need for betting money is of no concern to a fashion-conscious wife. As many of us can attest, wives often obstinately fail to understand the real purpose of race meetings.

Dennis hilariously captures the dilemma of the doomed husband whose 'logic', we all know from experience, will inevitably fail to impress. We are moved to laughter by the all-too-familiar pleas of a fellow sufferer when the husband tries appeasement.

As the 'battle' proceeds to its inevitable conclusion, victory for the wife, we share the Catch–22 frustration of the husband who knows that the only way he will get to the Cup is by being 'conned' out of his punting money.

LISTEN, ELAINE!

C.J. DENNIS

Listen, Elaine. Tho' I'm not mad on racing,
I like a little flutter now and then;
But I maintain you would not be disgracing
The family, or look like some old hen
If you just wore . . . Now, just a minute, please . . .
That pinkish frock . . . No, wait! Let me explain.
That pinkish frock with spots . . . You wouldn't *freeze*!
You've got your furs. Aw, listen, please, Elaine!

Now, look. We've twenty pounds. Don't let us quarrel.
Surely we can be sane and quite grown-up.
If you take most of that, what of the 'moral'
That Percy Podgrass gave us for the Cup?
Of course he's sure to win. What are vain dresses
Compared . . . My dear! I did not call *you* vain!
Nor selfish either. Gosh! What married messes
Start over clothes, and . . . Listen, please, Elaine.

We're partners, aren't we? Well, then, listen, darling.
We might discuss this calmly, don't you think?
Now! Please be sensible . . . I am not *snarling*!
Rubbish! Of course, you do look nice in pink.
I always thought that spotted pink looked dandy,
And comfy, too. Supposing it should rain.

Nice sight you'd look in . . . What's it called . . . organdie . . .
I was not *wishing* . . . Listen, please! Elaine!

Women just dress to spite some other tabby.
Who said you were a cat? One moment, pet.
Of course, I wouldn't have my wife look *shabby*.
Take what you need. We'll make a smaller bet . . .
Eight . . . ten . . . twelve quid! Whew! Not much left for betting.
Still, just a flutter and expenses . . . *What*?
Listen, Elaine. What could I be *forgetting*?
Hat? Stockings? Shoes to match? . . . Here . . . Take the lot!

Ouch! I can still feel the pain of the defeated husband 80 years after that piece was written. Some things don't change.

Dennis proved to be a man ahead of his time in his efforts to maintain gender balance and show the wickedness of husbands and the lengths to which they go to deceive their wives. Infidelity takes many forms, especially in Cup Week when there is a chance to get to the races and waste the housekeeping money on the punt.

Here is another one-sided conversation, written in 1933, in which the husband attempts to escape his family obligations and get to the Cup meeting. Of course, Melbourne Cup Day is a public holiday in Victoria and one might expect a family man to take the opportunity to spend time with his wife and children. With spring in the air and the prospect of a day away from housework with hubby to help with the children, a devoted wife is perfectly entitled to expect that a family picnic is 'just the thing'.

The husband, however, has other selfish and devious plans.

WHY A PICNIC, JANE?

C.J. DENNIS

But, why a picnic, Jane? We went last year,
And missed the Cup; and you know how you grieved
Because we lost . . . Oh! Yes, you did, my dear.
I had the tip, but I was not believed.

It's just sheer nonsense to deny it all.
And when he won, you said, if you recall,
You'd never miss a chance like that again.
Well, cut the Cup. But why a picnic, Jane?

You know how I hate picnics, sticky things,
The grizzling children and the dusty road,
The flies and all those crawlywigs with stings –
My dear, I am not selfish! But that load
Of baskets . . . Eh? Back him at starting price?
That's an idea. And then I could remain
To take you and the children? —M'yes. Quite nice.
Jolly, of course. But, why a picnic, Jane?

Wait! Have you thought of burglars? There you are!
The empty house. Remember that last case
Near here? . . . Bright thought, my dear! You take the car.
You've solved it. I'll stay at home and mind the place.
Lonely? Not I. You take the car, of course.
I've a good book; I'll be all right alone.
That's settled then . . . And now, about the horse.
Wait here, and while I think of it, I'll phone.

'Lo! That you, Sam? All set! I can't talk loud.
'Lo! Can you hear me? Listen, lad. It's on.
Tomorrow, yes. Count me in the crowd.
Your car . . . about eleven. They'll be gone.
Great stunt, that picnic! If we make the pace
We ought to get there for the second race.'
Well, Jane, that's all fixed up. I've backed our horse.
Eh? Help cut sandwiches? Why, dear, of course.

It wasn't in Dennis's nature to question or analyse the morality of racing or the social behaviour it generated. He was less concerned with the heroic deeds of the winners and the jockeys than he was with the everyday thoughts and schemes and disappointments of the nameless normal battlers, office workers, tradesmen and pretentious middle-class pretenders who adored his writing in their daily paper. He always pitched his writing in the common ruck; he was never concerned with attempting to be more 'informed' than all the other 'mug punters'.

In one Cup Week poem, he considers all the elements of the form guide and, after expressing the typical 'mug punter's' confusion, makes the obvious conclusion.

THE PONDERING PUNTER

C.J. DENNIS

> From now until Tuesday thousands of racing enthusiasts will spend a great deal of spare, and other, time in brain-racking attempts to sort out candidates and pick winners of the Melbourne Cup.

I've been watching them for weeks;
And if anybody speaks
Of a likely candidate, I test the truth
Of every tip and claim.
I am well up in the game,
And I follow form and figures like a sleuth.

I am fairly saturated
In the hopes and fears debated
By the seers and scribes who write the sporting notes.
I've the favourite's every feat;
Times, weight, distance . . . all complete.
And a black list, too . . . of all the hairy goats!

Now then, this one has a chance,
Certain winner at first glance,
But, his weight! Well, *that* one carries ten pounds less.
But the scribes, with strange insistence,

Say he cannot do the distance.
Well then, this one? Odds too short! Oh, what a mess.

Ah! And what about this other?
He has breeding, he's full brother
To . . . but someone told me he was over-trained.
Hang it all! I was forgetting . . .
Here's the nag for my tote betting . . .
Good long odds . . . but wait . . . I've heard his fetlock's strained.

What about this fast outsider?
Um! He's got a rotten rider.
Well *this*? If he could beat *that* he might win.
Or *this*! Or *that* might win it.
But . . . if . . . isn't it the limit?
Give it up! . . . Has anybody got a pin?

Dennis loved the confusion and enthusiasm of Cup Week, for him *not* picking the winner was far more 'Australian' than some tall tale of good luck or a dream which led to a fortune. This is illustrated in many of his Cup poems over the years. It was always the human spectacle and the human behaviour that fascinated C.J. Dennis.

In the year of Peter Pan's first Melbourne Cup win, Dennis wrote a wonderful parody of Adam Lindsay Gordon's famous racing poem 'How We Beat the Favourite', which features in Part 1 of this volume. Dennis's poem was called 'How We Backed the Favourite'.

While Gordon's poem is an heroic tale of a titanic struggle, which celebrates the nobility and bravery of the racehorse, Dennis's poem typically concentrates on the confidence shown by the everyday 'mug punters' in the Cup favourite, Peter Pan.

There are no heroic struggles and no tall tales of lost fortunes in Dennis's poem, simply the everyday hopes of the 'one shilling' punters. He sees the horse as merely another player in the whole drama and excitement of a week which gives the humdrum, mundane lives of Aussie battlers a yearly highlight.

Having been told that Peter Pan *will* win, the poet goes to see the horse and make up his own mind:

I saw Peter Pan; there was nothing he lacked.
And, as he looked willing, I plonked down my shilling
And triumphed, and that's how the favourite was backed.

Now, Peter Pan was arguably the most beautiful horse to ever win the Cup. He was a flashy chestnut with a silver mane and tail, and his bravery in recovering from illness to win two Melbourne Cups is the stuff of legend in the history of the Australian turf. C.J. Dennis sums up this champion horse in the understated and prosaic phrase 'there was nothing he lacked'. Really, you can't get more Aussie than that!

Similarly, when Trivalve won in 1927 Dennis wrote 'A Post-Cup Tale' in which a poor mug punter tells us how he 'switched' at the last minute from his own original choice for the race, the eventual winner Trivalve, to some other horse due to the 'urging' of a mate.

There is, however, no real concern with Trivalve, the wonderful three-year-old AJC Derby winner who valiantly and famously won the race against older, more seasoned stayers. Instead we have an amazingly accurate and timeless portrayal of the punter's eternal frustration with picking winners and *not* backing them as the protagonist tells us, over and over again, that he had the money in his hand.

A POST-CUP TALE

C.J. DENNIS

I 'ad the money in me 'and!
Fair dinkum! Right there, by the stand.
I tole me wife at breakfus' time,
Straight out: 'Trivalve,' I sez 'is prime.
Trivalve,' I sez. An', all the week,
I swear ther's no one 'eard me speak
Another 'orse's name. Why, look,
I 'ad the oil straight from a Book

On Sund'y at me cousin's place
When we was torkin' of the race.
'Trivalve,' 'e sez. ''Is chance is grand.'
I 'ad the money in me 'and!

Fair in me 'and I 'ad the dough!
An' then a man 'as got to go –
Wot? Tough? Look, if I 'adn't met
Jim Smith (I ain't forgave 'im yet)
'E takes an' grabs me by the coat.
'Trivalve?' 'e sez. 'That 'airy goat!'
'Trivalve?' 'e sez. 'Ar, turn it up!
'Ow could 'e win a flamin' Cup?'
Of course, I thort 'e muster knoo.
'Im livin' near a trainer, too.

Right 'ere, like that, fair in me fist
I 'ad the notes! An' then I missed –
Missed like a mug fair on the knock
Becos 'is maggin' done me block.
'That 'airy goat?' 'e sez. ''E's crook!'
Fair knocked me back, 'e did. An' look,
I 'ad the money in me 'and!
Fair in me paw! An', un'erstand,
Sixes at least I coulder got –
Thirty to five, an' made a pot.
Today I mighter been reel rich –
Rollin' in dough! Instid o' which,
'Ere's me – Aw! Don't it beat the band?
I 'AD THE MONEY IN ME 'AND!
Put me clean off, that's wot 'e did . . .
Say, could yeh len' us 'arf a quid?

The wonderful thing about Dennis's poem about Trivalve's win is that it has outlived any other poems written about Cup winners in various years because it contains a greater human story and captures an elemental truth about all punters, anytime, anywhere.

There is one poem which illustrates the poet's ability to capture the everyday human element of Cup Week not only dramatically, but with great understanding and humour. In 'An Anticipatory Picture', written in Cup Week in 1931, he gives us all the excitement of the race and concludes with a blank space in which we can live out our own Melbourne Cup dream.

AN ANTICIPATORY PICTURE

C.J. DENNIS

The scene upon the frock-flecked lawn
Is, as you please, a picture fair,
Or just a hunk of human brawn,
With blobs of faces here and there.
Stilled are the clamours of the Ring;
The famous race is on at last;
All eyes are on the lengthening string
Of brilliant jackets moving fast.

Torn, trampled tickets mark the birth
Of broken hopes all now would mend,
As quickening hoof-beats spurn the earth,
And the field thunders to the bend.
All men are equal for the nonce,
Bound by an urgency intense,
And eager questionings win response
From strangers tiptoe with suspense.

'What's that in front?' All faces yearn
Toward the track in serried rows.
The field comes round the homeward turn,
As, wave on wave, the murmuring grows,
Waxes and swells from out that host
Till pandemonium begins,
And flecks of colour pass the post
To mighty cries of '(________*) wins'.
[N.B. – Write your own ticket.]*

So, as you 'write your own ticket' each year and take a punt on a dream in the annual celebration that stops the nation, perhaps you might remember to raise a glass to the people's poet, the bard of the Cup, the man who understood Australians better than any other writer of verse in our history, C.J. Dennis . . . cheers!

FATTY—THE IMPRESSIONIST

Sir Robert Menzies once said that the art of Will Ashton 'will never become dated'. To me, that is as true a statement as I ever heard. Yet, Will Ashton's work has been out of favour for quite a while now—not 'dated', just unappreciated.

John William Ashton was the son of the English artist and art teacher James Ashton of York. Will, as he was known, was born in 1881 and when he was three his father 'made up his mind to go to Australia' and the family migrated to Adelaide.

His father, according to Will, had 'the heart of a boy' and a strong spirit of adventure. He was always known as 'Jimmy', even to the students at Prince Alfred College, where Will was educated. Jimmy was drawing master at the college for 40 years.

Jimmy also had a studio at Norwood in Adelaide, where he painted commissions, and he ran the Norwood Art School in the local town hall. Later he set up the Ashton Academy of Arts in the city itself, where he taught many future artists—including the great landscape artist Hans Heysen, a lifelong friend of Will's.

Will's school nickname was 'Fatty'. He was self-effacing and freely admitted that the name fitted him. He also claimed that he was not much good at anything at school—except art.

His only other claim to fame at school was that he once took a bicycle apart and put it back together. On the basis of that achievement his parents decided he should be an engineer, but Fatty Ashton was always destined to be an artist.

After leaving school he worked in his father's studio for five shillings a week and learned the basics of painting. Written on the wall of the studio was the motto, 'He that attempts to run before he can walk will stumble and fall.'

In 1900 Will travelled back to England where he studied under the seascapist Julian Olsson at St Ives in Cornwall, a town with a thriving artist community. He remained there for five years, also spending time in Paris, where he studied at the Académie Julian in the winter of 1902–03 with other Australian artists Hans Heysen and E. Phillips Fox.

In 1904 Ashton had work accepted by the Royal Academy in London, and the Salon de la Société des Artistes Français in Paris.

On his return to Adelaide to teach art he sold one of his French paintings, *Boulevard Montparnasse, Paris* to the National Gallery of South Australia for the huge sum of 150 guineas. And this meant he had enough money to propose to one of his students, May Millman, whom he married in January 1906.

Exhibitions and good reviews quickly followed in Sydney, Melbourne, Perth and Adelaide and, in 1908, Ashton won the prestigious Wynne Prize for landscape for the first time. He would win it again in 1930 and 1939.

Between 1912 and 1914 he was back in Europe and painted in Britain, France and Egypt. He returned to Australia briefly before moving the family to London in 1915. Although he suffered from arthritis, which prevented him from active service, he joined the Australian army as a driver.

By this time he was a recognised art authority, advised the South Australian gallery on acquisitions and was elected as an examiner by the Royal Drawing Society, of which he was a member.

Returning to Australia he settled in Sydney and received several commissions from the Commonwealth government, including a painting of the La Perouse monument that was given as a gift to the people of France.

Over the next twenty years Will Ashton spent his time equally in Europe and Australia, working almost exclusively in oils, and captured the light and beauty of both French and Australian landscape and seascape as few artists ever have, before or since.

He was the master of capturing the effects of changing light on snow, cloud and water, and his impressionist seascapes and landscapes are a delight to the eye of the art lover as well as the uninitiated observer. While he never departed from perfect technique and draftsmanship, he painted with what his friend Lionel Lindsay called 'such a fine truth and vision, that you will go far in Europe today to find so able a painter'.

The noted critic and artist William Dargie called Will Ashton's impressionist Australian landscapes 'a revelation', and his paintings of Paris and Brittany are often breathtaking and were described as 'poetic'.

He painted every bridge on the River Seine at least once, and often many times, not just those in Paris—every bridge along the full length of the river from its source to the sea.

Will Ashton was an old-fashioned man who believed in social responsibility and wanted to give something back to the art form with which he had a lifelong love affair so, in 1937, in the hope that he 'could be of value to the artists here', he accepted the position of director of the Art Gallery of New South Wales.

In that position he was responsible for the acquisition of many of the gallery's treasures that those of us lucky enough to grow up in Sydney came to love and admire. He improved the gallery's spaces and lighting and during World War II he took an Australian exhibition to the USA and studied galleries there in order to improve the NSW gallery.

He was a member of the Commonwealth Art Advisory Board from 1918, and its chairman from 1953 to 1962. He was also a member of the Royal Institute of Oil Painters, London, vice-president of the Australian Painter-Etchers' Society, and a member of the Society of Artists, Sydney. He was knighted in 1960.

Will Ashton made Sydney his home until his death from cancer in 1963. He lived at Mosman and loved the harbour and painted it often. He was not related to Sydney's other Ashton family of painters or associated with Julian Ashton's famous art school.

My advice is to buy his works whenever you can; one day they will again become fashionable. Today they often sell at ridiculously low prices but, when the cycle of artistic fashion turns, as it inevitably does, you could be well rewarded. Then again, how you could ever bear to sell a Will Ashton painting, I don't know.

If you love great art and especially great impressionist art, do yourself a favour and take a look at the paintings of a truly great and humble artist who claimed to be a painter of what he saw. When asked if he was an impressionist, Ashton answered:

> If the true aim of impressionism was to achieve ever-greater naturalism, by exact analysis of tone and colour, and by trying to render the play of light on the surface of objects . . . then, I too, am an impressionist.

ALONG THE ROAD TO BUNDABERG?

Jack O'Hagan was born in 1898 and lived all his life in Melbourne. He was a prolific songwriter and wrote hit after hit. His creations were the most popular and most played songs on radio in Australia throughout the 1920s, 30s and 40s.

Today few people could tell you who wrote the Australian classic, 'Along the Road to Gundagai', let alone all the other hits that poured from Jack's pen and piano over his long career.

Jack's dad, Patrick, was a hotelkeeper in Fitzroy. Jack was educated at Xavier College and was just old enough to serve as a corporal on home service in the Australian Imperial Force at the end of World War I.

In 1920 the famous musical retailers and publishers Allan & Co employed Jack as a 'song demonstrator'. His job was to play and sing the latest songs to customers in Allan's stores, in order to get them to buy the sheet music. He also worked as a 'song plugger' in the entertainment industry, trying to get Allan's songs played in cinemas, theatres and dance halls.

In the 1920s he wrote songs linked to silent films from the USA. When the latest blockbuster silent movie arrived in Australia, Jack would write songs relevant to the film in order to sell sheet music or gramophone records, and then get radio airplay for the songs in order to increase sales.

Sometimes these songs were used to advertise the movie but often it was just a way to cash in on a film's success. Jack's song 'In Dreamy Araby', for example, was popular around 1922 and

1923, when the Rudolph Valentino smash-hit film *The Sheik* was all the rage.

Recalling how his most famous song came to life, Jack said:

> Back in the early twenties, people weren't interested in songs about Australia. So, I called one of my songs 'Down Carolina Way' and took it to Hugh McIntosh, the great entrepreneur of the day. Very colourful he was—used terrible language. He looked at 'Down Carolina Way' and exploded. 'Why don't you write a blank, blank, blank Australian song?' he roared. So I went away and wrote 'Along the Road to Gundagai.'

Many years later, as guest of honour at Gundagai's centenary celebrations in 1956, Jack confessed that it was his first visit to the town. The song was originally called 'Along the Road to Bundaberg', but 'Burnett' (the river at Bundaberg) is a word with only two syllables. So Jack changed the town to Gundagai, 'where the blue gums are growing, and the Murrumbidgee's flowing'—and the river name has four syllables!

The song was published in 1922 and included in the pantomime *The Forty Thieves*. It was recorded and popularised in 1931 by Peter Dawson, and then it was chosen, in 1937, as the theme for the radio serial *Dad and Dave*. It has become an Aussie classic and is still being recorded and played 90 years after it was written. It has been recorded by singers, bands and orchestras thousands of times and was a favourite of the great jazz violinist Stephane Grappelli, who performed the tune as part of his repertoire all his life.

Jack wrote follow-ups in the 1930s, like 'Where the Dog Sits on the Tuckerbox', 'The Snake Gully Swagger', 'Snake Gully Home of Mine' and 'When a Boy from Alabama Meets a Girl from Gundagai'.

Jack O'Hagan was a great opportunist and would write songs almost overnight when heroic deeds were performed by sportsmen or aviators—and they mostly became instant hits.

His 'hero' songs include 'Kingsford Smith', 'Our Don Bradman' and 'A Lone Girl Flyer', which was dedicated to Amy Johnson.

He also wrote a song about Ginger Meggs, and 'Our Marjorie', which was about Olympic runner Marjorie Jackson. Jack also wrote the songs for Australia's first musical film, *Showgirl's Luck*, in 1931.

As well as songwriting, Jack had a long career in radio in Melbourne. He worked as a sales manager as well as on air. As early as 1924, the year that commercial radio began in Australia, he was singing his own songs on 3AR. At 3DB he produced musical shows; he also featured on 3LO and on 3AW and as an anchorman for 'live' Test cricket matches.

When Don Bradman was destroying the English bowlers in England in 1930, radio broadcasts were taken from coded telegrams of each over and these were then re-created on radio as if they were live broadcasts. Jack pushed a piano into the studio during a lunch break and played his latest song, 'Our Don Bradman'. Within a week, sales of the sheet music had exceeded 10,000 copies!

His last song 'God Bless Australia' (1967), using the tune of 'Waltzing Matilda', was tipped to become Australia's new national anthem. Jack was awarded an MBE in 1973 and died in 1987.

A PLEASANT MINOR POET

When my spirit needs restoring, or I am grieving the loss of someone I love, I turn to one poet, Roderic Joseph Quinn. To me, his poetry had a lyrical quality matched only in Australian verse writing by his close friend Victor Daley.

In an era in our literary history when bold stirring ballads were all the rage, Rod Quinn wrote the most beautiful, reflective, soul-searching and humble verses about the human condition and human spirit. Yet, today, he is unknown to the vast majority of Australians, even keen students of our verse tradition.

Quinn was born in Surry Hills, Sydney, in 1867. He was the seventh of nine children of Irish migrants, his father a postman.

Educated at Marist Brothers school in the Haymarket, where he met lifelong friends and fellow poets Chris Brennan and E.J. Brady, Quinn studied law for three years while working for a produce merchant and also taught at a country school near Wagga Wagga briefly before drifting into journalism and becoming editor of the *North Sydney News*.

Like his close friend Daley, Rod Quinn was much influenced by Celtic legends. He was a reflective poet and dreamer in an era when Australian poetry was very much about bush ballads and broad humour.

Here is a lovely lyrical poem he wrote about desires and false hopes and how they are very much part of the human spirit. It uses the notion of adult desire compared to childish naivety to make a point about human aspirations in a self-mocking and gently accepting tone that always brings a smile to my face.

STARS IN THE SEA

RODERIC QUINN

I took a boat on a starry night
And went for a row on the water,
And she danced like a child on a wake of light
And bowed where the ripples caught her.
I vowed, as I rowed on the velvet blue
Through the night and the starry splendour,
To woo and sue a maiden I knew
Till she bent to my pleadings tender.

My painted boat she was light and glad
And gladder my heart with wishing,
And I came in time to a little lad
Who stood on the rocks a-fishing.
I said 'Ahoy!' and he said 'Ahoy!'
And I asked how the fish were biting;
'And what are you trying to catch, my boy,
Bream, silver and red – or whiting?'

'Neither,' he answered, 'the seaweed mars
My line, and the sharp shells sunder:
I am trying my luck with those great big stars
Down there in the round skies under.'
'Good-bye!' from him, and 'Good-bye!' from me,
And never a laugh came after;
So many go fishing for stars in the sea
That it's hardly a subject for laughter.

Quinn was much favoured by the *Bullletin* editors J.F. Archibald and A.G. Stephens and his verse received excellent reviews and praise from critics and poets like Yeats. He also wrote many short stories for the *Bulletin*, the best of them being gripping melodramatic and romantic tales set in the bush.

By 1900 Quinn was regarded as one of the leading poets in Australia. He published four very popular collections of poetry over the next twenty years, as well as a novel and many short stories.

Rod Quinn was a painfully shy and reticent man. He never married and his personality was very restrained and proper. Although he was a member of Victor Daley's Dusk to Dawn Club, he was never known to utter a crude word or join in the satirical criticism of fellow poets or the bawdy recitations.

He would recite his own verse at times and also enjoyed telling Celtic fairy stories and ghost stories. He is associated with the poetic movement popularised by Yeats and known as the 'Celtic Twilight'.

He wrote about the joy of the human spirit, and music was one of his chief pleasures.

This is my all-time favourite of Quinn's poems. It is about the magic of music and the triumph of the positive spirit and joy of living over the mundane and less laudable elements of human nature.

THE FIDDLE AND THE CROWD

RODERIC QUINN

When the day was at its middle,
Tired of the limb and slow of pace,
Came a fiddler with his fiddle
To a crowded market place;
Lying, cheating, boasting, bragging,
Men and women walked together;
Heads were nodding, tongues were wagging,
Talk there was of trade and weather,
Talk there was of man's enslavement
To the tyrants, Toil and Worry;
Yet the fiddle on the pavement

Minding not the noise and hurry,
Singing low and singing loud –
Spoke its message to the crowd.

Said the fiddle –
'Pause and listen;
Can't you hear the waters running
Down the mossy mountain valleys?
Don't you see the lyre-bird sunning
Glossy plumes in fronded alleys?
Life is glory, life is glamour!'
Said the fiddle
In the middle
Of the tumult and the clamour.

Though unheeded seemed the fiddle,
Bidding each and all rejoice,
When the day was at its middle –
Yet beneath its magic voice,
Laughing, sobbing, teasing, fretting,
Men and women met together,
Smiled to find themselves forgetting
Troublous thoughts of trade and weather;
One bethought him of a cavern
Cool and sweet with running water,
And another of a tavern
And a tavern-keeper's daughter –
Ale to drink and lips to kiss . . .
'Twas the fiddle did all this!

Said the fiddle –
'Hush and hearken
To the song that I am singing,
For it is a song entrancing.
Telling now of gladness ringing,
Telling now of children dancing;

Life is music, life is glamour.'
Said the fiddle
In the middle
Of the tumult and the clamour.

Like Victor Daley and John O'Brien, Quinn's writing was very popular with Australia's large Irish Catholic community. A plain-living man of simple pleasures, Quinn supported himself almost entirely on the proceeds of his poetry and, from 1925, received a Commonwealth Literary Fund pension of £1 a week, which was supplemented by a similar grant from the New South Wales government.

Throughout his life he never owned a home of his own but boarded with other members of his large family who had a great affection for him. He was a tall man with a dignified bearing and a walrus moustache who was, by all accounts, gentle, kind and courteous and possessed of a great sense of humour. No one seems to have had a bad word to say about him and he himself was never heard to make a derogatory remark about a colleague or the work of any other writer.

Two of his brothers, Patrick and Jim, were also writers and Patrick was a member of parliament and deputy trade commissioner to the USA. Both brothers saw Rod as their mentor and inspiration.

Quinn was a modest man whose greatest praise of himself was to admit once that he was perhaps 'a pleasant minor poet'. Sadly, this humble underestimation of this great Australian poet became the accepted assessment of his work and, after World War I, his work was less and less appreciated. After World War II, with new movements in Australian literature, his work was all but forgotten.

This final poem, written in a female voice, and perhaps written after the death of Victor Daley in 1905, perfectly expresses the deep grief we will all feel someday, and the process of grieving that is the inevitable result of deep and intimate loss. I know of no more accurate an account of true grief.

DOING NOTHING

RODERIC QUINN

With the sorrow on me
Neighbours come and go –
Think me vain and foolish
Nursing up my woe.
With the grief-blade in me
Keen and chill as steel –
Can I laugh like others,
Feel the joy they feel?

Since he died and left me
Things don't matter much,
Life, that danced and capered,
Limps upon a crutch.
Night and day I ponder,
Drawing weary breath –
Since to love we're moulded,
Why should there be death?

Night and day I'm asking
Him Who dwells above –
Since to death we're going,
Why should there be love?
When he kissed and left me,
Oh, he looked so brave! –
God be with him sleeping
In his far-off grave!

What are dress and jewels,
What are meat and bread
To a lonely woman
Grieving for her dead?
Wan I am with weeping,
Tired of heart I sink –

Doing nothing . . . only
Trying not to think.

Roderic Quinn spent the last twenty years of his life boarding in the house of a Mrs Cassidy at Waverley and, after his death in 1949 at the Sacred Heart Hospice in Darlinghurst, his body returned to Waverley where he still lies, near his great friend Victor Daley and his supporter J.F. Archibald, in Waverley Cemetery, all but forgotten.

WHO REMEMBERS FRANK?

Many Australians are obsessed by nostalgia for past international stars like The Beatles, Abba and Elvis. There is even a hugely successful Elvis Festival held each year in Parkes, New South Wales.

But if Australians were asked to name the international superstar who lives quietly in the outer suburbs of Sydney and shares with Elvis the honour of three consecutive number-one hits in the UK, and had the first million-selling single ever, and had no less than *three* million-selling singles (and a few others that almost made a million sales), how many would immediately recall the name of the great Frank Ifield?

Frank is remembered for one song, 'I Remember You', and many Australians erroneously think that he was a 'one-hit wonder'!

But the handsome young lad from Dural was a big star here before he ever left to record in Britain, where he is remembered as a superstar and had many international hits and recorded hundreds of songs in a long and successful career.

Many people don't realise that Frank was actually born in England, in the city of Coventry in 1937; his parents were Australians who were living there while his dad, an ambitious and talented engineer, worked as a designer of fuel systems for the first jet plane engines.

Coventry was the centre of the aeronautical industry and it was highly secretive work. Once the war began, the Luftwaffe targeted Coventry and the town was infamously devastated in a bombing raid by 500 German planes on 14 November 1940, when Frank was three years old. The cathedral was destroyed; along with more than half the houses in the city and a third of the factories; 600 lives were lost.

After being evacuated to London, Frank remembers looking forward to the air raids as a small child, as he had the chance to sing and entertain the other schoolchildren in the air raid shelters.

After the war the family moved back to Australia when Frank was eight and settled at Dural, north-west of Sydney, where Frank would listen to his grandfather tell stories about touring in minstrel shows on Cobb & Co coaches as they milked the cows on the family's dairy farm.

One day little Frank, who loved listening to the hillbilly shows on early morning radio while milking, burst into the kitchen out of the blue and announced, 'Hey, Mum, I can yodel!' He received a ukulele for his eleventh birthday and his grandmother bought him his first guitar at thirteen—and a star was born.

The family moved to the Sydney suburb of Beecroft in 1950 and young Frank soon appeared on Australia's *Amateur Hour* on radio. One night he talked his way onto one of Tim McNamara's live shows at Hornsby when he heard an artist had not turned up to sing. He left school at fifteen to take up a regular spot on the very popular *Bonnington's Bunkhouse Radio Show*.

Signed to EMI in August 1953, Frank began his recording career with a very successful Regal Zonophone release featuring 'Did You See My Daddy Over There' and 'There's a Love Knot in My Lariat'. By the end of the 1950s, Frank had recorded more than 60 tracks in Australia and was a veteran of the show circuit. He was a familiar voice on radio and was the second singer to appear on Australian television. He also hosted his own weekly television show, *Campfire Favourites*.

Frank had done just about all he could in Australia and, when the first jet flight left Sydney bound for London in 1959, he was on board. His first release in the UK was 'Lucky Devil', which made it to number 15 on the pop charts and paved the way for Frank to start touring in Britain and release his biggest single, 'I Remember You'.

'I Remember You' was an international mega-hit and gained Frank a permanent place in *The Guinness Book of World Records* as the first single to sell a million copies in Britain. Other hits followed, such as 'Lovesick Blues', 'Wayward Wind' (making Frank the first artist in Britain to achieve three consecutive number-ones), and 'Nobody's Darling But Mine'. Frank teamed up with legendary manager Peter Gormley (who also managed The Shadows and Olivia Newton-John) to become a top international cabaret act, performing in Las Vegas, Tokyo, London, Sydney, and just about everywhere else.

Frank had four number-one hits in less than two years, and was the first artist in the world to have three million-selling singles. He also starred in a hit movie about himself, *Up Jumped a Swagman*, which co-starred James Bond girl Suzy Kendall.

People tend to forget that Frank was as big as Elvis and Cliff Richard in the 1960s and his favourite story concerns the time his manager was asked to do a favour for a mate, another manager.

Frank was doing a two-day event at Peterborough, north of London, and was asked to give a new band a chance as his support act. He agreed but the promoter insisted they play for nothing, do two performances and get themselves to the event.

The group drove all the way from Liverpool and arrived just in time to go on stage. They had a new drummer who was a bit lost and they played so loudly that Frank knew there would be trouble.

Sure enough, the promoter came looking for Frank and he had to tell the band to turn it down for their second performance.

The manager who asked the favour was Brian Epstein, the new drummer was Richard Starkey, better known as Ringo Starr, and the band was, of course, The Beatles.

Frank still laughs as he recalls that he actually told The Beatles to turn it down!

Frank continued touring until he suffered a health scare with collapsed lungs which caused pneumonia and his retirement in 1984. After recovering and finalising a divorce from his wife of many years, Frank remarried and returned to Australia.

These days Frank spends his time helping young artists starting out and still appears occasionally in a stage show about his fascinating life called *I Remember You,* in which Frank yarns about his life and all his hits are sung by internationally renowned country singer Wayne Horsburgh.

PART 3
UNLIKELY TALES FROM SMALL TOWNS

Here is a bunch of very unlikely Aussie tall stories, mostly humorous but with a few swashbuckling and sentimental tales thrown in.

These stories are only 'unlikely' in the sense that they mostly never happened at all, but 'could' happen—if enough coincidences stacked up. They are the kind of stories that get told locally but are pretty much unknown outside of the district or small town in which they supposedly took place.

The subject material of these stories is the stock standard stuff of bush and outback communities. Dogs, dunnies, fire brigades, pubs, ghosts, bushrangers and horses all figure prominently, along with 'bush characters'. In some stories quite a few of the above get together to provide the plot, and the humour.

For some reason Aussies find dunnies a great source of amusement. The word evidently derives from a gaelic word *dunnekin*, meaning a cellar or outhouse.

Australians took the word 'dunny' to heart and the men who serviced the dunnies and replaced the dunny-cans before sewerage arrived were affectionately known as 'dunny men'.

The narrow lanes used by dunny men became prime real estate in Sydney a few years ago and were the cause of several major court cases over ownership and encroachment. The 'dunny man' always left a card and poem at Christmas that went along the lines of:

Christmas comes but once a year,
We wish you all good cheer
May you have health and happiness
Throughout the coming year.
We try to leave your place quite clean
And never make a mess,
So you wouldn't know we've even been
Taking care of business.
We strive to make you happy
Take a load right off your mind
More reliable blokes than us
You'd rarely ever find.

Of course, the card was designed to remind householders that a few bottles of beer or a ten bob note was the normal Christmas gift for the dunny men!

ABC local radio turned up an odd story about our quirky obsession with dunnies a few years ago. Lindsey Dennis, who lives along the road between Bute and Port Broughton, in rural South Australia, put an old ceramic toilet out the front of his farm near the mailbox. Anyone passing the farmhouses on the Spencer Highway cannot help but notice his property, as his house is now the one with a line of toilet pans out the front.

The funny thing is, he only put the one pan outside and the others have all mysteriously turned up at night since.

A rather bemused Mr Dennis told ABC Radio, 'You'd be surprised how many people stop and sit there and have their photos taken.'

For two of the funniest dunny yarns I am indebted to Peter Watson Sproal and Bob Magor.

Peter is a native of Port Fairy. He was born and bred there and has a wealth of great local stories, all of which he assures me are true. Port Fairy is one of my favourite places and my connection with the town's festival and the annual Pat Glover Storytelling Award goes back a long way. Peter now runs a beaut gourmet food store in Collingwood in Melbourne but you only have to read the story to realise that his heart is forever in the wonderful little fishing town of Port Fairy.

Bob Magor and Grahame Watt are about the funniest and best bush poets I know. Grahame doesn't get around as much as he once did, but his verse is as whimsical and funny as ever. Bob travels across the continent performing and has written eight volumes of hilariously original award-winning verse. If you enjoy 'Motionless', you will love Bob's other verse.

Henry Lawson seemed to have a 'thing' about dogs, and I have included three of his dog stories, each one different in tone and style. 'We Called Him Ally for Short' is a tall story in the true tradition of deadpan tall stories, featuring a dog and a ghost. 'That There Dog O' Mine', with its stock characters of a faithful dog and an old bushman, is about as sentimental as Lawson gets, and 'The Loaded Dog' is, of course, about a dog and dynamite. It's hardly an 'unknown' story of Lawson's—but it fits the bill for this section and is always worth re-reading!

We all love ghost stories and delight in telling them around the campfire; the stories by Ernest Favenc and Rod Quinn are among the best ever published in the *Bulletin*, real ripping yarns both of 'em.

There are quite a few links between some of these stories and the 'characters' section of this book. Victor Daley, George Barrington and Rod Quinn all feature in that section and have stories by or about them here also.

I have always found small town pubs and volunteer organisations a source of hilarity and larger than life characters. There is a kind of real humour in small towns that's always funnier than anything you could ever make up. Every incident in my Weelabarabak stories actually happened, although not perhaps in quite the same order as they do here.

There's nothing like a tall tale well told and hopefully these very Aussie stories will entertain and delight you as much as they have me—and perhaps some may even raise a few laughs of recognition along the way.

THE DAY THE PUB DIDN'T BURN DOWN

JIM HAYNES

It was the palm trees in the courtyard that caused all the trouble.

The new publican at the Royal Hotel reckoned they were 'a bit of an eyesore'. They towered way above the galvanised iron roof and their thick grey trunks took up most of the space in the little courtyard bounded by the bar at the front, the wash house and store along the sides, and the guests' rooms along the back.

The ornamental berries and fronds used to shed regularly onto the pub roof and Old Jimmy the pub handyman reckoned he was 'getting too old to be forever climbing up on the bloody roof'.

Win Jenkins, who did the cleaning and laundry at the Royal, agreed with him. She was sick of the mess around the courtyard floor causing her a lot of extra work and she voiced that opinion to anyone who would listen. Indeed she spent a lot more time voicing the opinion than she did actually cleaning up the mess in the courtyard.

There wasn't that much cleaning done at the Royal, to be honest. Being the town's 'other pub' meant that a high standard of cleanliness was not really expected. There wasn't much laundry because people only stayed there by mistake, and usually only once. Mopping out the front bar and hosing down the verandah were the main cleaning tasks and, when the pub lived up to its reputation of being 'the bloodhouse' and fights erupted, the routine changed to hosing out the front bar as well, rather than persevering with a mop.

Nevertheless, Win was of the opinion that 'those bloody old palm trees' made her life a lot harder, and she joined with

Jimmy in telling the new publican that the pub would be better off without them.

The new publican listened and nodded.

The trees might still have been safe if Jimmy and Win had been the only voices speaking out against them. After all, Jimmy and Win had said the same thing to a succession of new publicans.

But this time there were other reasons why the trees were threatened.

The first of these was that Dot, the barmaid at the Royal, had also decided the trees were a 'bloody nuisance'.

This was a new development. As a rule Dot didn't bother herself with the territory beyond the bar at the Royal, she didn't need to. Dot ruled the Royal with a fist of iron from the front bar. She didn't need to visit the courtyard or the laundry as long as she controlled the front bar of the Royal.

Dot was a legend in Weelabarabak. Her usual greeting, 'Waddya want?', actually set the standard for small town hospitality for miles around. She could prevent a brawl with one word from twenty paces and she possessed an icy stare that could make a drunken shearer think twice about causing trouble.

Nobody really knew why Dot suddenly took an interest in the palm trees. I reckon she just got sick of Win and Jimmy whingeing and decided to resolve the matter by agreeing with them. Whatever the reason, she added her considerable weight to the decision by telling the new publican he should 'get rid of the bloody things'.

This onslaught on the new publican occurred very soon after his arrival at the Royal. The staff knew you didn't have much time to initiate change before a new publican sank into the same state of apathy as all his predecessors and did pretty much nothing except let Dot run the pub from the front bar. So the plot against the palm trees was hatched during his first week in the place.

Even then it might not have succeeded except for one other thing. The new publican had just come from managing a series of pubs that had all been destroyed by fire. He was not quite stupid enough to believe that these fires had been complete accidents; on at least one occasion he had been told to be away from the premises at a specified time. He was also well aware that the actual owners of these establishments had benefited rather nicely from the demise of each pub by moving the licence to a more heavily populated town.

These experiences had left him wary of sudden fires in the night. He hadn't *always* been told to be away from the premises on relevant dates, it seems, and he had consequently become a bit jumpy about the prospect of sudden fires.

So the new publican, perhaps in light of the staff conspiracy against the palm trees—or perhaps solely for reasons of his own—decided firstly that the palm trees *were* a fire hazard and decided secondly to solve this problem in a unique way. He would burn them down.

Well, they were too tall to cut down; they would have caused quite a lot of damage when they fell onto the roof. And that's where they would have fallen because the courtyard was so small. They could have landed on the bar, the store, the laundry or the guests' rooms, causing who knew how much damage.

The new publican no doubt thought the palm trees would burn in a quite orderly manner, disintegrating into a fairly neat pile of coal and ash within the courtyard.

He set fire to them quite early one morning, expecting the whole thing to be over and cleaned up by lunchtime. He soaked the trunks with kero and piled some kindling and stove wood around each base and up the fire went, racing on kero fumes into the foliage at the top of each tree.

An excited mob of kids and grown-ups assembled from nowhere to enjoy that strange communal thrill humans always seem to experience in the presence of a really destructive fire.

We were on our way to school as the fire took off, and quickly diverted from our normal course down the side street next to the pub to watch the proceedings, wheeling our bikes as close as we dared so we could see the whole scene inside the courtyard.

The fronds and greenery at the top of the trees burned away very quickly. In a quite spectacular display, the burning vegetation fell to earth in and around the courtyard and on the galvanised iron roof where it quickly burnt out, leaving a mess of ash to be cleaned up later by Win and Jimmy.

We 'oohed' and 'arrghed' in time to the bursts of flame and the descent of the largest pieces of burning vegetation and tried to ignore the adults who told us to 'look out' and 'get off to bloody school and out of the way'.

After that the fire settled down and became rather boring. The thick spongy trunks burned away slowly, apparently from the inside.

As they smouldered the trunks turned blacker and blacker and a steady column of grey smoke arose from each one and drifted lazily into the clear sky above the courtyard of the Royal Hotel. They looked like two industrial chimneys transplanted in a rural pub courtyard.

After the early spectacle of the blazing vegetation and fiery falling fronds, this was rather mundane to watch and soon the group of onlookers had completely disintegrated, we reluctantly headed to school and the town went about its business.

By lunchtime the new publican had discovered that burning palm trees smoulder for an amazingly long time. So long did they smoulder, in fact, that they had practically been forgotten when the wind strengthened out of the west at about three o'clock that afternoon, just about the same time that the trees really began to disintegrate and fall apart.

The tree trunks had now become two teetering columns of glowing coals and, as the wind picked up, they began raining red hot embers and quite sizeable lumps of fire all over the pub and its surroundings.

As the hot wind gusted out of a still-clear sky, the scene began to resemble something in a medieval painting of Judgement Day or one of those particularly lurid Old Testament illustrations we were shown in Sunday school—the ones where Egypt suffered plagues and torments because the pharaoh wouldn't let the Israelites go.

These falling embers were far more substantial than the morning shower of burning fronds. The coals continued to burn with substantial intensity upon hitting the ground, the roof, the dry grass around the pub, or the wooden verandahs and walkways inside the courtyard and along the main street in front of the pub.

In fact by three twenty, when Mrs Thompson was telling us to tidy up our desks and make sure we'd written our homework into our homework books, the Royal Hotel was in mortal danger of transforming itself from the town's 'other pub' into the town's 'ex-pub'.

The new publican and the few staff who were on duty, along with the few desperate afternoon drinkers, had been stirred into action. Some were filling buckets from the cement tubs in the wash house and others had been despatched to get help from nearby businesses and dwellings and meanwhile warn the residents of the possible danger.

In the midst of the growing hysteria, Dot the barmaid arrived to start her normal shift. She took one look at the scene, lifted the phone and told the postmaster to call out the Weelabarabak Fire Brigade.

Luckily this was back in the days when the postmaster kept a key to the fire shed, whether he was fire captain or not, so the postmaster closed the post office and, along with his postal clerk and a couple of farmers who happened to be collecting mail at the time, hastened to the nearby fire shed, opened the door and, by doing so, magically transformed himself, his clerk and the farmers into the adumbral phase of the Weelabarabak Fire Brigade.

The Weelabarabak fire shed contained the fire trailer which held the brigade's water tank, pump and hose. The brigade did not possess a vehicle; the trailer had to be attached to the towbar of the nearest vehicle which possessed a towbar and could be commandeered, in order to get the firefighting equipment to the actual fire.

As the small group of firemen entered the shed, however, the postal clerk, the brightest of the group, made the observation that the Royal was actually *downhill* from the fire shed and, if they filled the water tank *after* they arrived at the scene of the alleged fire rather than before they left the fire shed, the trailer would be light enough for them to push it to the Royal rather than waste time looking for a vehicle with a towbar. They could then fill the tank from the water mains at the pub and use the pump to direct the water with the necessary force onto the fire.

Gil Stafford had closed his produce store and dashed across the road to become part of the Weelabarabak Fire Brigade while the original group was opening the fire shed. It was Gil who made the suggestion at this point that perhaps the water mains could be connected directly to the brigade pump, thus making the water tank redundant.

Encouraged by the general response that 'it sounded like a good idea', Gil grabbed the length of hose designed to siphon water from rivers and dams into the pump and dashed back to his store to see if he had suitable fittings for its other end.

Meanwhile, the remainder of the Weelabarabak Fire Brigade (a remainder which was growing larger by the minute as local businesses closed and able-bodied men arrived) wheeled the trailer out of the fire shed and began pushing it in the direction of the endangered Royal Hotel. They left the water tank on board for two reasons: one was 'just in case' and the other was 'it took too long to get off'. Those who couldn't find a space to help push the trailer gathered up sundry items from the fire shed, shovels, buckets and axes, and ran behind, beside or in front of the trailer.

The arrival of this enthusiastic caravan outside the Royal Hotel coincided with the entire student body from Weelabarabak Public School arriving from the opposite direction.

The coming together of these two groups—one made up of kids yelling rather obvious news of fires and fire brigades to each another, and the other consisting of a trailer, on which everything rattled, bouncing along at terrifying speed, accompanied by a dozen or fifteen men thumping along in work boots and yelling at us to 'look out'—is certainly the noisiest memory I have of my childhood. But the visual memories I have of that scene, and what happened next, are even better.

In the midst of the confusion Gil Stafford had arrived with an armful of fittings and located the water main under the pub verandah. Stilsons were applied to the appropriate connections and, with a minimum of fuss and water wastage, the mains were connected to the pump.

Parts of the pub had now started to burn rather seriously and, of course, the remains of the trees themselves were now glowing chimneys of chaos and destruction.

The short hose from the mains was connected to the intake at the back of the pump and now the fire hose was rolled out and connected to the front of the pump. The pump was started after a few good pulls on the rotor and it sprang into deafening life with a roar and a billow of smoke much blacker than that now arising from various parts of the pub. The hose unwound up the steps, across the verandah, in the front door of the bar and out through the back door into the courtyard like a vengeful canvas python.

The men of the Weelabarabak Fire Brigade positioned themselves at intervals every few yards or so along the length of the fire hose. They were ready to take the strain like a tug-o'-war team, ready to control the deadly force of water about to be unleashed against the flames which threatened the Royal Hotel.

Us kids were told to 'stand well back' and the word was given to turn the valve and let the pump do its work.

Nobody could remember when the hose had last been checked. It was a rule of the Weelabarabak Fire Brigade that 'in the case of *no fire*' the hose should be checked annually. In other words, if the hose was not used for twelve months, there being no fires in that time, it should be checked to see that it was still in an operational condition.

The problem was that blokes got busy through the year and fire drill wasn't always as regular as it should be. Besides, no one really made a note of whether or not the hose had been used when the brigade was called out and there wasn't always time for a working bee between fires, even if the time between fires stretched into years.

Evidently the hose, made of some kind of rubberised compound covered in canvas, had not been checked for quite a while. The resulting attempt at fire-fighting was spectacular. I can still see it now after all these years.

The water hit the first kink in the hose, where it turned an angle of twenty degrees or so from the trailer to the pub steps and a jet of water shot out of the hose, soaked the postmaster and arced some fifteen feet into the air. A few yards further down the hose another stream of water shot out all over the postal clerk, then another stream broke out just under the verandah roof. It went straight up, hit the galvanised iron ceiling and cascaded down over all those on the verandah.

Just at the door of the pub a double stream shot out laterally hitting both sides of the door frame. Inside the bar jets continued to spout, at the floor, the wall and the ceiling. Each new spout was just as unexpected as the first and left men jumping and swearing along the length of the hose. It was as if the flow of water was accompanied by some weird electric current.

What we couldn't see from our position outside the pub was that each new eruption of water from the hose was measurably weaker than the last. The funniest scene of all, according to Old Nugget who was inside and told me and Dad later, through tears of laughter, involved the two burliest farmers who stood braced in the doorway from the bar to the courtyard with the hose nozzle directed at the worst of the fire.

As the jets of water breaking from the hose became weaker and weaker, they stood steadfast and resolute, waiting to give the force of water its final direction. But when the stream did reach them it was not a fearsome pub-saving gusher of white water which could be directed into the depths of the ravening fire. It was, in Nugget's own words, 'a woeful little piddle of water which dribbled out the nozzle of the hose and splashed around the farmers' boots'.

While chaos reigned in the bar and on the verandah, and a forlorn puddle formed at the firefighting farmers' feet, the fire raged on in the courtyard, totally unaffected by the large amount of misdirected human energy being expended in futile attempts to extinguish it.

Many theories regarding possible remedies for the situation abounded among the men of the Weelabarabak Fire Brigade, most of whom were soaked to the skin. Before the fearless firefighters had formulated a really useful Plan B, however, Dot had organised a bucket brigade from the wash house.

The fires in the courtyard, in the grass around the pub and in various other places, were quickly put out. The soaked firefighters joined in meekly, doing exactly as Dot told them until all was under control.

Sometime later the palm trees were replaced on one side of the courtyard by a half-hearted barbecue and on the other side by a new rotary clothesline. This was meant to make Win's life a bit easier, although she whinged a fair bit that it wouldn't keep still when you were pegging stuff on it.

Locals reckon that's the cleanest the bar of the Royal has ever been, before or since.

MOTIONLESS

BOB MAGOR

Now, you've no doubt watched with interest,
'Cos each animal's unique,
When it comes to motion passing,
Each adopts its own technique.

You find sheep and cows and horses
Wander off without a care,
While the cats and dogs and others
Have a look, to check it's there.

And most humans can't resist it,
When they squat out in the scrub,
To glance around with satisfaction
At the newly fashioned nub.

We were fencing north of Hawker
With a new chum jackaroo,
Who provided entertainment
As he made his bush debut.

He deplored his work conditions,
With no deli close at hand,
Cursing flies that shared his lunches
And the endless rocks and sand.

But the greatest bane that narked him
Was the lack of porcelain
In the twenty square mile toilet
On the dusty saltbush plain.

It was with great trepidation
From a fear of things unseen
That he'd bare his timid bottom
In behind the mulga screen.

'Course we'd fuelled his apprehensions
With some yarns that bent the truth,
About nasty saltbush bunyips
That will goose a bending youth.

But we went too far one morning,
As he answered nature's call.
When he bolted for the bushes
Up behind him did we crawl.

Our long-handled posthole shovel
Through the bushes we aimed plumb
And positioned it precisely
Underneath his nervous bum.

We could barely quell our laughter
When his load we deftly caught,
Then withdrew the laden shovel
Leaving jackaroo with naught.

Now, this prank might seem quite vulgar
But I still can see his face
As he stood with job completed
And gazed idly round the place.

His relief then turned to horror
When he viewed the vacant ground,
When no showing for his efforts
In the dirt there could be found.

Petrified he scanned the flora,
Under bushes he did scout,
As he searched for signs, or footprints,
Of his turd gone walkabout.

Hoisting pants, no time to buckle,
He stampeded through the scrub,
Blazing twenty miles of saltbush
To the bar in Hawker's pub.

Where he told his bunyip story
In between large quaffs of rum,
Of his morning constitution
Stolen out from 'neath his bum!

Then he caught the first freight southwards,
Hiding in with sheep and cows,
Till he found a public toilet
To relieve his tortured bowels.

And we later heard he settled
In a city near the sea,
Where his dunny locks from inside
With a padlock and a key!

THE DUNNY CART

PETER WATSON SPROAL

Old Treg knew it was the dunny cart as he leant against the front window of his hairdressing salon and watched as it made its way up Sackville Street.

How can you call it anything else but the dunny cart, that's what it was, the truck that was used by the council to collect the toilet cans from those houses in the town not rich enough to be able to afford a new septic and the grand flush toilets that had sent the water usage for certain areas in the town sky high.

Old Treg had lit his pipe and was enjoying the warm morning sun and the tobacco smoke as it curled into the air blue and rich. For some reason that he couldn't work out, he always enjoyed the spectacle of men shouldering the dropped burdens of others, hefting them onto the back of the truck, lidded and sealed to prevent the unsavoury aromas from creating too much havoc.

Not that they had too much to do in Sackville Street. After all, it was the main shopping street of the town and, though most of the shops had toilets in the backyard, these were emptied from either Coffin Alley on the one side or up some of the lanes that ran off Barclay Street on the other. For those few shops that didn't have rear access, they were subjected once a week to having the can from the toilet carried through their premises.

The dunny truck was now parked opposite his hairdressing shop and he watched as the two men hoisted a couple of empty cans from the rear of the truck and headed into Brown's Pharmacy and the boot and shoe repair shop next door.

The mornings were always quiet in the men's hairdressing

business. Men who wanted a haircut and didn't work never bothered to get up too early, and those who worked could only have it done in their lunch hour or after work. The exception was Friday and that was country day. On Friday he employed a retired hairdresser to help him out with the rush that started about eleven and didn't let up until five-thirty.

The usual chores he did when he opened. He had swept the shop, emptying the hair from the tin sunk into the floor that had a lid he lifted by pulling a string and into which he could easily sweep all the cut hair. He had served the men or women on their way to work, calling in for their day's supply of tobacco. It had all been done.

As Treg watched, the men came out of the respective shops carrying the now lidded cans filled with the week's contributions. He noticed that Harry Sawyer was up to his usual stunt and was carrying the can on the top of his bald head on which he had jammed a woollen hat. Harry had been told many times by the works foreman that this was a dangerous practice and one which, some day, could well see him in trouble. John Sands, the works foreman, had explained that the centre of some of the older cans had some rust problems and that the only safe way to carry a can was to take the weight on the side rim which was reinforced with a steel band.

Treg smiled to himself as he remembered the many jokes and jibes poked at Harry in Hearns Pub when his mates told him that one day he would indeed be 'inturd'.

Just at that very moment, Larry Baulch came around the corner in his truck, having been across to Warrnambool and collected the goods from the railway station from the evening train. Harry Sawyer turned his head to take a look at how much freight Larry had collected. As he did, the extra movement of his head against the already weak bottom of the can made it give way and Harry's head vanished into the contents of the can.

Later, when Treg had closed the shop and was having his usual pint or two at Hearns, the talk was that if Jim Smiley had not acted swiftly, dropping his own can and ripping the lid off the can that Harry's head had vanished into, he would have drowned in the evil vat.

As it was, the commotion of having the entire contents of two whole cans dumped into the middle of the main street in mid-morning had seen practically every shopkeeper slam his door shut as the aroma began to waft down the street.

Treg had done the same, closed his front door and put the sausage in place that he used in mid-winter to stop the drafts and watched through the parted curtains of his front window.

Luckily a quick-thinking shopkeeper, and no one admitted to this later, called the fire brigade and just said Sackville Street, whereupon the fire bell began to ring and all the firemen from whatever job they were doing immediately converged on the fire station and the truck, with firemen dressed in all manner of clothing, but each one wearing his brass helmet, roared up the middle of the street with its bell ringing loudly,

As the fire truck driver frantically searched for some telltale sign of the fire and found none, they arrived at the now solitary dunny truck, since anyone with a car had hastily removed it, leaving the main street resembling a war zone.

The fire truck approached the dunny truck and those firemen clinging to the rear of the fire truck, resplendent in shiny brass helmets, began to get the first whiffs of the pungent aroma of the spilled contents, onto which Jim Smiley had poured a whole bottle of phenyl which they carried in the truck in the event of a really smelly can. The phenyl added to the already potent smell,

Harry, upon extricating himself from the can and mess, had trotted straight around the corner into Bank Street and was heading for Gipps Street and the little bridge that crossed the Moyne River. As one or two of the fishermen watched in complete amazement, Harry did a sharp turn at the beginning of the bridge and used the track that the kids used to take the shortcut onto the wharf. He trotted onto the wharf, ran along about twenty yards, until there was a spare spot where no fishing boat was parked, and performed a perfect swallow dive into the river, clothes and all.

They were even more amazed as Harry struck out down the middle of the river and headed for the wharf up near the harbour master's yard, discarding his clothing as he swam. By the time

Harry reached the jetty, he was clad only in his long underpants. He climbed from the water, still holding his nose.

Jim Smiley had climbed into the cabin of the truck with the driver and wound up the windows, wondering just what would happen next. Both Jim and the driver were aware that they were supposed to carry a full sack of sand and a small shovel in the event that this could happen and both also knew that this was not on board. Their choices were limited to either sitting and waiting while the news of the accident filtered down to the foreman in Cox Street or driving off to the works yard and collecting the bucket of sand and leaving the unsightly mess.

As it happened, the decision was taken from them as the fire truck, driven by Tony Buzzard, the fire chief, careered wildly down the street.

Guessing that the accident with the cans may have been the reason they were called out and not wanting to miss the opportunity for some training, Tony Buzzard decided to take matters into his own hands and brought the truck to a complete halt 50 or 60 feet further on from the site of the mishap. He leapt from the truck and, in his usual brisk manner, ordered his men off and began pulling the hose out to connect it to the nearest fire hydrant, which turned out to be on the footpath up near the dentist.

The men, not sure if this was a serious decision on his part and not even sure what to do, had all gathered at the back of the truck as the fire hose began to feed off the spinning red spindle.

Tony barked his orders as he connected the end of the hose to the hydrant and, with the special tool, turned the water pressure full on. George Dusting, the one nearest the nozzle end of the hose, realised that unless he pulled the nozzle out and dragged it away from the truck, the pressure of water would cause the hose to swell on the spindle and burst. Grabbing the shiny brass nozzle he ran, as he had been trained to do, in the direction of the dunny cart and just as he reached the point where the hose was fully extended, the water pressure came in full and he was left struggling with the squirming hose.

Tony Buzzard, having completed his part in the job, was now running hell for leather down to the nozzle shouting and pointing at the overturned cans and the spilled contents that surrounded them. George realised that Tony's intention was to clean up the mess using the strong jet of water from the fire hose. Like many towns built in the previous century, Port Fairy was blessed with deep gutters that carried even the run-off from the heaviest rain safely away and deposited it into the river through some of the outlets connected to the drainage system. Tony grabbed the fire hose and, with a twist of the control, directed a blast of water at the offending mess. As he did so, it caught into the open can into which Harry had plunged and sent it into the air and clattering along the centre of the street, spilling what contents had not already been spilled.

The librarian, who had closed the library door and was watching the proceedings from one of the windows in the two front rooms, burst from the door waving her arms. Miss Ireland was a nature lover and conservationist when such was not a popular thing to be and immediately had become aware of what Tony Buzzard was intending. Knowing that the whole mess would make its way into the gutter system and, by natural fall, then into the river, and because she had been fighting the council for some time trying to stop them emptying the town's waste water into the river, she began waving and shouting for him to stop as she ran from the library's front door. Tony lifted his head from the water spray for a moment as he heard the shouting and, as he did so, raised the water spray just enough to lift it and the load it was carrying up from its path to the gutter and give Miss Ireland a thorough drenching and splattering with the can contents.

At this moment, several of the shopkeepers and their customers, who had been witnessing the scene from the relative pure air of the closed shops, decided that this matter required their personal intervention and joined the scene. Miss Ireland, completely incensed by the drenching and now doubly determined to make sure that Tony Buzzard would not succeed in his efforts, was continuing in a menacing way to stalk towards him and his hose. As she reached the hose, she gave Tony Buzzard a push that sent him backwards and, once again, Miss Ireland was given a thorough drenching. By this time, the water had succeeded in sluicing most of the can's contents into the gutter and it was now beginning its slow and stately amble down the full length of the main street, to take a left hand turn into Cox Street and thence to the river.

The contents of the cans had the added attraction of torn-up newspaper since most of the shopkeepers were too mean to supply toilet tissue and this, like the more solid contents, was decorating the whole mess as it made it's way towards the post office corner. Miss Ireland, galvanised into action now and in a fury, took off in hot pursuit of the travelling night soil (the current polite name) and was pursuing it, in full voice and shouting at anyone and everyone who would listen.

As she passed the State Saving Bank, which had remained open during the whole episode since the manager had read the regulation that absolutely forbid the bank's closure other than when a criminal event or activity was perpetrated or thought to be possible, she was watched by the whole staff who had at first climbed onto the rung of the ledger desk to get a better view out the window and then, unable to see properly, gone into the street. Mr Badger, the bank manager, unsure of just what was happening, had carefully collected the bank's revolver and was carrying it in his right hand, brandishing it in a way he hoped would dissuade any would-be robber from attempting a heist. Miss Ireland approached the bank, yelling at full volume and wet from head to toe with her hair hanging in forlorn ringlets from the carefully rolled-up and pinned hair-do she usually effected.

Mr Badger, certain that a robbery had taken place or was about to take place, raised the pistol into the air and let off a volley of four shots. The teller, Mr Dade, an Englishman who had joined the bank when he and his family migrated to Australia under the ten-pound scheme and who had requested a posting in a small and quiet country town, crumpled to his knees, certain that he had been shot. Mary Nightingale, the daughter of the local shoe-shop owner and the ledger keeper at the bank, let out a piercing scream that frightened even herself and fled indoors.

Mr Badger, having caught sight of Mary fleeing into the bank, was again unsure of what was happening and, thinking that the robber may well now be inside the bank, fired the pistol's last two shots, one of which ricocheted off a nearby awning and went straight into the window of his own office, smashing it to a million slivers of glass in a resounding crash.

Mr Dade, now recovered, turned on his heels and headed into the bank just in time to collide with Mrs Badger who, having previously been in the kitchen at the rear preparing the staff's morning cup of tea, had heard the commotion and was coming out to investigate.

Finding the bank deserted, she had climbed over the teller's cage window and was now going out the door when she was fallen upon by Mr Dade. Thinking it was the robber, Mr Dade, to his own amazement, quickly wrestled the wife of the bank manager to the ground and managed to grasp her hands behind her back. He only discovered his mistake when Mr Badger rushed through the doors with the intention of reloading the now empty gun and saw his wife being wrestled to the ground by Mr Dade.

In the meanwhile, the contents of the can, now with a number of the town's more important residents in hot pursuit, was making its way along past the Craig Lea Cafe, where eleven members from a tourist bus that included Port Fairy on its tours and had a special arrangement for an early lunch at the cafe had been sitting down to a mixed grill. Daryl Thomas, the owner of the Craig Lea and a member of the Port Fairy Shire Council, hearing the gunshots, had suggested to his customers that they move down to the next section of the dining room while he investigated the commotion. At the same time, he told his wife, Shirley, who did the cooking, that maybe she had better give them some free ice cream and a canned peach, which she called a Peach Melba when she had added a splosh of raspberry syrup on top, or they might lose the trade in the future.

As he stepped from the front door of the Craig Lea Cafe, Daryl was greeted by the sight of an apparently completely insane Miss Ireland, totally dishevelled and by now moderately distraught, gesturing wildly towards something in the gutter and shouting things he could not understand. As the smell of the phenyl and the contents of the gutter now passed the Craig Lea on a wave of water like small surfers on surfboards, Daryl realised that some awful accident had occurred. He unwisely reached into the shop, slipped the snib on the lock and slammed the door shut in case any of his guests from the tour bus were tempted to leave the premises.

Miss Ireland, recovering sufficiently to recognise that she had cornered Daryl Thomas, a shire councillor, promptly headed towards him and grabbed his arm, propelling him along with her as she followed the surfing night soil. Daryl, not a person overly endowed with bravery, was under the thumb of his wife. He had only stood for council because she said it would be good for business. He did not know what to do and allowed himself to be towed along by the now indignant and very angry Miss Ireland.

As the parade approached Alec Hill's Sports Store, Alec, also a member of the local shire council, was silly enough to walk out onto the footpath, just in time to be grabbed by the free left arm of Miss Ireland, whose right hand was clutching Daryl Thomas in a deathlike grip. Alec also was immediately swept into the fray.

David Brown, the second of the town's chemists, was contemplating a morning after the night before and was looking forward to one o'clock when he could shut the shop and head for Marty Hearn's pub to have a couple of beers to stop the trembling.

The sight of a completely wet Miss Ireland (whose figure, he noted, though past its prime was still very presentable) clutching two of the town councillors, one of them one of his drinking partners, was too much. He closed the shop, put a notice up that said he would be back in ten minutes, went into the street and straight up to Marty Hearn's for a drink.

As the post office came into sight and the whole wave began to take a left hand turn, one of the posties on his bicycle was about to cycle up with a telegram to Mrs Guyett informing her that her mother was ill. He rode straight into the three fleeing locals and his bike, with him on it, crashed straight into the gutter and into the mess that was heading for the river.

On smelling the mess, the postie, not completely sure about just what it was, leapt up and returned to the post office via the rear door. As he entered the portals of the office, which before had only ever smelled of cigarettes and ink, the smell of his dripping clothing changed the entire ambience of the place. Even the postmaster in his corner office, which was usually closed off with solid wooden doors because he was the one who had to send the telegrams in morse code and needed to concentrate, looked up and sniffed the air.

As the smell grew stronger, warmed by the warm air in the post office and the postie's body, the full impact began to be felt and the two officials on counter duty vaulted the counter and, followed by the postmaster, left the premises. The couple of colleagues still sorting the morning mail took one look at the dripping postie and fled.

By this time, the councillors and Miss Ireland were being followed by a good crowd who were remaining at a safe distance from the main body of the water as it carried its load and were hugging the fence as they ran.

The postmaster, who considered it his sacred duty to be well informed about the activities of the town and who, because of his unique position as sender and receiver of telegrams, had a good idea about the successes and failures of the whole town, joined the parade and, by asking questions of some of those who were struggling to keep up near to the back of the parade, ascertained that a major spillage of some offensive and very dangerous chemical had occurred and it was heading for the river where it was anticipated that unless it was stopped the whole fish population of the river was in jeopardy.

Just at that moment the fire truck came around the corner, following the action with its bell clanging and all the men, now in high spirits and still with their helmets on, hanging on to the sides and rear of the truck. The fire chief, who took his work seriously, had decided that it was his duty to pour water on the offending material and also his responsibility to see things through to a successful conclusion.

The truck sped past the crowd and stopped just at Coffin Alley outside the shire chambers where another hydrant was set into the footpath. Acting quickly, and this time well prepared, the firemen had unwound the hose and were in the process of turning on the water just as the wave reached them. With the advantage of being in front of the approaching water, Tony Buzzard felt sure that he would be in a better position to disburse the offending material and bring the whole matter to a safe and satisfactory conclusion.

Drawn by the madness of the activity outside, the shire president, accompanied by the shire engineer, was just stepping out of the door to investigate the hubbub when Tony Buzzard ordered the water turned on and directed the jet at the approaching wave. The resulting clash of waters raised both solid matter and liquid matter along with sheets of torn newspaper into free air in a complete and not unattractive fan shape into which the shire president and engineer walked and emerged from the other side like some showgirls stepping from a waterfall.

The shire president, who always wore a hat, that day had it decorated with an object that not even in his wildest dreams could he have imagined using. The result was that Tony Buzzard, concerned that he had offended the shire president and seeing the offending decoration on his hat, turned the full force of the hose onto him in order to wash away the unwanted decoration.

The wave, interrupted and widened now with the extra new water, surged forward and headed even further down Cox Street, preparing to cross Gipps Street and head for the river. By this time, Miss Ireland had gathered one or two supporters and, along with those willing and unwilling participants, some twenty people were accompanying the offending material on its journey to the river.

There was very little that anyone could do as the wave reached the intersection. At this point it plunged beneath the road in a freefall that carried it even faster to the river. The band of followers, realising that there was little they could do since the material was underground, grabbed the shire engineer and asked him where the outlet was that would allow the offending material into the river. The shire engineer, not at all sure just what this material was but having heard that it was an offensive and dangerous chemical, pointed towards the ice works and indicated that the drain came out just below.

The band of followers headed in the direction indicated, some through the ice works, others onto the wharf, all heading along towards the drain. Miss Ireland, with her two prisoners still gripped firmly and with not the slightest intention of letting go, had opted for the overland route with the aim of placing one or both of the bodies of the two councillors in front of the drain to block the final exit of the waste flotilla into the river. As she spotted the drain, she dragged the councillors down the riverbank just in time to see the surge of water beginning to pollute the river.

Without so much as a by-your-leave or beg-your-pardon she thrust the now exhausted and very unhappy Alec Hill, who was the lighter of the two men and was, by luck, closest to the drain, with a hearty thwack to his middle regions towards the drain and as he doubled over, she pushed again and, to her delight, his bottom fitted neatly into the drain hole and prevented the escape of the noxious raft of material that she was determined to stop.

Just at that moment, the water from the additional washing outside the shire chambers joined in. The pressure inside the drain, which was blocked by Alec Hill's bottom, began to build up and he found himself being pushed out. Miss Ireland, attempting to win at all costs, was pushing him back into the drain. She was urging her followers to join the fight, but many realised that this was not a fight she could win and they stood back to watch the outcome.

Alec Hill by this time was in considerable pain and was very aware of the build-up of matter now putting pressure on his rear end. He was howling in pain and protestation as he fought back against Miss Ireland. Then more water from the extra hosing arrived and Alec Hill popped from the drain hole with a sound like an enormous fart and was ejected into the river, accompanied by Miss Ireland.

They were soon joined by an generous amount of effluent which produced an aroma not usually associated with the calm waters of the Moyne River.

At the next meeting of the shire council, the shire president, at the urging of the shire engineer and foreman of works, had a motion passed calling for the replacement of all worn-out dunny cans. They also dealt with several requests for the allocation of the old cans but they were refused on the basis of possible misuse. Marty Hearn from the pub had suggested that a can be mounted on the wall of the public bar in recognition of one Harry Sawyer, who was the toast of the hotel for being the only man known to have been 'inturd' and survive, locally anyway.

Harry was able to get free drinks for the next three weeks, The only problem he had was that his children, who attended the local Catholic school, had to put up with the taunts of both the kids from their own school then face the taunts from the kids who attended the local state school and now chanted 'Catholic dogs smell like bogs.'

As he watched the antics, Old Treg decided there and then that he would mention to his wife the advantages of having their home in Gipps Street fitted with a septic toilet in order to avoid this ever happening close to her, since she was too delicate to ever survive such an experience.

At the next meeting of the town's conservation and nature group, Miss Ireland was urged to take a more active role and asked to stand for council elections due the following month, which she did and won a seat with a very handsome majority. The downside for Miss Ireland only came some weeks later when a long-term clandestine affair she had been conducting with the works foreman came to what she considered to be a premature end. With her new-found interest in local politics and conservation, she went on to become president of the annual Port Fairy show committee as well as convenor for the Gould Bird League of Bird Watchers.

David Brown, who had retired to Marty Hearn's hotel during the event, never did make it back to work. He spent the rest of the afternoon in the hotel and was roundly and soundly abused by his wife when he arrived home in a very bad state that evening. The next day he decided that it was time for him to dry out and he went on the wagon for a full week, at the end of which he was urged by his wife and family to take up drinking again, since he was too annoying when sober all the time.

Tony Buzzard was called into the office of the shire president and told that in the future he was only to attend actual fires and, unless this was strictly and properly adhered to, he would not be considered for the position of fire chief when the post was next due for consideration.

The manager of the State Saving Bank was asked by the local police why he had fired off all six rounds of his gun and a report was submitted to his superiors who sent him off to the local gun club for retraining. His wife never spoke to Mr Dade again but, for reasons that remain between them and them alone, when in his presence she always acted in a coquettish way.

Mary Nightingale resigned from the bank and went to work for her father in his electrical business. In the long run it was a good decision as she was due to marry Alan Sherman in three weeks and he was one of the fireman who had witnessed and heard the whole thing. In view of her doctor's reports as to her nervous condition as a result of the gun firing and crashing glass, she was offered a good compensation package which she would not have received had she, in the normal course of events, resigned for her marriage, since the bank did not employ married women.

Finally, and wisely, the foreman, in discussion with his men, decided that the rounds of the dunny cart would be rescheduled to a time in the day when less people were around and when any accidents were less likely to be a problem.

All of this was duly reported in full in the *Port Fairy Gazette.*

A BUSHMAN'S HOLIDAY

COLIN NEWSOME

It was not only just by chance, I heard old bushmen say
To get blind drunk and poo your pants was a bushman's holiday
A change from tucker in the scrub, he'd gorge on roasted fowls
And luscious meals cooked in the pub which loosened up his bowels.
Snoring in a hotel bed, he found that he had sinned,
And he had pooed the bed instead when he was passing wind.
Then he'd work for months again. Completely sobered up,
He'd leave to catch the bus or train to see the Melbourne Cup.
Soon he came back to the scrub and looked foolish when he said
'I got drunk at the local pub and pooed my pants instead!'
City folk would look askance, 'Bush' people all would say,
'Good on you mate! You pooed your pants! That's a bushman's holiday!'
Hard work was done by men who'd shear the sheep and cut the logs.
The bushman helped to pioneer the land with horse and dogs.
He used to live on billy tea and damper and corn beef,
And passing wind both ends would be his best form of relief.
A careless pattern, this, which grew from living on hard tack;
He didn't go so often to the toilet out the back.
Leaning from his saddle seat he'd let the loud winds pass;
His horse would shy and stoop to eat a blade of Mitchell grass.
'You'd better steady up, old mate', companions used to say,
'You are a perfect candidate for a bushman's holiday!'
Sometimes in company he'd forget; or to amuse the boys,
He'd lift his leg up and he'd let out some wind with roaring noise.
At Christmas Eve or Yearly Show he always came to town,
Where small town smarties had to go to try and take him down.
Soon everybody was his mate; he'd buy them all some beer,
Then to the toilet ran too late—confirming his worst fear!
He looked sheepish, though he grinned, and foolishly he said,
'I thought that I was passing wind, and pooed my pants instead!'

Wearing no pyjamas, while in a hotel bed;
He went to pass a gust of wind and pooed the bed instead.
When a bushman came to wed he had to change his ways;
No more to poo in hotel beds on bushman's holidays!
'Our newborn son is like his dad!' his wife would often say,
'I'll change his nappy. Yes! He's had a bushman's holiday!'

WE CALLED HIM 'ALLY' FOR SHORT

HENRY LAWSON

I don't believe in ghosts; I never did have any sympathy with them, being inclined to regard them as a nuisance and a bore. A ghost generally comes fooling around when you want to go to sleep, and his conversation, if he speaks at all, invariably turns on murders and suicides and other unpleasant things in which you are not interested, and which only disturb your rest. It is no use locking the door against a ghost, for, as is well-known, he can come in through the key hole, and there are cases on record when a ghost has been known to penetrate a solid wall.

You cannot kick a ghost out; he is impervious to abuse, and if you throw a boot at him, likely as not it will go right through a new looking-glass worth eighteen shillings. I remember, about five years ago, I was greatly annoyed by a ghost, while doing a job of fencing in the bush between here and Perth.

I was camping in an old house which had been used as a barrack for the convicts or their keepers (I'm not sure which) in the lively old days of the broad arrow. He was a common-looking ghost of a skeleton kind, and was arrayed in what appeared to be the tattered remnants of an old-time convict uniform.

He still wore a pair of shadowy manacles, but, being very elastic and unsubstantial and stretching the full length of his stride, he did not seem to notice them at all. He had a kind of Artful Dodger expression about his bare jaw-bones, and in place of the ordinary halo of the ring variety, he wore a shining representation of a broad-arrow which shed a radiance over his skull. He used to come round and wake me about midnight with a confounded rigmarole about a convict who was buried alive in his irons, and whose representative my unwelcome visitor claimed to be.

I tried all I knew to discourage him. I told him I wasn't interested and wanted to go to sleep; but his perseverance wore me out at last, and I tried another tack. I listened to his confounded yarn from beginning to end, and sympathised with him, and told him that he, or the individual he represented, had been treated confoundedly badly; and I promised to make a poem about it.

But even then he wasn't satisfied. Nothing would suit him but he must spin his old yarn, and be sympathised with about seven times a week, always choosing the most unbusinesslike hours (between one and three in the morning) for his disclosures.

At last I could stand it no longer. I was getting thin and exhausted from want of sleep, so I determined on a course of action.

I had a dog at home, a big black dog with unpleasant eyes, and a chewing-up apparatus that an alligator might have envied. He had a most enterprising appetite, and wasn't afraid of anything on the surface of this earth—or under it—as far as he could burrow. He would gnaw a log to pieces rather than let the possum it contained escape him.

He was not the sort of dog to stand any nonsense even from a ghost. His full name was Alligator-Desolation (we called him 'Ally' for short): and, as I considered that if any person on earth could lay the ghost that annoyed me, that person was Alligator-Desolation, I decided to bring him along.

The next time I journeyed home for rations I brought Alligator-Desolation back with me. On the trip back he killed five kangaroos, sixteen possums, four native rats, two native bears, three sheep, a cow and a calf, and another dog that happened by; and before he had been two hours at the hut he had collected enough carcases of indigenous animals to stink a troop out in a week, or to feed all the dogs in Constantinople.

I had tea and a smoke while Ally was resting, and about eleven o'clock I lay down in my bunk, dressed as I was, and waited. At about one I heard the usual unearthly noises which accompanied the arrival of my friend the ghost, and Ally went out to investigate.

While the dog was gone, the ghost strolled in through the door of the end room, apparently unconscious of his danger. He glided straight up to the side of my bunk, took his accustomed seat on a gin-case, and commenced in a doleful voice to pitch his confounded old yarn again; but he hadn't uttered half-a-dozen ghostly words when Alligator-Desolation came in through the side door.

The ghost caught sight of Ally before the latter saw him, and made for the window. Ally wasn't far behind; he made a grab at the ghost's nether garments, but they gave way easily, being of a ghostly material.

Then Ally leapt out through the window and chased the ghost three times round the house, and then the latter came in through an opening in the wall where a slab had fallen out. Being of an easily compressible constitution he came through, of course, with the facility peculiar to his kind, but the crack was narrow and the dog stuck fast.

His ghostship made the best of his opportunity, and, approaching my bed, hurriedly endeavoured to continue his story, as though his ghostly existence depended on it. But his utterances were drowned by the language of Alligator, whose canine oaths were simply terrific. At last, collecting all his energy for one mighty effort, Alligator came through, bringing down the slabs on each side of him. He made for the ghost at once, and the ghost made for the window.

This time Alligator made a grab for the spectre's ankle, and his teeth came together with a crash that threatened their destruction. Ally must have been greatly astonished and disgusted, because he so seldom missed anything he reached for. But he wasn't the kind of dog to give up. He leapt through the window, and, after a race round the hut, lasting some minutes, the ghost gave it up, and made for the scrub.

Seeing the retreat through a crack in the slabs, I immediately rose, went outside and mounted my horse, which I had kept ready saddled in case of emergency. I followed the chase for about five miles, and at last reached a mound under some trees, which looked like an old grave. Down through this mound the ghost dived.

Alligator-Desolation immediately commenced to dig, and made two feet in no time. It appeared that a wombat had selected the grave as a suitable site for the opening of his burrow and after having sunk about three feet, was resting from his labours. There was a short and angry interview between Alligator and the wombat, during which the latter expired, and then Ally continued his work of excavation. After sinking two feet deeper he dragged out what appeared to be the leg-bone of a human being, attached to which was a pair of heavy leg-irons, such as were used in the old convict days.

Ally went down the hole again, but presently he paused in his digging operations, and I heard a noise like a row in the infernal regions. Then a thin shadowy form issued from the grave and made off through the scrub with the dog in pursuit. My horse was knocked up, so I left the chase to Alligator and returned home to await developments.

Ally came back about three days later with his hair badly singed and smelling strongly of brimstone. I have no doubt that he chased the ghost to the infernal regions and perhaps had an interview with Cerberus at the gate, or the boss himself; but the dog's tail was well up and a satisfied grin oozed from the roots of every fang, and by the same tokens I concluded that the other party, whoever he was, had got fatally left. I haven't seen the ghost since.

DALEY'S DORG 'WATTLE'

W.T. GOODGE ('THE COLONEL')

'You can talk about yer sheep dorgs,'
Said the man from Allan's Creek,
'But I know a dorg that simply knocked 'em bandy!
Do whatever you would show him,
And you'd hardly need to speak;
Owned by Daley, drover cove in Jackandandy.

'We was talkin' in the parlour,
Me and Daley, quiet like,
When a blow-fly starts a-buzzin' round the ceilin',
Up gets Daley, and he says to me,
"You wait a minute, Mike,
And I'll show you what a dorg he is at heelin."

'And an empty pickle-bottle
Was a-standin' on the shelf,
Daley takes it down and puts it on the table,
And he bets me drinks that blinded dorg
Would do it by himself –
And I didn't think as how as he was able!

'Well, he shows the dorg the bottle,
And he points up to the fly,
And he shuts the door, and says to him – "Now Wattle!"
And in less than fifteen seconds,
Spare me days, it ain't a lie,
That there dorg had got that insect in the bottle.'

THE LOADED DOG

HENRY LAWSON

Dave Regan, Jim Bently, and Andy Page were sinking a shaft at Stony Creek in search of a rich gold quartz reef which was supposed to exist in the vicinity.

There is always a rich reef supposed to exist in the vicinity; the only questions are whether it is ten feet or hundreds beneath the surface, and in which direction. They had struck some pretty solid rock, also water which kept them baling.

They used the old-fashioned blasting-powder and time-fuse. They'd make a sausage or cartridge of blasting-powder in a skin of strong calico or canvas, the mouth sewn and bound round the end of the fuse; they'd dip the cartridge in melted tallow to make it water-tight, get the drill-hole as dry as possible, drop in the cartridge with some dry dust, and wad and ram with stiff clay and broken brick. Then they'd light the fuse and get out of the hole and wait. The result was usually an ugly pot-hole in the bottom of the shaft and half a barrow-load of broken rock.

There was plenty of fish in the creek, fresh-water bream, cod, cat-fish, and tailers. The party were fond of fish, and Andy and Dave of fishing. Andy would fish for three hours at a stretch if encouraged by a 'nibble' or a 'bite' now and then—say once in twenty minutes. The butcher was always willing to give meat in exchange for fish when they caught more than they could eat; but now it was winter, and these fish wouldn't bite. However, the creek was low, just a chain of muddy water-holes, from the hole with a few bucketfuls in it to the sizable pool with an average depth of six or seven feet, and they could get fish by baling out the smaller holes or muddying up the water in the larger ones till the fish rose to the surface.

There was the cat-fish, with spikes growing out of the sides of its head, and if you got pricked you'd know it, as Dave said. Andy took off his boots, tucked up his trousers, and went into a hole one day to stir up the mud with his feet, and he knew it. Dave scooped one out with his hand and got pricked, and he knew it too; his arm swelled, and the pain throbbed up into his shoulder, and down into his stomach too, he said, like a toothache he had once, and kept him awake for two nights—only the toothache pain had a 'burred edge', Dave said.

Dave got an idea. 'Why not blow the fish up in the big water-hole with a cartridge?' he said. 'I'll try it.'

He thought the thing out and Andy Page worked it out. Andy usually put Dave's theories into practice if they were practicable, or bore the blame for the failure and the chaffing of his mates if they weren't.

He made a cartridge about three times the size of those they used in the rock. Jim Bently said it was big enough to blow the bottom out of the river. The inner skin was of stout calico; Andy stuck the end of a six-foot piece of fuse well down in the powder and bound the mouth of the bag firmly to it with whipcord.

The idea was to sink the cartridge in the water with the open end of the fuse attached to a float on the surface, ready for lighting. Andy dipped the cartridge in melted bees'-wax to make it water-tight.

'We'll have to leave it some time before we light it,' said Dave, 'to give the fish time to get over their scare when we put it in, and come nosing round again; so we'll want it well water-tight.'

Round the cartridge Andy, at Dave's suggestion, bound a strip of sail canvas—that they used for making water-bags—to increase the force of the explosion, and round that he pasted layers of stiff brown paper—on the plan of the sort of fireworks we called 'gun-crackers'.

He let the paper dry in the sun, then he sewed a covering of two thicknesses of canvas over it, and bound the thing from end to end with stout fishing-line.

Dave's schemes were elaborate, and he often worked his inventions out to nothing. The cartridge was rigid and solid enough now—a formidable bomb; but Andy and Dave wanted to be sure. Andy sewed on another layer of canvas, dipped the cartridge in melted tallow, twisted a length of fencing-wire round it as an afterthought, dipped it in tallow again, and stood it carefully against a tent-peg, where he'd know where to find it, and wound the fuse loosely round it.

Then he went to the camp-fire to try some potatoes which were boiling in their jackets in a billy, and to see about frying some chops for dinner. Dave and Jim were at work in the claim that morning.

They had a big black young retriever dog—or rather an overgrown pup, a big, foolish, four-footed mate, who was always slobbering round them and lashing their legs with his heavy tail that swung round like a stock-whip. Most of his head was usually a red, idiotic, slobbering grin of appreciation of his own silliness.

He seemed to take life, the world, his two-legged mates, and his own instinct as a huge joke. He'd retrieve anything: he carted back most of the camp rubbish that Andy threw away.

They had a cat that died in hot weather, and Andy threw it a good distance away in the scrub; and early one morning the dog found the cat, after it had been dead a week or so, and carried it back to camp, and laid it just inside the tent-flaps, where it could best make its presence known when the mates should rise and begin to sniff suspiciously in the sickly smothering atmosphere of the summer sunrise.

He used to retrieve them when they went in swimming; he'd jump in after them, and take their hands in his mouth, and try to swim out with them, and scratch their naked bodies with his paws. They loved him for his good-heartedness and his foolishness, but when they wished to enjoy a swim they had to tie him up in camp.

He watched Andy with great interest all the morning making the cartridge, and hindered him considerably, trying to help; but about noon he went off to the claim to see how Dave and Jim were getting on, and to come home to dinner with them. Andy saw them coming, and put a panful of mutton-chops on the fire.

Andy was cook to-day; Dave and Jim stood with their backs to the fire, as Bushmen do in all weathers, waiting till dinner should be ready. The retriever went nosing round after something he seemed to have missed.

Andy's brain still worked on the cartridge; his eye was caught by the glare of an empty kerosene-tin lying in the bushes, and it struck him that it wouldn't be a bad idea to sink the cartridge packed with clay, sand, or stones in the tin, to increase the force of the explosion. He may have been all out, from a scientific point of view, but the notion looked all right to him. Jim Bently, by the way, wasn't interested in their 'damned silliness'.

Andy noticed an empty treacle-tin—the sort with the little tin neck or spout soldered on to the top for the convenience of pouring out the treacle—and it struck him that this would have made the best kind of cartridge-case: he would only have had to pour in the powder, stick the fuse in through the neck, and cork and seal it with bees'-wax.

He was turning to suggest this to Dave, when Dave glanced over his shoulder to see how the chops were doing—and bolted. He explained afterwards that he thought he heard the pan spluttering extra, and looked to see if the chops were burning.

Jim Bently looked behind and bolted after Dave.

Andy stood stock-still, staring after them.

'Run, Andy! Run!' they shouted back at him. 'Run!!! Look behind you, you fool!'

Andy turned slowly and looked, and there, close behind him, was the retriever with the cartridge in his mouth—wedged into his broadest and silliest grin.

And that wasn't all. The dog had come round the fire to Andy, and the loose end of the fuse had trailed and waggled over the burning sticks into the blaze; Andy had slit and nicked the firing end of the fuse well, and now it was hissing and spitting properly.

Andy's legs started with a jolt; his legs started before his brain did, and he made after Dave and Jim. And the dog followed Andy.

Dave and Jim were good runners—Jim the best—for a short distance; Andy was slow and heavy, but he had the strength and the wind and could last.

The dog leapt and capered round him, delighted as a dog could be to find his mates, as he thought, on for a frolic.

Dave and Jim kept shouting back, 'Don't foller us! Don't foller us, you coloured fool!' but Andy kept on, no matter how they dodged.

They could never explain, any more than the dog, why they followed each other, but so they ran, Dave keeping in Jim's track in all its turnings, Andy after Dave, and the dog circling round Andy—the live fuse swishing in all directions and hissing and spluttering and stinking.

Jim yelling to Dave not to follow him, Dave shouting to Andy to go in another direction—to 'spread out'—and Andy roaring at the dog to go home.

Then Andy's brain began to work, stimulated by the crisis: he tried to get a running kick at the dog, but the dog dodged; he snatched up sticks and stones and threw them at the dog and ran on again.

The retriever saw that he'd made a mistake about Andy, and left him and bounded after Dave.

Dave, who had the presence of mind to think that the fuse's time wasn't up yet, made a dive and a grab for the dog, caught him by the tail, and as he swung round snatched the cartridge out of his mouth and flung it as far as he could: the dog immediately bounded after it and retrieved it.

Dave roared and cursed at the dog, who seeing that Dave was offended, left him and went after Jim, who was well ahead.

Jim swung to a sapling and went up it like a native bear; it was a young sapling, and Jim couldn't safely get more than ten or twelve feet from the ground. The dog laid the cartridge, as carefully as if it was a kitten, at the foot of the sapling, and capered and leapt and whooped joyously round under Jim.

The big pup reckoned that this was part of the lark—he was all right now—it was Jim who was out for a spree.

The fuse sounded as if it were going a mile a minute. Jim tried to climb higher and the sapling bent and cracked. Jim fell on his feet and ran.

The dog swooped on the cartridge and followed. It all took but a very few moments.

Jim ran to a digger's hole, about ten feet deep, and dropped down into it—landing on soft mud—and was safe.

The dog grinned sardonically down on him, over the edge, for a moment, as if he thought it would be a good lark to drop the cartridge down on Jim.

'Go away, Tommy,' said Jim feebly, 'go away.'

The dog bounded off after Dave, who was the only one in sight now; Andy had dropped behind a log, where he lay flat on his face, having suddenly remembered a picture of the Russo-Turkish war with a circle of Turks lying flat on their faces (as if they were ashamed) round a newly-arrived shell.

There was a small hotel or shanty on the creek, on the main road, not far from the claim.

Dave was desperate, the time flew much faster in his stimulated imagination than it did in reality, so he made for the shanty.

There were several casual Bushmen on the verandah and in the bar; Dave rushed into the bar, banging the door to behind him. 'My dog!' he gasped, in reply to the astonished stare of the publican, 'the blanky retriever—he's got a live cartridge in his mouth—'

The retriever, finding the front door shut against him, had bounded round and in by the back way, and now stood smiling in the doorway leading from the passage, the cartridge still in his mouth and the fuse spluttering.

They burst out of that bar.

Tommy bounded first after one and then after another, for, being a young dog, he tried to make friends with everybody.

The Bushmen ran round corners, and some shut themselves in the stable.

There was a new weather-board and corrugated-iron kitchen and wash-house on piles in the back-yard, with some women washing clothes inside. Dave and the publican bundled in there and shut the door—the publican cursing Dave and calling him a crimson fool, in hurried tones, and wanting to know what the hell he came here for.

The retriever went in under the kitchen, amongst the piles, but, luckily for those inside, there was a vicious yellow mongrel cattle-dog sulking and nursing his nastiness under there—a sneaking, fighting, thieving canine, whom neighbours had tried for years to shoot or poison.

Tommy saw his danger—he'd had experience from this dog—and started out and across the yard, still sticking to the cartridge.

Half-way across the yard the yellow dog caught him and nipped him. Tommy dropped the cartridge, gave one terrified yell, and took to the Bush. The yellow dog followed him to the fence and then ran back to see what he had dropped.

Nearly a dozen other dogs came from round all the corners and under the buildings—spidery, thievish, cold-blooded kangaroo-dogs, mongrel sheep- and cattle-dogs, vicious black and yellow dogs—that slip after you in the dark, nip your heels, and vanish without explaining—and yapping, yelping small fry.

They kept at a respectable distance round the nasty yellow dog, for it was dangerous to go near him when he thought he had found something which might be good for a dog to eat. He sniffed at the cartridge twice, and was just taking a third cautious sniff when—

It was very good blasting powder—a new brand that Dave had recently got up from Sydney; and the cartridge had been excellently well made. Andy was very patient and painstaking in all he did, and nearly as handy as the average sailor with needles, twine, canvas, and rope.

Bushmen say that that kitchen jumped off its piles and on again. When the smoke and dust cleared away, the remains of the nasty yellow dog were lying against the paling fence of the yard looking as if he had been kicked into a fire by a horse and afterwards rolled in the dust under a barrow, and finally thrown against the fence from a distance. Several saddle-horses, which had been 'hanging-up' round the verandah, were galloping wildly down the road in clouds of dust, with broken bridle-reins flying; and from a circle round the outskirts, from every point of the compass in the scrub, came the yelping of dogs.

Two of them went home, to the place where they were born,

thirty miles away, and reached it the same night and stayed there; it was not till towards evening that the rest came back cautiously to make inquiries. One was trying to walk on two legs, and most of 'em looked more or less singed; and a little, singed, stumpy-tailed dog, who had been in the habit of hopping the back half of him along on one leg, had reason to be glad that he'd saved up the other leg all those years, for he needed it now.

There was one old one-eyed cattle-dog round that shanty for years afterwards, who couldn't stand the smell of a gun being cleaned. He it was who had taken an interest, only second to that of the yellow dog, in the cartridge.

Bushmen said that it was amusing to slip up on his blind side and stick a dirty ramrod under his nose: he wouldn't wait to bring his solitary eye to bear—he'd take to the Bush and stay out all night. For half an hour or so after the explosion there were several Bushmen round behind the stable who crouched, doubled up, against the wall, or rolled gently on the dust, trying to laugh without shrieking.

There were two white women in hysterics at the house, and a half-caste rushing aimlessly round with a dipper of cold water. The publican was holding his wife tight and begging her between her squawks, to 'hold up for my sake, Mary, or I'll lam the life out of ye.'

Dave decided to apologise later on, 'when things had settled a bit,' and went back to camp. And the dog that had done it all, 'Tommy', the great, idiotic mongrel retriever, came slobbering round Dave and lashing his legs with his tail, and trotted home after him, smiling his broadest, longest, and reddest smile of amiability, and apparently satisfied for one afternoon with the fun he'd had.

Andy chained the dog up securely, and cooked some more chops, while Dave went to help Jim out of the hole.

And most of this is why, for years afterwards, lanky, easy-going Bushmen, riding lazily past Dave's camp, would cry, in a lazy drawl and with just a hint of the nasal twang—'El-lo, Da-a-ve! How's the fishin' getting on, Da-a-ve?'

MY KELPIE

WILBUR HOWCROFT

Who barks and wags his tail with glee
And greets the new day joyously
Each morning as he welcomes me?
My kelpie

Who, with his head upon his paws,
Waits patiently while I'm indoors
And plainly shows who he adores?
My kelpie

Who sticks with me the whole day through
No matter what I say or do
And does most things I ask him to?
My kelpie

Who digs great holes in garden beds
And tears his sleeping mat to shreds
And never worries where he treads?
My kelpie

Who often whimpers in the night,
Perhaps through some canine foresight
Or nightmares of a long-past fight?
My kelpie

Who looks at me with faithful eyes
And never cheats and never lies
Nor puts me off with alibis?
My kelpie

Who is my mate – not just a pet –
A mere brown dog, perhaps, and yet
I know I never shall forget?
My kelpie.

THAT THERE DOG O' MINE

HENRY LAWSON

Macquarie the shearer had met with an accident. To tell the truth, he had been in a drunken row at a wayside shanty, from which he had escaped with three fractured ribs, a cracked head, and various minor abrasions. His dog, Tally, had been a sober but savage participator in the drunken row, and had escaped with a broken leg. Macquarie afterwards shouldered his swag and staggered and struggled along the track ten miles to the Union Town hospital. Lord knows how he did it. He didn't exactly know himself. Tally limped behind all the way, on three legs.

The doctors examined the man's injuries and were surprised at his endurance. Even doctors are surprised sometimes—though they don't always show it. Of course they would take him in, but they objected to Tally. Dogs were not allowed on the premises.

'You will have to turn that dog out,' they said to the shearer, as he sat on the edge of a bed.

Macquarie said nothing.

'We cannot allow dogs about the place, my man,' said the doctor in a louder tone, thinking the man was deaf.

'Tie him up in the yard then.'

'No. He must go out. Dogs are not permitted on the grounds.'

Macquarie rose slowly to his feet, shut his agony behind his set teeth, painfully buttoned his shirt over his hairy chest, took up his waistcoat, and staggered to the corner where the swag lay.

'What are you going to do?' they asked.

'You ain't going to let my dog stop?'

'No. It's against the rules. There are no dogs allowed on premises.'

He stooped and lifted his swag, but the pain was too great, and he leaned back against the wall.

'Come, come now! Man alive!' exclaimed the doctor, impatiently. 'You must be mad. You know you are not in a fit state to go out. Let the wardsman help you to undress.'

'No!' said Macquarie. 'No. If you won't take my dog in you don't take me. He's got a broken leg and wants fixing up just—just as much as—as I do. If I'm good enough to come in, he's good enough—and—and better.'

He paused awhile, breathing painfully, and then went on.

'That . . . that there old dog of mine has follered me faithful and true, these twelve long hard and hungry years. He's about—about the only thing that ever cared whether I lived or fell and rotted on the cursed track.'

He rested again; then he continued: 'That . . . that there dog was pupped on the track,' he said, with a sad sort of a smile. 'I carried him for months in a billy, and afterwards on my swag when he knocked up . . . And the old bitch, his mother, she'd foller along quite contented, and sniff the billy now and again, just to see if he was all right . . . She follered me for God knows how many years. She follered me till she was blind, and for a year after. She follered me till she could crawl along through the dust no longer, and . . . and then I killed her, because I couldn't leave her behind alive!'

He rested again.

'And this here old dog,' he continued, touching Tally's upturned nose with his knotted fingers, 'this here old dog has follered me for—for ten years; through floods and droughts, through fair times and . . . and hard . . . mostly hard; and kept me from going mad when I had no mate nor money on the lonely track; and watched over me for weeks when I was drunk . . . drugged and poisoned at the cursed shanties; and saved my life more'n once, and got kicks and curses very often for thanks; and forgave me for it all; and . . . and fought for me. He was the only living thing that stood up for me against that crawling push of curs when they set onter me at the shanty back yonder . . . and he left his mark on some of 'em too; and—and so did I.'

He took another spell.

Then he drew in his breath, shut his teeth hard, shouldered his swag, stepped into the doorway, and faced round again.

The dog limped out of the corner and looked up anxiously.

'That there dog,' said Macquarie to the hospital staff in general, 'is a better dog than I'm a man . . . or you too, it seems . . . and a better Christian. He's been a better mate to me than I ever was to any man . . . or any man to me. He's watched over me; kep' me from getting robbed many a time; fought for me; saved my life and took drunken kicks and curses for thanks . . . and forgave me. He's been a true, straight, honest, and faithful mate to me . . . and I ain't going to desert him now. I ain't going to kick him out in the road with a broken leg. I . . .. Oh, my God! my back!'

He groaned and lurched forward, but they caught him, slipped off the swag, and laid him on a bed.

Half an hour later the shearer was comfortably fixed up.

'Where's my dog!' he asked, when he came to himself.

'Oh, the dog's all right,' said the nurse, rather impatiently. 'Don't bother. The doctor's setting his leg out in the yard.'

THE MONGREL

GRAHAME WATT

'Who owns the mong in the corner?'
The bloke at the bar loudly said,
He's breathing his last breath, I reckon,
That poor blessed dog looks near dead!
And dogs aren't allowed, where I come from,
To frequent hotels in the town.
Who owns this excuse for a canine?
He'd be much better off if put down!'

A silence hung there for a minute,
Then a whiskery old drover spoke up.
'That's my dog, young feller, he's my dog,
I've had him since he was a pup.
You're right, he's old and decrepit,
Like me he has not long to go.
But that mong as you call him's my best friend,
And no better mate could you know.

'For me and that dog have enjoyed life.
We both talked a language the same.
We shared the hot days and water-bag thirst
As we worked at the mustering game.
And that dog saved my life in the outback
When thrown from my horse, far away,
That dog ran for help and led the men back,
I owe him my life you could say.

'I reared him on scraps from my feed bag,
I taught him to fetch and to heel.
I'd say you're a stranger to these parts
Or you'd know just the way that I feel.
Yes, he's old, and it's cruel now to see him,
No dog should have earned such a fate.

Last Friday I picked up my rifle,
But how could I shoot my best mate?

'I even asked that young vet bloke
"How much to give my dog rest?"
"Fifty dollars," he said, "is the fee for the job."
But with money I've never been blessed.'
The stranger grew quiet at the story,
He glanced at the bar drinking crew.
He said, 'Sorry, old timer, I spoke out of turn,
I can see what that dog means to you.

'Here's fifty dollars to have him put down,
And you'll have to excuse me I fear,
I know it's hard to lose a good friend,
One so close, and so near.'
The stranger shook hands with the drover
And quickly departed the room.
A silence hung over the drinkers,
A sort of a sadness and gloom.

But then the old drover said, 'Spark up!'
Things aren't that bad, for you see,
That city bloke left fifty dollars
So now all the drinks are on me!
Drink up you blokes, name your poison,
And drink to that mong—he's a swell!
If his owner were here, well, I'd kiss him,
And shout him a few drinks as well!'

BAILIFFS I HAVE MET

VICTOR DALEY

It has been remarked that the worst use to which you can put a man is to hang him. A mistake. You can put him to a still worse use. You can make him a bailiff.

I am writing this article in bed, using as a desk a box which, at one time, according to the printed legend pasted on its lid, contained seven pounds net of cocoanut ice. It commenced its career coldly, this poor little box; but it shall end warmly and famously. Tomorrow morning I shall split it up into neat little splinters, to which I shall deftly set fire, and therewith boil my coffee. I know that in years to come, when I shall have lost my taste for coffee and all other worldly pleasures, relic collectors will wish that I had not done this thing; but one can't boil coffee on posthumous glory.

Alexander Pope is said to have written most of his translation of the *Iliad* in bed, but that was mere luxurious laziness on his part. I am writing in bed for the reason that, if I were up, I would have to sit on the floor to write—a position which, besides being uncomfortable, is apt to make one round-shouldered.

The intelligent reader will gather from the foregoing remarks that the bailiff has been with me. He has been, with a vengeance, and liked my taste in furniture so well that he took it all away with him, including even my little Japanese tobacco-jar, and a Satsuma spittoon of fantastic elegance.

I shouldn't have cared so much if he had left me my engraving of Don Quixote, which used to bring the tears to my eyes every time I looked at it. The noble knight-errant is shown sitting in his chamber, with all his armour around him. His withered hands, with their bony knuckles and outstanding veins and sinews, are clasped on the hilt of his long, cross-hilted sword, and there is a look of visionary exaltation in his faded eyes, which is in itself an inspiration. The valourous Manchegan had also his troubles with the world, even as I have mine.

It is now twelve years ago since I gathered my first practical knowledge of bailiffdom. Even then I did not see a bailiff in the flesh, but I stood in the place (he had left nothing to sit upon) where a bailiff had been, only a few hours before. It was after dusk, one evening in autumn, and, as I knocked at the door of the house in which dwelt my guide, philosopher, and friend of those early days, I thought that the knock sounded singularly loud, as though the house were empty. So it was, in a sense, its sole contents being my philosopher friend and his wife and family. They were seated on the floor, in a circle, around a sheet of newspaper, upon which were displayed two or three loaves of bread, a paper bag containing sugar, a large billycan of tea, and some tinned sardines.

They were eating with their fingers, and drinking in turns out of a pannikin, which passed from hand to hand, in the manner of a bottle at a small and informal convivial gathering of friends.

'You observe,' said my philosopher, with a nod at the newspaper, and a wave of his hand towards the bare walls, 'you observe, my young sage, how little the natural man really needs to satisfy his legitimate requirements. All else is mere superfluous luxury. The bailiff relieved me of my superfluous luxury this morning. I bear him no malice on that account. A man of letters' (my philosopher was a contributor to the weekly papers, but always called himself a man of letters) 'should fly light in the matter of furniture.'

I looked at the squabbling children on the floor, and thought that the remark might be extended to include family as well as furniture. My philosopher, however, had his revenge on bailiffdom in due course, as will be seen later on.

A year or so after the foregoing incident, which occurred in Melbourne, I was in Sydney lodging in the house of a friend, who also described himself as a man of letters. He was, as a matter of fact, a reporter on one of the daily papers, but was endowed with tastes and aspirations far above his position. These found expression in speckled-green jars, papier-mache statuettes of classical shepherds and shepherdesses, vases of every size and shape, brackets, tables with spiral legs like crossed corkscrews, and other articles of virtue too numerous to mention.

The front room of the little house in which he lived was so crowded with these things that it was seldom opened, except when his wife went in to dust them. He had also a library, contained in a carven bookcase with glass doors. It consisted of some forty or fifty volumes, works of the old dramatists. These were carefully numbered and catalogued, and it was (as Artemus Ward called the Tower of London) a Sweet Boon to me to see him, when he required a book, gravely refer to a small ledger, neatly lettered from A to Z on its outer edge, and then, having discovered the registered number of the volume, take the latter out of the bookcase with the air of a man who had found what he wanted on the shelves of the Bodleian or the Bibliotheque Nationale.

Of course, Simson (this was not my friend's real name, but it will answer quite as well for present purposes) could have put his hand upon the book at once, without going through this elaborate mummery, but that would not have been Simson's style.

'My father,' he observed to me upon one occasion, 'always kept an index to the books in his library, and I do my best to follow in his footsteps. I haven't the number of books he had—his library contained several thousand volumes; but I can, at least, have an index.'

This filial sentiment was expressed with so much dignity that I almost felt ashamed of myself for having laughed at the index. The true shrine of the Simson household, however, was the room in which was stored the gimcrackery previously referred to. Simson himself entered it but rarely, and then trod softly with slippered feet.

I accused him once of going in there to worship in secret a hideous porcelain image of the Chinese dragon god which stood on the mantelpiece, but he merely smiled and said I was a hopeless Philistine.

One morning I came downstairs and found the door of the shrine open. I went in, half expecting to surprise Simson in the midst of some mysterious rite, but he was not there. There was somebody in the room, however. A man with tousled hair, a dirty-reddish beard, and a face that looked as if it had been (which was, no doubt, the fact) soaking in beer for years, was lying in a loose heap on the dainty green satin sofa, with one of his huge feet, encased in a broken blucher, resting carelessly on the glory of the shrine—a tall Japanese vase embellished with illustrations of the story of the Forty-seven Ronin.

I stared hard at the man, who winked familiarly at me with one bloodshot eye, and I walked out of the room, greatly wondering.

In the dining-room I met Simson with hair on end, and eyes glaring wildly.

'Who's your friend?' I asked, nodding in the direction of the front room.

'He's no friend of mine!' replied Simson—and then a base inspiration seemed to come to him, for he added, 'He's the wife's uncle.'

Of course, the man was a bailiff. He had insisted on camping in the front room, because he saw that it contained all the really valuable articles in the house. I am glad to say that Simson managed to raise the money required to meet the ruffian's demand, and to get rid of him before he had been in the house more than a few hours. As it was, he left behind him an effluvium of stale alcohol, which hung around the place for days afterwards.

Two or three years passed without my making any further acquaintance with bailiffdom. And then it came about that I stopped one night at a house in Woolloomooloo, wherein dwelt a happy family, consisting of a poet, a piano-tuner, a professor of mathematics, and an artist who painted religious subjects for preference, but, owing to lack of orders in this direction, painted panels of bar-screens and picturesque whisky advertisements for living.

The house was taken in the name of the artist, he being the only member of the party who did any regular work. The piano-tuner came next in financial importance, but he was not a perfect character in other respects. When he earned a few shillings by tuning a piano, he often started to tune himself up with beer to such an extent that the artist, who was a fastidious person when not himself intoxicated, always insisted on his sleeping in the wood-shed till he became sober again.

As for the poet and the professor of mathematics, they also made a little money occasionally, the poet by writing elegies and epitaphs and the professor by 'coaching' students for examinations. They brought home their money man-fully, and handed it over to the artist, who as man-fully expended it in the purchase of liquor and tinned provisions for the use of the establishment.

Taking them altogether, the happy family was the most genial set of Bohemians I have ever had the fortune to meet with. I do not even except the piano-tuner from that category, as he made up for his periodical drinking bouts by long spells of self-sacrificing total abstinence, and put the money he earned during these intervals into the common fund like a hero.

If they had a fault at all it was that they were almost too convivial. They used to drink rum at breakfast, and bottled beer in cups at tea-time.

Of course, an arrangement of this kind was too good to last. The end came, as luck would have it, on the morning when I happened to be a guest of the household. I was awakened by hearing a sound of voices in the passage—the artist had made up a bed for me on the floor of the front room with newspapers, and had covered me, in the kindest manner, with one of his great historical cartoons, representing the landing of Captain Cook at Botany Bay, the paint upon which was alone sufficient to keep me warm, without taking the canvas into account.

I knew at once what the trouble was—the bailiff was in possession. So far, however, he had not penetrated beyond the passage, and the artist, with a ring of pathos in his voice which revealed to me unsuspected depths of feeling in his nature, was imploring him not to take away the furniture without giving him (the artist) a chance to find the coin required, or, at any rate, to come to some arrangement with the landlord. (The distraint was, I may remark, about to be made for arrears of rent.)

'Not me!' said the bailiff, a brutal miscreant bloated with intemperance; 'I'm not that kind of bloomin' goat. Fork out the coin at once or I clean out the furnicher.'

'Heartless wretch!' exclaimed the artist, turning away with a choking sob, 'do your worst!'

The bailiff, signing to his assistant to remain in the passage—a wily precaution against any of the furniture being removed on the sly—went through the house to take an inventory of its contents. He had not been gone five minutes before he was back in the passage again, cursing and blaspheming in a most shocking style. 'What's the matter!' his assistant asked.

'This is what's the matter!' he replied bitterly, kicking a table made out of an old packing-case into the passage, 'this is the kind of thing they have the blanky cheek to call furnicher. Why, s'elp me gawd, there isn't enough in the whole place to pay our blanky fees!'

It was so. Every article of furniture in the house was literally home-made out of palings, packing-cases, and pieces of old deal board, picked up from time to time by the artist and his friends.

I then appreciated the full burlesque significance of the pathetic appeal made to the bailiff with regard to sparing the furniture.

'I am glad to see,' observed the artist by way of a parting shot, 'that your better feelings have prevailed, and that you intend to leave me my little household treasures.'

The bailiff scowled horribly, and went away threatening unutterable things.

'We shall have to move now, boys,' said the artist, addressing the others; 'we can't stand off the landlord any more on the strength of our furniture.'

I have said that my philosopher ultimately had his revenge on bailiffdom. I was on the spot when the revenge was consummated, having occasion to call on the philosopher with reference to some impracticable scheme peculiarly in his line.

There was a van in front of the door, into which a van man was piling tables, chairs, washstands, bedsteads, and other articles of domestic use. The philosopher, in his shirt-sleeves, and with beads of perspiration rolling down his intellectual forehead, was vigorously assisting.

'Lend a hand here!' he exclaimed, as he caught sight of me.

I followed him into the house and saw, lying on a sofa, snoring stertorously, a man who looked like Simson's wife's uncle.

'Take hold of his head!' said my philosopher.

I took hold of his head. The philosopher grasped him by the feet.

'Now, lay him gently down on the floor—steady!'

We laid him on the floor. The movement didn't awake the sodden ruffian, who simply turned over on his side, and grunted drunkenly.

'Now, take hold of one end of the sofa and we'll run it into the van.' Which was accordingly done.

The house was now empty of anything in the shape of furniture.

My philosopher, after placing a bottle of beer by the head of the unconscious man in possession, locked the front door and threw the key through the window into the front room.

'I don't pretend to be a practical man, but I think I managed that little affair pretty well,' he remarked, making a sign to the van man to drive on.

'How did you do it?' I enquired.

'Well, I happened to meet the bailiff on his way down to the house. I knew who he was, and where he was going. I also knew he couldn't refuse a drink to save his life, and so I took him into a hotel, with the result you have seen.

'He knew me as a man of letters, but didn't know my name or that I lived in the house we have just left. I couldn't make him stay in the hotel, however. Drunk as he was he had still a muddled idea of responsibility, seeing which I offered to accompany him, and brought a flask of rum with me to top him off with.

'He topped off with it, and the moment he sat down on the sofa where you saw him he went to sleep like the debauched beast he is. For all that, I had to leave him something to recover upon. *Noblesse oblige* you know, even in dealing with a bailiff. He'll be glad to find that bottle of beer when he wakes.'

I have met other bailiffs since then, and the result of my experience is that, as I said in the beginning of this article, the worst use to which you can put a man is to make him a bailiff.

WHEN THE POLICE FORCE COULDN'T SPELL

JACK MOSES

Years ago when our land was new,
Scholars then were very few,
A poor old cabbie's horse dropped dead
In Castlereagh Street, it was said.
Policeman '9' was standing by
And saw the neddy fall and die.
'On this I must at once report –
Can I spell Castlereagh?' he thought.
God bless the force! They are never beat.
He dragged the horse into K-I-N-G Street!

BARRINGTON

JOHN LANG

A few years ago I made the acquaintance of an elderly lady, whose husband, so far back as 1799, held an official position, both civil and military, in the colony of New South Wales.

Many anecdotes she told me of celebrated characters who had, in the words of one of them, 'left their country for their country's good'. With most, if not with all, of these celebrities the old lady had come in contact personally. Here is her story.

One morning I was sitting in my drawing-room with my two little children, who are now middle-aged men with large families, when a gentleman was announced. I gave the order for his admission; and on his entering the door of the apartment; I rose from my chair, and greeted him with a bow, which he returned in the most graceful and courtly manner imaginable.

His dress was that of a man of fashion, and his bearing that of a person who had moved in the highest circles of society. A vessel had arrived from England a few days previously with passengers, and I fancied that this gentleman was one of them. I asked him to be seated. He took a chair, opposite to me, and at once entered into conversation, making the first topic the extreme warmth of the day, and the second the healthful appearance of my charming children, as he was pleased to speak of them.

Apart from a mother liking to hear her children praised, there was such a refinement in the stranger's manner, such a seeming sincerity in all he said, added to such a marvellous neatness of expression, that I could not help thinking he would form a very valuable acquisition to our list of acquaintances, provided he intended remaining in Sydney, instead of settling in the interior of the colony.

I expressed my regret that the major (my husband) was from home; but I mentioned that I expected him at one o'clock, at which hour we took luncheon; and I further expressed a hope that our visitor would remain and partake of the meal.

With a very pretty smile (which I afterwards discovered had more meaning in it than I was at the time aware of), he feared he could not have the pleasure of partaking of the hospitalities of my table, but, with my permission, he would wait till the appointed hour, which was then near at hand.

Our conversation was resumed; and presently he asked my little ones to go to him. They obeyed at once, albeit they were rather shy children. This satisfied me that the stranger was a man of a kind and gentle disposition. He took the children, seated them on his knees, and began to tell them a fairy story (evidently of his own invention, and extemporized), to which they listened with profound attention. Indeed, I could not help being interested in the story; so fanciful were the ideas, and so poetical the language in which they were expressed.

The story ended, the stranger replaced the children on the carpet, and approached the table on which stood, in a porcelain vase, a bouquet of flowers. These he admired, and began a discourse of floriculture. I listened with intense earnestness; so profound were all his observations. We were standing at the table for at least eight or ten minutes; my boys hanging on to the skirt of my dress, and every now and then compelling me to beg of them to be silent.

One o'clock came, but not the major. I received, however, a note from him, written in pencil on a slip of paper. He would be detained at Government House until half-past two.

Again I requested the fascinating stranger to partake of luncheon, which was now on table in the next room; and again, with the same winning smile, he declined. As he was about, as I thought, to depart, I extended my hand; but, to my astonishment, he stepped back, made a low bow, and declined taking it.

For a gentleman to have his hand refused when he extends it to another is embarrassing enough. But for a lady! Who can possibly describe what were my feelings? Had he been the heir to the British throne, visiting that penal settlement in disguise (and from the stranger's manners and conversation he might have been that illustrious personage), he could scarcely have, under the circumstances, treated me in such an extraordinary manner. I scarcely knew what to think.

Observing, as the stranger must have done, the blood rush to my cheeks, and being cognizant evidently of what was passing through my mind, he spoke as follows:

'Madam, I am afraid you will never forgive me the liberty I have taken already. But the truth is, I could not resist the temptation of satisfying myself that the skill which made me so conspicuous in the mother-country still remained to me in this convict land.'

I stared at him, but did not speak.

'Madam,' he continued, 'the penalty of sitting at table with you, or taking the hand you paid me the compliment to proffer me, yourself in ignorance of the fact I am about to disclose, would have been the forfeiture of my ticket-of-leave, a hundred lashes, and employment on the roads in irons. As it is, I dread the major's wrath; but I cherish a hope that you will endeavour to appease it, if your advocacy be only a return for the brief amusement I afforded your beautiful children.'

'You are a convict!' I said, indignantly, my hand on the bell-rope.

'Madam,' he said, with an expression of countenance which moved me to pity, in spite of my indignation, 'hear me for one moment.'

'A convicted felon, how dared you enter my drawing-room as a visitor?' I asked him, my anger again getting the better of all my other feelings.

'The major, madam,' said the stranger, 'requested me to be at his house at the hour when I presented myself; and he bade me wait if he were from home when I called. The major wishes to know who was the person who received from me a diamond necklace which belonged to the Marchioness of Dorrington, and came into my possession at a state ball some four or five years ago—a state ball at which I had the honour of being present.

'Now, madam, when the orderly who opened the front door informed me that the major was not at home, but that you were, that indomitable impudence which so often carried me into the drawing-rooms of the aristocracy of our country, took possession of me; and, warmed as I was with generous wine—just sufficiently to give me courage—I determined to tread once more on a lady's carpet, and enter into conversation with her. That much I felt the major would forgive me; and, therefore, I requested the orderly to announce a gentleman. Indeed, madam, I shall make the forgiveness of the liberties I have taken in this room the condition of my giving that information which shall restore to the Marchioness of Dorrington the gem of which I deprived her, a gem which is still unpledged, and in the possession of one who will restore it on an application, accompanied by a letter in my handwriting.'

Again I kept silence.

'Madam!' he exclaimed, somewhat impassionedly, and rather proudly, 'I am no other man than Barrington, the illustrious pickpocket; and this is the hand which in its day has gently plucked, from ladies of rank and wealth, jewels which realized, in all, upwards of thirty-five thousand pounds, irrespective of those which were in my possession, under lock and key, when fortune turned her back upon me.'

Barrington, the pickpocket! Having heard so much of this man and of his exploits (although, of course, I had never seen him), I could not help regarding him with curiosity; so much so, that I could scarcely be angry with him any longer.

'Madam,' he continued, 'I have told you that I longed to satisfy myself whether that skill which rendered me so illustrious in Europe still remained to me, in this country, after five years of desuetude? I can conscientiously say that I am just as perfect in the art; that the touch is just as soft, and the nerve as steady as when I sat in the dress-circle at Drury Lane or Covent Garden.'

'I do not comprehend you, Mr. Barrington,' I replied. (I could not help saying Mister.)

'But you will, madam, in one moment. Where are your keys?'

I felt my pocket, in which I fancied they were, and discovered that they were gone.

'And your thimble and pencil-case, and your smelling-salts? They are here!'

He drew them from his coat-pocket.

My anger was again aroused. It was indeed, I thought, a frightful liberty for a convict to practise his skill upon me, and put his hand into the pocket of my dress. But, before I could request him to leave the room and the house, he spoke again; and, as soon as I heard his voice and looked in his face, I was mollified, and against my will, as it were, obliged to listen to him.

'Ah, madam,' he sighed, 'such is the change that often comes over the affairs of men! There was a time when ladies boasted of having been robbed by Barrington. Many whom I had never robbed gave it out that I had done so, simply that they might be talked about. Alas! Such is the weakness of poor human nature that some people care not by what means they associate their names with the name of any celebrity. I was in power then, not in bondage. "Barrington has my diamond ear-rings!" Once exclaimed the old Countess of Kettlebank, clasping her hands.

'Her ladyship's statement was not true. Her diamonds were paste, and she knew it, and I caused them to be returned to her. Had you not a pair of very small pearl-drops in your ears this morning, madam?'

I placed my bands to my ears, and discovered that the drops were gone. Again my anger returned, and I said, 'How dared you, sir, place your fingers on my face?'

'Upon my sacred word and honour, madam,' he replied, placing his hand over his left breast, and bowing. 'I did nothing of the kind! The ear is the most sensitive part of the human body to the touch of another person. Had I touched your ear my hope of having these drops in my waistcoat-pocket would have been gone. It was the springs only that I touched, and the drops fell into the palm of my left-hand.'

He placed the ear-rings on the table, and made me another very low bow.

'And when did you deprive me of them?' I asked him.

'When I was discoursing on floriculture, you had occasion several times to incline your head towards your charming children, and gently reprove them for interrupting me. It was on one of those occasions that the deed was quickly done. The dear children were the unconscious confederates in my crime, if crime you still consider it, since I have told you, and I spoke the truth; that it was not for the sake of gain, but simply to satisfy a passionate curiosity. It was as delicate and as difficult an operation as any I ever performed in the whole course of my professional career.'

There was a peculiar quaintness of humour and of action thrown into this speech; I could not refrain from laughing. But, to my great satisfaction, the illustrious pickpocket did not join in the laugh. He regarded me with a look of extreme humility, and maintained a respectful silence, which was shortly broken by a loud knocking at the outer door. It was the major, who, suddenly remembering his appointment with Barrington, had contrived to make his escape from Government House, in order to keep it. The major seemed rather surprised to find Barrington in my drawing-room; but he was in such a hurry, and so anxious, that he said nothing on the subject.

I withdrew to the passage, whence I could overhear all that took place.

'Now, look here, Barrington,' said my husband, impetuously, 'I will have no more nonsense. As for a free pardon, or even a conditional pardon, at present, it is out of the question. In getting you a ticket-of-leave, I have done all that I possibly can; and as I am a living man, I give you fair warning that if you do not keep faith with me, I will undo what I have already done. A free pardon! What! Let you loose upon the society of England again? The Colonial Secretary would scout the idea, and severely censure the Governor for recommending such a thing.

'You know, as well as I do, that if you returned to England to-morrow, and had an income of five thousand a year, you would never be able to keep those fingers of yours quiet.'

'Well, I think you are right, major,' said the illustrious personage.

'Then you will write that letter at once?'

'I will. But on one condition.'

'Another condition?'

'Yes.'

'Well, what is that condition? You have so many conditions that I begin to think the necklace will not be forthcoming after all. And, if it be not, by . . .'

'Do not excite yourself to anger, major. I give you my honour . . .'

'Your honour! Nonsense! What I want is, the jewel restored to its owner.'

'And it shall be, on condition that you will not be offended, grievously offended, with me for what I have done this day!'

'What is that?'

'Summon your good lady, and let her bear witness both for and against me.'

My husband opened the drawing-room door, and called out, 'Bessie!'

As soon as I had made my appearance, Barrington stated the case all that had transpired, with minute accuracy; nay, more, he acted the entire scene in such a way that it became a little comedy in itself; the characters being himself, myself, and the children, all of which characters he represented with such humour that my husband and myself were several times in fits of laughter.

Barrington, however, did not even smile. He affected to regard the little drama (and this made it the more amusing) as a very serious business.

This play over, my husband again put to Barrington the question, 'Will you write that letter at once?'

'Yes,' he replied, 'I will; for I see that I am forgiven the liberty I was tempted to take.' And seating himself at the table he wrote:

> MR. Barrington presents his compliments to Mr.--, and requests that a sealed packet, marked DN. No. 27, be immediately delivered to the bearer of this note. In the event of this request not

> being complied with, Mr. Barrington will have an opportunity ere long of explaining to Mr.--, in Sydney, New South Wales, that he (Mr.--) has been guilty of an act of egregious folly.

Fourteen months passed away, when, one morning, my husband received a letter from a gentleman in the Colonial Office. He clapped his hands, cried 'Bravo!' and then read as follows:

> MY DEAR MAJOR, The great pickpocket has been as good as his word. My lady is again in possession of her brilliants. Do whatever you can for Barrington in the Colony, but keep a sharp eye upon him, lest he should come back and once more get hold of that necklace.

My husband sent for Barrington to inform him of the result of his letter, and he took an opportunity of asking the illustrious man if there were any other valuables which he would like to restore to the original owners.

'Thank you—no!' was the reply. 'There are, it is true, sundry little articles in safe custody at home; but, as it is impossible to say what may be in the future, they had better for the present stand in my own name.'

THE SILENT MEMBER

C.J. DENNIS

He lived in Mundaloo, and Bill McClosky was his name,
But folks that knew him well had little knowledge of that same;
For he some'ow lost his surname, and he had so much to say –
He was called 'The Silent Member' in a mild, sarcastic way.

He could talk on any subject – from the weather and the crops
To astronomy and Euclid, and he never minded stops;
And the lack of a companion didn't lay him on the shelf,
For he'd stand before a looking-glass and argue with himself.

He would talk for hours on lit'rature, or calves, or art, or wheat;
There was not a bally subject you could say had got him beat;
And when strangers brought up topics that they reckoned he would
baulk,
He'd remark, 'I never heard of that.' But all the same – he'd talk.

He'd talk at christ'nings by the yard; at weddings by the mile;
And he used to pride himself upon his choice of words and style.
In a funeral procession his remarks would never end
On the qualities and virtues of the dear departed friend.

We got quite used to hearing him, and no one seemed to care –
In fact, no happ'ning seemed complete unless his voice was there.
For close on thirty year he talked, and none could talk him down,
Until one day an agent for insurance struck the town.

Well, we knew The Silent Member, and we knew what he could do,
And it wasn't very long before we knew the agent, too,
As a crack long-distance talker that was pretty hard to catch;
So we called a hasty meeting and decided on a match.

Of course, we didn't tell them we were putting up the game;
But we fixed it up between us, and made bets upon the same.

We named a time-keep and a referee to see it through;
Then strolled around, just casual, and introduced the two.

The agent got first off the mark, while our man stood and grinned;
He talked for just one solid hour, then stopped to get his wind.
'Yes; but –' sez Bill; that's all he said; he couldn't say no more;
The agent got right in again, and fairly held the floor.

On policies, and bonuses, and premiums, and all that,
He talked and talked until we thought he had our man out flat.
'I think Bill got in edgeways, but that there insurance chap
Just filled himself with atmosphere, and took the second lap.

I saw our man was getting dazed, and sort of hypnotized,
And they oughter pulled the agent up right there, as I advised.
'See here –' Bill started, husky; but the agent came again,
And talked right on for four hours good – from six o'clock to ten.

Then Bill began to crumple up, and weaken at the knees,
When all at once he ups and shouts, 'Here, give a bloke a breeze!
Just take a pull for half a tick and let me have the floor,
And I'll take out a policy.' The agent said no more.

The Silent Member swallowed hard, then coughed and cleared his
throat,
But not a single word would come – no; not a blessed note.
His face looked something dreadful, such a look of pained dismay;
Then he gave us one pathetic glance, and turned, and walked away.

He's hardly spoken since that day – not more than 'Yes' or 'No'.
We miss his voice a good bit, too; the town seems rather slow.
He was called 'The Silent Member' just sarcastic, I'll allow;
But since that agent handled him it sort o' fits him now.

BILL'S YARN: AND JIM'S

A. CHEE

BILL'S YARN

'You don't believe in 'em?' said Bill. 'I didn't, either, one time. But if ever you see one, like I did, and you lose your girl through it, like I did, you'll believe in 'em right enough, I promise you!'

'Did the girl see it too, Bill?'

'My word.'

'Were you scared?'

'Was I scared? Would you be scared if you saw six foot long of ghost coming at you?'

'Tell us about it, Bill.'

'Well, mind you, this is a true yarn, and you'd better make up your minds there's nothin' funny in it. And there's nothin' to laugh at in it, either. So, if any of you fellows wants to laugh, he'd better start now, and we'll go outside an' see whether he can give me a hidin' or I can give him one. Lend's a match.'

And Bill lit his pipe.

We promised Bill that we would take his yarn seriously, because we could see he would be annoyed if we didn't, and Bill scales at around 12st 13lb.

'They was havin' races at Bogalong,' said Bill, 'at the pub. And there was a little girl working there that I was shook on, name of Mary, Mary . . . darned if I don't forget her other name. Now, that's curious, too! Mary . . . well, no matter. Never mind her other name. But I thought a lot of that girl those days.

'There was a jockey, though, named Joe Chanter, and I always thought he was the white-headed boy with Mary, and I had no show. But she was only stringing him on, after all. Only Joe never found it out. He was ridin' a colt for the publican this day in the maiden handicap, and the colt bolted and ran into a fence and chucked Joe, and they picked him up with his face stove in and his neck broke. He wasn't a bad sort, Joe; a long, slim chap he was, tall as me, but thin, some of you chaps might ha' knowed him? No? Lend us a match.

'Mary didn't seem much cut-up over the accident, though she was keeping the other women company in howlin' most of the afternoon. But all the women cheered up a bit after supper, and it was decided not to put off the dance at night, because there was a great crowd there, and the publican said it didn't matter about Joe—Joe wouldn't mind. Landlord was thinking about what he'd lose, you see, if they broke up the party.

'So they cleared the kitchen, and the fiddles played up, and at it they went. Now, I never was much of a dancer, and Mary wasn't dancin', either; she was helpin' in the bar; so I went in and talked to her instead.

'By-and-by I got her to come away and sit in the best parlour with me. There was nobody there, and we sat down on the sofa, and got a bit confidential, and she said, when I asked her wasn't she shook on Joe, "No, indeed, not on Joe."

'"There was somebody else," she said.

'I asked her who was he? She says, "A lot you care!"

'"Indeed I do care a lot, Mary," I says. "I don't believe you care anything at all about me," she says, half crying. "Why," I says, "Mary, you ought to know (an' she did know, too, only she was foxin') that there's nobody in all the world I do care about except you."

'Then she began to say something, but couldn't get it out for crying, an' I cut in. "Don't you know, Mary, that I love you?"

'"I don't know," says she. "Well, I do, then," I says, "more than anything else in the whole world. Tell me, do you like me a little?"

'(I got that out of a book I'd been readin'. Sounds silly rot, doesn't it?) Lend's a match.

'"Yes, I do, Bill," says she, "and I never liked anyone else."

'Well, then, of course you know what a fellow'll do when a girl talks that way, and they're by themselves. By the Lord, boys, it was a treat to kiss that girl. She was just an armful of loveliness. Funny thing I can't think of her name.

'The music was going it out at the back all the time, and they were dancin' away no end. Presently Mary says she'd have to go; she might be wanted; and, of course, I said she'd have to give me another kiss before she went. And she was just doin' it, when, all of a sudden, she turns white an' says, "Oh, Bill, how wicked we are!"

'"Why, Mary," says I, "what's wicked about this lot?"

'"Just think, Bill," she says, "here we are, talkin' love and kissing, an' poor Joe Chanter lyin' dead in the very next room!"

'"Great Scott!" says I; "is he?" And then Mary began to cry and laugh both together like, but she was hardly started when I hears an almighty bump on the floor in the next room, and then we both looks up, and there was Joe!

'He was standing at the door, wrapped up in his windin'-sheet, and his face was covered with blood. Mary gave one yell and ran out by the other door, and me after her, like blazes! Scared! Now, wouldn't that ha' scared you? Lend's a match.'

'Well, and what was it, Bill?'

'Great Scott, ain't I tellin' you! It was Joe! Can't a man trust his own flamin' eyesight?'

'And what happened after?'

'Nothin'. Joe was dead enough when the rest came in and looked, and they wouldn't believe what I told 'em. Only Mary wouldn't look at me next day—seemed frightened like—so I came away. I've never been to Bogolong since.'

We all thought Bill's yarn a very unsatisfactory one, yet we couldn't get any more out of him. But six months afterwards I heard Jim's yarn.

JIM'S YARN

'Bogalong?' said Jim. 'Yes, I've been there, and I don't want to go there any more. It was a bit funny, though, all the same. Oh, all right, I'll tell you all about it.

'I'd just delivered a mob of stores at Pilligi, and as I was comin' back, I made Bogalong about dusk. I thought I might as well be a swell for once, havin' a bit of stuff, so I reckoned I'd stay at the pub all night. So I put my horse up, and had a drink, and asked if I could have a bed. But the place was full up as they'd been havin' races that day and they said there was no bed for me, so I was goin' away. But the publican called me back. I s'pose he guessed I had a cheque on me and he said he'd find room for me somewhere.

'"There's a double bed," says he, "if you don't mind sharin' it with another man. He's a very quiet fellow," he says; "I'll answer for him not disturbin' you."

'So I said all right, and after I had a few more drinks I went to bed. They had a dance on, but I wasn't in the humour for dancin', for it was a hot night, and I was tired.

'The other fellow must ha' been that way, too, I thought, for he was in bed already, I saw, when I went in. I didn't take much notice of him, except that he seemed pretty well covered up, for such a hot night. But after I put the light out, an' lay down, I found that I'd have to cover up, too, or else the mosquitoes would eat me.

'So I pulled the sheet off the cove an' rolled it round myself, and went to sleep. But the noise of the music and the dancin' woke me up after a bit, and I lay awake, growlin' a bit to myself for a time, an' I was just goin' off again, when I heard someone talkin' in the next room.

'I had left the door open, an' could hear quite plain. I was goin' to sing out to them to clear out, or shut the door, or something, but when I heard what they were sayin', I thought it was too good to miss, so I listened.

'It was some fellow doin' a mash with a girl, and I couldn't help laughin' to myself to think how mad he'd be if he knew somebody was listening. He was pretty solid with the girl, I could tell, and by-and-by he started kissin' her, an' I nearly burst myself laughin' when that began, and he called her sweetheart, and darling, and all that.

'I was goin' to wake up my mate, and let him share the fun, but I thought they might hear me, so I lay very quiet, until presently the girl says, "Oh, Bill! And poor Joe lyin' dead in the very next room!"

'I shoves out my hand as quick as lightning, and feels for my mate's face, and . . . Great Lord! It was as cold as a snake!

'"Holy Wars!" I says, and I gives one bound out of bed, forgetting all about the sheet bein' wrapped round my legs. I came down an awful buster, and my nose hit the side of the bed, and started to bleed like a waterspout but I picked myself up and made for the door, and then I saw the fellow and the girl sitting together on the sofa.

'They had one look at me, I was still rolled up in the sheet, and the blood was running down my face, and then they cleared. By Jove they did travel! I got my clothes on, I didn't much care about going back in for them, though, and went out to the stable and got my horse and took the road for it, and went on to Blind Creek, and camped there.

'But you'd ha' laughed to see how them two footed it!'

THE GHOST OF THE MURDERER'S HUT

A.B. 'BANJO' PATERSON

My horse had been lamed in the foot
In the rocks at the back of the run,
So I camped at the Murderer's Hut,
At the place where the murder was done.

The walls were all spattered with gore,
A terrible symbol of guilt;
And the bloodstains were fresh on the floor
Where the blood of the victim was spilt.

The wind hurried past with a shout,
The thunderstorm doubled its din
As I shrank from the danger without,
And recoiled from the horror within.

When lo! at the window a shape,
A creature of infinite dread;
A thing with the face of an ape,
And with eyes like the eyes of the dead.

With the horns of a fiend, and a skin
That was hairy as satyr or elf,
And a long, pointed beard on its chin –
My God! 'twas the Devil himself.

In anguish I sank on the floor,
With terror my features were stiff,
Till *the thing* gave a kind of a roar,
Ending up with a resonant 'Biff!'

Then a cheer burst aloud from my throat,
For the thing that my spirit did vex
Was naught but an elderly goat,
Just a goat of the masculine sex.

When his master was killed he had fled,
And now, by the dingoes bereft,
The nannies were all of them dead,
And only the billy was left.

So we had him brought in on a stage
To the house where, in style, he can strut,
And he lived to a fragrant old age
As the Ghost of the Murderer's Hut.

HIS MASTERPIECE

A.B. 'BANJO' PATERSON

Greenhide Billy was a stockman on a Clarence River cattle-station, and admittedly the biggest liar in the district. He had been for many years pioneering in the Northern Territory, the other side of the sun-down—a regular 'furthest-out man'—and this assured his reputation among station-hands who award rank according to amount of experience.

Young men who have always hung around the home districts, doing a job of shearing here or a turn at horse-breaking there, look with reverence on Riverine or Macquarie-River shearers who come in with tales of runs where they have 300,000 acres of freehold land and shear 250,000 sheep; these again pale their ineffectual fires before the glory of the Northern Territory man who has all-comers on toast, because no one can contradict him or check his figures. When two of them meet, however, they are not fools enough to cut down quotations and spoil the market; they lie in support of each other, and make all other bushmen feel mean and pitiful and inexperienced.

Sometimes a youngster would timidly ask Greenhide Billy about the 'terra incognita': 'What sort of a place is it, Billy—how big are the properties? How many acres had you in the place you were on?'

'Acres be damned!' Billy would scornfully reply; 'hear him talking about acres! D'ye think we were blanked cockatoo selectors! Out there we reckon country by the hundred miles. You orter say, "How many thousand miles of country?" and then I'd understand you.'

Furthermore, according to Billy, they reckoned the rainfall in the Territory by yards, not inches. He had seen blackfellows who could jump at least three inches higher than anyone else had ever seen a blackfellow jump, and every bushman has seen or personally known a blackfellow who could jump over six feet.

Billy had seen bigger droughts, better country, fatter cattle, faster horses, and cleverer dogs, than any other man on the Clarence River. But one night when the rain was on the roof, and the river was rising with a moaning sound, and the men were gathered round the fire in the hut smoking and staring at the coals, Billy turned himself loose and gave us his masterpiece.

'I was drovin' with cattle from Mungrybanbone to old Corlett's station on the Buckadowntown River.'

Billy always started his stories with some paralysing bush names.

'We had a thousand head of store-cattle, wild, mountain-bred wretches that'd charge you on sight; they were that handy with their horns they could skewer a mosquito. There was one or two one-eyed cattle among 'em—and you know how a one-eyed beast always keeps movin' away from the mob, pokin' away out to the edge of them so as they won't git on his blind side, so that by stirrin' about he keeps the others restless.

'They had been scared once or twice, and stampeded and gave us all we could do to keep them together; and it was wet and dark and thundering, and it looked like a real bad night for us. It was my watch. I was on one side of the cattle, like it might be here, with a small bit of a fire; and my mate, Barcoo Jim, he was right opposite on the other side of the cattle, and had gone to sleep under a log.

'The rest of the men were in the camp fast asleep. Every now and again I'd get on my horse and prowl round the cattle quiet like, and they seemed to be settled down all right, and I was sitting by my fire holding my horse and drowsing, when all of a sudden a blessed 'possum ran out from some saplings and scratched up a tree right alongside me. I was half-asleep, I suppose, and was startled; anyhow, never thinking what I was doing, I picked up a firestick out of the fire and flung it at the 'possum.

'Whoop! Before you could say Jack Robertson, that thousand head of cattle were on their feet, and made one wild, headlong, mad rush right over the place where poor old Barcoo Jim was sleeping. There was no time to hunt up materials for the inquest; I had to keep those cattle together, so I sprang into the saddle, dashed the spurs into the old horse, dropped my head on his mane, and sent him as hard as he could leg it through the scrub to get to the lead of the cattle and steady them. It was brigalow, and you know what that is.

'You know how the brigalow grows,' continued Bill; 'saplings about as thick as a man's arm, and that close together a dog can't open his mouth to bark in 'em. Well, those cattle swept through that scrub, levelling it like as if it had been cleared for a railway line. They cleared a track a quarter of a mile wide, and smashed every stick, stump and sapling on it. You could hear them roaring and their hoofs thundering and the scrub smashing three or four miles off.

'And where was I? I was racing parallel with the cattle, with my head down on the horse's neck, letting him pick his way through the scrub in the pitchy darkness. This went on for about four miles. Then the cattle began to get winded, and I dug into the old stock-horse with the spurs, and got in front, and began to crack the whip and sing out, so as to steady them a little; after awhile they dropped slower and slower, and I kept the whip going. I got them all together in a patch of open country, and there I rode round and round 'em all night till daylight.

'And how I wasn't killed in the scrub, goodness only knows; for a man couldn't ride in the daylight where I did in the dark. The cattle were all knocked about—horns smashed, legs broken, ribs torn; but they were all there, every solitary head of 'em; and as soon as the daylight broke I took 'em back to the camp—that is, all that could travel, because I had to leave a few broken-legged ones.'

Billy paused in his narrative. He knew that some suggestions would be made, by way of compromise, to tone down the awful strength of the yarn, and he prepared himself accordingly. His motto was 'No surrender'; he never abated one jot of his statements; if anyone chose to remark on them, he made them warmer and stronger, and absolutely flattened out the intruder.

'That was a wonderful bit of ridin' you done, Billy,' said one of the men at last, admiringly. 'It's a wonder you wasn't killed. I suppose your clothes was pretty well tore off your back with the scrub?'

'Never touched a twig,' said Billy.

'Ah!' faltered the inquirer, 'then no doubt you had a real ringin' good stock-horse that could take you through a scrub like that full-split in the dark, and not hit you against anything.'

'No, he wasn't a good un,' said Billy decisively, 'he was the worst horse in the camp. Terrible awkward in the scrub he was, always fallin' down on his knees; and his neck was so short you could sit far back on him and pull his ears.'

Here that interrogator retired hurt; he gave Billy best. After a pause another took up the running.

'How did your mate get on, Billy? I s'pose he was trampled to a mummy!'

'No,' said Billy, 'he wasn't hurt a bit. I told you he was sleeping under the shelter of a log. Well, when those cattle rushed they swept over that log a thousand strong; and every beast of that herd took the log in his stride and just missed landing on Barcoo Jimmy by about four inches.'

The men waited a while and smoked, to let this statement soak well into their systems; at last one rallied and had a final try.

'It's a wonder then, Billy,' he said, 'that your mate didn't come after you and give you a hand to steady the cattle.'

'Well, perhaps it was,' said Billy, 'only that there was a bigger wonder than that at the back of it.'

'What was that?'

'My mate never woke up all through it.'

Then the men knocked the ashes out of their pipes and went to bed.

INCOGNITO

ANONYMOUS

Every station in the country keeps a pony that was sent
Late at night to fetch a doctor or a priest,
And has lived the life of Riley since that faraway event;
But those stories don't impress me in the least.

For I once owned Incognito – what a jewel of a horse!
He was vastly better bred than many men,
But they handicapped so savagely on every local course
I was forced to dye him piebald now and then.

For I needed all the money that a sporting life entails,
Having found the cost of living rather dear,
And my wife, the very sweetest little girl in New South Wales,
Was presenting me with children every year.

We were spreading superphosphate one October afternoon
When the missus said she felt a little sick:
We were not expecting Septimus (or Septima) so soon,
But I thought I'd better fetch the doctor quick.

So I started for the homestead with the minimum delay
Where I changed and put pomade on my moustache,
But before I reached the slip-rails Incognito was away
And was heading for the township like a flash.

First he swam a flooded river, then he climbed a craggy range,
And they tell me (tho' I haven't any proof)
That he galloped through the township to the telephone exchange
Where he dialled the doctor's number with his hoof.

Yes, he notified the doctor and the midwife and the vet,
And he led them up the mountains to my door,
Where he planted, panting, pondering, in a rivulet of sweat
Till he plainly recollected something more;

Then he stretched his muzzle towards me, he had something in his
teeth
Which he dropped with circumspection in my hand,
And I recognised his offering as a contraceptive sheath,
So I shot him. It was more than I could stand.

But I've bitterly repented that rash act of injured pride –
It was not the way a sportsman should behave,
So I'm making my arrangements to be buried at his side,
And to share poor Incognito's lonely grave.

A LUCKY MEETING

ERNEST FAVENC

'What do you make of it, Jim?'

'Looks remarkably like an E, but what can be the meaning of the extraordinary triangular thing that follows?'

'That's the puzzle. The first mark one could swear had been made by a white man; but the other is apparently one of those native carvings.

'There, however, is the scar plain enough, where the bark was stripped, and from the shape of the piece removed I think it's like a white man's work.'

'Moreover,' added Jim, 'it has been done with a steel tomahawk.'

The two men were standing in front of a dead coolibah tree of some size, on which the marks they were trying to decipher had been deeply cut. It was on the shore of a broad, shallow lake surrounded by a forest of similar dead trees—white skeletons, lifting heavenwards their writhing, bare limbs.

A stranger, set down there suddenly, would say that the axe of the ring-barker had been at work; but the locality was away in the far interior, where the white man had only just intruded on the solitude. Round the lake, which at its deepest only averaged a few feet, was a border of green, luscious grass; back from which was only desolation and sterility.

Loose, puffy soil, broken into mounds and hollows, seamed with gaping cracks. On these dusty mounds were heaped thousands of tiny shells; in the hollows drooped a few withered stalks of nardoo. On all sides were the gaunt, lifeless trees. Two exceptionally wet years had, in some remote time, obviously deluged the plain, and the long-standing, stagnant water destroyed the timber.

This state of things is not uncommon in many parts of the North Australian interior. In the deepest hollows of these dry lake-beds lie the bones of fish, which have escaped their feathered enemies, to perish slowly as their native element evaporated.

On the broader expanse, bleached skeletons are mouldering; the grotesque-headed pelican and the dingo, with a wild-dog snarl on his fleshless jaws. Bird and beast have made for the lake after long, long flight, and hot, dusty tramp, only to find there drought, disappointment and death.

To the north-west, where a bank has been formed by the action of the steady south-east monsoon, layer after layer of dead shells has been deposited by the constantly-lapping wavelets, forms of life that have lived and died in the waters of the ephemeral lake.

Beyond and around these depressions wherein the overflow of a rarely heavy rainfall accumulates, are the great plains whose treeless edges meet the sky in an unbroken straight line. Where the tall columns of dust revolve in a wild waltz; where, in summer time, the air is so aglow with heat that it throbs like a living thing, and in this fierce atmosphere is born the treacherous mirage: a bush becomes a tree, a stone, a rock, and the hard, baked clay-pan a blue lake. This is riverless Australia, the sun-god's realm, the region of short-lived creeks, lost for ever in these dead, dry lake-beds.

The elder of the brothers who had been regarding the tree copied the inscription in his note-book, and the two strolled back to their camp where a young Aboriginal boy was watching the boiling of a piece of dried beef. They sat down and commenced smoking.

'How long do you suppose these trees have been dead?' said Sam Gilmore, the elder of the two.

'Impossible to say, for certain, but about ten or fifteen years.'

'Yes,' returned Sam, after some silent puffs, 'that would be about it. There was a devil of a wet season all over the north in '72 and '73. That mark was made before then, when the tree was alive.'

'Certainly it was, and if you remember the Herbert was settled in the sixties. Some fellow from the tableland has been out here, that's about all it is.'

Sam looked at his note-book. 'I've got it!' he exclaimed. 'E. Triangle! It's a station-brand. Many fellows have a trick of cutting their brand on a tree instead of their initials.'

'That will be it,' replied his brother, 'there were no registered brands, all of one pattern, in those days.'

The two thought little more about the matter, but were busily employed the next two days in examining the surrounding country, it being part of a large block they had taken up in the Northern Territory.

One evening their young native companion, who had been left in camp to look after the spare horses and see that they did not get bogged, remarked with the laconic suddenness of the Aboriginals: 'Old man horse sit down,' indicating by a motion of his hand the far side of the lake.

'Which one horse?' said Sam, thinking he meant that one of their own had got bogged.

'Baal mine know. Long time that fellow sit down. Old man bone.'

'A skeleton of a horse?' queried Jim, looking at his brother.

Sam nodded. 'We will have a look at it to-morrow—too late to go all round there this evening.'

Next morning they were soon beside the bones of the animal, which lay in a patch of grass, almost concealed from view. Evidently the moist border of the lake had saved them from destruction by the bush fires that annually swept the surrounding country.

'A horse, but how it came here, there is no evidence to show,' said Jim.

Their young guide was poking about with a stick. 'That fellow bin carry saddle,' and from the mouldering rubbish he dragged out the corroded iron-work.

Inspired by this discovery a closer search was made. The plated buckles of a saddle-pouch were found, a plated sandwich-case, such as hunting-men carry in England, and the blade of a large pocket-knife. Everything in the shape of leather had long vanished.

They devoted all the morning to examining the vicinity, but no further relics were forthcoming, and, taking what they had found with them, the brothers returned to camp.

During the afternoon Sam set to work cleaning the old sandwich-case. By dint of hard rubbing he succeeded in restoring it to something like cleanliness, and although time and exposure had dealt hashly with the metal, a monogram became faintly visible on one side, and on the other was roughly scratched the mark they had found on the tree, E and a triangle.

'Now,' said Jim, after the examination, 'let's have a look at the inside.'

He inserted the point of his knife beneath the half-cover and, after some trouble, raised it. Inside were some papers, loose sheets, torn from a note-book, on which the pencil-writing was faint and illegible; but there was a larger sheet of blue letter-paper, on which the writing was in ink and, although slightly yellow, plain and distinct.

The battered old case had been true to its trust and, despite all, had preserved the message confided to it.

The brothers perused their strange find and, at the conclusion, looked at each other in silence for a few moments.

'This is a strange document to drop across in such a howling wilderness,' said Sam at length.

Jim whistled in sympathy. 'I suppose,' he remarked, 'the writer came to grief, and his horse made it back to the water, got bogged and died. Is that how you read it?'

'I think so. At any rate, it's too long ago for us to bother looking up tracks. The date on this, December 4th, 1870, coincides with the time we surmised.'

'I suppose you'll keep it?' queried Jim.

'Most carefully. It belongs to the man's children, and may be valuable, or, perhaps, only waste paper. Possibly we shall find out when we get back to civilisation; meanwhile I vote we make a start for home tomorrow. We are satisfied, I suppose, that this country is good enough.'

'All right,' said the younger; and for the rest of the day they devoted themselves to preparations for an early departure on the morrow, dismissing the subject of their strange discovery from their minds.

*

Young Simpson propped himself up against the slabs and gazed disconsolately down the sunny road. He was suffering a bad recovery, his pockets were empty, and his credit exhausted.

He had lately finished a job of horse-breaking, and had knocked his cheque down in orthodox style. Now, life was all dust and ashes, and everything a mockery and a delusion. He was only thirty-six, and had already managed to break every breakable bone in his body, and pull through several bad attacks of delirium tremens. He was the son of a well-to-do squatter, but ere he was twenty had managed to incense his father so bitterly that he had been cast forth without even the proverbial shilling, and a younger brother, a good and well-behaved youth, reigned in his stead.

Since his expulsion from home he had steadily gone to the dogs, and it was a pity, for, however weak, he was a good-hearted young fellow. A strong, helping hand would have saved him, but he never got it, and now it was too late. At least so everybody thought and said.

Simpson had been dozing on a rude bench in the verandah, and had just got on to his feet, under the impression that somebody had ridden up and aroused him. Presumably this impression was correct, for a horse was hitched up to the rail outside, and voices could be heard in the bar. Possibly there was a drink on hand. He licked his dry lips with a still dryer tongue, and lurched inside.

A deeply sun-tanned man, with bright eyes, was talking to the landlord. 'Here, Joe,' said the latter to Simpson, 'come and have a drink, you look sleepy.'

This was most astonishing; only that morning his credit had been peremptorily stopped, and now he was invited to refresh himself. The landlord shifted down the bar a bit and Simpson followed him.

'This gent,' said the publican in a subdued tone, 'has got a mob of cattle going north, and wants another hand badly. I'll put in a good word for you, and, perhaps, he'll be right for a bit of an advance, so that you can square up with me before you go.'

Simpson took to the suggestion at once. He immediately poured out a drink so long that it made the landlord eager to clutch the bottle again. Refreshed by this, he accosted the stranger, and with few words a bargain was struck, and Joe Simpson went off to roll up his scanty belongings in his blanket.

'As good a man as ever crossed a horse,' said the effusive publican; 'only keep him off the booze. Born a gentleman, too.'

Jim Gilmore, for it was he, on his way out with cattle to stock the country he and his brother had lately examined, looked curiously after the retreating form. He was warm-hearted, and something in the ne'er-do-well had appealed to him.

The long trip drew to an end, and tired men, leg-weary horses, and listless cattle all desired the arrival of that morning when they should mutually take leave of each other.

Dry stages had been successfully crossed, wet, blustering nights experienced, and death in many forms had taken toll of the herd before Jim, with a sigh of relief, dismounted on the bank of a long serpentine lagoon, some twenty miles from the shallow lake where they had formerly camped. Leaning on his horse he watched the long string of cattle troop in to the water.

'Poor Joe!' he thought, as he caught sight of Simpson steadying the leaders, 'he's got a bad touch of this northern fever. Glad we are here so that he can get a spell.'

The publican's blatant recommendation had turned out true. A better man than Joe Simpson had proved himself could scarce be found. Ever ready when the weather was bad and the cattle rowdy on camp; always alert during the long sleepless nights across the dry plains, and alas! never neglecting the opportunity of a short spree in the few townships they had passed, Joe had been young Gilmore's right hand throughout the tedious journey.

Now, the malarial fever had seized on him. The day after the herd was turned out Joe lay delirious under a bough shade.

Jim devoted all his spare time to him, and at last had the satisfaction of witnessing his return to reason. But Simpson was very weak—he had played too many tricks with his physique to be able to stand a severe attack of fever with impunity, and lay almost apathetic as regarded his chances of final recovery.

One morning Jim noticed that the patient had been idly tracing letters and signs on the dusty earth alongside his rude bed of dry grass. Amongst them he recognised with a start the E followed by a triangle. 'What are you up to, Joe?' he said quietly.

'Just trying to remember a lot of brands,' returned Simpson, in his weak voice.

'Whose brand is that?' asked Gilmore, indicating the one he was interested in.

Simpson's wasted face flushed hotly. 'When a fellow gets down in the world,' he said, after a pause, 'he does not always stick to his right name. That brand was our old station brand on my father's place. There were three partners at first, Emerson, Unthorpe, and Charters, and, as their initials made the first syllable of Euclid, they took the triangle as a brand with my father's initial before it. Finally he bought them out, and my brother has the place now.'

'Then,' said Jim, staring hard at him, 'your name is . . .?'

'Emerson.'

'Good God!'

'What is the matter? What do you know about me?' cried the invalid anxiously.

'Nothing, nothing, go on. Tell me, where did your father die? How is it you were left so badly off?'

Joe Emerson looked at his questioner with some surprise, but answered quietly enough. 'My father died in his bed on Bellbrook station, where I was born. He and I had quarrelled some years before and finally he disowned me. I was a bad lot, there's no denying.'

'Was your father ever up this way?'

'Yes. He had a share in a station in the north of Queensland, and took a trip out west, I know. In fact, it was through some terrible hardship he endured that he afterwards died. He was too old to stand it. I never heard the rights of it, but I believe through some stupid blunder of one of the men some of their horses got away from them on a dry stage with packs and saddles on. My father and the others managed to get into water, but the horses made back and probably perished.'

'Your brother then took your place in your father's will, and you were left out in the cold. Do you know the date of that will?'

'It was the time of our final row, in the beginning of '69.'

Jim strode outside and thought for a moment, then he returned.

'This is the strangest thing I ever came across outside of a novel. I have good news for you. Your father must have been in a tight place before the horses were lost, and when he anticipated death he repented of his harshness to you, and wrote out another will. It commences: "I, George Henry Emerson, now expecting death, and being desirous of making amends to my dear son Joseph for my stern conduct." I do not remember any more, but it was duly witnessed by Isaac Wright and Thomas Peberdy. Do you know anything about them?'

Young Emerson was looking at Jim as though bewildered by what he heard, and answered slowly. 'Peberdy was an old servant of my father's, and went north with him; he has a selection now, down south. Wright I don't know. But surely you remember the purport of this will?'

'Certainly. It left the whole of his property to you, subject to certain charges on it for your brother and sister.'

'But—but, Mr. Gilmore!' cried the sick man, impatiently, 'how did you find it? Who has it now?'

'My brother has it now. We found it with the remains of your father's horse, preserved in an old-fashioned sandwich case. Do you remember it?'

'Yes, with his monogram on it; he brought it from England.'

'If the two witnesses are alive, it seems to me that the will cannot be disputed. My brother may be here at any time; he knows when we are due, and is bringing up supplies from Burketown, and will probably push ahead.'

There was silence for a short time; then Emerson reached out and felt for Gilmore's hand. He grasped it and sat upright. 'Look here,' he said, 'I'm going to do three things.'

'Don't be in a hurry,' murmured Jim.

'I'm going to get well.'

'Hear, hear!'

'I'm going to knock off liquor.'

'Hear, hear, hear!' from Gilmore.

'And I'm going to get the skeleton of that old horse set up and mounted on a pedestal.'

'When the will is proved, I presume,' said his companion.

No need to tell much more. One witness was alive and able to swear to the signatures. Joe kept to his three resolutions. The skeleton of the old horse adorns the hall of Bellbrook station, and Jim Gilmore's wife was once Miss Emerson.

BUCKED OFF ITS BRAND

'RAF'

Take my word, he could buck, Brown Baron;
And to ride, who could ride like Long Jack?
There was never a thing born with hair on
Could throw him when once on its back.

In the crush went on saddle and bridle
And he set Jack a go pretty hard;
But his previous efforts seemed idle
When he flung down the rails of the yard.

A few bucks, and the gear was all lying,
Busted girths, broken bit, on the sand;
And away through the trees he went flying,
Nothing on him but Jack, and the brand.

Through the paddock the Baron went sailing
Jack keeping him straight with his hat,
We saw him jump over the railing
At the creek on the Kurrajong Flat.

And then, where on earth were they hidden?
The boss swore he'd soon have 'em back,
And rode as he never had ridden,
The traps had to start on their track.

But Jack was not beaten by trifles,
When he and the Baron were found,
It took four police, ditto rifles,
Ere Jack would set foot on the ground.

When we came to examine the Baron,
All the brand mark had disappeared clean;
'Twas the horse, we could swear, with a scar on
The place where the 'Z9' had been.

Jack explained, in the dock at his trial,
That the horse slung his brand on the track;
To the charge gave indignant denial,
Said, when caught, he was bringing him back!

For a saddle, Jack sits now on stone
And for reins has a hammer in hand,
'Cause the ignorant judge would not own,
That horses could buck off their brand!

NOBODY KNEW WHO THE FIRE CAPTAIN WAS

JIM HAYNES

Nobody knew who the fire captain was.

Mind you, everyone was taken a bit off guard.

We were trying to conduct a golf club social committee meeting and not particularly thinking about who the fire captain was. In fact, nobody's mind was on anything to do with fires. Everybody was busy thinking about kegs and entertainment and other very important golf club end-of-season party business.

I was there only because I could play the guitar, sort of, and that made me an honorary member of the golf club social committee. However, I did play golf and I was a member of the golf club. I played golf slightly worse than I played the guitar but that was immaterial.

I was only eighteen or nineteen at the time, but, as I said, I played the guitar, sort of, and therefore was co-opted onto the golf club social committee. I always thought I was honorary—I don't think I was ever elected. In fact, I'm sure I was never elected. I'm not even sure there were elections. I was there, however, when the question was asked, and nobody knew who the fire captain was.

The sergeant had arrived at the Tatts looking for Jersey Mason. There was a fire reported from just down the river. The sergeant had taken the call himself at the police station residence.

Usually the sergeant's wife answered the phone but the sergeant was there at the time and, as he was also on duty, he took the call himself.

'Looks like one of those weekenders on the river, one of the unoccupied shacks down near the O'Shea's place, judging by the smoke,' the caller had said. 'If the O'Sheas were around they'd no doubt go and put it out but perhaps you could get the fire brigade to do it.'

'Not a problem, Bernie,' the sergeant had replied. 'I'll try to get the fire boys down there. I used to have a key to the fire shed but I don't seem to have one now. Who's the fire captain? Do you remember?'

Bernie had no idea who the fire captain was at present. He thought the sergeant would know a thing like that. But mightn't it be Jersey Mason? Bernie was sure it used to be Jersey Mason at one time.

The sergeant wasn't sure that it was Jersey Mason, but that was as good a starting point as any. So, he headed for the Tatts, because he knew there was a golf club social committee meeting there that night and Jersey, he was fairly certain, was on the golf club social committee.

The reason that the sergeant knew that there was a golf club social committee meeting that night was that he was on the golf club social committee.

The reason that the sergeant wasn't at the golf club social committee meeting yet was that he was on duty that night. Although being on duty didn't mean he was actually doing anything that would prevent him from attending such a meeting, he always preferred, when on duty, to arrive late at meetings and say, 'Sorry I'm a bit late, I'm on duty.'

Anyway, as he seemed to remember that Jersey was also on the committee, the sergeant collected his hat and headed to the Tatts to ask the question, 'Who's the fire captain these days?'

Having arrived at the Tatts and found the meeting in progress in the back room, the sergeant said his 'g'days' and asked the question and he was soon 'assisted in his enquiries' from a number of sources.

The only problem was that most of the information he received was negative and unhelpful. Jersey wasn't on the golf club social committee, hadn't been for quite some time most members reckoned, and no one seemed to know who the fire captain was. Most of the blokes present, however, were certain about who the fire captain *wasn't*—Jersey Mason wasn't.

The funny thing was nobody could be equally as certain about who was the fire captain. Some thought it was Bindi Williams and there was a bit of support for a couple of blokes who lived out of town, because they had vehicles easily adapted for firefighting, although they wouldn't have been the most suitable blokes to keep the key to the fire shed, living so far out of town.

Others thought it could be the postmaster for no reason other than the fact that the post office was opposite the fire shed and it seemed to make sense for him to keep the key, if the sergeant didn't.

Weelabarabak Fire Brigade didn't actually have a vehicle as part of its firefighting weaponry, so ownership of a 'suitable vehicle' was a paramount and desirable requisite for anyone being fire captain.

Weelabarabak Fire Brigade had a hose, shovels, spades, buckets, backpacks with hoses and nozzles, a trailer and a one-hundred gallon welded water tank which fitted on the trailer, a small pump . . . and no vehicle. This accounted for the fact that the building housing this array of firefighting technology and artifacts was always referred to as the 'fire shed' rather than the 'fire station', as a 'fire station', in most people's minds, would be expected to contain a vehicle of some kind—perhaps a fire engine.

The Weelabarabak fire shed was built from rough poles and galvanised iron sheets and had a dirt floor. It was certainly a 'shed' if anything ever was. It was also the size of a shed, not the size of a fire station.

No one seeing the fire shed would have assumed that it could have held a vehicle capable of firefighting. We didn't like to put on airs and graces in Weelabarabak and we would certainly have been accused of putting on airs and graces if we had called our fire shed a 'fire station'.

The *modus operandi* of the Weelabarabak Fire Brigade was to open the shed, load the trailer and push it along the main street until a 'suitable vehicle' with a towbar was encountered. The vehicle was then commandeered, hopefully with the permission of the owner, in order to play the role of fire truck by transporting the brigade and its equipment to the fire.

There had been a few altercations with vehicle owners over the years, but most locals understood the way it worked.

There was one time when a cocky, who lived about fifty miles out of town, had refused to allow his ute to be commandeered. He claimed he had to get back home as he was shearing and had only dropped into town for a few supplies. Moreover he stated that he wasn't concerned about a 'bloody grass fire on a vacant block that was probably started by a few bloody kids!'

We were saddened by his attitude. He was almost considered to be a local until that day, but then we remembered that he wasn't born in the district and his wife was from the city. So, in retrospect, we weren't too surprised by his un-neighbourly attitude.

That night at the Tatts, however, we were not thinking about anything but the puzzling question of just who might be the current fire captain.

It was quite odd. A dozen blokes and not one of us seemed to be able to recollect being at a meeting in recent years where the appointment was made. We all tried to remember who had called us out last time we attended a fire, but every name that was mentioned seemed to be that of an ex fire captain.

Admittedly our minds were on other things. It was harvest time, it was hot and there was the important business of the end-of-year do at the golf club to think about.

Still, it was odd.

I certainly didn't know who the fire captain was. Perhaps I'd erased the memory from my memory banks because of the embarrassing incident that had occurred on the one and only occasion I'd actually been called upon to fight a fire.

If it had been just the usual grass fire or rubbish set alight by kids behind the produce store it would have been fine. Unfortunately it was a 'real' fire, in another district.

Weelabarabak had been asked to provide volunteers for a serious fire burning through grazing land and scrub near Cooper's Junction.

The only available 'men' at the time were Old Nugget and myself. We tried to uphold the honour of the Weelabarabak Fire Brigade . . . but we failed.

We had set out in a borrowed truck with the equipment from the fire shed and arrived at the headquarters of the firefighting operation, a cattle property about twenty miles past Cooper's Junction.

The bloke in charge was pleased to see us and directed us to fill the tank from a dam a few miles away and proceed on to the edge of the fire.

We found the dam and filled up but we were in red soil country and forgot to let some air out of the truck tyres.

Consequently we became bogged about a hundred yards from the dam in the first patch of red sand we struck.

Then we did let some air out of the tyres but the weight of the water had us a fair way down in the soft red sand by then.

I don't really remember whose idea it was to let some of the water out onto the sand, but the idea was that we might be able to drive the truck out on moist sand, rather than dry sand.

I never blamed Nugget and he never blamed me.

We soon discovered that being bogged in red mud is pretty much the same as being bogged in red sand.

Rather than upholding the reputation of the Weelabarabak Fire Brigade as a brave bunch of fearless firefighters, Nugget and I spent thirty-six hours bogged about a mile from the fire in a borrowed truck.

Meanwhile the other brigades had managed to fight the fire to a standstill and then found time to come and tow us out of the bog we had created for ourselves. It had more or less dried out by then, anyway.

We attempted to restore the town's reputation by helping put out the spot fires that were left and we put out burning logs and carried water to where it was needed and helped out by doing a few back burns to prevent a similar fire breaking out again later in the summer.

When we thought we had done enough so that the memory of our involvement in the fire would amount to more than being bogged when we were most needed, we headed home.

Sitting at the Tatts that evening I tried to remember who had been in charge of the brigade when Nugget and I had been asked to represent the town at the Cooper's Junction fire, but it was useless. I remembered the shed was open when we arrived and I could remember the few blokes who helped us load the truck.

I tried to remember who had called to see if anyone was available to go . . . But I remembered that Mum took the call and said something like, 'They want you to help fight a fire, you might as well go. There's nothing much to do around here at the moment.'

By this time the sergeant had left to follow some of the other suggested leads as to who might be fire captain on the pub's telephone.

When he came back twenty minutes later we had already made a number of important decisions in record time. We had decided on the number of kegs, the entertainment (me on guitar and Nugget on squeezebox and Trevor Jackman on piano if he was sober enough).

We had decided that Old Sexy Rex would be Santa Claus, as usual, and we'd let the CWA ladies do the food, as usual.

So when the sergeant popped his head around the door and said he'd had no luck at all trying to locate the fire captain, the dozen or so blokes in the room simply changed from being the golf club social committee to being the Weelabarabak Fire Brigade.

Squeaky Campbell, who worked on the roads, still had the work truck parked outside the pub, so we all piled into the truck and the police wagon.

We used a crowbar from Squeaky's truck to break into the shed and loaded up the gear and went off to fight what was left of the fire.

What was on fire turned out to be a shed at the back of the weekender, which Bernie had mentioned as the likely source of the smoke.

There wasn't much in the way of vegetation around the shed, it had been a hard season, so it had burned almost to the ground without the fire spreading.

There was no obvious sign of what had caused the fire. Suggested causes were 'kids smoking' or 'sunlight through broken glass on a hot day'.

The shed was really just a shelter for the owner's vehicle when he took his family there on weekends to swim and fish in the river. He was a bloke who had a large sheep run out of town. He used the shack now and then, he'd drink while the kids swam and mucked about in the river and his wife visited relatives in town.

There was nothing much left except some charred sheets of galvanised iron and a few smouldering posts.

He was a good bloke so we were glad his shack was okay. We hosed down the ashes and checked that there were no other fires around the buildings.

He'd probably thank us for saving his shack, although we hadn't done anything of the kind. He'd probably park in the shade of the river gums from now on.

It turned out that the fire captain had been a really enthusiastic school teacher who'd been transferred in the middle of the year to a town hundreds of miles away.

Neville Swan his name was, a real nice bloke, too.

We'd given him a send-off at the golf club. It had been a real beaut evening, with much the same line-up of entertainment and catering as we had just planned for the end-of-year do.

In fact, the entertainment and catering had been exactly the same, except that there was a speech by the school principal instead of Santa Claus.

A few blokes remarked that it was odd that we didn't think about him being fire captain when he left town, especially seeing we planned his farewell and all that.

Then again, we weren't thinking about fires at that time. It was winter and we didn't get fires in winter much. Come to think of it, we didn't get many fires at all in Weelabarabak, which was just as well, really.

There was a lot of talk about electing a new fire captain as we drove back to the Tatts.

'What about Jersey Mason?' someone suggested. 'Or the postmaster, he's handy.'

Someone also suggested that whoever was elected might write to Neville Swan and thank him for doing such a good job as fire captain, as we seemed to have neglected to do that when he left town.

There'd be no need to ask him to send back the key to the shed. We needed a new padlock now anyway.

SOMEONE PINCHED OUR FIREWOOD

JIM HAYNES

Someone pinched our firewood, what a mongrel act!
It's about as low as you can go – but it's a bloody fact!
We spent a whole day cutting it – bashing round the scrub,
I bet the bloke who pinched it spent the whole day in the pub.

We nearly got the trailer bogged – flat tyre on the ute,
So when we finally got it home we thought, 'You bloody beaut!
No more cutting firewood, at least until the Spring.'
We unloaded it and split it up to size and everything.

Stacked it really neatly, a ute and trailer load,
Trouble was we stacked it too close to the road!
And some miserable mongrel started sneaking 'cross the park,
Every night or two, to pinch some – after dark.

Now, as luck would have it, we'd gunpowder in the shed,
We hollowed out one log and packed that in instead.
Then back up on the pile it went . . . next night he took the bait,
We'd soon know who the bugger was, we settled back to wait.

He was a contract shearer, only new in town,
I never got to meet him 'cos he didn't stick around.
The house was only rented, the whole town heard the pop,
They say the Aga Cooker split right across the top.

'Tho justice is its own reward, I wish I'd heard that cove,
Explaining to the landlord the condition of his stove.
Folk in our town mostly are a warm and friendly lot,
Until you pinch our firewood – and then we're bloody not!

A STRIPE FOR TROOPER CASEY

RODERIC QUINN

The magpies had said goodnight to the setting sun, and already darkness was moving through the dead timber. The first notes of night birds came from the ridges, and a curlew mourned in the reeds of a creek.

My brother Will shook his reins and rode away.

'Good-bye, Sis,' he said; 'I will be home pretty early.'

I smiled, knowing that he reckoned without his host. Will was visiting Lizzie Lacy, and Lizzie had a sweet face. Love's pretty trickeries upset many promises, and I knew that my brother would not return till the small hours. But what was love to me—a simple country girl with a heart to lose and nobody to find it?

The cold chilled my fingers, and I shuddered. I was alone, with no one to talk to. Mother and father had gone to Bathurst that day, and evil men walked the roads, lured west by the gleam of gold.

As Will disappeared in the distance, fear struck through me like a chill wave. There was a dance at Staunton's, and Mary had invited me. I was sorry now that I had refused her. Still, if Mary's heart had been as perfect as her face, she would not have said hard things of poor me. She should have schooled her tongue, although she might be a fine woman—which was trooper Casey's estimate of her. The little successes that please a woman had spoilt her, gilding her pride till it dazzled one painfully. If I had grey eyes, it was God who had coloured them; and someone has since told me that it is the pleasantest colour of all. She had said, as well, that my cheeks were red—country complexion. I blessed God for that also, because it meant health and strength. They could be pale enough at times—but pale only when hers would have been ashen.

I remembered myself and laughed. All this bitterness because Will was visiting Lizzie Lacy, and no one was coming to kiss my hand! Silly Carrie, I said to myself, you must bide your time—You are over-young yet to harbour these thoughts. Time will surely bring you the rose, and as surely the thorn that wounds.

I had turned to enter the house when Sally whinnied from a distance, and came down the green lane between the cultivation paddocks at a high trot, her silver tail lifted in excitement and streaming out behind her. She halted at the slip-rails and stretched her head over them, coyly inviting a caress. I gave her a cake, smoothed her velvet nose, and talked to her till the trees in the distance were very dim.

Now, while I fondled, I noticed a curious inattentiveness in the mare's manner. She seemed to heed me with one ear only. The other continually flickered back and quivered as though distracted by a distant sound. Listen intently as I might, I could discover nothing. Peer as I would, I saw dead trees and naught else. But this listening and peering made me fretful and afraid; and, with a final pull at Sally's forelock—a lingering pull that told how loath I was to leave her—I turned and entered the house.

The fire burned steadily. All the little sticks that splash and splutter and noise so much were in white heaps, and only two great logs of ironbark glowed sullenly. I lit a lamp, sat down, and gazed into the fire: sweet pastime for pensive moments. At a girl's age-of-dreams, questions come in troops, and a log's red side is often rich with fancy-food. My head pillowed on an arm, I looked sideways down. The fire drowsed my eyes, and in a little while sleep shut them wholly.

Remember, at that period Crime went down the roads in many guises! I awoke with a start and looked towards the door. Two men stood in the room—a tall and a short man. They were dressed in sailor clothes, and the eyes of one squinted horribly.

'Who are you? ' I said, rising to my feet and feeling strangely nervous.

'Weary men, lassie,' said the tall man.

'All the way from Sydney,' added the other

'With not a bite for two blessed days,' continued the first.

'And ne'er a sup,' said the second.

'Indeed,' I remarked, pretending sympathy with their lie; 'that is hard. But I will give you full and plenty, and when you're satisfied you must go—for,' I continued, thinking to soften the words, 'we do not allow any strangers to sleep here.'

'Yes,' said the tall man; 'feed us well, good lassie.'

'And,' added the other, 'being satisfied, we'll leave you all alone.'

Then they both chuckled, and moved to the table.

As I laid cold meat and cream and bush honey before them, a nervousness assailed me that made my hands dance.

'All alone, lassie?' said the tall man at last, throwing himself back in his chair.

'Yes,' I replied, but—recognising my mistake instantly—continued: 'That is, for a little while. I expect my brother every instant—he is with trooper Casey.'

The short man lit his pipe, the tall one following suit. 'Time to be gone, then,' remarked the latter. The other drew the stem from his lips and expelled a long white plume.

'Which first?' he said.

'The gilt,' said the tall man.

I heard the words, and suddenly sprang up and ran for the door. 'Money first,' I thought; 'what second?'

'Ah, would you!' said the short man, leaping in front.

'Let me pass!' I cried; 'someone is coming.'

He did not move, but stood with folded arms, smiling coarsely. 'A sweetheart, perhaps, lassie?'

'My brother,' I answered.

The tall man opened the door, put out his head, and listened. A moment after he drew in and shut the door.

'No one,' he said; 'the lassie's mistaken.'

'Come!' said the short man, extending his arms. I retreated as he advanced, till at length I stood by the fire. I was all flushed with rage, and cold with fear.

'My brother is a big man,' I said; 'he could kill you both with one blow.'

They laughed brutally, and the short man said, 'He has a pretty sister.'

'If you are men you will not harm me. Tell me what you want, and I will give it you.'

'Take her at her word,' interrupted the tall man, coming forward.

'I will,' replied the other. 'What will you give us?'

'What do you want?' I asked, brightening.

'One thing and another, lassie,' said he.

'Tobacco,' suggested his companion; 'tea and sugar and flour.'

'A word in your ear, lassie!' interrupted the short man, touching me with an outstretched hand.

But I drew away, and tried to look down from my little height. 'Go out of the door, sir!—This is my father's house!'

'Pert words from pretty lips,' said the short man. 'A kiss!—a kiss!'

With that he had me in his arms, and drew me in close. I struggled, at first in silence, but at the touch of his bearded face threw back my head and filled the house with cries. He did not desist—only grew fiercer; nor did his fellow make any motion to release me. His grasp was like that of a vice, and blue marks remained long after.

Once in the struggle I saw stars, and thought a wicked dream had passed. A gust of cold wind struck my cheeks, and I strove to free myself. Then the wind blew again, and again I saw stars—the door was open and someone stood in the doorway. It was a man—tall as a giant, I thought, and the curse he thundered seemed like a great song. The sailor released me and drew apart, laughing to lighten his guilt.

'God bless you!' I said, moving to the door—both hands on my heart, for it was panting fiercely. Before I reached him the stranger raised a hand to make me pause. He had a gun at his shoulder—a long, bright barrel that gleamed fitfully.

'In the nick of time,' he said calmly; 'which first?'

I looked at the two sailors. They stood close together, distressed by fear. The tall man slanted sideways, like a sapling from the wind, and the short one cowered behind an upraised arm as if to ward a blow.

'Which first?' said the stranger again.

'Neither!' I replied, shuddering.

He sloped his rifle a little, looked at me cynically, and hinted something that filled me with shame.

'No, no,' I cried; 'do not say that! I never saw them before, and I am a good girl.'

A smile crept across his lips, and his wide, dark eyes softened.

'I believe it,' he said shortly.

He stepped forward and halted in the centre of the room.

'You were hungry?' he said to the short man. The man nodded.

'And she fed you on cream and honey—the best she had?'

The man did not answer. The gun went to the shoulder again, and the dark eyes looked along the levelled barrel.

'And you wanted to pay her in your own foul coin. Now for this,' he continued, 'I've a mind to put hot lead in your brain.'

I ran forward with a great dread lest he should do as he threatened.

'Go away!' I cried to the sailors; 'go quickly, while you are safe!'

The men turned as if to slink off but the stranger warned them to stand very still.

'You must be punished for this night's work,' he said; 'and then you may go—both of you—as far as Berrima.'

The two men started and eyed him keenly. 'Just so, just so,' he said, nodding from one to the other; 'a guilty conscience, eh?'

They scowled and sank their eyes, and he turned to me.

'Get your whip!' he said. I stood irresolute, and he continued:

'My arm is tired holding this gun. They should have been dead long ago. Get your whip!'

I ran away, got my whip, and returned. 'Go forward and strike that man across the face.'

'It would be cruel,' I replied.

'Quick! Or he will be dead before you reach him!'

Then I was in front of the sailor.

'Lift your arm,' the stranger said. Then he told me to strike with all my force—'As you would a wicked steer.'

I obeyed with some hesitation, and struck lightly. But presently faint-heartedness forsook me. At the second lifting of the whip a sudden spirit of mastery surged my arm with fierceness, so that I dealt some savage blows. The sailor sheltered his eyes with his hands and cried aloud for mercy. Then I suddenly remembered myself and drew away, shuddering and half in tears.

'Good!' said the stranger. 'And now for the other—they are mates.'

'He did not offer me any hurt,' I replied.

The stranger looked at him.

'You are lucky,' he said. The man's face lightened with pleasure. 'But less lucky than you think, my good man,' he continued. I noticed the white fear that came into the tall man's face, and the sudden upward look of his companion. 'Come here!' said the stranger, beckoning to the short man. The sailor approached, trembling.

After a few paces had been taken, 'Halt!' the stranger cried. The man stood still on the instant. 'Squint-eyed, and with the limp of the leg-iron—dressed like a sailor!' said the stranger, in loud, clear tones. 'Get some saddle straps, my girl!'

'Why?'

'Get them!' he said, shortly.

I went away, and displeasure at his brusque manner made my cheeks burn. Did it paint them also—that he spoke so gently on my return?

'I am not used to ladies, and I mean no offence,' he said.

I forgave him, and said that I had felt none.

'Your action to-night shows that you are a good man.'

'Perhaps,' he replied; 'but one star does not make a heaven.'

He was silent, and I forebore to ask what he meant. He motioned for the straps, and I gave them. Then he turned to the men, and his voice hardened. 'Down on your faces!' he thundered, 'quick! Quick! Both of you, or . . .'

They were down on the instant, abject as worms.

'Now take this gun, my girl,' he said, 'and if that man so much as wriggles, shoot him. I will manage the other.'

The man was fashioned to command. I took the gun, and if the prostrate figure had moved then it would never have moved again. But the sailors were utterly cowed, and did not murmur while the stranger pinioned their hands behind them. This done, he rolled them over and looked down at them.

'What does this mean?' I said.

'A stripe for trooper Casey,' he replied, and laughed.

'For trooper Casey? I do not understand?'

'You will, in time,' he replied. With that, I had to content myself. Who this man was, with the command on his lips, and the disobey-me-if-you-dare in his eyes, I did not know. I only know that he had reserves of gentleness, which spoke through his harsher moods like a bird's song in a storm.

'You, there!' he said to the short man; 'do you know what they are doing at Weatherley's?'

The sailor turned his face aside, and was mute.

'Or you?' to the tall man.

'No,' the man replied. 'Where is Weatherley's?'

'Liars—both of you!' said the stranger. 'Weatherley's, under the Range.'

'What are they doing?' I interposed.

'Burying a dead woman,' he replied, looking from one to the other of the prostrate men, and nodding as he changed his gaze.

'How sad!' I cried. 'Poor Mrs. Weatherley! When did she die?'

'Yesterday.'

'She was a strong woman.'

'She met someone stronger.'

'You mean Death!'

'Death, and two devils!'—he ground his teeth.

I looked at him in wonder.

'Two devils—what do you mean?'

The short man lay on his side, looking up as a beaten dog looks at his master. The stranger spurned him with a foot.

'Answer!' he said; 'which of you killed her?'

'Not me,' groaned the sailor; ''twas the bushrangers.'

'You liar!' cried the stranger in a rising, incredulous voice, as though he doubted his own ears.

'We do not . . .' He paused and looked at me, and saw that he had revealed himself.

'Ah!' I whispered as he turned away. I understood now, and yet he did not seem as black as people painted him.

'I tried to hide it,' he said; 'but it slipped out. It is a bad thing even at its best.'

Then he looked very downcast, and I pitied him. An angel impulse stirred me, and I stepped forward, raised my face, and kissed him.

'Good!' he said, his fine eyes flashing, ''tis a long time since.' He lowered his voice and continued, as if to himself: 'But what does it matter? She is only a child.'

'To-night has made me a woman,' I replied.

'No, no! You are a child. No woman would do a thing like that. But some day you will be a woman. Then you will kiss with the lips only, not with the heart—cheating the heart that loves you.'

It was some minutes before he spoke again.

'I saw a horse in the stockyard,' he said; 'bring him round. I want you to go somewhere.'

And when Sally was ready at the door and I in the saddle, he continued: 'Ride to Staunton's—Casey is there. Tell him'—this with a low laugh—'that the man who borrowed his horse at Weatherboard waits here to give him a stripe in exchange. Come back with him yourself.'

I turned Sally's head to be gone immediately.

'Wait—another word! Would you like to see me dead or trooper Casey dead?'

'Oh, no; how can you ask?'

'I distrust women,' he returned, 'since I met Judas in petticoats.'

'Try me,' I replied; 'I could not be false after what you have done.'

'When you come to the bridge, coo-ee! I will be here watching these brutes, and when I hear your cry I will up and away.'

As Sally moved off some words followed from the door, where he stood in the light.

'Good-bye, little girl!'

'Good-bye! And I will always remember you.'

A curlew wailed, and the stranger laughed—to make the parting easy, it seemed. Yet something that Nature had put into the curlew's wail went through the man's voice and saddened me for many days. It seemed that both bird and man mourned something lost.

I galloped along the track that made a siding in the green hill and slanted to the creek. Sally's hoofs rattled on the turpentine planking of the bridge, and presently struck fire from the ironstone on the farther side. Where the track wound through wild hops I gave her free head; for there was open country. Where the scrub crept in she slackened of her own will, not liking the rebound of the bushes.

In a little while we came to a second creek, where bullocks' heads in a white line made stepping-stones. She crossed it with a bound and a splash, and climbed the slope beyond in a few strides. Another mile brought me to Staunton's log-fence, and through the trees I saw bright windows. A little later there came to me a concertina's music and other sounds of merry-making.

I fastened Sally to the stockyard gate, and walked through the doorway. A number of couples were there, swinging round and round in a dance. As I walked into the room I felt strangely out of harmony with the surroundings, the music having put a spirit in my feet that made them seem to drag.

Mary Staunton had trooper Casey for a partner. She looked very fine and pale, but as she went by she scarcely deigned to notice me.

Trooper Casey was six feet high, and had curly hair—the hair that women fancy. Every time he wheeled his metal buttons flashed. When the dance finished he was near me. I touched him on the arm.

'Mr. Casey!'

'Hallo, Carrie!' said Mary Staunton, in affected welcome; 'how late you are!'

'I didn't come to dance, Mary—only to see Mr. Casey.'

'Ah, I should have known,' she answered, with a little mocking laugh, and with a glance at my dress where Sally had splashed it in crossing the creek.

I tossed my head and turned from her.

'Trooper Casey, can you spare a moment?'

'What do you want? Say what you want, here and now,' said Mary Staunton. 'That is, if you're not afraid of us hearing it.'

'I intended this for you alone'—I addressed the trooper—'but now'—with a sidelong look at his sweetheart—'everyone may hear it.'

'What is it, Miss Anson?'

'Do you want a stripe?'

'Why, one'd think you were the Governor's lady,' said Mary Staunton, laughing so that I blushed.

I took no notice of her, other than turning my back, and then I smiled quietly as I spoke.

'A gentleman waits at our house to pay you for a horse he borrowed at Weatherboard.'

I watched him keenly to see how he took the news. On his cheeks two red spots stood out and burned. He gnawed his under-lip, and there was a suppressed anger in his eyes, that glowed like covered fires. From those standing around there went up a great laugh, and Casey turned to a group who forced their merriment overlong.

'You are great laughers,' said he; 'but are you men enough to fight?' None of them made a movement to accept the challenge; but, on the other hand, it was curious to see how speedily the laughter faded from their faces, giving place to something almost sad.

Then up spoke Mary Staunton. 'Carrie Anson,' said she, with tremulous white lips, 'if you come here to insult people, you'd better stay away.'

'Don't mind her, Mary,' said the trooper; 'it's a trick some fool has made her play.'

'Indeed it is not,' I replied. 'The man who gave me that message is waiting at our house with two sailors, and one of them'—I dropped my voice so that only he and Mary heard—'killed Mrs. Weatherley.' The trooper started, as though shot through; looked me in the eyes, and drew a long breath.

'By God!' he cried, and moved towards the door. 'It is three to one, Mary,' he said.

'Do not go!' she answered; 'you may be killed.'

'It is man to man, trooper!' I interrupted; 'two are bound and the third keeps watch.'

'Stuff!' exclaimed Mary, viciously: 'he keep watch! You will not go alone, trooper.'

'Alone! I must take the man. Where are my carbine and cap?'

'Take someone!' pleaded Mary.

'No,' Casey replied, 'I will do this myself. If I succeed you know what it means'—and he looked earnestly into her eyes.

I laughed pleasantly. 'I shall be a bridesmaid—eh, Mary?'

She did not smile, but went off with a set face, swaying her skirts behind her.

'With the help of God, Miss Anson,' whispered Casey, confidentially, 'I shall make three prisoners to-night.'

'With the help of God, you shall not, trooper Casey!' I whispered to myself.

As the trooper turned to leave the room, his carbine on his back, his sabre at his side, and his cap pressing a cushion of brown curls, I did not wonder Mary Staunton had lost her heart to him. He was a man to delight any eyes.

Some came forward and offered to assist him, but these he refused coldly. I was in the saddle before he had mounted. Then he said, in surprise, 'You must stay here, Miss Anson.'

'I must go home, trooper Casey.'

'There may be bloodshed.'

'There must be none.'

'You are very brave,' he said, suspiciously; 'are you sure it is no hoax?'

'Follow me, if you are not a coward!' I replied.

As I passed her, Mary Staunton muttered something about 'an interfering minx'. The trooper she warned to be careful. In my heart I believe that she thought his chief peril lay in me, and I laughed to think that, after all, an outlaw may not be the greatest danger in a man's path.

As the trooper rode after, his bridle jingled in the silence. 'Miss Anson,' said he, 'these sailors that you spoke of—was one a tall man?'

'Yes.'

'And the other short?'

'With a squint.'

'Just so'—and he relapsed into silence.

The track was narrow, with no room for two horses. This prevented us from riding abreast, and gave me an excuse to keep in front. Several times Casey urged his horse forward, but I patted Sally and she kept her place. At the creek he made a bold bid to front me, but the mare flashed forward and headed him at the farther side.

'Draw aside, and let me ride in front, Miss Anson.'

I answered that I knew the way quite well.

'That may be, but I have a different reason.'

I was dumb, having nothing to answer.

'There may be danger ahead,' he continued; 'and you are foolish.'

I cast about for an answer, and remembered a last week's storm. 'There is danger,' I replied; 'a fallen tree, and you might flounder in the branches.'

He muttered something under his breath, but I did not catch the word. In a little while we reached the fallen tree and rode round it. Beyond he spoke again.

'You can have no objection now.'

'None whatever,' I said, 'only that a little way along a swarm of bees have fastened to a limb. You might mistake them for a wart and brush them with your shoulder. That would not be pleasant, would it?'—and I laughed to gild the prevarication. But Casey, seeing no humour in the situation, remained dumb.

Presently I cried out to him to beware of the bees, and he listed in his saddle.

'Now?' he asked.

'Not yet, trooper; we are in the bush and I prefer to stay where I am, because if you rode in front the branches would come back and sting Sally's eyes.'

'Rubbish!' muttered Casey.

When we were through the bush and among the hops, he suddenly bade me halt.

'You must play no tricks, Miss Anson!'

'La! Who is playing them, Mr. Casey?'

'The man at your house is a desperado.'

'Is he, indeed?'—with all the innocence of the world in my voice.

'And you are an accomplice?'

'Dear me, what does that mean, trooper?'

'It means that you must stay where you are.'

'But I must go home.'

'Then I shall arrest you.'

'Arrest me, and let three grown men go free!'

'But you make it necessary,' he said.

'Trooper, the desperado is a brave man, and would be as likely to kill you as you would be to kill him.'

'Have no fears for me, Miss Anson.'

'I have none.'

'Then they are for . . .'

'The man who saved me?'—and I went away like an arrow.

It was the first time I had come into conflict with the law, and the situation thrilled me. Casey with a great oath thundered close behind, calling on me in a low voice to hold up, and muttering dire consequences. I laughed, bent forward, and bade Sally do her best. It was necessary, since his horse had better pace and gained greatly at every stride. Now the animal's nose was at my saddle, now at Sally's shoulder, and now we raced level to the bridge.

I rose in the saddle, threw up my face, and sent a long, long 'Coo-ee! Coo-ee!' speeding across the open.

'Hush, you hoyden!'

I tugged at the reins, throwing Sally back on her haunches, and again I cooeed. Then I sat back and listened. The trooper was now a fading bulk in the dark. The speed of his horse on the siding was terrible, and his rein and sabre jingled fiercely.

Then, one—two—three, came the sounds of slip-rails falling. I sat back in the saddle with a sigh of deep content, and breathed as I had not for many minutes. Far and farther away I heard another horse, his hoof-thuds in the dead timber sounding like footfalls in an empty house.

'You have done good work to-night,' said trooper Casey, when I entered the room a little later; 'fine work for a decent, self-respecting girl.'

I picked up his sleeve where the silver braid circled it.

'This looks lonely, trooper: it would be prettier if there were two of them, would it not?'

He smiled in a wintry way, and this gave me heart to say that the stranger was not so bad, after all. Casey shook his head.

'Bad enough,' he replied.

Will came in shortly after, and these words followed: 'Where did you meet him?'

'At the boundary gate,' Will answered.

'What did he say?'

'Looked along his gun and ordered me to hoist my hands.'

'And then?'

'Took my horse and watch—and left me his animal.'

'Never mind,' said the trooper quietly, 'I have two prisoners. And he was not so bad, after all—eh, Miss Anson?'

'No, trooper; especially if it should happen that the horse he left is the same that he borrowed.'

Casey rose to look out at the dawn.

DAN WASN'T THROWN FROM HIS HORSE

HENRY LAWSON

They say he was thrown and run over,
But that is sheer nonsense, of course:
I taught him to ride when a kiddy,
And Dan wasn't thrown from his horse.
The horse that Dan rode was a devil,
The kind of a brute I despise,
With nasty white eyelashes fringing
A pair of red, sinister eyes.
And a queerly-shaped spot on his forehead,
Where I put a conical ball
The day that he murdered Dan Denver,
The pluckiest rider of all.

'Twas after the races were over
And Duggan (a Talbragar man)
And two of the Denvers, and Barney
Were trying a gallop with Dan.
Dan's horse on a sudden got vicious,
And reared up an' plunged in the race,
Then threw back his head, hitting Dan
Like a sledge-hammer, full in the face.
Dan stopped and got down, stood a moment,
Then fell to the ground like a stone,
And died about ten minutes after;
But they're liars who say he was thrown.